THE UNREQUITED

SAFFRON A. KENT

This is a work of fiction. Names, characters, places, and incidents are either the product of the author's imagination or are used fictitiously, and any resemblance to actual persons living or dead, business establishments, events, or locales, is entirely coincidental.

The Unrequited © 2017 by Saffron A. Kent
All rights reserved. No part of this book may be used or reproduced in any manner whatsoever without written permission of the author except in the case of brief quotations embodied in critical articles or reviews.

Cover Art by Najla Qamber Designs
Editing by C. Marie
Proofreading by Kaitie Reister & Leanne Rabessa

July 2017 Edition
Published in the United States of America

OTHER BOOKS BY SAFFRON A. KENT

Gods & Monsters

Medicine Man (Heartstone Series Book 1)

Dreams of 18 (Heartstone Series Book 2)

California Dreamin' (Heartstone Series Book 3)

St. Mary's Rebels Series

Bad Boy Blues (SMR book 0.5)

My Darling Arrow (SMR book 1)

The Wild Mustang & The Dancing Fairy (SMR book 1.5)

A Gorgeous Villain (SMR book 2)

These Thorn Kisses (SMR book 3)

Hey, Mister Marshall (SMR book 4)

The Hatesick Diaries (SMR book 5)

This one, hands down, goes to my husband. This book wouldn't be here without him. I'm sorry for all the grief I put you through. You deserve so much better than me and my absent-mindedness, but I'm not letting you go. Also, I owe you a strawberry cheesecake, and I'm gonna make it this time. I promise.

PART 1

THE STARLET

CHAPTER ONE

My heart is not an organ.

It's more than that. My heart is an animal—a chameleon, to be specific. It changes skin and color, not to blend in, but to be difficult, unreasonable.

My heart has many faces. Restless heart. Desperate heart. Selfish heart. Lonely heart.

Today my heart is anxious—or at least it's going to be anxious for the next fifty-seven minutes. After that, who knows?

I'm sitting in the pristine office of the school's guidance counselor, Kara Montgomery, and my heart is going haywire. It's fluttering, dipping up and down in my chest, bumping against my ribcage. It doesn't want to be here, because it takes offense at seeing the guidance counselor, which is really just a euphemism for therapist.

We don't need a therapist. We're fine.

Isn't that what crazy people say?

"Layla," says the guidance-counselor-with-a-psychology-degree/therapist, Ms. Montgomery. "How was your vacation?"

I glance away from the window I've been staring out of, forgoing the scenery of the snowy outdoors to focus on the smiling woman behind the desk. "It was all right."

"Well, what did you do?" She is rolling a pen between her fingers, and then it slips out of her hand and falls to the floor. She chuckles at herself and bends to pick it up.

Kara is not a typical guidance counselor/therapist. For one, she's clumsy and always appears frantic. There's nothing calm about her. Her hair is never in place; strands are flying everywhere, and she's forever running her fingers through them to make them behave. Her blouses are always wrinkled, which she hides under her corduroy jackets. She talks fast, and sometimes things she says aren't very therapist-like.

"So?" she prompts, giving me her full attention. I want to tell her that her glasses are tipped to one side, but I don't; she is less intimidating this way. My heart doesn't need any more threats than what her degree represents.

"Um, I took walks, mostly." I shift in the cushioned chair, tucking a strand of my loose hair behind my ear. "Watched Netflix. Went to the gym."

Lies. All lies. I binged on Christmas candy my mom sent—or rather her assistant sent, because my mom didn't want me to come home for the holidays. I sat on the couch all day and watched porn while sucking on Twizzlers and listening to Lana Del Rey in the background. I'm addicted to that woman. Seriously, she is a goddess. Every word out of her mouth is gold.

I'm not addicted to porn or Twizzlers, however. Those are just for when I get lonely...which is most of the time, but that's beside the point.

"That's great. I'm glad." She nods. "You didn't feel lonely without your friends, then? It was all good?"

Now, this is what I don't get: why is she smiling at me? Why are her eyes curious? Is she trying to dig deep? Is she trying to fish for answers?

Her questions could be a cover for other loaded questions, like, *Were you good, Layla? Were you* really *good? Did you do something crazy, like calling him in the middle of the night? Because you've done this before when you were lonely. So, did you call him, Layla? Did you?*

The answer to all of this is a big fat no. I did not call him. I haven't called him in months. *Months.* All I've done is stare at his photo on my phone—the photo no one knows about, because if my mom knew I was still pining after him, she'd send me to a real therapist, a real live one who would ask all sorts of questions rather than disguising them with euphemisms.

So *no*, I did *not* call him. I have only stared at a stupid picture like a pathetic lovesick person. There, happy now?

I shift in my chair and open my mouth to tell her exactly that when I realize she hasn't even asked the question. I'm only *thinking* she has. It's all in my head. I tell my anxious heart to calm down. *Relax, would you? We're still in the clear.*

I exhale a long breath and answer, "Yeah, it was good. I kept myself busy."

"That's great. That's good to hear. I don't like when students have to stay back for holidays. I just worry about them." She laughs and her glasses become even more crooked. This time she straightens them up and folds her hands on the desk. "So have you given any thought to what electives you'll be taking this semester?"

"Sure."

Of course not. I'm not made for education. The only reason I agreed to college was because I was given the choice between school in Connecticut and the youth rehabilitation center in New Jersey, and I'm not setting foot in New fucking Jersey *or* going to a rehab center.

"Well?" Kara raises her blonde eyebrow in question.

I lick my lips, trying to think of something. "I think I'm gonna stick with the regular courses. College is hard as it is. I don't wanna pile on new things."

Kara smiles—she's always smiling—and leans forward. "Look Layla, I like you. In fact, I think you're great. You have great potential, and to be honest, I don't think you need these thinly disguised therapy sessions with me."

I sit up in my seat. "Really? I don't have to come here anymore?"

"No, you still have to come. I'd like to keep my job."

"I won't tell anyone. It could be our secret," I insist. I don't like to keep secrets, but this one I'll take to the grave.

"It's tempting, but no. Cookie?" She chuckles, offering the chocolate chip cookies sitting on her desk, going all friendly on me again.

She gives me whiplash and sometimes I want to ask her, *Are you here to analyze me or not?* Not that there is anything to analyze. I'm a simple girl, really. I hate winters, Connecticut, and college. I love the color purple, Lana Del Rey, and him. That's all.

I reach out to take one cookie but then change my mind and take three instead. I never say no to sugar.

Kara watches me carefully and I am about to snap at her when she speaks up. "So as I was saying, I think you have great potential, but you need set goals and you need to work on impulse control." She gives me a pointed look as I take a bite out of my cookie. "You don't have any, or at least, what you have is very little."

"Huh." I sag back in the chair. "Well, I knew that already."

Kara threads her fingers together on the desk. "Great. So we've already conquered the first step: acceptance. Now we need to work on the next step."

"And that is?"

"How to control it."

I hold up my finger. "Way ahead of you there. I've totally got it under control." Kara raises a skeptical brow and I continue, "I've been going to all my classes even though I wanna walk around aimlessly all day, and I've got C's across the board even though I hate college. Not to mention, I'd kill for a drag or a drop of Grey Goose, but I haven't touched any of those things. I don't even go to parties, because we all know parties are just breeding grounds for pot, alcohol, and sex."

I shoot her an arrogant smirk then finish my cookie. She can't get me after that. I've been good. I've busted my ass to be good.

"That's commendable. I appreciate your restraint, but that's also the bare minimum. You shouldn't be drinking and partying it up anyway." She pushes her glasses up. "College is your time to learn, to discover yourself, to see what kind of things you like, and for that, we have electives. So, I ask you again, any thoughts?"

Sighing, I look away. I'm back to staring out the window. The grounds are white and the trees are naked. It's all desolate and sad, like we're living in a post-apocalyptic world where things like electives are mandatory.

"What are my choices?" I ask.

Kara beams at me, swatting at a wayward curl that's getting in her eyes. "Well, we've got a great writing program. Maybe you should try some of the writing classes."

"You mean, like, *writing* writing?" At her nod, I shake my head. "I don't even like reading."

"You should probably pick up a book sometime. Who knows, you might end up liking it."

"Yeah, no, I don't think so." I sigh. "Do you have anything else? I don't think I'm cut out for writing."

"In fact, I think you'd be great at it."

"Really?" I scoff. "What do you think I should write about?"

This time her smile is both sweet and sad. "Write about New York. I know you miss it. Or maybe something about winter."

"I hate winter." I wrap my arms around my body and hitch my shoulders to huddle in my purple fur coat. Another thing I like: fur. It's soft and cuddly, and it's the only thing that can somewhat keep me warm.

"Then why do you keep staring at the snow?" I shrug, and she dips her head in acceptance of my non-answer. "How about you try writing something about what you felt when Caleb left? About the way you acted up?"

Caleb.

I'm jolted at the mention of his name. It's not an outward jolt, more a tremor on the inside, like when you hear a sudden loud sound in a quiet apartment and you know it's nothing, but your body tenses nonetheless.

I don't think I've heard his name spoken out loud since I moved here six months ago. It sounds so exotic in Kara's voice. On my tongue, his name sounds loud, shrill, wrong somehow. I shouldn't be saying it, but hey, I've got no impulse control, so I say it anyway.

I hate her for bringing him up. I hate that she's going there in a roundabout way.

"I didn't act up. I just...got drunk...every now and then." I clear my throat, pushing my anger away when all I want to do is storm out of here.

"I know, and then *every now and then*, you went shoplifting, crashed your mom's parties, and got behind the wheel."

Should therapists be judgy like this? I don't think so. And why are we talking about these things, all of a sudden? Mostly, we stick to neutral topics like school and my teachers, and when things get a little personal, I evade and make jokes.

This one time when she tried talking about the days leading up to Caleb's departure, I took my top halfway off and showed her my newly acquired belly button ring, and maybe even the underside of my bra-less boobs.

"I didn't kill anyone, did I?" I say, referring to her earlier comment about drinking and driving. "Besides, they took away my license, so the people of Connecticut are safe from the terror that is me. Why are we talking about this?"

"Because I think you can channel all of your emotions into something good, something constructive. Maybe you'll end up liking it. Maybe you'll end up liking college." She lowers her voice then. "Layla, I know you hate college. You hate seeing me every week. You hate being here, but I think you should give it a chance. Do something new. Make new friends."

I want to say I do have friends—I do, they are just not visible to the naked eye—but I don't, because what's the point of lying when she knows everything anyway?

"Fine."

Kara looks at the clock on the wall to her right. "Tell me you'll think about it, *really* think about it. The semester starts in a couple days so you've got a week to think about the courses, okay?"

I spring up from my seat and gather my winter gear. "Okay."

"Good."

It takes me a couple of minutes to get ready to go out in the snow. I snap my white gloves on and pull down the white beanie to cover my ears.

Winter is a cruel bitch. You gotta pile on or you'll get burned by the stinging wind, and no matter how much I pile on, I'm never warm enough, not even inside the heated buildings. So, I've got it all: hat, scarves, gloves, thermal tights, leg warmers, fur boots.

I'm at the door, turning the knob, but something stops me.

"Do you think…he's doing okay up there? I mean, do you think he misses me?" I don't know why I ask this question. It simply comes out.

"Yes. I do think he misses you. You guys grew up together, right? I'm sure he misses his best friend."

Then why doesn't he call? "Boston is cold," I blurt out stupidly, my throat feeling scraped. A chill runs through my body at the thought of all that snow up there.

"But I'm sure he's fine," she reassures me, with a smile.

"Yeah," I whisper. I'm sure Harvard is taking good care of their genius.

"You know, Layla, falling in love isn't bad or wrong or even hard. It's actually really simple, even if there's no reciprocation. It's the falling out that's hard, but no matter how much you convince yourself otherwise, reciprocation is important. It's what keeps the love going. Without it, love just dies out, and then it's up to you. Do you bury it, or do you carry the dead body around? It's a hard decision to make, but you have to do it."

I know what she's saying: move on, forget him, don't think about him—but how can you forget a love of thirteen years? How can you forget the endless nights of wanting, *needing*, dreaming? *I love you.* That's all I ever wanted to hear. How can I let go of that?

With a jerky nod, I walk out of her room. Outside the building, the air is cold and dry. It hurts to breathe. My heart is still fluttering with residual anxiety when I take my phone out, and stare at the last picture I have of him. He's smiling in it. His green, green eyes are shining and his plump, kissable lips are stretched wide. It's fucking beautiful. I don't think I can ever delete it. Not in this lifetime.

I put the phone away when I see a couple. They are up ahead of me on the cobblestone pathway, and they are wrapped around each other. The girl is cold, her cheeks red, and the guy is rubbing his hands over hers, trying to warm her up. They are smiling goofy smiles, reminding me of a smile from long ago.

Caleb as the ring bearer and me as the flower girl. Caleb stopping in his confident but boyish stride to take my small hand in his, me looking up at him with a frown. Oh, how I hated him in that moment. Caleb flashing his adorable smile and me returning it, despite the frown, despite the strange surroundings, despite the fact that my mom was marrying his dad. I hated getting a new brother. I hated moving across town to a new house with no rooftop garden.

At the fork, the couple takes a right turn and I'm supposed to go left, but I don't want to go left. I want to go where they're going. I want to bask in their happiness for a while. I want to see reciprocation.

What does requited love look like? I want to see it.

I take the right turn and follow the couple.

It's cold, *so* fucking cold. Also, dark—super dark, and the Victorian lamps flanking the street don't do shit to light up my path.

But none of that deters me from taking a harried pace. I'm walking down Albert Street, heading toward Brighton Avenue where the university park entrance is. Sleep is hard to come by, especially after Kara mentioned writing about my unrequited love.

Once upon a time, six-year-old Caleb Whitmore smiled at five-year-old Layla Robinson. She didn't know it then, but that was the day she fell in love with him. Over the years, she tried to get his attention without success. Then one night, in her desperate, desperate attempt to stop Caleb from going off to Harvard, she kind of, sort of...raped him a little bit. She's not entirely sure. Caleb went off to college one month earlier than he was supposed to and Layla was stuck acting up. The end.

Two years later I'm here, walking the streets, feeling ashamed of my love, ashamed of having ever fallen for my stepbrother and then driving him away.

For the record, Caleb Whitmore isn't even my stepsibling anymore. My mom divorced his dad a few years ago, but I think some stigmas never go away—like, you don't sleep with your best friend's ex-boyfriend, and you don't date your friend's brother. Caleb will always be my stepbrother because we kind of grew up together.

I don't even have memories of the time before him. I can't remember the house I lived in before I lived with him, except that it had a rooftop garden. I can't remember the friends I had before he came along. I can't even remember my own dad before his dad came into the picture.

All I remember is one day when I was five, Mom said we were leaving, and that I was going to get a brother. Then the dark days followed where I cried because I hated the idea of a sibling.

And then a burst of sunlight: a tiny six-year-old boy holding the rings on a velvet cushion, standing next to me. I remember thinking I was taller than him in my frilly, itchy dress, flowers in my hand. I remember thinking that I liked his blond hair and green eyes as opposed to my black hair and weird violet eyes. Together, we watched our parents get married, and together, we grimaced when they kissed each other on the lips.

It was beautiful, with white lilies and the smell of cake everywhere.

Now, I make my way toward the solitude. Slipping and stumbling on the transparent patches of ice, I enter the park. The cold wind curls around my body, making me shiver, but I keep going, my booted feet trudging through the snow. I'm looking for a particular spot that I like to frequent during the nights when I can't sleep, which happens often.

Unrequited love and insomnia are longtime friends of mine. They might even be siblings—evil and uncaring with sticky fingers.

Frustrated, I stomp and slip, falling against the scratchy bark of a tree. Even through the thick layer of my fur coat, I feel the sting.

"Motherfucking..." I mutter, rubbing the burn on my arm. My eyes water with the pain, both physical and emotional. I hate this. I *hate* crying. I wipe my tears with frozen fingers and try to control my choppy breaths.

"It's fine. It's totally fine," I whisper to myself. "I'm gonna be fine." My words stumble over each other, but at least I'm not crying now.

Then I hear a sound. Footsteps on the iced ground. A wooden creak. Fear has me hiding against the tree, but curiosity has me peeking out.

A tall man dressed in all black—black hoodie and black sweatpants—is sitting on the bench, my bench, under my tree with the network of empty branches.

That's my spot, asshole, I want to say, but I'm mute. Terrified. Who is he? What's he doing here at this time of night? People sleep at night! I'm an exception though; I'm heartbroken.

He sits on the edge, head bent and covered by the hood, staring at the ground. Slowly, he slides back, sprawls, and tilts his face up. His hood falls away, revealing a mass of black hair illuminated by the yellow light of the lamp. It's long and wavy, almost sailing past the nape of his neck and touching his shoulders. He watches the sky and I do the same. We watch the moon, the fat clouds. I smell snow in the air.

I decide the sky isn't interesting enough. So, I watch him.

He is breathing hard, his broad chest puffing up and down. I notice a thick drop of sweat making its way down his strained throat, over the sharp bump of his Adam's apple. Maybe he's been running?

Without looking down, the dark man reaches back to get something from his pocket—a cigarette. He shifts, brings his face down, and I see his features. They are a system of angles and sharp, defined lines. His high cheekbones slant into a strong, stubbled jaw. Sweat dots his forehead and he wipes it off with his arm, stretching the fabric of his hoodie over his heaving chest.

Any moment, I expect him to light the cigarette and take in a drag. I realize I'm dying to watch him smoke, to see the tendrils of smoky warmth slip away into the winter air.

But he...doesn't.

He simply stares at it. Wedged between two of his fingers, the cigarette remains still, an object of his perusal. He frowns at it, like he is fascinated. Like he hates it. Like he can't imagine why a blunt stick of cancer is holding his attention.

Then he throws it away.

He reaches back again and gets out another cigarette. The same routine follows. Staring. Frowning. My anticipation of seeing what he does next.

This time he sighs, his chest shuddering up and down as he produces a lighter from his pocket. He throws the stick in his mouth and lights it up with a flick of his finger. He takes a drag and then lets the smoke seep out. His eyes fall shut at the ecstasy of that first pull. He might've even groaned. *I* would have.

Watching him fight his impulse to smoke was exhausting. I feel both sad and happy that he gave in. I wonder what I would've done in the same situation. Kara's face comes to mind, her saying I need to work on restraining myself.

I know the smoke coming out of his mouth is virgin, not a drop of marijuana in there, but I want it in my mouth too. I *so* want it.

Abruptly, he stops and shoots up from his seat, pocketing the lighter. This guy is tall, maybe 6'3" or something. I have to crane my neck to look at him even though I'm standing far away. He skips on his feet, takes one last drag, flicks the cigarette on the ground, crushes it, pulls the hoodie over, and takes off jogging.

I come unglued from the tree, run to the bench, and look in the direction where he vanished -- nothing but darkness and frosty air. I might as well have conjured him up, like a child makes up an imaginary friend to feel less lonely. Sighing, I sit where he sat. The place is cold as ever, as if he never sat there.

My exhaustion is taking its toll and I close my eyes. I breathe in the lingering smell of cigarette and maybe even something chocolatey. I curl up on the bench, my cheek pressing into the cold wood. I hate winter, but I can't fall asleep in my warm bed. It's one of those ironies people laugh about.

Drifting into sleep, I pray that the color of the stranger's eyes isn't green.

CHAPTER TWO

I live in a tower.

It's the tallest building around the area of PenBrook University, where I've been banished to go to school. I'm on the top floor in a two-bedroom apartment overlooking the university park. In fact, I can see the entire campus from my balcony—the umbrella of trees, red rooftops of squatting houses, spiked buildings. I like to sit up on my balcony and throw water balloons at people down on the street. When they look up, outraged, I duck behind the stone railing, but in those five seconds, I feel acknowledged. They knew someone was up there, throwing things at them. I like that.

The lower floors will be rented out in a few months, but currently I'm the only person living in this posh, luxurious, tower-like building. Henry Cox, my current stepdad, is the owner, hence the early access. My mom thought living in a dorm would make me more susceptible to drugs and alcohol. As if I can't score here if I want to.

Since my heart is lonely today, I decide to go to the bookstore and get the books on my course list. Might as well since classes begin tomorrow.

I throw on some sweatpants and a large hoodie, then cover myself up with my favorite purple fur coat, a scarf, and a hat. My dark hair falls around my face for extra protection from the cold.

Ten minutes later, I'm at the campus bookstore, pulling up the list of books on my phone. One by one, I collect the required texts in the nook of my arm. I'm sad that it took only a few minutes and now I'll have to go back to my tower.

Then I get an idea. I walk toward the literature section of the store. Rows and rows of books with beautiful calligraphy surround me in shoulder-height wooden bookshelves. There's a smell here that I can get used to, warm and sharp. Heaven must smell like this.

Unlike Caleb, I'm not much of a reader. He's a great lover of books and art.

With Lana crooning in my ears about "Dark Paradise," I run my fingers over the edges of the books, trying to decide how best to mess things up. My lonely heart perks up. It flips in my chest, telling me how much it appreciates my efforts to fill this giant, gaping hole.

Don't mention it.

Then I get to work. I trade books on the G shelf with the ones on the F. I laugh to myself, cackling as I imagine people getting confused. It calls for a little twerking so I move my ass—only a little, mind you—to the sensual beats of the song.

As I turn around, my movements halt. The book in my hand remains suspended in the air and all thoughts vanish from my head.

He is here.

Him.

The dark smoker from last night.

He stands tall and intimidating with a book of his own in his hands. Like last night, he is frowning at the object. Maybe it pissed him off somehow, offended him with its existence. If not for the ferocity of his displeasure, I never would've recognized him under the industrial light of the bookstore.

He looks different in the light. More real. More angry. More dangerous.

His dark hair gleams, the strands made of wet, black silk. The night muted their beauty, their fluidity. I was right about his face though.

It is a web of square planes and valleys, sharp and harsh, but regal and proud. Nothing is soft about him except his lips, which are currently pursed. I picture the cigarette sitting in his full, plump mouth.

Then, like last night, he sighs, and the violence in his frown melts a little. He hates the book, but he wants it. I think he hates how much he wants it.

But why? If he wants it so much, he should just take it.

My heart has forgotten its loneliness and is invested in this dark stranger now. I study him from top to bottom. A leather jacket hangs from his forearm. He's wearing a crisp white shirt and blue jeans and…

Oh my God! He's wearing a white shirt and blue jeans.

He's dressed like my favorite song, "Blue Jeans" by Lana Del Rey.

My heart starts to beat faster. Faster. Faster. I need him to look up. I need to see his eyes. I will him to do just that, but he doesn't get my vibes. I'm just about to go up to him when a girl skips into my vision.

He looks up then. In fact, he whips his eyes up, irritated.

They are blue—a brilliant blue, a fiery blue, like the hottest part of a flame, or like the water that puts out that flame.

"Um, hi," the girl says as her blonde ponytail swishes across her back.

He doesn't reply but watches her through his dark, thick lashes.

"I was wondering if you could help me get a few books from over there." She points to the tall wooden shelf across the room that almost touches the roof. A couple of girls are standing by it. They giggle among themselves when he looks over.

Really? That's so cliché, hitting on a guy like that at a bookstore.

Well, who am I to judge? I've done things like that multiple times with Caleb, playing the damsel in distress just so he'll come save me.

The girl is waiting for him to say something. He's been holding his silence for the past few seconds, and I begin to feel embarrassed for her. Silence is the worst response when trying to get someone to notice you.

Then he breaks his tight pose and shrugs. "I'd love to help you, but I forgot my ladder at home today."

Low and guttural—his voice. It's a growl, really, and it makes me shiver.

He delivers the line with such dryness that even I'm confused. Don't they have a ladder here at the store? But then the complete, yet fake, innocence on his face tells me he's making a joke, and despite the shivery skin, I chuckle quietly.

"They have a ladder here. Look," the girl says, pointing to the dark brown wooden ladder slanting against the bookcase. Her friends are still staring at the exchange between them.

"I see," he murmurs, scratching his jaw with his thumb and then drumming his fingers against his biceps.

There are tight lines around his eyes, flashing in and out of existence. He's trying to control himself yet again. He hated the interruption, and now he's deciding how to deal with it. It's all guesswork on my part, but I'm right. I just know it.

"I'm totally scared to climb it in my heels," the blondie explains.

"You shouldn't be," he encourages. "I do it all the time."

"Do what all the time?"

"Climb ladders in my heels," he deadpans and studies something on the floor—her shoes, maybe? "Ah, I can see where you're having trouble. Pencil heels. You don't want to mess with those. Dangerous contraptions. People have lost their lives."

There's a moment of silence. Then, "You're kidding, right?"

"No, I never kid about heels." He rubs his lips together. "Or skirts that make my calves look slimmer. I never kid about them either."

"What?" the girl screeches.

He draws back, looking affronted. "You don't think my calves can look slim in a skirt? Are you calling me fat?"

"Wh-What? I'm not... I never..."

"Yes, so I just had a tub of chocolate ice cream, and yes, I promised myself I'd cut down on sugar"—a sharp, dramatic sigh—"but I slipped up. You think just because you're blonde and pretty you can question a man's wardrobe choices?" The blue in his eyes is amused, as are the crinkles around them. I press my lips together to stop the snort from bursting out.

"I don't...I don't even know what you're talking about. I just came here asking for help." The girl is irritated and indignant.

The crinkles around his eyes snap back into tight lines. "Let me tell you a little secret." He lowers his voice and I find myself inching closer. "I'm not the helping kind." He tilts his head to point toward her friends. "You should run along and play with people your own age and IQ level."

Then he throws the book on the shelf, looks at his watch, and strides away, leaving us both stunned. The blondie huffs and heads toward her friends.

So the blue-eyed smoker is a giant asshole. I feel bad for the girl, even though a trapped laugh escapes me.

If that was his show of control, I don't know what he'll do if unleashed. I walk to where he was standing and pick up the abandoned book. *A Lover's Discourse: Fragments* by Roland Barthes. It looks harmless enough with an unassuming black cover. I wonder why he was mad at this book. I wonder how our conversation would go if we ever talked. I wouldn't even know what to say to him, except, *Hi, I'm Layla, and you remind me of a song.*

Hours later, I'm back at home. I'm tired and want to go to sleep. I don't even want to watch porn, which I would normally do while munching on my Twizzlers. I don't watch porn to get myself off, no. I don't even touch myself. I watch it to feel something, a sense of closeness to someone, maybe. I study the naked, writhing bodies, the erotic frown on the girl's face, the look of focus on the guy's. I listen to the sounds they make, albeit fake.

I try to understand their dynamic. It looks surreal to me. I try to compare it with the one time I had sex. It was nothing like that. The guy didn't look at me like he'd die if he didn't get inside me, and the girl—me—wanted him to get out as soon as he got in.

Well, that's what you get when you force someone to sleep with you.

First day of the spring semester. I wonder why they call it the spring semester; it's still January and freakishly cold. The snow is sprawled around like a white nightmare and the wind blows it sideways, slapping our faces with chilled flurries.

Even so, there's an enthusiasm in the air. New classes, new professors, new love stories.

The street outside my tower is flooded with people carrying book bags and wearing puffed-up multicolored jackets. I'm bombarded with shrieks of laughter and conversations as I walk down the street to Crème and Beans, my favorite coffee shop.

It seems as if it's become everyone's favorite overnight because it's jam-packed this morning. I wait in a long line that stretches to the back of the store.

The line moves slowly, like molasses, and as I take a step forward, I see him. Again. The blue-eyed smoker. He is up ahead at the counter. I can only see his profile—square jaw and untamed hair—as he steps out of the line, fishes his wallet out, and pays for the coffee.

He walks out, clenching a cigarette between his teeth, and lights it up. No hesitation this time. Has he already lost the battle?

My legs move of their own volition and I abandon the line, running after him. Even the blast of the cold wind isn't enough to deter me from pursuing the dark stranger.

He is eating up the distance, leaving a trail of smoke behind. He is more lunging than walking with his long legs, and I have to speed-walk to keep up. He walks toward McKinley Street where the quad is located, dodging the stream of people easily. I'm not as graceful. I bump and crash into bodies.

But somehow, I keep the broad line of his shoulders in sight. It's hard not to, really. He's taller than most people, his back broader, and I bet when that black sport jacket is peeled off, that back is an expanse of thick cuts and sleek lines, much like his face.

The chilled breeze ruffles his hair and scatters the smoke billowing out of his cigarette. I can taste it in my mouth, taste the ashy smoke and languid relief that only nicotine can provide. This man makes me want to buy a pack of cigarettes and smoke my day away. He makes me want to whip out my fake ID and get liquored up.

That reminds me—I am a good girl now.

So what the fuck am I doing? I've got class, and I should be scrambling like everyone to get to it.

But we want to follow him, my heart whines.

Fine. Just this once.

I keep following my smoker. We cross the quad and he climbs the steps leading up to the bridge that stretches over the two sides of campus. I hardly ever take it since all my classes are on the south side, where I live, but we're going to the north side, I guess.

The other side of campus is quieter. Cobblestone pathways and benches are almost empty. There are hardly any stragglers here. Even the air is sharper as it blows through my loose hair and swishes around my red-checkered skirt. Here, the leafless trees are dense as they line the path, making it seem like we're walking through woods.

At last, he stops in front of a building and I stop a few feet behind him. The golden letters on the red-bricked high-rise building say *McArthur Building*, and on the side in a smaller cursive font, it says *The Labyrinth*—whatever that means.

I enter the building behind him and sounds bombard me from every side. Murmurs, laughter, footsteps. A phone rings somewhere. A drawer is snapped shut. A door thuds closed. It is a hub of activity in contrast to the quietness outside, as though every soul on this side of campus resides within this archaic building.

The floors gleam under my feet and the unpolished brick walls give the space a homey feel. I want to look around and see what exactly this place is, but I don't dare take my eyes off him. He walks down the hallway and enters the very last room.

I follow him and as I'm about to enter the room, it happens.

He turns and looks at me.

His mysterious, otherworldly blue eyes are on me, and I'm rendered paralytic. I can't move. I can't think. His stare lulls me into a foggy stillness.

He leans against something...a table. The windows in the wall behind him let the sunlight in, which dissolves as soon as it touches his body, making him glow. He takes a sip of his coffee and watches me over the rim of the mug. Somewhere along the way he got rid of his cigarette, and oddly, I mourn the loss.

"Hi," I say breathily.

"Are you going to take a seat?"

His rich, mature voice slides over my skin, causing a slight sting, like that of an aged liquor.

"What?" I ask stupidly, thoughtlessly.

"Take a seat," he says again, sighing.

"I don't..."

He stands up straight. "Take. A. Seat." He enunciates every word like I'm an imbecile. "Or get the fuck out of my class."

Class. That word pierces the bubble around me, making me wince. I break his gaze and look around. Sure enough, we're in a class with twenty or so people, and they're all staring at me.

I look back at him, frowning, and study his features. The *aged*, *mature* features. The lines around his mouth and eyes. His confident manner. The fact that he is intimidating when he wants to be.

He doesn't look like a college-going guy...because he is not.

This blue-eyed smoker is a professor.

CHAPTER THREE

"You're...a professor." I repeat my thoughts out loud; I don't know what else to say.

A tight, barely tolerant smile. "What gave me away?"

Plenty of things, actually. I open my mouth to answer his question but my heart whispers, *He's kidding, you idiot. Sarcasm alert.*

Right. I close my mouth but open it again. "I-I didn't realize that when I followed you here."

"You followed me." He's studying me with shrewd eyes. I wonder what I look like to him—not like that blondie, I hope. Not like anyone else either.

"No," I answer immediately, without a thought. *Did you steal Caleb's underwear? No, Mom.* "Of course not. I mean, I didn't mean it that way. I just... I didn't realize this is a class."

"It is, as you can see." He puts down his coffee mug, ready to dismiss me. "So either take a seat or get out."

"Right." I nod. I'm on the verge of leaving, putting this whole thing behind me, but my legs move forward instead of backward, and then I'm walking through the rows of red plastic chairs. An uncomfortable prickle needles the back of my neck and I know he is watching me.

I take a seat in the back, look up at him—*the professor*—and find him unzipping his coat. He takes it off, revealing a starched grey shirt over black jeans. As he drapes the jacket over the chair, his movements are deft and fluid, like a melody. I was right—he's like a song.

The realization brings heat, and I feel hotter than I've ever felt in winter. My skin sizzles and my breath skips. It's so odd. Drops of sweat bead and trickle down my spine.

With trembling hands, I take my white beanie off and shake out my messy hair. Next to go are my fuzzy scarf, my gloves, the purple fur coat, and at last, the black cardigan, leaving me in a full-sleeved white top and red-checkered skirt. I pile everything in the next chair and take a deep breath.

As I look up, my eyes clash with the tiny blue balls of fire. The professor stares at me with a raised eyebrow and hands in his pockets. By the looks of it, he—along with everyone else—has been staring at me for a while now.

"Cold hates me," I mumble and shrug, jerking my shoulders up.

He shakes his head once and runs his gaze over the class. The students sit on the edges of their seats as they wait for him to speak. I lean forward too. What class is this?

"Well..." He rocks on his heels. "I'm T—"

"We know who you are," a girl says from the front row, and the entire class breaks into excited murmurs.

Yeah, but I don't. What's his name?

"Okay then." He seems to be a little taken aback at their enthusiasm.

"I loved your latest collection," she chirps. "I mean, we all did. We even had an *Anesthesia* night after finals. We read the entire thing. I got the title piece. It's hands down the best poem in the book."

Wait, what? He is a poet?

The guy next to her interrupts her. "I beg to differ. I think I like *The Nighttime* the best. It's got a certain mystery to it. It starts in one place and then, *boom*, the ending completely blows your mind."

"Yeah. See, that's the thing. I think it's deceiving the reader. I hate deceiving the reader. I think it's just cheap tactics, you know. That's why *Anesthesia* is the best one. It's simple and pedestrian and just so powerful."

"Yeah, it is simple, but *Nighttime* has...flair to it. It's dramatic. Sometimes drama is important—big gestures, you know, that kind of thing."

They argue some more. Words like syllables, *stressed* syllables, flow, form, rhythm—things I've never even heard of—are thrown around. Meanwhile, the professor watches them with a certain shock. It's comical, really. Finally the girl gets tired of it and addresses him. "What do you think, professor?"

He shakes his head as if waking up from sleep. "Think about what?"

"Drama or simplicity, what do you think is better?" This comes from the guy.

The professor folds his arms across his chest and squints his eyes, as if he's thinking about the answer. If yesterday's incident is any indication, he is pretending to indulge them.

"That's a tough one. I might need something a little stronger than coffee to come up with an answer, and unfortunately, it's frowned upon to drink in a class. So, why don't we begin with something a little ordinary? Like names, perhaps?" He lifts his chin to the front-row girl. "Do you want to start us off?"

"Uh, okay." The girl wasn't expecting that. "So, uh, I'm Emma. Emma Walker."

Just like that, the spotlight falls away from him as people start introducing themselves.

He adjusts the cuffs of his shirt, fiddles with the buttons with his thick, long fingers. I feel especially drawn to them. He is a writer. He writes, with those hands. They are little gods, aren't they? They create things, words, poems. For someone like me, that's extraordinary.

I've got zero knowledge of poetry, but he makes me want to crack open his book and read. *Huh.* No one has ever made me want to do something as innocent as reading while simultaneously, making me want to get high and drunk.

Who *is* this man?

He's like candy-coated toxin.

I'm so caught up in my musings that I almost miss the golden glint of a ring on his hand. For a split second, I'm confused as to what it is. Then I realize it's a wedding band.

The blue-eyed professor is married.

My heart slows down for a few beats, making me dizzy, and then it picks back up. Thundering, galloping; it's anxious. I almost want to rub my palm in circles where it's making a fuss inside my chest. It's bizarre. What do I care if he's married?

Biting my lip, I look up and find his gaze on me. It's one of those things where you accidently meet someone's eyes. It's not deliberate. It's not like he was watching me watch his hands. And yet, my skin crackles with the tiny bit of electricity that is left behind after a gaze touches the body. I shift in my chair, crossing and uncrossing my legs.

Before long, it's my turn to talk. "I'm Layla. Layla Robinson."

His focus stays on me a beat longer than it did on other students. "Why do you want to take Introduction to Poetry, Miss Robinson?"

Great. The first thing he asks me is the one thing I have no clue about. Maybe I can say my therapist/guidance counselor suggested I try something new and here I am, but I don't want him to know I'm crazy.

We are not crazy, my unhelpful heart chimes in.

I sit up straight and clear my throat. "Well, because it's interesting. I like poetry."

"What do you like about it?"

My breaths bubble up from my chest but don't reach my mouth. I can't exhale a proper puff of air as I contemplate his question. I'm under scrutiny, and I hate it. I feel everyone judging me, picking me apart. It feels like home, and I want to disappear.

But, like always, I keep my chin up and my eyes unblinking. The question churns inside my brain and I have an epiphany.

"The words," I exclaim.

"Yes?" He raises a sarcastic brow. *Asshole.*

"It's like lyrics without music." I forge on. "It's so easy to lose yourself in the beat of music, but lyrics keep you grounded. It keeps your mind active, you know. You have to pay attention, listen to it over and over to get its meaning, to read between the lines." I nod, agreeing with my own analysis. "Yeah. That's why I like poetry. Because of the words. They ground me."

The silence is absolute. No one even breathes, or maybe it's just me who doesn't. I've never thought about lyrics in that way, but maybe it's true. Words. Lyrics. Poetry. Aren't they all the same?

The professor has the same look on his face as he did while he watched the cigarette and the book. His control is tick-tocking and I'm afraid. I'm...thrilled, which is a very strange reaction to have.

Then he turns his gaze away. "Let's discuss the syllabus, shall we?"

A relieved breath whooshes out of me. This man has some serious self-control, if you don't count the cigarettes. I should take lessons from him. I should register for this class. At least Kara will be happy.

He moves around the desk and fishes out a stack of papers from the drawer. It's copies of the syllabus. He keeps one and hands the rest to Emma in the first row. For the next few minutes, the room is filled with rustling of papers and scratches of pen.

The sheet reaches me and I see it. His name. On the top right corner of the page with his office number and hours, and his extension.

Thomas Abrams.

Thomas.

Professor Abrams.

I bend down and retrieve a pen from my bag and underline his name. Once. Twice. Three times in purple glitter ink. Then I draw a circle around it. I tell my hands to stop, but they don't. They dig the nib of the pen in, even more furiously at my protests.

Once we all have a copy, Professor Abrams proceeds to read out the important parts. This class is part workshop and part lit, meaning we will have to write our own poems and have them critiqued, along with reading poems by some famous people. Honestly, I don't know the names of half of them—Dunn, Plath, Byron, Poe, Wilmot.

Professor Abrams' voice has very little inflection to it, making me think he doesn't have much interest in the syllabus. He frowns at certain places especially, like when the syllabus outlines the homework to be given and the grading system.

There are a few moments when Emma tries to engage him in a conversation, but he evades smoothly. I can feel her frustration from where I sit in the last row. Either Thomas Abrams doesn't care, or he has no idea how to be a teacher. I'm guessing it's a little bit of both.

Before long, the class is over and we have our first assignment: write a one- to two-page essay on our reasons for choosing this class and authors that inspire us. The assignment is enough to send me dashing and never return to this side of campus.

As I'm exiting, I pause at the threshold and look back. Professor is fiddling with the cuffs of his shirt again, and sunrays reflect off his golden wedding band. Rolling his shoulders, he puts the jacket on and shakes his arms out. Still graceful. Still fluid like a song. Still potent enough to make me shiver.

Before he can catch me staring, I walk away and almost collide with someone out in the hallway. It's the guy from the front row; I forget his name. He's got messy hair and black-rimmed glasses. He is cute in a nerdy sort of way with the hood of his jacket crooked around his neck.

"Hey." He greets me like he knows me.

"Hey?" I cock my head to the side, trying to remember if I know him.

"You're Layla. Layla Robinson."

"I am." *Did I do something to him?*

"I'm Dylan Anderson. We had history together."

"We did?"

"Uh-huh. Professor Allen? He used to pick at his nose while writing on the board?"

"Oh yeah. Oh my God, how did I forget that?" I shudder. "Ugh. That was the worst."

Dylan laughs. It's a goofy, awkward kind of laugh, and I love it. He turns to the girl who sat beside him. "This is Emma Walker."

"Hey." I raise my hand and wave at her.

"It's nice to meet you."

Her greeting is wary, and I don't understand why that would be. "You were in history too?" I ask her.

"No. I passed on that after Dylan told me about the professor."

"Yeah. You coward." He elbows her playfully and coaxes a reluctant smile out of her. "She's a big chicken when it comes to taking risks. We'd decided to do the class together, but then she abandoned me."

"You're such a drama queen." She pretends to be annoyed, but I can see she's not. She's loving this, basking in his attention.

They argue some more, and it becomes clear. I am quite an expert at sniffing out heartbreak and one-sided love after years of practice. Emma is in love with Dylan but he doesn't know it, and that wary glance? She was jealous of me. Me, the discarded girl. I want to tell her she has nothing to be afraid of. I'm not a threat—maybe to myself, but not to other people.

I study them together. Dylan: messy dark hair and hazel eyes with a boyish, somewhat shy charm about him, and Emma: brown hair and eyes, sparkling with intelligence and maturity.

They're a perfect match. I think anybody who's in love with anyone is a perfect match. I don't believe in crap like *There's somebody better for you out there.* I don't want better. I want the guy I'm in love with.

There goes my selfish heart. It's thundering in my chest with anger and frustration. *Why doesn't Caleb love us?*

The clicking footsteps have us turning toward the classroom. Thomas emerges, tall and unapproachable, hardly sparing us a glance. As he passes our little group, I feel the buzz of his energy waking up my body in goose bumps. He strides down the hallway to the stairs at the end and takes them two at a time.

Dylan exhales a sharp breath. "That guy is…not what I expected."

"Is it me or is he totally boring? He's nothing like what I was hoping." Emma frowns, folding her arms. "I thought he'd be friendlier or something, or would at least answer my questions. I was so excited to actually learn something from him, you know."

Dylan rubs the top of her head playfully and Emma swats his hand away. "Told you. You were expecting too much, Emmy. He's just a guy who writes poetry."

"Just a guy!" Emma is enraged. "You have no idea how amazing he is. He's one of the best poets we have right now. Do you know how many awards he's won? He's magic."

Dylan turns to me. "He's really not. She's got a little crush on him, that's all."

"I do not!"

Dylan's eyes hold a twinkle at seeing Emma so riled up, and I chuckle. Guys can be so clueless. He likes her too, he just doesn't know it yet.

They begin arguing again, and I feel like this is how they are with each other. This is their sacred ritual, and I'm the intruder. I'm about to excuse myself when a series of footsteps thump on the second floor and we all look up.

"What is that?" I ask, wincing.

"The theatre people. They have a conference room upstairs they use to practice when the auditorium isn't free," Dylan informs me.

"Wow." I'm impressed. "You guys have theatre people here?"

Emma laughs. "Yup. This is the Labyrinth. We've got all kinds of weirdos and artsy people here."

After my detour to the north side of campus, I rush back to reality. I attend the rest of my classes in a certain daze, here one second but gone the next. It's odd, to say the least.

By the end of the day, I'm still trapped in those flaming eyes, looking at the world through a blue fog.

He's magic.

I don't know why, but that word affects me so much. Once all my classes are done, I find myself at the bookstore again. This time around, I don't want to buy a required book or create chaos. I want to get to know him through his words.

His book is called *Anesthesia: Collected Poems*. According to Wikipedia, this is his first full-length collection of poems. It was released almost a year ago and since then, it has been named one of the best poetry books of the year and has received a bunch of awards. Most specifically, he is the youngest recipient of the McLeod genius grant at the age of twenty-nine. He's a big deal.

I hold the thin, leafy book in my hands. The pages are crisp white with black, bold letters. I flick through them as Lana's "Blue Jeans" plays in my ears. My fingers trace the curly letters of his name on the front.

Thomas Abrams.

Thomas, dark smoker and blue-eyed professor.

This side of the store is almost empty. There are a bunch of stragglers in the popular fiction section, over to the left side, partially hidden behind the sprawling staircase and flanking bricked pillars.

Knowing the coast is clear, I bring the book to my nose and smell the clean, sharp pages. I take a large sniff and strangely, catch a scent of warm smoke. I sway with the rush of warmth skating down my spine and the rhythm of the music echoing in my ears. Beginnings of a moan surprise me and I whip my eyes open.

There he is, as if conjured by my own imagination.

The eyes that have been haunting me, following me everywhere today, bore into me and slowly sweep down to the book currently covering the lower half of my face. I feel a tug in my stomach, behind my navel, as though someone is pulling on the silver ring adorning my belly. I clear my throat and lower the book, taking my headphones off.

"I love the smell of books."

He doesn't look like he believes me. His contemplative stare makes me aware that I'm wearing layers upon layers of clothing. Too many layers. Too much heat.

I put the book away with trembling hands and shrug. "You can say it."

"Say what?" He cocks his head, as if analyzing me.

Kara does the same. She tries to figure me out and I hate it, but hate isn't the word I'd use to describe what I'm feeling right now. It's something else. Bolder. Thrilling. Unknown.

"Whatever you're thinking. I can see it on your face—you think I'm crazy, think I'm an idiot for smelling a book."

I'm waiting for him to acknowledge it, to say, *Duh, you're right*, though I don't think he'd say it exactly that way.

"That's...impressive." He nods, his mouth curling into a one-sided smile. "You can read me like a book—though I'd rather you not smell me."

A surprised chuckle escapes me. "You're funny."

"Guilty. One of my many talents."

"Right. What are your other talents? No wait, I know—teaching, right?"

"Yes. I was born to teach," he deadpans, his face made of smooth stone except for the deepening crinkles around his eyes.

"Ah, delusion. Got it. You're *insanely* talented."

His beautifully carved jaw tics. "Are you insulting my teaching skills, Miss Robinson?"

My name sounds like tendrils of chocolate in his rich, deep voice. I feel it drenching me in a sticky, excited buzz. How is it that he makes me hot while at the same time giving me shivers? How is it that he does any of these things *at all*?

"No, Professor Abrams. I wouldn't dare. You kinda scare me."

Truth. Absolute and utter truth. He scares me, because he has a strange effect on me, mystical and unprecedented.

"Good. I am scary. Never forget that," he says approvingly, ready to leave, but then he turns around to face me. "Do you know it's illegal to mess up the order of the books?"

It takes a moment for me to get what he means. He's talking about what I did yesterday. "I didn't—"

He throws me a disbelieving stare. "It was dumb, not to mention ineffective. G to F? No one cares about that. If you really want to scare someone, go with something like S to A. Wider stretch, ergo, bigger panic."

I swallow. "Okay."

"Don't tell anyone I said that."

"Okay," I repeat.

He ducks his head down and smiles.

"I thought you didn't see me. Yesterday, I mean."

Until I said it, I hadn't realized I'd wanted him to see me. In another drastic epiphany, like the one I had in class about words, I realize I don't want to be invisible to him. *Not to him.*

But why? I don't get it. What is this madness?

"I told you, I have many talents. Sniffing out crazy is one of them."

I gasp and he chuckles. He called me crazy. I absolutely *hate* that, but as I watch him leave, it's not anger that I'm feeling.

It's something else. Something magical.

CHAPTER FOUR

I'm dense when it comes to art, be it a book, a painting, or whatever. I don't understand the allure of it. I don't understand how bland circular lines on a painting, nonsensical words in a book, or a broken piece of clay inspire devotion in people.

Even so, I've read Thomas' book of poems at least a hundred times since Monday. In fact, this book has kept me company throughout the week when I couldn't sleep at night. The tiny words on the paper seem to have risen and attached themselves to my skin. I feel them everywhere, all the time, as if I know them. They are my friends. I know where they are coming from.

As if I know what Thomas was thinking when he wrote these lines.

Emma was right—Thomas is indeed a genius. He is magic. He went to school here before moving to Brooklyn, and he was the one who started the Labyrinth, an online journal that features varied pieces from both upcoming and established poets, prose writers, playwrights, and so on.

I'm so far removed from him, from these people, but still, I'm back at the Labyrinth, the artistic maze. I'm skipping political science—the class I missed last week—again, but I don't care. I want to be inside this mysterious building.

I enter and feel an instant warmth seeping into my body. Now that I'm not in pursuit of someone, I give myself time to study things. It smells like campfire: smoky and marshmallow-y. The sounds are still there, lively and energetic as ever.

My boots hit the polished cement floor as I walk farther in. The walls have a chipped brick façade, giving it an industrial look. It is dotted with countless colored flyers and photos. I take in every single face displayed up there; most of them are group shots, and the location is eerily similar: a bar. The flyers are for readings—some outdated, some upcoming—or for singing auditions, band performances, theatre productions, et cetera.

I turn the corner and almost bump into someone. He's carrying a stack of papers and speed walking. I mutter my apologies but he doesn't pay me any mind. A burst of laughter floats out of a classroom and I find myself smiling in return. Running footsteps above indicate that the theatre people still haven't found an auditorium to practice in.

This place is something, isn't it? This building is a living, breathing thing.

I go inside the classroom and take my seat in the back like the last time. A few minutes later, Professor Abrams comes in. He takes off his coat and drapes it on the chair, revealing a black shirt that molds over the tight arches of his shoulder and pecs. The languidness in his demeanor while at the bookstore is gone. He's strained inside these four walls, chiseled from a rock, but no less handsome.

Like last time, he fiddles with the cuffs of his shirt. I realize it's a ritual of some sort, as if he's preparing himself for the torture ahead.

"I want a circle," he declares when he is comfortable with the state of his cuffs.

Confused, we stay still and silent. He studies us with uncanny eyes. "How many of you have taken a workshop before?"

Without giving us a chance to answer, he shakes his head. "Never mind. I don't care. In my class, you'll sit in a circle, and..." He folds his arms across his chest. "You're going to read your work out loud. We'll take some time to ponder, and then we'll talk about it. I want everyone to pitch in, and I don't want repeated comments. If someone has said what you were going to say, then think of something else. Is that clear?"

Not a word, not even a breath.

Professor Abrams lets out a sharp puff of breath. "Are we *clear*?"

Broken out of the shocked trance, we all nod our heads and spring up from our seats. The room is filled with the screech of chairs being dragged across the floor. Five minutes later, we're all seated in a semicircle around the professor, who perches on the edge of his desk, elbows on his thighs and fingers laced.

Somehow, I've ended up directly in front of him. This is the line of fire, and I'm going to get burned before this class is over.

He straightens and picks up a thin yellow folder from the desk, perusing it. "When I call your name, tell me about your essay, who your favorite author is, and how he or she inspires you and your writing." He looks up and grimaces. "I'm boring myself just talking about it, but it's in the syllabus."

Emma smiles, sitting up in her chair. She is loving the chance to interact with her rock-star poet. Me? I'm crouching, because I completely forgot about the homework.

Hide. Hide.

Just as the thought occurs, I dismiss it. As it turns out, I want him to pay attention to me. I don't want him to gloss over me like he's doing other students. I want him to see me even though I'm doing everything I can to curl up and become invisible in a room full of students.

Again, what *is* this madness?

He keeps reading off names from the list in his hands and dismissing them right as they begin speaking. His eyes glaze over. I can see it. I wonder if it's visible to other students.

Even though I'm restless, shifting in my seat, fiddling with my skirt and my top, I'm fascinated by how these people talk about their ideals.

I want to be like Hemingway. Direct. Precise.

I love Shakespeare. If I manage to write a single poem like him, I'll die happy.

I'm fascinated by the passion in their voices, the goals they have set for themselves—to be something, to be someone. It makes me jealous of their brand of love, a love that doesn't make you selfish or lonely, a love that gives you purpose.

Milton, Robert Browning, James Joyce, Byron, Edgar Allen Poe, Stephen Dunn, Joyce Carol Oates, Gillian Flynn, Jennifer Egan, Neil Gaiman, Sylvia Plath.

I don't know any of them, and I have an urge to find out. My restlessness is swelling, expanding. My breaths have escalated with the hint of possibility in the air, the possibility to tip over the edge into a different world with brick façades and cement floors, a world with surly professors with eyes the color of hot flame and cool water.

My musings are cut short when Professor Abrams jumps down from his perch on the desk, his hands on his hips. *What's wrong?*

"I wasn't planning on saying anything because it's none of my business, but I'm your teacher, and apparently I'm supposed to care about these things. Also, I don't think I can stop myself, but that's beside the point." He paces, then pauses to scowl at the class, at no one in particular.

"All I've heard so far is how amazing an author is and how you want to write like him or her. I don't think you understand what inspiration is. It's not ripping off Hemingway or Shakespeare or Plath. It's not the ambition to *be* like someone. That's no ambition at all. If that's truly what you want, then I'd rather not teach you. But, unfortunately, I need this job, so..." He puffs out an exasperated breath as he runs his thick fingers through his hair.

"I'm only going to say this once: there's a difference between writing and creating art. Anyone can write, but only a few can create art, and for that, you need to find your own voice. Reading is good. Read as much as you want, but make your own rules. Don't just follow. Strive to create something that comes from you. Strive to create *your* art, not recreate what someone else did, because frankly, you should rather want to be dead than be a rip-off."

He is panting, his chest punching the taut fabric of his shirt. The hard planes and hollows of his face shift with emotion. This is the poet Emma was talking about. Passionate. Volatile. Genius. Magical.

I've got goosebumps under the sleeves of my sweater, followed by flashes of heat. I touch the spine of his book, going up and down the length with my finger. The smooth texture of it causes something heavy to swirl inside my chest. It causes me to bite my lip. As if he's attuned to my actions, his gaze falls on me. We stay connected a beat before we both look away. For that one beat, I saw his eyes flare, and the blue was so prominent, it took my breath away.

Professor Abrams' fervent speech has sparked interest and from there, the class practically carries itself. Emma is the first one to ask questions. *Who was your inspiration? Who did you read while growing up? Did you always know you wanted to be a poet? Do you write every day?* He dodges every one of those, never divulging anything about his favorite writers or his writing ritual—as Emma calls it—answering every question with a question of his own.

I stare at him. I observe him, his little habits. The tic in his jaw when someone seems to bother him. How he swallows down cutting comments when the same someone doesn't get that he's irritated. Every time he controls himself, I feel the familiar tug in my belly button.

As soon as the class is over, everyone submits their homework on the desk, reminding me that somehow, I've been spared. Happy or disappointed, I can't decide. I gather up my winter gear, ready to leave, when his voice, sharp as a whip, stops me.

"Miss Robinson, can I talk to you for a second?" Not even a glance at me. His focus is on the essays as he bundles them up.

The room has almost emptied as I approach the wooden expanse of the desk, the solidness separating us. Is it weird that I notice how he's changed since the class ended a few minutes ago? He isn't the rigid professor anymore. He is... Thomas.

The reappearance of the guy from the bookstore injects a shot of mischief and boldness in me. I'm reckless in the moment, light and airy. I give him a smile and my most innocent look: wide, blinking eyes and a hint of a frown on my smooth forehead. "Yes, Professor?"

But he isn't in the mood to indulge. He thumbs through the essays while staring at me, and I know I've been found out. Any second now, he's going to give it to me about my missing homework. My heartbeat gallops.

"What are you doing in my class?" he asks instead, with the typical tic in his jaw. Yeah, I'm in trouble.

"What do you mean?"

"You're clearly not a poet." He studies me. "In fact, I don't even think you like books. So, it begs the question: what are you doing in my class?"

"I like books! I read all the time." I'm outraged that he knows this about me, that he *sees* my deception in being here.

But isn't that what I wanted? I wanted him to see me. It doesn't make any sense. My reactions to him *don't* make sense.

"What was the last book you read?" he challenges.

Yours. But I don't say that.

"It was called, um, something...I forget the name, but it was about love. Uh, childhood sweethearts getting married and having a bunch of kids."

"So who's your favorite author, then? I'm sure you'd remember something like that."

He is relentless, but what he doesn't know is that I'm relentless too. "There are too many to count."

Thomas puts his palms on the desk and leans toward me, curling his athletic body over the desktop. "Name one."

From this close, I breathe him in, his scent. The intoxicating combination of cigarettes and chocolate is turning my brain to mush. I take a step back. "You know what, I'm late for class, and I have to go all the way back to the south side of campus, so—"

"Name one author you love and I'll let you go."

I'm ready to wave the white flag and peace out of here. Instead, another lie blurts out of me. "Sh-Shakespeare."

The vein on the side of his neck looks alive and breathing, like it could leap off any second, separate from his body, and attack me with the anger pulsing through it.

Slowly, he shakes his head. "Try again."

"That wasn't the deal. I told you—"

He straightens and lifts a thick, ridged finger. "One. Just one."

Oh God. I almost groan out loud as I study the bumps on his finger. It looks worn, well-used. It looks like...yeah, magic, a magic that spins out words and poems, poems I can't stop reading. I wonder what would happen if he ever accidentally touched me. I'd pass out, most likely.

"Y-You. I love you."

Wait...what?

I clap my hand over my mouth, my eyes going wide. I did *not* just say that. I've never said that to anyone except Caleb—not that he ever understood my meaning. He thought it was in fun, in friendship.

But here and now, I rush to explain, "I mean I love your work. I—"

His jaw is ticking again, but this time around it's more dangerous, because it comes with a twitch in his right eye. "I know you're not in my class because you're not on the official roster, so technically, you're trespassing, and I want you to stop. Next time, don't be here."

I'm tempted to say okay, but the thought of not showing up is even worse than braving his wrath.

"Or what?" I swallow and curl my fingers around the edge of the desk.

"You don't want to do this."

"Do what, exactly? This is a class and I'm a student—why can't I be here?"

He pins me with his gaze before hitching one side of his lips up in a tight, mocking smile. "You really think this is going to work?"

"What are you talking about?"

He leans forward again, and I'm hit by the desire to push this desk away. It feels like miles and miles of ocean rather than a few inches of polished wood. His proximity has upped the sounds of the world. The talking, the laughing, the footsteps. The earth is shifting, rolling side to side, and he seems like the only anchor. How crazy is that?

"You want me to spell it out, huh." His voice has dropped an octave. Low and gravelly. Words slurring together. "I know your secret, Layla."

A blip in my heartbeat. Firecrackers burst over my skin at the way he said my name. As far as I'm concerned, my name is average, but his voice, the movements of his tongue against his lips, make it special. A squeaky sound escapes me because I've forgotten how to speak.

"You think I don't know? It's in your eyes." He flicks his gaze left to right, studying said eyes. His blue and my violet. The colors with just a pinch of a difference, belonging to the same part of the spectrum of a rainbow.

"What about them?" I breathe at last, gathering my scattered thoughts.

His lips twitch and my cold, dry fingertips want to touch it, feel the tiny dance of muscles. "They do a shit job of hiding your emotions." His lopsided smile morphs into a chuckle. Dark and rich, like chocolate. *We want to taste it.* For once, I agree with my stupid heart.

"What emotions?" I'm just saying things now, robotically. A doll made of plastic.

"You have a thing for me."

It takes a second for me to register what he just said. "Wh-What?"

He draws back and shrugs. "It's obvious."

"What?" I screech again. My plastic brain is coming to life. "That's ridiculous. I don't...I don't have a *thing* for you." He shrugs again, so cocky and arrogant, as if the whole world revolves around him. My palms ball into fists. "I don't. I don't have a crush on you—or on anyone, for that matter."

Thomas nods. "Sure."

"I don't." I huff out a frustrated breath.

"Okay."

His careless dismissal, his disbelief, his beautiful, condescending eyes—they make me want to hit him. They make me want to spill my secrets. I'm taken aback. I *never* want that. I never want anyone to see the dark, needy hole inside me. Even *I* don't want to see it.

This is sick, Layla. How can you think that about your brother?

My mom's voice in my ears angers me further. She pops up every now and then to be my tormentor, to tell me how much I need Kara to straighten me out.

I take a deep breath and tighten my features. I hate Thomas Abrams in this moment, and I want him to know it. My pelvic bone digs into the edge of the desk as I let my anger loose. "I hate to break it to you, Professor Abrams, but old guys don't do it for me. They've got a sickly smell that I don't like, and correct me if I'm wrong, but doesn't that thing down there increasingly shrink with age?"

I'm angry enough to not care about what I just said, but not angry enough to ignore the flame flickering in my stomach or to not look at the...thing I just mentioned, the slight bump hidden by the zipper of his jeans. Heat spans the entire length of my body as I imagine what it looks like...bare and hard.

"I wouldn't know, Miss Robinson." His soft, smooth voice brings me out of my trance. "I think I have some good inches left in me, but thanks for the tip. Might come in handy in a few years when I start measuring my dick."

Dick. He said dick. In front of me. His student. Everything about this is inappropriate. My skin is throbbing, pulsating with too much energy. I'm saturated with sweat and tingles.

What is happening?

He shrugs on his coat and buttons it up with deft movements. His eyes are on me as he says, or rather commands, "Don't be here next time."

Then he walks out.

The night is sleepless and snowy. I watch the snow through the door of my balcony, pressing my naked body to the chilled glass.

I am hot, too hot. I look down and find myself covered with a constellation of scarlet splashes, almost hiding the web of blue veins under my pale skin. My thighs slip against each other due to the wetness leaking out of me. I break my cardinal rule and touch my swollen pussy. My hips jerk at the sensation. It's foreign and so fucking good. The folds are creamy and sensitive, begging for something.

You have a thing for me.

That's all I can hear, all I could hear throughout the day. I shiver, imagining his wispy whispers over my skin.

Yeah, I do.

Somehow, someway, I have developed this crush on him. I know he's married. I know he's an asshole, rude and mean and some kind of a genius poet—but maybe that's the appeal. I don't want him to love me back. I don't want the hope of reciprocation. Hope kills. It tortures. I just want this.

This viral need that is eating through my heart, my brain, all my organs, starting up a pulse deep below. It swells and slickens, like every time I watch porn. I never bring myself relief because it feels dirty, illicit to be jerking off to something like that. Besides, after what I did to Caleb, I don't think I deserve any kind of pleasure. Hence, my cardinal rule: no touching my own body.

But this pulse is hard to ignore. It's too strong. Too forceful. Too alive, as if my pussy is breathing and has a mind of its own. It's making me do things. *He's making me do things to myself.* He's making me touch my clit, my slippery cunt. Slow, at first. Slow, measured, lazy circles. Then fast, rushed, frantic flicks that cause my body to writhe. My small tits jiggle and shudder, pink nipples beading in excitement as I twist them with my other hand.

He's making me play with myself. He might as well be cradling my hand, dusky digits curled over my small, smooth ones. I'm his puppet and he is my invisible master, holding my strings from miles away.

"Thomas," I whisper and shatter at the same time. I come, wrapped in Thomas' heat and his poems. The orgasm vibrates through my body, making me moan, exhausting me so much that I have to press my forehead against the chilled glass.

Even through the arousal, I'm aware that it's wrong and sick and inappropriate. But, it's also freeing. A cleansing ritual. I'm shedding my old obsession. I'm moving on. Being normal.

Before this, I was Layla Robinson, crazy in love with her stepbrother. Now, I'm Layla Robinson, crushing on her poetry professor.

I slide open the balcony door. The curtains whip and billow in the frosty wind. Snowflakes catch on my fevered skin, cooling me down, freezing me, turning me blue.

And I throw my arms open and laugh.

CHAPTER FIVE

"I've got a crush." I grin at Kara.

"You've got what?"

"A crush. You know, when you fantasize about someone?"

"Yes. I know about that." She smiles. "So who's the guy?"

"That's the best part." I chuckle. "He's like, the most unavailable guy out there."

He is my professor, an asshole, *and* he is married. This crush is triple doomed.

Kara frowns at me and laces her fingers together on the desk. "I'm sorry. You lost me."

"Don't you get it?" I spring up from the chair and pace. "It's hopeless and I know it and I have no urge to date him. No urge, whatsoever. I don't expect him to tell me he loves me because I don't want him to and I know he won't."

"Because he's unavailable," Kara jumps in.

"Uh-huh. That's right." Laughing, I sit back down.

"That's...interesting. Kind of backward, but interesting. But what if it changes? What if you begin to want those things?"

"I won't, because he's like cancer." Kara raises her eyebrows at my analogy. "I know the endgame with him. I *know* the cancer is going to kill me, so I'm not begging for my life anymore. I just..." Sighing, I try to put my feelings into words. "He distracts me, you know...from Caleb. He makes me feel normal. If I can fantasize about someone else then that means Caleb's hold on me is weakening, going away." I swallow as sadness and fear and tiny excitement overwhelm me. "And I want that. I want a life of my own where I don't think about him all the time."

Our session goes fast after that. Kara is happy I'm moving on, but I can see the guardedness in her eyes. She doesn't need to worry though. My crush is harmless, just a distraction, and I need that right now.

After finishing, I go to Crème and Beans to get my coffee fix and run into Emma. She's at the counter, paying for a large mug of coffee, and I come up behind her.

"Hey." She waves at me awkwardly, and I do the same. She is still wary of me and I can't take it, especially when there's nothing to be wary of.

"So Emma, uh…" She gives me her full attention and I stumble over my words a little. "I don't…know how to say this but, uh, I'm just gonna say it. I kind of know that you don't like me for some reason and I also know that you like Dylan." She freezes, her eyes wide, blush burning her cheeks. "I-It's okay. I'm not…I'm not judging or anything. I just wanna say that you have nothing to fear from me. I shouldn't even be on your radar."

I whoosh out a breath when I'm done. She is in shock, opening and closing her mouth at my frankness. After a few seconds, she manages to gather herself. "I…don't know what to say. I don't even know what you're talking about."

Denial. I've done the same thing before.

"It's fine. You don't have to say anything. Just know that I'm harmless."

At that, she scoffs. "Right."

"I am."

"You're the violet-eyed goddess."

"Huh?"

She smiles sadly. "That's Dylan's nickname for you. He's crazy about you. Last semester when you guys had that class together? He wouldn't shut up about how much he liked you."

"What?" I bark out a disbelieving laugh.

"It's fine. His feelings are not your fault. I'm being stupid."

"But he *doesn't* have feelings for me." Emma doesn't look like she believes me, and I continue, "Do you want me to prove it?"

"Prove what?"

"That he doesn't like me that way. He can't. He doesn't even know me—not like he does you. Trust me when I say this: Dylan likes you."

Dylan might think I'm attractive, what with violet eyes and black hair, but liking is taking it too far. Back in New York, I always knew guys liked my face —I take after my mom, after all, the beauty queen of the Upper East Side— but they never liked *me*. All they saw was my beautiful face, never me. I was invisible to them.

Caleb was the only one who knew the real me, but that wasn't enough.

Hope flares in Emma's brown eyes and my heart hurts for her. She is me, so very much like me in her unrequitedness.

"I don't think so." She shakes her head and sips her coffee.

"Will you at least give me a chance to prove it to you?"

"Okay. Yeah."

"All right then."

We throw small smiles at each other and I think this could be the beginning of something. There is a delicate truce between us. I get my coffee while Emma waits for me and then we head out together. She tells me she went to see an apartment a few streets over because she's planning to move out of the dorms.

"It was the worst. I don't think I've seen such a small room in my entire life, and I've been to the city, numerous times." She shudders.

"Why don't you live with me?" It's a spur of the moment decision and I don't even know I've made it until after the words come out of my mouth.

"What?"

"Yeah." I nod. "I think it's a great idea. I live just up the street, and I've got a spare room you can use."

"I don't... Are you sure?"

"Yes. Do you wanna come see it?"

"Right now?" She stops walking. "Yeah. I'd love to."

"Great." I grin.

Five minutes later, I let her in my tower. The ground floor smells like paint and new floors. Emma raises her eyebrow at the construction equipment but remains silent. We take the elevator up and she walks into the apartment after me.

Now that she is here, I see the space through her eyes and am embarrassed. The open floor plan has a living room and kitchen separated by a large island, which is hidden under the empty pizza boxes and Chinese takeout containers. A blanket is sprawled on the beige couch with a bag of chips and a package of Twizzlers on it. My laptop sits on the coffee table, lid half open, beside a stack of notebooks.

The only good thing about this large space is the sliding doors that lead to the balcony beyond the kitchen.

I smile at her in embarrassment and walk her to the spare bedroom on the left, adjacent to mine. This room is empty and, quite frankly, the cleanest one in the apartment since there's no stuff in here.

"This would be your room," I tell her, almost cringing at what she must be thinking about my living conditions. It feels oddly intrusive and vulnerable to show someone where you live. I'm beginning to regret this idea.

Emma walks in and circles around the room, passing by the closet, the en suite, and at last, standing at the window overlooking Albert Street and the university park. I'm at the edge of the room, feeling anxious. I tell myself it's no big deal if she hates it, but really, when is rejection not a big deal?

"I love it." She faces me and grins.

"You do?"

"Yeah. It's super big. I love the building. The location is great." She frowns. "Though how much is the rent for this place? I don't think I can afford it."

I enter the room and wave my hand at her. "Oh, don't worry about that. My stepdad owns the building."

"Whoa, really?"

"Yeah. It's still not ready to rent out, but they made an exception for me. I call it my tower."

"So that's why it looks like a construction zone." She nods her head as if coming to a conclusion. "You're rich, aren't you?"

"My parents are. I'm just lucky, I guess." I shift on my feet, feeling embarrassed when she remains silent. "What about your parents? I mean, are you close with them?"

"No. I don't...I don't talk about them." Now it's her turn to be embarrassed, and I want to tell her it's okay, that sometimes we just don't get along with the people who gave birth to us, but she doesn't let me talk. "Anyway, I can't just not pay rent. I mean, I don't wanna live for free."

I puff out a breath, thinking. "Okay, so how about this? You can chip in some other way. Like, maybe you can grocery shop? And also cook? I'm terrible at that kind of stuff. I never remember to buy anything other than Twizzlers."

Her eyes squint as she mulls it over. "I can do that. I mean, I'm not a great cook, but I do like cooking. I cook for Dylan all the time, so I'm totally in."

"So you'll do it? Move in?"

"Yes." She laughs, and in a surprising act, wraps me in a tight hug. "Thank you, thank you, thank you. I can't believe I finally found something great. I am so freaking happy right now."

Her hug makes me feel all choked up, like a frog is croaking in the depths of my throat. "It's gonna be great."

"Yes." She moves away, beaming.

She continues touring the house and balcony. We decide on a move-in day—tomorrow.

"I'd do it today but we've got the poetry night and I won't be able to find anyone to help me move my stuff."

"Poetry night?"

"Oh yes." She shakes her head. "I forget you're new. So every other Saturday we meet up at this bar called The Alchemy, just outside of campus. It's pretty informal. We read our stuff to each other. Sometimes theatre people do their shows, but tonight is poetry night and I'm reading some of my poems. You should come."

"Sure."

I am bundled up in my white beanie and my purple fur coat, which is buttoned up to my chin. My thigh-high boots crunch over the pavement as I reach the red door of The Alchemy and enter.

It's a small space with exposed brick walls and vaulted ceilings, the kind you find in a church. Wooden beams run along the length of the roof, lit up with Christmas lights. The air is warm and laced with a fruity aroma. Just like the Labyrinth, this place is bursting with energy.

My eyes take in the artwork on the walls, the mock guitars, the musical notes, the framed newspaper clippings, the silhouettes of people dancing in various poses, along with black and white photos of some of the famous writers I've only come to know this week.

"Hey, Layla!" I hear Emma's voice over the crowd and find her waving at me from the bar. "Over here!"

"Hey!" I barrel through to get to her and greet her with an amused smile when I see she's balancing three drinks in her hands. I take one glass from her and we wind our way through the scattered layout of tables.

"Hey guys, this is Layla, my new roommate," she says as we reach her table. There are a couple of guys sitting; one's Dylan, and the other one I don't know.

"Hello." I finger-wave at them.

Both wave back and the guy introduces himself as Matt. Dylan stands up and gives me his chair. "Hey Layla. So glad you came."

Now that Emma has revealed that Dylan likes me, I analyze his behavior. He's both shy and chatty, adorably awkward. It's a harmless crush, the kind I have on Thomas, which ties my tongue, gives me wet dreams, and makes my crazy heart pound faster. It's not easy and comfortable. It's not what he feels for Emma.

I'm aware that I'm sitting wedged between the two would-be lovebirds, but I'm not budging. I need to prove to Emma that Dylan is into her.

Leaning toward Dylan, I ask, "How are you guys drinking alcohol? Aren't you all underage?"

Dylan gulps as I shoot him a flirty smile. Emma is sitting strained in her seat. I hope she trusts me.

"It's all, uh, props. They don't serve alcohol on Labyrinth night."

"So what is it that you're drinking?" I grab his glass and take a sip.

His mouth hangs open before he closes it and clears his throat. "A Hemingway. It's just...a dummy martini."

"Sounds boring." I bat my eyelashes and Dylan almost spits out his drink. I take pity on him and turn toward Emma. Matt is talking to her, but I know she isn't listening. She is more attuned to what's going on between me and the love of her life.

I nudge her with my elbow. "Walk with me to the bar."

I don't wait for her agreement and get up from my seat. I know she'll follow. We make our way to the bar and I order a purple drink on their menu, then lean against the dark wood.

"So here's my plan," I tell her. She looks sad. "Cheer up. I'm ready to prove you wrong."

"By flirting with him?"

"Yes, among other things."

"You know what, I'm just gonna go—"

"Would you relax? I asked you to trust me." I give her a meaningful look until she nods. "Okay. So I want you to flirt with Matt, or at least talk to him. I'm going to keep Dylan busy, and I bet you anything he'll come out of this jealous and totally irritated by me."

"I don't..." She shakes her head.

"Come on. It's going to be fun. Besides, he should get a little taste of what you go through every day."

She scrunches her nose and thinks it over. My drink is here so I take a sip and watch her. "Don't you think it's...vengeful to do that?"

"Yeah, it is, but if you don't do anything, he'll never realize how much he likes you and will miss out on the awesomeness that is you. Now *that's* vengeful." Emma laughs and I steer her to our table. "Think of it as a favor to him, okay?"

"Okay."

As we walk through the crowd, my legs come to a halt. I feel something moving inside me. It spans my chest and my belly, going around to my spine, an urgent, incessant pulse. My gaze jumps to the door and he's there.

Thomas. Professor Abrams. My crush.

Maybe I'm regressing, going back to those precocious years in high school when girls giggle and gossip about their handsome teachers. Back then, everything was invisible to me but Caleb. I never cared enough to look elsewhere or have a life of my own.

But I'm ready now. I need the control back. I need the normalcy. It's so ironic that the very unrequitedness that destroyed me is going to keep the pain at bay.

Thomas strides to the opposite side of the bar and comes to stand beside another man, one who's shorter than him and dressed in a more formal style.

I scurry back to the table and take my seat. Emma gives me an admonishing look and I mouth, *Sorry*. Then I resume flirting with Dylan while Emma talks with Matt.

We're a sad pair, Dylan and I. While we're both talking to each other, our attention is diverted. He keeps glancing toward Emma, who has upped her game and is now laughing at whatever Matt is saying. The move may be cliché, but I'm so proud of her. It's hard to keep my face straight.

And me? I can't help but shift my eyes to Thomas. He is a tall, dark figure leaning—or rather, sprawling—against a wall, away from the crowd gathered around the table. He's taken his jacket off, leaving him in a plain black t-shirt. It stretches across his sculpted chest when he runs his fingers through the strands of his hair. He takes lazy sips from the beer bottle in his hands, quirking up small smiles as the shorter man beside him talks.

Just then Emma barks out a loud laugh and Dylan gives up all pretenses of talking to me. "What's funny?" he grumbles, and I can't hold back my chuckle.

My intuition was fucking right. Dylan's such a moron. Shaking my head, I sneak a glimpse at Thomas. This time, our gazes catch. Tiny blue flames stare at me from across the space and I'm suspended in his attention. I have the straw in my mouth, but I'm not sucking on it. I'm not even drawing breath.

He found me.

The thought runs on a loop even when he looks away and turns to the stage. Something tells me he's thinking of me; I spy the subtle movement of his sharp jaw as he clenches his teeth.

He *hates* me.

A small smile blooms on my lips. I *love* that he hates me. *See, hopeless.* I've never loved hopelessness so much before.

I look away when the static of the mic fills the room as Thomas' friend takes his place on the stage. He announces the commencement of poetry night and introduces Emma.

I wish her good luck as she walks up on the stage with a piece of paper in her hands.

"Thank you, Professor Masters, for the lovely introduction." She laughs, looking giddy and flushed. "And thank you all for having me up here. I'm going to read something I wrote a long time ago. It's called *You*, and I hope you enjoy."

She looks at the paper once before tucking it back in her jeans pocket. Her gaze falls on Dylan, who sits riveted next to me. She starts with a clear voice and confident demeanor. Her words are simple but filled with longing.

During the entire narration, she never takes her eyes off Dylan, letting him know the poem is an homage to the love she feels for him. It's beautiful, and for the first time in my life, I feel like I've done something right. I've brought them together, made both of them the star of the show, and who doesn't want to be a star? It's a dream for everyone, that one moment in the spotlight.

People are catching on to what Emma is doing. They watch Dylan's astonished face and Emma's flushed one, alternatively. Tears brim in my eyes as I witness their love story reaching its peak right in front of me.

This is what requited love looks like.

Shimmering. Grinning. Teary-eyed.

We want it too.

But I'll never have that.

CHAPTER SIX

When the poem is done, I notice that Thomas is gone. I look around, but I can't see him anywhere. I spring up from my seat before the clapping subsides, and no one notices my departure in the midst of love.

The hallway in the back is littered with people leaning against the brick walls, some fondling their dates, some waiting in the bathroom queue. The industrial lights above are dimmed, lending the narrow passageway an intimacy that begs for illicit touches and grey-tinted, slippery kisses.

Thomas might have simply left or gone to the bathroom, but my attention is snagged by the rusted maroon door with the exit sign. It stands ajar, bringing in the chilly draft from the outside. I push it open, stepping into the dark, cold alley. The wall opposite is lined with trashcans.

The cold, stinging air punches my nose and forehead, and I sneeze. Once. Two times. My boots almost slip over the patch of ice on the ground but I manage to keep my balance.

"Fuck!" I right myself, patting my heavy ensemble of a coat, a scarf, and a beanie.

"I don't think you're old enough to curse."

I gasp at the familiar guttural voice. Thomas emerges from beside the fire escape, ringlets of smoke rising from his lips. The yellow light lends him a certain glow. My drunk-on-crush heart jumps in my chest, pounding, pumping my blood furiously.

Even outside, he's without his jacket, leaving his elbows and his veiny, hair-dusted forearms exposed. What is it with me and his hands? I can't stop looking at them. I can't stop imagining them over mine. As if my lust was waiting for a single glimpse of his magical fingers, it bobs to the surface and I'm thrust back into my dark apartment, in front of the sliding door, watching the snow, playing with myself.

"You can stop staring any second now." He takes in a drag and blows out a cloud of smoke.

"I wasn't staring," I lie.

"Sure."

Thomas leans against the damp wall and crosses his arms across his chest, careful to keep the burning end of the cigarette away. The glowing orange embers tumble to the frosty ground, appearing like fireworks. I almost regret missing out on his battle with his impulse. His flickering anger giving way to his defeat—it's fascinating to me.

Before I know it, I am walking closer to him, catching a hint of his chocolatey scent, and snatching his cigarette away. I put it in my mouth and almost moan out loud at the relief.

"You're right. I was staring," I confess, puffing out smoke. "But only because you've got this."

The hit of nicotine is instant, liquefying. It dissolves my brain, one puff at a time. I'm bolder, invincible with it in my body—or maybe it's my hopeless crush making me feel immortal tonight.

"Stealing is a sin," he tells me.

"I'm not stealing." I smile. "I'm borrowing. And don't worry, I only borrow things that make me high."

He shakes his head at me and scratches his jaw. "You probably missed school the day they taught that smoking causes cancer."

I burst into laughter. His words remind me of the analogy I made to Kara the other day. I look back at his shimmering face. He is like my personal moon—unattainable, to be admired from afar. He is my cancer, slowly killing me, and I don't even mind.

"I'm not afraid to die," I divulge, taking another puff. He is watching me with an unknown glint in his eyes. I can't decipher it, and I don't want to. Let it be a mystery; mysteries can't hurt me. "Besides, it's not impossible that I might have missed that class. I wasn't the type to attend classes."

"What type were you?"

"I don't know, the bad type. I used to cut school. I was always behind on homework. My teachers thought I was a nightmare to deal with."

"Is that really something you should be telling your professor?"

His hands are in his pockets and his ankles are crossed. He has black snow boots with grey soles, and something about the ruggedness of them makes me smile. "But then you're not my professor, are you? And I'm not your student. I'm just the trespasser."

"I'd be careful then. Bad things happen to those who trespass," he says in a voice that steals my own.

Thomas' lips twitch with a restrained smile as his eyes rove over my face. My skin flushes, blooms in a million goose bumps. He has become the single point of my focus. He has absorbed the edges of my world, and all I see is his wind-ruffled hair, his magnificent chiseled features. I'm so engrossed in him that I don't notice his hand reaching over and snatching the cigarette back, until it's already gone.

"As much as I find you annoying, I'd rather you not kill yourself on my cancer stick," he says before sucking in a drag.

"Fine. Whatever," I grumble. "What are you doing out here in the cold, anyway? Without a jacket? Aren't you missing the readings of your own students?"

He gives me a side glance. "You're wearing enough clothes for the both of us, and I can ask you the same question."

"I'm getting fresh air."

Cigarette clenched in his teeth, he throws me a knowing look. His eyes are saying what his mouth said last week: *You have a thing for me.*

Like him, I let my eyes do the talking. I narrow them and cock my head to the side. *You're full of yourself.*

His chuckle is soft and airy. "Yes, I was too, until you came out and ruined it."

"You're such a people person, aren't you?" I shake my head. "Why did you take this job when you so clearly hate teaching and the students?"

"It's not just students. I hate all humans, in general," he explains. "But I still need a job, don't I?"

"Actually, I don't think you do. Aren't you some big-shot award-winning poet? Shouldn't you be working on your book somewhere? Isolated and drunk, growing out a beard or something?"

"Are you sure you're describing a poet and not your life goals?"

"I can't grow a beard. In case you didn't notice, I'm a girl."

Something changes in his demeanor. I don't know what it is, but he seems more aware of me, like I touched him without lifting a finger. It awakens every nerve ending in my body.

"I noticed," he murmurs.

It seems he also touched me without putting a hand on me because I feel something rustling over my skin, electric and hot, causing seismic shivers. I huddle inside my coat and rub my arms, chasing the sensation away.

Thomas flicks his finished cigarette off and crushes the butt with his boots, the wintry breeze catching his dark hair. "You should probably head back now. Your boyfriend must be looking for you."

"What boyfriend?"

"The one you were sharing drinks with."

It takes me a second to understand what he means. "Oh, you mean Dylan?" I chuckle. "It fooled you too? I didn't know I was that good. I was trying to prove a point to someone."

"And what point is that?"

"That love doesn't always have to be one-sided."

"What do you know about one-sided love?"

"More than you think."

"Yeah? Did your date ditch you for prom? Or let me guess, he took you out on a date but didn't call back the next day. Isn't that how all high school love stories go?"

Anger, hot and fierce, burns through me. How is it that in the last however many minutes, I've run a gamut of emotions with him? How is it that with him, all I do is feel and feel until I'm about to burst? And none of this scares me—not his rudeness, not his callous comments. I want to give as good as I get.

"Just because you've got everything figured out doesn't mean you can be an asshole, okay? And what, you can't fall in love in high school? Is that what you're saying to me? That age has something to do with love?" I shake my head. "God, you're so fucking narrow-minded."

"You think I've got everything figured out?"

"Haven't you? I mean, look at you. People can't stop talking about how much of a genius you are. The entire class wants to talk to you but you won't give them the time of day. You're married, and I'm assuming you got the one you wanted, so what do *you* know about one-sided love?"

I hate him. I hate him so much. I hate that he's got it all. I hate that he belittled my feelings for Caleb even though he didn't know he was doing it. I hate that he is the happiest man alive.

Although, if that's the case, why doesn't he look it?

Why are the lines around his mouth tight and rigid? Why is there a heartbreaking sheen in his eyes? His hands are curled in fists. In fact, his entire body is curled, drawn into itself.

"Yeah, what the fuck do I know about one-sided love?" he says at last with a humorless smile.

Oh God, did I say something wrong? Is there something wrong in his marriage?

I know firsthand that marriages aren't always black and white. My mom is on husband number three. Over the years, I've realized that her marriages were convenient. No love. No passion. They were bound to fail.

But I can't think of Thomas that way. I can't think of this passionate, surly poet as being anything but in love with his wife, and love has to be enough, right? It *has* to be. Because if it isn't, then what else is sacred in this big, bad world?

Then out of nowhere, something else strikes me.

"Hold on, you saw that? You saw that I was sharing a drink with a guy from across the room. Were you...?"

"Was I what? Watching you?" He pierces me with his stare, so intense, so serious.

"Yeah?" I lick my dry, cracked lips. Is it my imagination, or has he moved closer?

Thomas dips his head, catching my confused gaze with his, making this moment fraught with intimacy. "Yeah." His words drag in a lazy manner. "I was. In fact, I can't stop watching you."

How did we get to this? From trading insults and me hating him to this... conversation. My body is going into a weird mode: panicked and aroused at the same time. Sweat runs down my spine and heat fans out in my lower body.

"Wh...?" Words are drying out on my tongue. I can't...I can't compute this, can't compute that he's been watching me, and yet it has happened twice now —once at the bookstore, and now here. A dangerous concoction of feelings is swishing around in my chest. I can't recognize them all, but I know I'm afraid, among other things.

Thomas snorts out a chuckle. "Teenagers. I fucking hate teenagers," he mutters to himself. "You should see your face."

I growl, enraged. He was fucking kidding.

I growl again. *We hate him*, my angry heart says. *Yeah, we do*, I agree.

Thomas is watching me with amused eyes, and that just pisses me off even more. I take a breath, and keeping our gazes connected, lift my right leg and whip it right down on his foot. Hard.

He doesn't even flinch. *Asshole.*

"How's that for a teenager?" My harsh breaths echo around us. In the back of my mind, I know I shouldn't have done that. This is the reason my mom sent me to therapy. I have zero impulse control.

"I'd say it's more middle school-ish, but what do I know about what kids are doing these days?" I'm still reeling from what I did, and he takes this opportunity to inform me, "You hit like a girl, by the way."

"I am a girl." I grit my teeth. "And I *stomped*. I did not *hit*."

"Either way, it was an assault, and on a teacher, no less." I feel the rumbles of his chest as he speaks, making me realize how close I am to him, to his body.

It's warm and hard and breathing. It feels exotic, like something I've never felt before, which is an absolute lie because I *have* felt a masculine body before—the night Caleb and I had sex. Why does this feel so different and new?

I should step back. I know it, but I can't. My anger is slowly draining out of my body and something else is filling up the emptiness inside me. My unruly foot inches closer, blindly searching for his foot. Once found, I tap the toe of his boot. "You're not my teacher, remember?"

Thomas looks down at our feet, connected on the ground, my pointed tip attached to his blunt one. It's a childish gesture without any importance, but still, I love how our feet look on the snow-patched earth. We gaze up at the same time, and together, we swallow, part our lips, exhale foggy breaths.

Before I can analyze what's happening, the screech of the door opening breaks the moment and I step back.

"Thomas. I had a feeling I'd find you here." It's a woman, short and sleek, with a blonde bob.

"Sarah. Want to join us?"

Her shrewd eyes flicker between Thomas and me, and I feel anxious, like I've been caught doing something wrong, something illicit.

"No thank you. I—"

"Are you sure? We were having an illuminating discussion about gender roles. Do girls really hit like girls or is it merely a stereotype created by modern literature?"

My breath hiccups as Thomas refers to my stomping so smoothly. I try to school my features, but I know I'm blushing. I hope the dim lighting conceals it.

"I'm sure it's fascinating," Sarah says in a suspicious tone. "But you're needed inside."

Thomas smiles but I can tell he isn't amused. "And who's doing the needing? You? I thought the day would never come."

Sarah throws him a strained smile. Clearly, these two don't like each other.

"I like your jokes, Thomas, but I don't think Professor Masters will be amused to be kept waiting. He wants everyone to meet the stellar addition to our staff."

"Well, I'll be right in then."

Sarah nods, ready to leave, but stops. She focuses on me and I shrink inside my big, giant coat. "Are you new? I've never seen you on the Labyrinth night before."

"Um, yes. I am. I'm Layla Robinson."

She nods. "I'm Sarah Turner. If you need any help with gender roles in literature, you should come find me. It's one of my specialties."

Again, her gaze switches to Thomas, and then it flicks back over to me. There isn't anything in her eyes that I can decipher, but still, I feel there is something there. With a last glance at us, she leaves, and the breath I've been holding whooshes out. "Who's she?"

Thomas shrugs, whipping out his phone from his pocket. "No one." His fingers fly as he types something. Once done, he heads toward the street.

"You're leaving?" I ask.

"Looks like it," he replies without turning around.

"But shouldn't you go in there?"

"I wish I could, but I don't want to."

He keeps walking and I jog after him. "Why not?" I'm pushing it but I don't know why.

Halting in his tracks, he turns around. The night is dark and the lighting is atrocious so I can't really study his expression, but I know he doesn't like being questioned. "Because it's almost midnight and if I stay any longer, I might turn into a toad, and I like this getup too much to risk that."

He turns back around but pauses again. Giving me his profile, he says, "And I haven't forgotten, Miss Robinson—don't be in my class next time."

CHAPTER SEVEN

Emma moves in the next day and it goes smoothly with Dylan and Matt and me helping her. Plenty of heated glances are exchanged between the two lovebirds, and I couldn't be happier. Turns out, after I left last night, there was a hug with a kiss and an all-nighter where they talked and got their feelings out.

At lunchtime, we order pizza and discuss all things poetry. I ask about Sarah Turner, and Emma tells me she was gunning for Thomas' job. Apparently it was all pretty much set until Jake Masters, dean of creative writing, brought Thomas in to attract more students to the program, hence Sarah's hostility; not to mention, Jake and Thomas have known each other since their college days, and, naturally, Sarah doesn't like that.

It's a fun afternoon, except for one heated phone call from Emma's mom. She goes into her room to talk so I can't hear what they are arguing about. Dylan calms her down though and from there, things get light.

Dylan, Emma, and Matt accept me easily. Apart from a few awkward silences where Dylan and Emma make googly eyes at each other, it feels natural—so natural, in fact, that Matt kind of becomes my favorite person in the world because he loves Twizzlers. We share a pack between us and argue its nutritional values against crappy foods like apples or leafy vegetables. By the end of it all, I decide I really want these fragile bonds of friendships to hold. Loneliness doesn't feel like an option anymore, not since I stumbled upon the Labyrinth.

Once Dylan and Matt are gone, Emma suggests a walk and coffee. I never say no to either of those, so I pile on my winter clothes and we set out into the quiet Sunday afternoon.

The street is wet and flanked by melting banks of snow. It hasn't snowed since the semester started so the air seems saturated, swollen with the nightmare of it. We pass by the neighboring buildings, which are smaller than the one we live in, a salon, and a deli before getting to Crème and Beans. The smell of coffee and warm chocolate hits us as we enter.

But it's more than that. There's a potency in the air, and I instantly know why. *Thomas*. He is at the counter, paying for his coffee. He is so tall that he has to lean down to speak to the barista. His fingers flick through the bills in his wallet as he counts them, and hands them over with a distracted smile.

Last night I became his puppet again and played with myself. This time I did it in darkness. It made the strings tighter, more urgent. It made me bolder, dirtier. Criminal, even. Unlike the last time, my fingers plunged in and dug deep, felt the flesh from inside out. It was warm and velvety and dripping and noisy. I heard the sounds my pussy makes when it's greedy and horny. I never knew. I never knew that part of my body so intimately. It felt brilliant and shameful. I basked in my arousal until I was gasping for breath, gushing cum on my purple sheets. I was writhing on my bed with no control over my body whatsoever. It was scary and erotic as fuck.

"Hey, you coming?" Emma calls out, bringing me out of my lust-induced trance.

Her voice is loud in the otherwise empty café and it snags Thomas' attention. In a flash, his relaxed stance changes and he is on alert, his jaw pulsing. His reaction is so predictable, his hatred so glorious that I bite my lip to keep from smiling.

My smile is lost when I notice he isn't alone. There's a woman a few steps behind him in a loose white sweater and a soft pink coat. Her hair is blonde and smooth with layered bangs falling over her forehead. She is petite, shorter than my five feet six inches, and a lot thinner than me.

Even though I've never seen her, I know who she is. She is Thomas' wife.

She is beautiful. So perfect. Ethereal. Like a soft feather or a soap bubble. Her skin is silky and her lips are pure pink. She seems the total opposite of me. Shy, quiet, and well-mannered.

Having seen them too, Emma makes a beeline in their direction. "Hi, Professor Abrams. It's so nice to see you here."

"Yes. Pleasure," he replies without enthusiasm.

Emma introduces herself to Thomas' wife with a polite smile. "Um, hi, I'm Emma Walker and this is Layla Robinson. We're in Professor Abrams' class."

"Hello. I'm Hadley," she says with a slight smile. Her voice...I can't even describe it. It's the tiniest of sounds, the lowest of decibels, and so...melodic.

I bet Thomas fell in love with her at first sight. How could he not have? She inspires that kind of devotion.

There's a clench in my chest, as if my heart is shrinking. I wonder what it takes to be loveable. Maybe you have to be less crazy or less selfish or less...ruining.

I swallow and try to smile as Hadley's golden gaze reaches me. I feel ashamed. It's the same feeling I had last night with Sarah. I want to hide behind Emma. My harmless crush seems not so harmless anymore.

With reluctance, Thomas jumps into introductions, moving closer to Hadley. "Yes, this is my wife, and that little guy over there is Nicky—Nicholas, our son."

Did he just say son? A son.

He has a son. A child. He's a dad.

This is getting worse by the minute. *Let's hide*, my frantic heart squeaks. I've been masturbating to thoughts of a man who has a son.

A son I can't stop staring at.

A blue-eyed, dark-haired baby with rosy cheeks. He's kicking up his feet in a stroller, gurgling over his chubby fist. He's bundled up in a black and white beanie and scarf with a puffy purple jacket. He's wearing purple. My favorite color.

"Oh my God, he's so cute." Emma comes down to her knees. "And so tiny. How old is he?"

"Six months next week," Thomas answers.

He is watching Nicky with pride, with tenderness. It's a look I've never seen on him before. It softens the chisels of his face, tempers the perpetual intensity in his eyes. It makes him look young, happy. His fingers graze Nicky's head gently, reverently.

My gaze lands on Hadley. Maybe the sunrays are hitting her wrong, but I swear I see...apprehension on her face as she looks at Nicky. Her soft lips are turned down and dark bags have erupted under her eyes. I don't understand her reaction. She snaps her gaze away as if she can't look at Nicky or her husband anymore.

I dismiss the stupid thought and turn to Emma. She is playing with Nicky, trying to get him to hold on to her finger, but he isn't biting. I kneel next to her and smile at him and instantly, he looks at me.

His eyes are blue, much like his dad's. I finger-wave at him. "Hi Nicky, I'm Layla." He wiggles on his cute butt and drools. "I love your jacket. It's purple." I grin, and he shoots me a toothless grin of his own. "Do you know purple is my favorite color? I just love it. Look!" I point to my jacket and he looks dutifully, still chewing on his fist. "I'm wearing purple too, though it's a different shade. But, you know, purple's cool in any shade."

He giggles as if he understands. Chuckling, I finger-wave at him again, this time close to his soft button nose. In a flash, he catches my finger in his wet fist, beaming.

I circle my lips in an O and he mimics my action, drool hanging on to his chin. "You caught me!"

"Why didn't he grab my finger?" Emma whispers.

"I'm way cooler than you."

We both make to stand up but I pause as my gaze falls on Thomas' boots. They're the same ones from last night, black with grey soles. They point toward Hadley's maroon, low-heeled boots, but hers are pointed to the opposite side, to the door. I picture the toes of Thomas' and my boots touching, pointing dead center, like a compass.

Something about the opposite direction of their boots strikes me as wrong. It gives me a bad feeling.

I sense a hot prickle on my scalp, tingling down to my neck and spine. I know Thomas is staring down at me with his gorgeous eyes. My body tightens as I come up to my feet and look at him. There's a microsecond of connection between us, and suddenly, I get it. I get the hidden depths of his eyes. I get the sharpness of his expression, every purse of his lips, every throb of his vein.

I get everything. I get why he didn't look like the happiest man alive last night.

I even get his poem. *Anesthesia* is about loneliness, heartbreak, one-sided love. It's about him, and it's about me. It's about people like us.

My heart is racing with the awful, *awful* knowledge.

Just then, Nicky's gurgles morph into fussing. His chubby cheeks shake as he chews on his knuckles. His distress is causing me distress, and I've only met him a few minutes ago.

Emma looks down, frowning. "Oh no, I guess he needs his mommy."

I swear I see Hadley flinch. What is going on?

Thomas notices it too and breaks into action. Setting his mug on the counter, he bends down and gathers Nicky in his arms. He presses him to his chest, cradling his head and rocking him. His movements are expert and fluid.

"I think we should get going. It's close to Nicky's feeding time, anyway," Thomas says.

We say our goodbyes and Thomas and Hadley leave. As Emma places her order with the barista, I watch them walk down Albert Street. They walk separate from each other, aloof. Thomas is pushing the stroller and Hadley is huddled in her coat, tucking her flying blonde hair behind her ears. She slips on a patch of ice and Thomas' hand shoots out to steady her, but it never makes contact with her body. Hadley shrinks away at the last second and straightens herself. She continues walking as if nothing happened, and Thomas follows.

With a sinking heart, I realize Thomas is like me. He is the unrequited lover.

For the past weeks, Thomas has claimed my nights. He is all I think about, but tonight is different. Tonight, Caleb is intruding on Thomas. The awful, breath-stealing, gut-wrenching love that I feel for him is rushing to the surface.

In my mind, I see purple flowers, the same ones I saw through the window of that strange house Caleb left me in.

Most days I don't think about those flowers, but tonight I can't stop thinking about them. I can't stop thinking about how beautiful they were and how I *hated* seeing them when I was at my worst. I hated them for being so pretty and delicate. The agony is multiplied a thousand-fold, as if I'm sad for not only myself, but someone else too.

Turns out, Thomas Abrams isn't a mystery anymore. He's just a man in love with someone who doesn't love him back. It demystifies everything about him, and it breaks my heart in a million ways. I pick up his book and read the poem again. I lick his words as if I'm licking his soul, his heart, his wounds.

Now that I know this about Thomas, the allure should be gone...but it's still there. It makes me want to run and run until I find him and ask him, *What does it feel like? Are you as lonely as me? As lost and angry? Are you insane like me?*

My agony, curiosity, anger, heartbreak...everything pours out of me onto a blank piece of paper. My trembling fingers fly and I write my very first poem.

For Thomas.

CHAPTER EIGHT

The Bard

Love is a scary thing. It's too powerful, too awe-inspiring, too life-changing for a man like me. I've seen it. I've believed in it, but I never wanted it for myself.

But when I saw her, it didn't matter. It didn't matter what I thought, what I wanted. At the first sight, I fell.

Hadley.

She was walking down the corridor, her arms laden with books, her honey blonde hair fluttering in the air. A frown marred her forehead. All I wanted to do was rub my thumb between her eyebrows and erase it. There was something about her that spoke to me. Maybe it was the way she walked, huddled, shrunken into herself, or it could have been her parted lips, dragging in air out of exertion. Whatever it was, it called to something inside me, something I didn't know I had—a sort of protective instinct, perhaps. She passed me by without sparing me a glance, without knowing how she shifted my world with that one frown.

Years later, I still feel the same. I see the bunched lines between her brows and downturned angles of her mouth, and I want to crush the source of her distress.

Trouble is, this time it's me.

I put those lines on her beautiful face. They rest when she's silent, simply listening to what Grace, Jake's wife, is saying to her, but they come alive when she throws Grace a tight smile.

Hadley has lost weight, the shine of her skin is gone, and the dark bags under her eyes give her a haunted, weak look. These outward signs make me feel helpless, angry—at myself, at the world, I don't know.

A distinct pain originates in the back of my skull and travels up my scalp. I know it won't be long before my head is full-on aching.

"You okay, man?" Jake thumps his hand on my shoulder.

We are at Jake and Grace's house for dinner. It's sort of a welcome-to-the-neighborhood kind of thing. Hadley and Grace are busy in a conversation at the kitchen island, though it's mostly Grace talking; Hadley is a listener. Jake and I are here, occupying the couch in the living room.

The chill of the beer bottle seeps into my overheated fingers as I take a long pull, looking away from my wife. "Yeah. Everything's fine."

"You can talk to me, you know. I'm here for you." His eyes move from me to Hadley and back again.

My teeth grit at his interference. *It's not interference*, I tell myself. Jake is the kind of a guy who'd be concerned, but I'm not the type to share. Words have the power to make things true. Just like some people don't talk about their nightmares because it might make them come true, I don't want to discuss what's wrong in my life, in my marriage.

"There's nothing to talk about. Everything's fine."

Jake senses my unease and lifts his hands in surrender. "Okay. No pressure." He takes a sip of his own beer. "So Sarah pretty much hates you."

Glad for the subject change, I say, "Sarah pretty much hates everyone."

"Yes, but not everyone argues with her at staff meetings, and not everyone points out—and I quote—'how shitty the syllabus is.' That's all you."

"It *is* shitty."

"You're not going to make my job easier, are you?" He shakes his head, growing serious. "You can't pull stuff like this now, Thomas. You can't text me and dash out when I want to introduce you to people. You can't insult your colleagues. You aren't a poet anymore. You're a teacher. A team player."

Not a poet.

Jake didn't mean anything by it, but it needles me all the same. The throbbing in my skull intensifies, on the verge of exploding with a thousand thoughts. It makes me feel tired, exhausted—the feeling I get when I've labored over a poem for hours, polishing it, chiseling it until it shines...or until I can't work on it anymore because all my words have dried up.

"Yeah. I know." I sigh, running my hand through my hair. "I know you're doing me a favor, man. I don't mean to piss all over it. It won't happen again."

And I mean it. If this job rights all the wrongs I've done, I'll take it.

"Good." Jake salutes me with his bottle. "How are the students? We got a decent batch this year, right?"

As if Jake's question is a trigger, I see her in flashes, as if my consciousness has clicked snapshots of her without my knowledge. Impish, wild, violet-colored eyes. Loud, uninhibited laughter. Smoke threading out of her pouty lips. The savage, dark curls that never seem to stay still. Her purple fur coats—*who wears fur coats, anyway?* Her voice that digs up the buried words inside me. Merciless words. They make me forget I'm not a poet anymore.

I can't be—it's the fate I chose months ago—but words come to me now because of her, as though she is my muse. I don't want a muse. I don't *want* Layla Robinson in my thoughts.

I grip the neck of the bottle tightly, restless, unable to sit still. I take another long pull of my beer. "Yeah. Decent," I say in reply to Jake's earlier question.

"That bad, huh?" He rests his arms on his thighs and gives me a meaningful look. "Listen, go easy on them. Not everyone is Hemingway in the making. Look at the spirit, not the talent."

"Is that my first lesson on how to be a teacher?"

"If you want it to be."

"You're full of wisdom tonight, aren't you?"

"I'm always full of wisdom." He grins, making me scoff.

We talk until it's time to go. Hadley thanks Grace for having us over and they hug. Jake and I pat each other's shoulders.

It's a bit of a drive to our place from Jake's house since they live off campus. As I start my car, I see Grace and Jake kissing and giggling like teenagers in the rearview mirror. It intensifies my headache even more.

When Hadley is all buckled up, I pull out. An instant sense of relief overtakes me at her nearness. My fingers twitch on the wheel with the desire to touch her skin, the curve of her cheek, her graceful neck—but I don't. She won't like it.

"So, uh, did you have a good time?" I cringe at my question, my eyes on the snowy road. Might as well have asked about the useless weather. I've never been a conversation starter, but for her, I try.

"Yes." She nods, giving me a glance that lasts only a second before turning back to the window.

The silence is oppressive. My fingers tighten, white-knuckling the wheel. "Do you think it's…going to snow tonight?"

I am nauseated as soon as the words are out, so empty and impersonal. It's like we've never met before, never touched each other, never felt each other's heartbeats or skin.

It's like we've never been in love before.

She shrugs in answer to my pathetic question. "Probably."

The nausea lurches and I feel hot all over. The car seems to have shrunk in the past five seconds. I want to stomp on the brakes, jerk us to a halt, and shove out of this tight space. I want to leave it all behind. Every fucking thing.

But there's nowhere else to go. So I keep on driving.

In fact, I'm so absorbed in this mundane task that I miss the turn that leads to our house. I keep driving straight and come to a stop in front of the park entrance. Only then does Hadley notice where we are.

"What…What are we doing here?" She turns to me. I'm ashamed to admit it gives me pleasure to see her disorientation. It gives me pleasure to see her need me, even if it is for something as inconsequential as seeking the answer to her question.

"I want to show you something." My voice is quiet, despite the roar inside my body.

Her golden-brown eyes flick over my face. It's probably the first time all night that she's been aware of me, and like a fucking beggar, I take it. I rejoice in her undivided attention.

It's gone too soon though. She jumps out of the car and I follow her. I'm beginning to think this was a bad idea, but I'm running out of options. I need her to understand.

Our footsteps crunch, filling the silence as I direct her to our destination: the bench under the white-flowered tree, the very spot where I proposed to her.

As the bench comes into view, surrounded by heaps of snow and spotlighted under the lamp, the night changes into that day from eight years ago. I'm thrown back to that rainy afternoon, when I told her I wanted to spend my life with her. I was going to go away to the city for grad school and I wanted her to come with me.

"Do you remember this place? You waited for me, as always." I swallow. "And as always, I was late. I thought you'd be gone. I was rehearsing all the apologies in my head, but there you were, and I just stopped. I had to catch my breath for a second. You were so beautiful and calm and...soft." I plow my numb fingers through my hair. "I felt so inadequate, like I didn't deserve you. I've always been such a...moody asshole."

My words trail off as Hadley turns around and faces me. I don't know what I was expecting to see on her expression, but it wasn't this...deathly stillness. She is like a blank piece of paper. She is almost one-dimensional in her absence of emotions, as if she has no depth whatsoever, nothing beyond the surface.

"I want to go home." Her voice is the same, quiet and soft, but it sounds all wrong with her expressionless, indifferent face.

"Hadley—"

"I don't want to be here."

"You promised." My voice thunders. I clench my fists to get it under control. "You promised you'd try. We both did. And I'm trying, Hadley. I swear to fucking God, I'm trying to be the kind of husband you deserve."

Anger and fear are warring inside me. What if I can never get through to her? What if I can never make her understand how much I have changed? What if she asks for a divorce again? I remember the invisible jolt I felt when she asked for it that day months ago. Her demand was a boom inside my body, an implosion of organs, my heart. I hadn't even realized things had gotten so bad.

"Is that why we're here? In this town?"

"Yes, because you love it here. You always wanted to move back."

"But you hate this town."

"I don't care. I'd do anything for you."

"Even give up your writing?"

I flinch at this. I'm not used to hearing it out loud. It's not something we talk about. For years, I lived on words, on creating them, molding them. Somewhere along the way, I forgot that I loved Hadley too. Words made me forget my wife, and I fucking hate them now. I don't want them. For her, I'll give everything up.

"Yes. Nothing means more to me than you." I shake my head, tired of this longing, this need for her. "Don't you get it? You give up anything for the people you care about. I'm just doing what you're supposed to do in love."

Her eyes shine with unshed tears, hurting me but making me happy because they mean she still cares. This display of emotion makes me take a few steps forward, but I come to a halt when her face changes. The emotions are erased and her expression has turned blank again.

"I want to go home. I'm tired." She doesn't give me time to respond, simply begins walking back to the car.

It takes me a few seconds to move. Anger is like hot lava, burning my flesh. She keeps rejecting me at every turn. Why the fuck can't she see what I've given up to be with her? Why won't she forgive me? Why aren't things getting better when I'm doing everything I can to make them so?

Ten minutes later, we are home.

We enter the house through the kitchen door. *Home* is a bit of stretch. It doesn't feel like home. It doesn't have a personality yet. It's too new, smells too much of paint and wood. Unlike in the city, it's too quiet in here; I'd rather be sleeping through the blaring siren of a fire truck than sitting in the unnatural silence. Small towns make me think I'm all alone in the world.

Hadley moves like a ghost, with light feet and grace, as if she's floating. She drifts up the stairs and just as she reaches the landing, a shrill cry echoes. Nicky is up. Hadley winces at the sound, pauses a moment in front of his door, but then moves on.

I fist my hands at my sides. I can take her indifference toward me. It fucking hurts, but I can take the pain—but her indifference toward Nicky makes me want to throttle her. I breathe in deep and climb up the same stairs. I come to Nicky's white door and my sweaty palms slip over the knob as I turn it.

The room is lit by moonlight and a lamp with sea animals on the shade. It stands on the dresser right next to the rocking chair Susan, our nanny, is currently occupying. She has Nicky in her arms, gently cooing in his ears. I pad inside the room and she looks up at me, smiling slightly.

"He's just being a little fussy," she tells me as she stands.

I reach over and take Nicky in my arms, relieving her. I rock him with practiced ease and kiss his forehead. "It's okay. I got him. You should go on home."

She rubs circles on Nicky's back, trying to soothe him alongside me. "Are you sure? I can stay. You should get some sleep. You have work in the morning."

Nicky fists the collar of my shirt and tries to put it into his mouth. I clutch his chubby fist and place a soft kiss on it. "I'll be okay." She doesn't know how many sleepless nights I've spent under this roof.

Susan studies me with a frown on her weathered face. Maybe she *does* know. She opens her mouth to say something, but I stop her. "Do you need help packing up your things?"

"No. I can do it." She throws me a sad smile. "I'll go then. Good night." She leans over, kisses Nicky on the cheek and leaves.

I let out a relieved breath. Finally, I am alone. I welcome the solitude after the roller coaster of tonight.

Nicky has calmed down and is drooling over my shoulder. I lay him down in the crib and watch him sleep. I trace the curves of his cheeks, the soft, cute chin with my eyes. His hair is dark and mussed, his fists lifted up by his face. He jerks and his blue onesie-covered feet twitch. I pat his chest, run my palm in circles, hoping to soothe him. Soon, his breathing goes back to normal as his mouth falls open slightly.

The words tumble out of my mouth on a whisper. "I love you. I'll always love you."

And I love your mom.

The thought pulsates like an ache in my skull and a churn in my gut. I'm restless again.

I need to remind Hadley how much I love her. I need to remind her that we share a child. We are a family. You never turn your back on your family. I have learned that in the worst of ways.

But how do you remind someone who doesn't want to remember?

PART 2
THE TRESPASSER

CHAPTER NINE

Monday morning, the start of another week of school. Emma and I walk to class together and sit side by side, in the middle of the semicircle. Dylan enters a few minutes later and walks straight to Emma, smiles, and takes a seat by her. They begin talking and I look at my notebook, grinning.

Who would've thought my life would entirely spin around in a week? A week ago I didn't even have friends, and now I have three, and I've got the Labyrinth too—or at least, I can hang out here until they realize I don't belong.

My heart thumps in my chest as I flip pages of my notebook and come upon the very last page filled with my squiggly handwriting. I'm scared to look at the words I wrote. They seem childish, inadequate, unworthy of the dynamic man to whom they are dedicated.

I snap the notebook close and stare ahead.

Before long, Thomas enters the class, carrying a bundle of papers in one hand and running the other through his hair. My body tingles, goosebumps erupting over my skin.

He takes off his jacket, throws it on the chair with a tight, jerky flick of his arm. Fiddling with the cuffs of his shirt, he opens the button and folds the sleeves up to his elbows. I watch his hands cradling the papers, flicking through them, and picture him cradling Nicky's fragile neck, soothing him.

Thomas Abrams is magic. He's a wordsmith, a baby whisperer, a blue-eyed asshole, but most of all, he's like me: brokenhearted.

"Miss Robinson." Thomas' voice lashes through the room, and I wince. He looks at me—glares, actually—and my stomach is filled with terrified butterflies.

"Do you have some work for us?"

"W-Work?"

"Yes. Do you have any?"

"Uh, I don't…I don't remember you giving us any homework last class."

He throws the papers on the desk and folds his arms. "It's a writing class, Miss Robinson. It requires you to write, to hold the pen and put it on paper—sound familiar?"

I gulp, twisting the pages of my notebook. Yup, a major asshole—but why does his anger turn me on so much? I'm a fucking masochist.

"Read us a poem you've written."

Fuck. Fuck!

The butterflies inside my stomach freeze and die, dropping to the bottom like dead weight. The silence is so thick that I hear the rustle of clothes as people shift in their chairs. All eyes are staring at me and I hate that, *hate* the stabbing gazes.

"Do you think you're special, Miss Robinson? Do you think I should completely ignore the fact that you've failed to turn in your assignment from last week? Or maybe you think your fellow students are fucking idiots for following the rules. Which is it?"

I grit my teeth against the onslaught of emotions that seem eerily similar to betrayal and choke out, "I have some work."

He looks surprised, and that gives me a teeny sense of pleasure. "Let's hear it." Thomas leans against the desk and crosses his ankles.

Okay, I'm not so turned on right now as I feel the class watching me with pity. This must be so natural for them, reading their 'work', and here I am quaking in my boots.

I clear my throat and begin.

"*The day we met you watched the moon*

While I watched you.

Tall and alone. Dark and lonely.

You looked like my mirror.

Cracked and empty.

Dried up and chewed out.

I could have been yours.

If only you had looked at me."

My voice is scratchy, and words sound garbled and thick to my ears. I'm afraid to look up and see Thomas' reaction. I keep dog-earing the page and shifting restlessly in my seat. Even though I'm not looking, I know the exact moment he is about to say something.

"Well, an A for the effort and courage to read it out loud. No, actually..." He scratches his jaw with his thumb. "I'd say A+ for the courage. You must have a lot of it to read something this choppy and unpolished. Tell me, Miss Robinson, how many times did you revise your work?"

I almost open my mouth and blurt out, *Was I supposed to?* but I control myself and manage to lie. "Once?"

"Once," he clips.

"Uh, twice." I hold up two fingers; they are shivering, barely able to stand on their own, so I lower them.

I can see Thomas doesn't buy it. "It shows. The structure is choppy. It's abrupt. And your word choice is horrendous."

My body heats up in shame, his words hitting me like fire darts. I poured out every fucking emotion I had into this stupid poem and that's all he has to say to me? Is he even the same person from yesterday? Is he even capable of vulnerability? Is it all in my head?

"Isn't a poem supposed to be a snapshot of a moment?" I ask with clenched teeth.

"If I have to tell you what a poem is, I think you're in the wrong class."

With one flick of his gaze, he dismisses me, and I'm left seething. I feel Emma squeezing my hand on the desk and I want to snap it away and shrink in my seat. I'm happy being the weird loner. I don't need pity.

Thomas calls out other names, asking them to read. He is impatient with his comments, snappy and rude, but not as rude or condescending as he was to me. I think by the time the class is over, he's enjoying the back and forth, the healthy debate over his precious 'word choice,' though he would never admit it. *Fucking egomaniac.*

The only person to get a fraction of positivity from him is Emma. Thomas said her poem has *potential*. Potential. I'm so jealous, and it's so ridiculous that my breaths are coming in pants.

And it has nothing to do with being turned on.

All day I've been seething over what happened in Thomas' class, so much so that once my other classes are over, I trek back to the north side of campus and inside the Labyrinth. The building is as alive as ever. I wonder when these people even go home. It's almost five in the evening and I can still hear the thumping footsteps above—the theatre crew. *Fucking hippies.*

I take the flight of stairs to the second floor, which is similar to the first floor with its long hallway and flanking rooms. A few are classrooms, but mostly this floor is for faculty offices. I stop at the last door. It sits right above our classroom downstairs and reads, *Thomas Abrams, Poet in Residence.* I grimace. *More like asshole in residence.* The door is ajar and I push it open.

Thomas is sitting in a high-backed chair, pen poised in his hands, head bent over a bundle of papers. He looks up as the door opens.

"Miss Robinson. Did we have an appointment?"

I enter and close the door behind me. "No."

"Then you should make one and come back later." He goes back to reading the paper in front of him.

If he doesn't look up any time soon, I might throw something at him. By the looks of it, it's going to be the small Tiffany lamp sitting by the door on a polished wooden stool.

"What was that?" I release a pent-up breath. "You humiliated me in class."

For the longest time, all I hear is the scratch of his pen, and all I see is the dark hair on his bent head. My hand creeps up toward the lamp, almost touching it. I'd do it too. I'm that mad and that fearless.

At last, he is done. He sets the pen aside and looks up. "And when was that exactly?"

A laugh of disbelief breaks out of my lips. "Are you serious right now? You fucking humiliated me, tore my poem apart like it was some...some..." Dammit, I can't find a word for it.

His fingers are laced together on the desk and with inscrutable eyes, he watches me struggle. "Like it was some what?"

"You're enjoying this, aren't you?" I swallow the scream that itches my throat.

"No." He stands up and walks around the desk, leaning against it. "I don't enjoy being cornered for giving my honest opinion. Maybe you didn't understand the first time: this is a creative writing class. If you can't take the heat, then get out. Besides, aren't you *not* in my class already?"

"Oh, you'd like that, wouldn't you?" I bring my backpack around to my front and fish out the printed document. I walk up to him and pin it to his chest. "Here, my official registration confirmation. I am not a trespasser anymore."

He lets the paper float down to the ground where it lands next to his boots. *Fucking boots.* I have no idea why I am so obsessed with them—*and* his hands.

"Is there a purpose to this visit?"

I focus on his face. "Yes."

"And what exactly is it?"

I stare at the slant of his jaw. The stubble over his face has grown thicker over the course of the day. It casts a shadow that contrasts with the brightness of his eyes. Twin blue flames. There's so much anger in them—anger, irritation, frustration.

I should be wary of him. I should want to stay away. But I don't.

Thomas Abrams is a wounded animal. It's a wound of the heart, bleeding and gaping. It makes him snap out and snarl.

I want to…lick him like I did his words. I want to kiss him.

Holy shit!

My broken heart wants to kiss him better. Stupid, *idiot* heart.

Swallowing, I lick my lips, studying the curve of his. I want to suck on those angry lips, vacuum his plump mouth between *my* mouth, my teeth, until the anger drains away and only his fire remains.

I breathe out misty breaths. They thicken the air. Under my gaze, the pulse on his neck jumps rhythmically, like my heart. I want to suck on that patch of skin too, soothe it. I want to suck the pain away from his heart.

Oh God, I'm crazy. I've lost my mind.

My mouth is dry even though I'm slippery between my legs. A wrong and dirty sort of quickening rises in my stomach.

"I have to go." I pant like a fool and lift my eyes up to his. His gaze is searing. It burns through my flimsy cover. The tic in his jaw is violent in conjunction with his flared nostrils. He's ready to kill, the wounded animal.

I gulp and back away. My registration slip crinkles beneath my boots, sounding like a gunshot in the silent but charged room.

"Writing is not for everyone, Miss Robinson," Thomas says when I'm almost at the door. "It takes a certain depth of soul, a certain sort of sensitivity, if you will. Not very many people possess that. It's good to know when to give up."

I don't know if he's taunting me or telling the truth, and I don't have the energy to find out. My lust has made me stupid, more stupid than I normally am.

"Thanks for the advice, Professor." I turn to look at him. "But depth is misleading from the surface. Sometimes taking a plunge is the only way to find out if the water is too deep or just deep enough."

We stare at each other. I don't know what he sees when he looks at me. When I look at him, though, all I see is someone brokenhearted. I see him trying to catch his wife as she slips. I see him following her, like I did with Caleb.

I wrote that poem for you.

Thomas locks his jaw in a clench and walks back to his chair. The legs squeak as he sits down and his hands get busy sifting through the papers.

I turn around too, facing the door. Right next to the Tiffany lamp I was planning to throw at him lies a black, sleek book. In my anger, I hadn't noticed it before. It's the same book from the bookstore—*A Lover's Discourse: Fragments* by Roland Barthes—though this copy is old and frayed.

As I step out of his room, I stick my hand out and swipe the book. I cradle it to my chest and walk away.

Sitting in bed with Lana's voice blasting through my headphones, I open the first page of the stolen book. It holds a message in curly handwriting.

To Thomas. Hope you enjoy reading this piece of literature (again) that no sane person can understand. Love, Hadley.

I run my fingers over the smudged ink while picturing scenarios in my head. I weave a story in which Hadley and Thomas have been dating for a year now, and it's his birthday. Hadley gifts him his favorite book, a book he's read countless times before. He's surprised, happy, and he kisses her like *she* is his greatest gift. Gentle, tender kisses. Kisses worthy of a queen—not the kind I want and probably deserve, filthy and rough and messy and wet.

With a sigh, I focus on the pages that have been yellowed, flipping through them. Every once in a while, I stop when I see a passage underlined or a word scribbled. *Agony. Fire. Passion. Loneliness. Destroyed. Crumble. Burn. Sleepless.*

The letters are straight and clear, severe, like Thomas, but there is an extra swirl in his esses, making them playful, somewhat soft. I want to keep touching them, want to lick them.

Then all at once, my heart stops beating.

Unrequited.

The word is written next to a passage that has been underlined with thick black lines. It says that the unrequited lover is the one who waits. He waits and waits, and then waits some more. He is the one who drops vital moments of his life, lets them scatter away, lets *himself* scatter away piece by piece for those three words. *I love you.* He is desperate and lonely, both by choice and circumstance.

It's the story of my life packed into a neat, tidy script.

Thomas and I, we share the same story. We might have gotten there differently, but now we share the same fate.

I look at the time: twelve past eleven. I get up, pile on winter clothes, and head out the door. I'm going to the place I went to last night. I'm going to trespass. Again.

I've got a confession to make: after seeing Thomas with Hadley at the coffee shop, I watched him...in his house...through the window, at night.

I know it sounds bad. Borderline criminal. Psychotic. Stalkerish. If Thomas ever knew, he'd kill me. If Kara ever found out, she'd shit her pants. So, I'm never going to tell them. I'll be taking this one to the grave.

Thomas' address was easy to find. It was on the university portal, under employee directory. I sat on that address for hours until I couldn't, until the night fell and I wrote that shitty poem with horrible word choices.

I've always felt like an outsider, a freak of nature to love someone who'd never love me back, to love my own stepbrother, who for all intents and purposes is considered to be my actual brother by everyone...by my mother.

And now I've found someone who's going through the exact same thing. So, I broke my rule to never stalk again and went to Thomas' house last night. I watched him through his living room window. He sat on a colorless couch, sprawling, his hair sticking up. He graded papers, pen tightly clutched in his hands, a t-shirt clinging to the valleys of his body, a permanent frown sitting on his forehead. He'd look up every now and then, stare out the window. Thank God for the oversized foliage surrounding his house that kept me hidden. Then he'd stab a grade on the sheet and throw it on the coffee table. Rinse and repeat.

I could feel the frustration taking him over until he tossed the papers aside and began pacing. He'd stop and look behind him—I don't know at what—and then pace again. It went on for hours, a hypnotizing ritual until he passed out on the couch, sitting up, his head pointed to the ceiling.

Tonight it's snowing. Thick flakes fall from the sky, burying the sidewalks under small hills of snow. I walk with slow, measured steps, feeling the bite of the cold. The tall campus buildings give way to arched-roof houses, squatting far apart from each other. I shouldn't be doing this. I shouldn't be snooping. It's crazy, not to mention illegal, but I keep walking.

Up ahead, I see a house, separate from the others. Thomas' house. The overgrown foliage and un-mowed lawn peppered with heaps of snow make it look abandoned. It's a house, not a home.

My stomach feels the usual tight pull when Thomas is around, but it's a false alarm, because Thomas isn't there. The lights in the living room are out. This is the time to turn back—maybe they aren't home—but my psychotic heart pushes me forward.

I brave the savage and cold yard and walk around the house. A lone tree towers over the roof, its sharp, naked branches grazing the siding. My eyes home in on the last window. Its light is on, and white curtains flutter with movement.

Slowly, I forge ahead.

I run my terrified gaze around but see no sign of civilization. The houses are dark; the nearest one seems an ocean away from my position. I reach the window and squat down in hiding.

I hear murmured sounds and it takes me a moment to gather the courage to look up. The drapes are partially drawn, leaving a slice of an opening. I see Thomas clearly. He is standing, giving me his side profile. He is wearing black drawstring pajamas and is bare-chested.

Holy fuck. He's almost naked.

He is not huge but tall and sleek, each muscle defined and curled. My eyes travel from his cheek down to the tendon of his neck merging into his strong shoulders. The veins on his toned arms flicker as he opens and closes his fist. His wedding band shines against his pants. He's got an artist's body: mysterious terrains, moody sheets of muscles that are tightened right now.

The murmurs are hard to place. Words run together. Their voices are low but the strain is unmistakable. I catch something about Nicky, about leaving him alone, about going somewhere for a few days. All of this is in Hadley's high-pitched, feminine voice. I don't know what Thomas says to that, but he's agitated. He plows a hand through his hair, pulling on the contours of his ribs and stomach.

Looking at him like this, his body on display, made of hard muscles, he seems unbreakable. Oh, how stupid to think that.

He *is* breakable, more fragile than even his wife, Hadley. She can break him into pieces, mangle him, leave him ruined if she wants. No one can save him.

But we want to. We just want to kiss him. One kiss.

As if my one kiss will magically cure his wounded heart. As if he'll even want to kiss someone like me. Besides, this isn't what I'm supposed to be thinking about. I'm not here to perv over him. I'm here to…see him, without his usual bullshit. I'm here to see someone else like me.

A flash of yellow—a nightgown?—passes through until it disappears. The murmurs stop. The silence is thick and dark.

Thomas faces away from the window, giving me a glimpse of his back. It's tight and strained. What were they talking about?

He shifts his stance and picks up an empty vase, his fingers fisting around its sleek neck. He raises his arm, getting ready to throw it in anger. I am already cringing at the impending crash, but at the last moment, he sets the vase down and walks out, following her.

Always following her.

CHAPTER TEN

It's Saturday and I'm sitting at Crème and Beans. My table is slouched under the myriad of books I picked up from the bookstore last week.

I've got another confession to make. No, it's not something horrendous or criminal like stalking or peeping through the window. Here it is: I bought some books on poetry after Thomas told me to give up on it. They are supposed to teach you how to be a poet, things like technique and form and syllables and types of verses. It's all very intimidating and foreign-looking.

I'm so engrossed in the debate regarding the importance of blank space in a poem—it is as important as the words themselves, apparently—that I'm caught off guard at the strong waft of chocolate and something spicy.

My fingers heat up and I find Thomas peering down at me. He's got a mug of coffee and a pastry bag in his hand, and the most devastating thing is the baby strapped to his chest, facing out. Nicky is kicking his legs and nibbling on his fist as he looks around the room. Thomas' hand is splayed on his tummy in a protective gesture.

Dear God, this man is sexy.

Thomas is staring down at my book and I try to slide it toward me, inch by inch. But he puts his coffee and pastry aside, bends with Nicky still secure, and drags it back to the center of the table.

Smirking, he pins me with his gaze. "What are you doing?"

"Nothing," I grumble, and try to tug the book away from his hold, but his hand is like a rock. "Let it go."

He does and I jerk back in my chair with the force, earning a soft chuckle from Thomas. He takes a seat then. I can't look away from the expert way he's holding Nicky, safe and secure against his chest.

His chest that I saw naked last night.

Don't think about it.

But my shameless heart doesn't listen and I'm bombarded with flashes of my adventure. I press my lips together. If I'm not careful, I'll end up blurting it all out. Thomas can never find out what I saw. *Never.*

He sips his coffee and fishes the pastry out of the bag—chocolate croissant.

"Is that your go-to food?" I ask, thinking about his delicious smell.

"Pretty much, yeah. And in case you were wondering..." He takes a bite of it. "I don't share chocolate."

I watch him chew, the smooth movements of his jaw and the bob of his Adam's apple as he swallows. It's mundane, something he does multiple times every day, and that makes this common occurrence so uncommon for me. It's a peek into his daily activities.

As if I haven't gotten enough peeks. Disgusted, I lower my gaze.

Thomas goes ahead and picks up the book, reading the title, effectively hiding his face. "*Coming of Age as a Poet.*"

I'm doubly ashamed now. I don't want him to see how I'm struggling, how deep his words from the other day cut me. "Can I have it back? I'm working."

I tug it free from his grip and he lets me, revealing his playful gaze. "But you just said you're doing nothing."

I roll my eyes at his childish statement. "I lied, okay."

"Lying's a very bad habit, Miss Robinson," he informs me, his voice anything but childish now. "It might land you in trouble."

"I think I can handle a little trouble, Professor Abrams."

He remains silent and drinks his coffee, watching me with speculation. I can't believe I'm saying this, but I want him to leave. I've committed so many crimes in the past couple of days that I can't even look at him without going hot and flushed all over. I bet I resemble a tomato, and I don't even like tomatoes, especially on a hamburger. I always gave them to Caleb.

He knows. Thomas knows I saw him last night.

"Do I make you nervous, Layla?"

"No," I scoff—or try to; it comes out all squeaky and high.

"Yeah, I didn't think so," he murmurs then takes another sip. "Have you done something?"

"What, no," I say quickly, playing with the pages of the book. "Look, do you mind leaving? I'm working here."

"How can you work here? Isn't it too loud?"

"I like it. It reminds me of home," I mumble.

"Where did you live, a playground?"

"No. New York."

He grows serious at my answer, and the crinkles around his eyes disappear as he studies me. Great, more microscopic observation. I should just tell him so this torture is over. Why can't I be normal and hide things like other people?

Learn to eat your feelings, Layla. Learn it!

"You miss the noise of the city," he concludes, breaking my inner monologue. I nod with hesitation. Taking another sip of the coffee, he says, "Me too."

I barely suppress a gasp at his revelation. I'm shocked that he chose to tell me something personal about himself. Now, along with drowning in embarrassment about my nightly actions, I'm thoroughly confused.

"What?" he asks.

"I... You're so weird." He arches his eyebrow at me. "No, really. Why are you being so nice to me?"

"I'm always nice."

"No, you're not. You hate me. You're always giving me a death glare, like I'm responsible for, I don't know, terrorism or global warming or something."

He chuckles or maybe laughs. It's a bark of a sound, rusty and awkward but still. I made him do that. Me.

Thomas goes to take a sip of his coffee, but I snatch it away before he can. I'm feeling gutsy now. His weird laugh/chuckle has made me brave. Embarrassment is still there, but like every time we're close, I become bolder.

Thomas gives me a meaningful look as I take a sip. "What? You know I only steal stuff that gives me a high." I shrug.

Shaking his head, he looks out the glass wall we're sitting by. I realize that outside of the Labyrinth, Thomas is much more receptive to me. Outside of class, he's more playful, relaxed. *The man really hates teaching, doesn't he?*

Nicky chooses this moment to gurgle and whip his fists up and down. I've been avoiding looking at him. Somehow entertaining sordid thoughts about

Thomas and spying on him, and then looking at Nicky's innocent face feels... wrong.

"Hey, Nicky." I greet him with a wave of my fingers, and the little man with the black beanie and fat cheeks turns his bright eyes to me. He lunges—as much as he can while still strapped to his daddy's chest—to grab my finger. Chuckling, I reach out and let him wrap his dimpled fist around it.

"Aren't you cute?" I blow kisses at him, making him laugh. "I wonder where you get it from." I widen my eyes at Thomas playfully.

Thomas' eyes are anything but playful. They are twin peaks of intensity, and they are trained on me. I shift in my chair, craving some sort of friction between my legs.

I want to keep looking, but I bring my focus back to Nicky. He's playing with my finger happily. "Oh look, you're wearing purple again. Good boy. You know what I think? I think you and me, we're soul mates. We should have matching outfits."

Thomas breaks his silence. "Don't give him ideas. I don't want my son to dress up like a clown."

Affronted, I glare at him. "Are you calling me a clown? What's wrong with what I wear?"

He pops a bit of the croissant in his mouth. "What's that on your head?"

My free hand goes up and I take off my hat, ruffling my hair. Waves fall around my face and I push them away. Thomas' gaze flicks over the loose mass of curls and it has me wondering if something is stuck in there. My hair tends to catch things—dead leaves, snow, twigs.

I feel shy all of a sudden so I glance down and clear my throat. "This is a Russian-style Arctic fur hat."

"And this is what, Russia?"

I purse my lips at Thomas and the crinkles around his eyes deepen, as he chews on another piece of croissant. To Nicky, I say, "Tell him, Nicky. Tell him he's a judgmental moron."

Nicky abandons my finger and stares at my hat. He coos at it while chewing on his finger. God, he's so adorable. I almost can't look at him.

"Do you want this Russian hat by any chance, little man?" I offer it to him and he grabs at it, and then promptly goes on to drool on it. "See? He loves it so much he wants to eat it." I throw Thomas a pitying glance. "It's okay, not everyone can be cool."

"Don't get too excited. He's at a stage where everything looks like food and drool-worthy." He whips out a tissue from his pocket, removes the hat from Nicky's mouth, and wipes off his drool. I take this tiny moment to study him and his expert movements.

"Is this your way of not giving up?" Thomas asks, pointing to the open book I'd completely forgotten about.

Shyness stabs my cheeks again and I lower my eyes. "Maybe."

"Show me what you've written so far"

I jerk my gaze up at him. "No—not that I've written anything. I *can't* write. I don't know how. Isn't that what the problem is?"

He shakes his head and snaps my notebook shut, making Nicky chuckle. *Thanks for the support, buddy.* "Now, I'm only going to say this once, so you better listen."

His professor-y voice makes me raise my hand as if we are in a classroom.

"What?"

"That's exactly what you said in class," I say, thinking about the time he blew his lid when people talked about their favorite writers. I lower my voice and imitate him, "I'm only gonna say this once..."

Nicky chortles again and I beam with pleasure.

"Do you want the advice or not?"

I nod enthusiastically.

"These books are no help to you unless you actually write something. They can't teach you to write. They can only teach you to polish what you've written." Sighing, he looks around, then settles his eyes on his coffee mug.

"Wrap your hands around the coffee mug and close your eyes," he tells me.

Confused, I don't do either of those things and he shakes his head at me. He leans forward, careful of Nicky, and drapes his big, thick fingers over my hands, bringing them to the mug.

My breath hitches at the very first contact between us. His rough, bumpy hands over my tiny, pale ones, it's...it's jarring. It's what I imagine touching a lightning rod feels like. Electric. Humming. Bubbling with energy.

"Layla, you with me?" Thomas asks, and I gulp, jerking out a nod. "Close your eyes."

I do, because I've got no other option but to obey. He holds the functions of my body hostage with his touch, and my eyelids fall shut at his voice.

I become awake, hypersensitive. I can hear the rasp of his breaths, punctuated by Nicky's gurgles. I feel the sun on my face even though we're sitting inside and the morning is grey. I want to shift in my chair, rub my thighs together. I want to ask him to increase the pressure of his grip so the feel of his skin is tattooed onto mine.

"Tell me how the coffee mug feels."

Can you taste sound? I don't know, but I can taste his voice in this moment. It's viscous and thick and sweet. "I-I... Well, it's hot." *But not as hot as your hands.*

"What else?"

Under his palm, I move my fingers, feeling the rough contours of the coffee mug. It's yellow in color with a brown ridged sleeve. "It's rough, scratchy." *But the roughness of your hands feels so much better.*

"And?"

I try to feel more and come in contact with something metallic. I bend my digit and touch something smooth with the knuckle. It's the wedding band, cool against his patent heat, icy cold. The rhythm of my breathing changes—or maybe it's his altered breaths, choppy and broken.

Feeling the wrongness of it, I snap my finger straight and away, taking refuge in the sensations of our skin rubbing together. "It feels like...like sunshine, like just by touching it I'm —I'm awake and alert and I don't know...just, alive." *And I'm not talking about the stupid coffee mug.*

Thomas removes his hand and I'm forced to open my eyes. There's color on his cheeks, not quite red, but something similar that brightens up his flesh. It flips something in my chest.

He shrugs. "There you have it. A cup of coffee is a pocketful of sunshine for you. Writing isn't only about technique, though that's important. It's not about what you see; it's about what you feel. You have to go in deeper, turn stones, look where you'd rather not look to be able to write. Ergo, you don't need these books right now."

I put my hands in my lap, covering one with the other—a poor attempt to preserve the heat left by him. "Is that what you do? Look where you'd rather not?"

"Sometimes."

"Aren't you afraid of what you'll find?"

I don't have to wonder what I'll find when I look inside me—a selfish, crazy girl who fell in the wrong kind of love—so I'd rather not look.

"Terrified," he murmurs, answering my question. "Art is painful, Layla. It's potentially dangerous. Explosive. It takes everything from you, sometimes more than you can afford. It's a beast, and it's always starving. You feed it and feed it...until you have nothing left." He sucks in a breath. "But you don't mind because you'd rather chase the high of creating something than live in darkness. It's insanity."

It's the most truthful and the most miserable thing he's ever said to me. His words lodge somewhere in my cracked heart, breaking it further. I realize he could be talking about love—an insane, hungry beast who takes and takes.

"Are you going to take that?" Thomas asks after a while.

"What?"

Vibrations echo on my thigh, alerting me that my phone is ringing. I take it out of my pocket and almost drop it like I'm holding an icicle in my hand.

It's Caleb.

Caleb, with his green eyes and dirty blond hair, grinning at me through my phone screen.

I don't...I don't understand. I keep staring at it, keep listening to the shrill tune, hoping it will change, hoping Caleb's face will dissolve, hoping this is a joke.

It has to be, right? Why would he call me after two years?

The phone stops ringing and I manage to take a halting breath.

"Layla."

I look at Thomas like I don't remember him.

Before I can say something, the phone rings again, buzzing on the table. Without a second thought, I hop up from my seat, gather my things, and throw Thomas a distracted glance.

"I-I have to go."

I run out of the café as if Caleb is here, rather than in fucking Massachusetts, as if Caleb has come to tell me how much he hates me.

CHAPTER ELEVEN

"No." Emma is shaking her head. "I won't wear that. I won't."

"Why not?" I look at her in the mirror and then back to the dress in my hands. "What's wrong with it?"

"The color. It's...orange."

"Tangerine," I say for the millionth time. "It's tangerine."

"They're the same thing." She puts her hand on her hip and turns to me. "Ugh. I just...don't know about this." She walks over to my bed and plops down on the pile of clothes.

"Do you trust me?" I ask her seriously, and she laughs at my expression. I thrust the dress in her face to make her stop and she swats at it. "Just try it, okay? Tangerine is fucking awesome. It'll look great on you. Trust me." When she throws me a dubious look, I add, "Dylan's gonna love it. It's like you're wearing...sunshine."

My lips curve up in a smile at the word. *A cup of coffee is a pocketful of sunshine for you.*

"Wow, aren't you the poet?" Emma teases.

"Yeah, I might be." I pull her up and shove her in the direction of my en suite. "Now, go change."

She gulps. "What if he doesn't like me? You know, we've been friends for so long, and now, everything is changing. I don't—"

"Do you love him?"

She rolls her eyes. "Yeah."

"Then it's enough. Love is magical. It can do things, things you can't even imagine." I smile. "Just have a little faith."

"Okay." Emma returns my smile with one of her own and leaves to change. I cross my fingers and toes, hoping, *begging* that what I said turns out to be true for her.

My prayers are interrupted when I hear the depressing buzz of my phone from somewhere on the bed.

Caleb.

That's all I think about as I frantically search for it under the pile of clothes and books and rumpled sheets.

By the time I manage to find it, I miss the call, but it wasn't from Caleb. It was my mom. What was I thinking? Of course Caleb wouldn't call me. Maybe he butt-dialed me earlier or something. We have nothing to say to each other.

The phone starts up again—my mom.

"H-Hello," I say as I try to tamp down my anxious heart. I have a bad feeling about this.

"Layla. How are you?"

Even though her tone is distracted, I can't stop the pleasure of hearing from her. Her voice is soft and always manages to stay at the same decibel, but her face changes when she is angry, becomes even more beautiful—painfully beautiful. It's hard to look at her. "I'm great. How-how are you?"

"Good. Good. I wanted to talk to you about Henry's party."

"Right. Sure. I remember. It's next week. Don't worry, I'm not gonna be there."

I made a mess at her Valentine's party last year; I was drunk and high, and I vomited all over the Cupid ice sculpture. It was in the papers. Mom was so embarrassed that she decided to banish me. Since then, I've barely been to the city or her parties.

"Yes. That's very thoughtful of you, but I just wanted to remind you anyway. It's imperative that you not come."

"Okay. I won't be there. Pinkie promise." I flop down on my back, my toes grazing the floor. How pathetic is it that your own mother calls you to remind you about your non-invitation?

"It's not a joke, Layla. This party is especially important, and I don't want anything to ruin it."

Meaning: *I don't want* you *to ruin it.*

"Care to share?" I ask, curling a strand of my hair.

"Pardon me?"

My mom would never say *excuse me* or *sorry*. That's too common and uncultured for her. *Pardon me*, on the other hand, is a sign of being ladylike, which I am not, by the way.

"About the party. What's so important about it? It's just Henry's birthday."

"It's not important."

"But you just said it's important."

"No, I didn't."

Frowning, I sit up. "Mom, why are you being weird?"

"Layla." She sighs again.

"Mom, just tell me, or I might decide to show up after all."

Instant fear. I can almost hear her gasping. Oh, the *horror* of her crazy daughter showing up to ruin everything. I'm like the plague.

I hear the tinkle of her bracelets through the phone. She changes hands when she is uncomfortable. "Caleb has agreed to attend."

Cold seeps into my bones, starting up in my ears, traveling down the side of my neck, pervading my entire body. I can fucking *feel* it moving. "C-Caleb?"

"Yes. He responded to my invitation."

Even though Caleb doesn't have anything to do with Henry, my mom insists on having him around for every occasion. Caleb is the son she never had.

"Okay," I mumble.

"And I don't want to spook him." I clutch the phone harder as she continues. "Because I want him to move back to the city. His place is here, working for his father's company. I want things to go as planned."

My eyes scrunch closed. "Sure. Yeah. It's better if I'm not there." The pressure increases and tears threaten to fill the shuttered confines of the sockets.

"I'm glad we're on the same page."

"Yeah."

There's silence after that, long and stretched. I don't know why we're holding on to the connection, why we're listening each other breathe. Maybe Mom wants to add something. Maybe I'm afraid to be alone after she hangs up.

I'm still thinking about the maybes when Mom speaks up. "Okay then. Call me if you need anything."

That's what she always says at the end of a conversation. "Yeah. I will."

I won't. I never do.

A click and she is gone. My tears lose the battle and fall down my cheeks, a river of guilt and sadness, maybe even anger. I'm not sure. I fall back on the bed and curl into a fetal position with the phone tucked beneath my cheek. Sobs rack my body—guttural, animalistic sounds I don't recognize, never thought I could even make. I never thought my chameleon heart could break this much. I've never felt so alone in my entire life.

So unloved. Such a freak of nature.

I feel a soft hand on my shoulder. "Layla," Emma says softly, glowing in the tangerine dress. "Layla, what happened? What's wrong? Why are you crying?"

Through hot tears, I look at her. She is a stranger to me. We hardly know anything about each other. She doesn't know how rotten I am, the things I have done. Her concern for me is unwarranted. If she knew, she wouldn't be here, consoling me, looking distressed on my behalf.

If I were stronger, a better person, I'd turn her away. I wouldn't grab on to her blind kindness, but I'm not a good person. Haven't I proved that already?

I sit up, turn on my side, and hug her like a child. Emma is surprised, but she puts her arm around me anyway. I tuck my face in her neck. It's unfamiliar. It smells of watermelon, sweet and comforting.

She pats my back. "Hey, what's wrong? What happened?"

"N-Nothing." I clutch her harder. I need the connection. I need to know I'm not repulsive, like my own mother thinks.

We stay like this for a few minutes before I move away, embarrassed. "I'm sorry for pouncing on you."

"It's okay. I don't mind. What happened?"

I can't tell her. I can't. She'll hate me and then she'll leave.

"It's nothing." I sniff, smiling awkwardly. Then I swing my legs down and jump to my feet, clapping. "Let's get you all ready for your date."

Emma looks at me like I'm crazy.

I'm contained in a bubble, thick as glass. I can barely hear and see through it. It feels like I've traveled back in time and I'm going through the same cold numbness I felt when Caleb left. I'd drench that numbness with Grey Goose or pot or creating chaos in the world. My favorite was drunk driving. People would look at me with accusing eyes, would honk at me, and I'd laugh. It soothed something inside me, being accused. I was a bad person, and people needed to know that.

Being good sucks, by the way. I need the drugging fumes of pot to forget Caleb's out-of-the-blue call. Why the fuck did he call me? Maybe to un-invite me to the party like my mom did. It's all for the best, really. I don't care about the party, nor do I want to see Caleb. I never want to see him again, if I can help it. How would I even face him? What would I say?

Everything is *fine*. So why do I feel like crying?

I don't even realize class is over until I hear the screech of chairs shifting across the cement floor. People are murmuring and packing up their bags, ready to leave.

Emma puts her hand on my shoulders. "Hey, you ready to go?"

"Yeah. Yes. Let me pack up."

I've just put my notebook in my backpack and picked up my winter gear when I hear my name called.

"Miss Robinson, I'd like to see you after class."

I gulp as I hear Thomas use his formal, curt voice. I don't know if I'm strong enough to confront him today. I tell Emma to go ahead without me and she leaves with Dylan. The class is almost empty as I shuffle to Thomas' desk, leaving my belongings behind.

He watches me with open fascination, his arms folded across his chest. I glance up at him and catalog the separate parts of his appearance. Maroon shirt paired with black jeans. Wild hair. Glinting eyes. Sleek lines of his jaw. Thumb grazing his lower lip in soft caresses. I want to both keep looking at him and escape from his masculine beauty. It's too soothing and too overwhelming for my senses.

This is the second time he's stopped me after class. The first time he told me I had a crush on him, which turned out to be true. I wonder what he'll say now.

"How did you like the class today, Miss Robinson?"

Busted. I wasn't paying attention—he knows it, I know it, but still I keep up the charade. "Great, as usual."

"Is that right?"

I nod, keeping my gaze on the desk.

"Remember what I said, Layla?" His powerful, rich voice creates a buzz inside my body. "Lying might land you in trouble."

I lift up my eyes to look at him. The buzz escalates into a restless trembling and words slip out of my mouth in a thick whisper. "I'm not afraid of a little trouble."

His thumb arcs in a long sweep across his lip, before he straightens his arms and thrusts them in his pockets. The silence between us has a certain drama to it. Thomas is preparing to unveil something. My pulse is pounding.

"Who's Caleb?"

My breath tangles up in my throat and all I can do is gasp. It's both quiet and loud, a breeze and a gust.

How does he know that name?

The name of the boy I love in Thomas' low, thick voice sounds wrong. Caleb is so gentle, so soft. His name needs to be spoken quietly, with reverence. He is nothing like Thomas—or me, for that matter.

Thomas frowns when I don't say anything. "Did he do something to you?"

"What?" The idea is so insane that I can only stand there and mutter useless words.

"The guy who called you yesterday," he explains. "Did he do something to you? Did he hurt you in some way?"

I shake my head once, still reeling from the fact that Thomas knows *anything* about Caleb. "It's none of your business."

It's a default response, but instead of coming out commanding, my voice wobbles and distorts into a broken whisper. It is none of his business. It's no one's business what happened with Caleb.

Even as I think it, confession balloons up in my chest and rushes into my mouth. For a split second, I entertain the thought of telling him. Everything. Every single thing.

It's a novel feeling, completely alien and terrifying. I can't. I can't tell him what I did. He'll hate me. *But I like that.* I need the accusation. Someone to remind me that I deserve to be shunned by my own mother. *Tell me how bad I am, how pathetic and sick and insane.*

God, I am so confused.

"I'm leaving," I tell him, because if I don't leave, I'll spill all my secrets.

I make to go but his fingers clamp around my wrist, stopping me from moving. This is the second time he's touched me. Skin to skin. This time around it isn't as shocking, but it's still as vibrant. A boom in the air, and then all falls silent. The world goes mute before it starts back up. I know the door is open. I know there are people in the vicinity. I know he shouldn't be holding my hand this way, but I don't care. I can't...

Like him, his fingers are magic.

Thomas tugs me toward him, forcing my pelvis against the desk. The edge bites into my bone but I don't wince. I lean into it.

"What'd he do to you?" he asks again, harshly. The lines of his beautiful face are stiff and there is a severe glint in his eyes. He is angry—at what? Maybe it's there on my behalf. It's such a sweet delusion.

I can't help but feel warm as I shake my head at him. "Nothing."

"Layla," he warns.

His raspy voice, like his touch, is a form of hypnosis. My body relaxes, gives in. My rationality is trapped under the rubble of my languid, obedient muscles.

"He just...he didn't love me. Ever."

"And you loved him?" His fingers flex over my wrist, gripping even tighter. Does he realize how tight he is holding me? What does my skin feel like to him?

"Yes." I loved him. Do I still love him, though? I don't know. I've been in pain and agony for so long that I can't really tell.

The angles of Thomas' face shift. He looks at me in a way he never has before, in a new light, maybe. I bask in it, even though I don't deserve his fresh eyes.

I'm like you, I want to say.

A fleeting thought enters my mind: maybe I was always meant to find him, to find this symmetry to my disfigured soul. Maybe I was always meant to find Emma and Dylan too. I was meant to pick up their tiny broken hearts and patch them back up. I wonder how I can help Thomas do that, how can I mend his cracked heart.

Licking my lips, I tell him, "I'm the one who hurt him."

His blue gaze smolders, as if my words are gasoline, stoking the flame. "What did you do?"

"I forced him to sleep with me."

There. I said it. It's out there. Thomas remains silent, waiting for me to explain.

"We were at this party. He was, actually. I just went there to see him. He was leaving for college the next month and I was desperate. I'd always loved him but he never returned my feelings. So I, uh, got him drunk." I cringe but keep going. "B-But that's not all. I got him high, too, and I lied about it. I told him it was just a cigarette but it wasn't, and...and then I took advantage of him."

I remember the dazed look in Caleb's eyes as he kept shooting me lazy smiles. That was the night his touch lingered on me. He caressed my cheeks while talking. His arms looped around my waist as we danced. We'd never danced so close to each other before. I could hear his racing heartbeat and for those few seconds, I pretended it was for me and not because of the marijuana and the liquor.

I'd never felt so loved and so disgusted before. I still don't understand it. It was awful, but like a dog, I lapped up his attention, his love, because what other choice did I have? He was leaving. He didn't love me for who I was. My body was the only thing I had left to give and I knew he wouldn't take it sober, so I tampered with his judgment.

"We ended up in a room, away from the party and...and I kissed him. He, uh, he didn't respond at first, but then he gave in and..." I take in a quivering breath. "And then I took my clothes off and put his hands on me. I-I could see he was confused and didn't want to but I straddled his lap and...and yeah. We slept together. I thought if I gave him my virginity, he'd come to love me, but he left the next day." I blink once and a single tear streams down my cheek. "So I hurt him. He was my best friend, my only friend, and he was my stepbrother. And I forced him to have sex with me."

That's all of it. All my ugly parts. All the reasons why I'm a freak. Why I've been banished to my tower. Why my own mother hates me. I wonder what she'd do if she found out what I did to Caleb. She knows I love him, but she doesn't know how many lines I've crossed for that love.

Thomas lets go of my wrist and the pressure on my lower body eases. The pain in my pelvis becomes a dull throb.

He is letting me go.

It brings forth more of my tears—salty, useless water that never fixes anything. He's disgusted by me, and who could blame him? A sob is preparing to escape, but it dies down into a hiccup when I feel his rough hand envelop my jaw.

His magic hands are on me.

This is the third time, and it's by far the most intimate. His calluses drag across my trembling chin, stabilizing it, keeping it calm. Keeping *me* calm, like some sort of anti-anxiety drug.

"I'm scared..." I whisper brokenly.

"Of what?"

Of always being this miserable and alone.

I don't say it because we have come closer now, and I've lost my voice. I can see the pores of his skin, the hidden flecks in his irises. His eyes sweep across my face, left and right, up and down.

I palm his hand that cups my cheek. The dusting of hair over his knuckles grazes my skin. It teases my senses, liquefying them, heating them up. I want to suck on his fingers. I want to taste them after he touches me, taste his flesh after it comes in contact with mine.

I'm assaulted by images of him—his fingers—inside me. Inside my needy core. Petting it, soothing it, stroking it. I picture them curling, hooking inside my channel to coax out my juices and then feeding them to me.

The desire is so strong, so alive that I can't stop myself from nuzzling in his hand. He grows even hazier, covered by a certain mist, sparkling.

Fuck it. I'm doing it. I'm tasting his skin. *Just one lick*, I promise myself. It won't hurt anyone.

I turn my face and peek my tongue out. I make contact with the juncture where his fingers meet the palm. The touch is barely existent. It barely registers in this vast, vast universe, but his taste bursts in my mouth—the strongest, most provocative flavor of salt and chocolate.

Belatedly, I realize he's grown rigid. The haze clears and I'm jarred back into reality. I move away from the desk, out of his reach, but he's staying still. His hand falls to his side, lax.

"I'm sorry," I blurt out, ashamed of myself, ashamed of my lack of impulse control. Kara was right—I need to work on it. I need to do better.

He doesn't say anything. His speechlessness and his blank face scare me more than his shout would have. I would've gladly taken his bark over this silence.

God, I'm so stupid.

"I have to go."

CHAPTER TWELVE

It's Saturday and I'm at The Alchemy with Emma, Dylan, and Matt. We find a table in the middle of the room and Emma thumps the big bag of goodies down on it. It's prompt night for the Labyrinth and Emma is in charge of producing the prompts.

"Explain to me one more time why you need this giant-ass bag again?" Matt says, taking off his coat and hanging it on the chair as he takes a seat.

Dylan gives him a disdainful look. "She's got her prompts in it, dumbass."

Emma smiles in pleasure, her eyes on the bag as she looks for something. It's adorable how shy she is in front of him when she's normally so self-assured. Dylan and Emma have gone on a few dates this week. Turns out, Dylan loved the tangerine. I knew it.

"And why can't you show them a picture or something on your phone?" He bumps his shoulder with mine. "Back me up here, Layla. This freaking bag is a monstrosity."

"I don't have a problem with it, actually," I say. "It's kind of fun to look at something while writing about it."

When Emma told me about the Labyrinth's prompt night, my first reaction was panic. I didn't think I could be a part of it. I wasn't prepared. I haven't even read all the books I own.

Reading has become a vital part of my life, now. In the past week, I've only roamed on the street once. I haven't been to Thomas' house at all. I stay up late reading. There's so much to discover, and I've been living inside this fog for so long. I feel like time is running out on me. I'll probably die before reading all the books out there.

I try to calm myself. I'm here to be a part of something greater than me—art—and I don't have to be perfect. The only thing I should be worried about is seeing Thomas.

It's been six days since I cried in front of him, told him my ugly love story, and sort of licked his hand, trying to taste him. Since then I've seen him all around campus, at Crème and Beans with Nicky, in the corridors at the Labyrinth when Emma dragged me to a play reading. I've even seen him in the park, at the bench, the one time I went out at night. He was smoking and battling with himself, as usual, and I was hiding behind the tree.

It's like he's everywhere. My secret keeper. The one person who knows what I did.

And he is disgusted by me. He never looks at me. To him, I'm invisible. Somehow, this hurts even more because deep down I thought he could relate to me, but he doesn't.

I really am a freak of nature.

The front door of the bar opens and in strides Sarah Turner, followed by Professor Masters and Thomas. The snowflakes swirl behind his back as he enters and the door swings shut.

"Hello children," Professor Masters greets us in a jovial voice as he saunters forward. There is a chorus of chuckles and *Hi Professor* around the room.

Without paying attention to anyone, Thomas breaks off from the trio and heads for the bar. Sarah throws him an annoyed look but Professor Masters steers her toward their destination.

Thomas orders a drink and sits on the barstool, his long legs straddling the small seat. He takes off his jacket, revealing a plain grey t-shirt that stretches across his shoulders and biceps. His jean-covered thighs bulge as he bounces his right leg with impatience.

The bartender sets down a chocolate martini in front of him and I look away, embarrassed. His weakness for chocolate awakens something raw and melty inside my stomach. I haven't thought about what I'll do come Monday. Will I go back to class? Will I hide and never show my face again?

Emma gets up from beside me, greets the room, and explains the instructions. She digs inside her bag and fishes something out. "So the first prompt is this bottle of hot sauce. You have to write a short poem, no more than twenty lines, with whatever comes to mind when you see a red bottle with H.O.T. written on it. I'm going to pass this around for a bit so you guys can look at it."

My first thought is that I hate hot sauce. I'm more of a sweet-loving person. In fact, I'm the only sweet-loving person in my family or the families I've had over the years. My mom, Caleb, my dad, Caleb's dad, even Henry—they all shy away from sweet things.

The thought of Caleb makes me aware of the phone in my jacket pocket. Since those missed calls at Crème and Beans, he's called several times, but I haven't picked up. I was hoping he'd leave a message or something so I'd know what it's about, but he hasn't.

Why does he keep calling me? As impulsive as I am, a strange fear is keeping me from taking his call.

Emma bumps my elbow and tells me to get writing.

Right, hot sauce. I nibble at my pen, trying to think...no, trying to feel. How does hot sauce make me feel? H.O.T. Feel. *Feel.*

I close my eyes and the first thing I see is Thomas' face. His beautiful, intense gaze. How every molecule of my body, every inch of my flesh burns when he is near. How he has the power to change the weather, cold to hot.

Gasping, my eyes whip open. Thomas Abrams is a fire-breather. He breathes flames and lust, makes me forget everything and say yes. Yes to obsession. Yes to stalking. Yes to insanity. Yes to *licking*.

With shaking hands, I begin to write and capture him in words. The pen moves and the words flow out. They keep flowing without my knowledge. All I can feel is the heat seesawing through my body.

Next thing I know I'm jolted by Emma's clap and shrill voice. "All right guys, it's time to stop. Put down your pens."

Murmurs escalate and the room breaks out in conversation, as Emma asks someone to volunteer their poem first. With flushed cheeks, I pocket my small notebook. While the entire room is busy, I get up and shuffle into the hallway in the back. I need to get to the ladies' room and calm myself down.

I rub my arms at the unexpected chill in the dank hallway and take a deep breath. My legs can barely support themselves. Is this how poets feel when they put feelings into words? Is this how Thomas feels? It's like bleeding. It's like running for miles and running out of breath.

Before I can reach my destination, I'm being hauled into a dark, tiny room. I don't even have time to squeal before the flimsy wooden door is shut, and I'm surrounded by a very familiar heat.

It's Thomas.

He has me trapped inside what looks to be a storage room, his hand banded around my elbow, pushing me back against the dank wall.

"T-Thomas." I'm panting. "What... What's happening? What're you doing?"

His chiseled face is a study of thick shadows and thin slices of light under the flickering yellow bulb. The only bright spots on his features are those fire-starting eyes of his. I can smell the delicious smoke rising from my body, can feel the sting.

Now that the initial shock is gone, my body sags, relieved to be the center of his attention after days. *He sees us.* There are things to worry about, I know that, but I can't muster the energy to.

"Thomas?" I whisper when it's clear he won't say anything. "Wh-What are you doing?"

His breaths are choppy, short jabs of air inhaled and exhaled as he stares at every inch of my face. "Do you still love him?"

"What?"

"Do you still love that guy?"

"I... Yes."

"How much?"

My breaths match his, succinct and sharp. I study him, this man in front of me. There's a hint of vulnerability to him. His usually cool persona is frayed. Is it because I told him my story? Maybe he relates to me after all.

"Thomas, what's going on?"

"How much do you love him, Layla? Do you love him so much that you hate yourself? That you can't stand your own sight? Do you constantly think about how to fix it? How to make it better? How to *be* better?"

He isn't merely frayed—he's coming apart. Naked agony dances on his features. It's too bright and glaring. It's too similar to mine, but I'm not worried about that right now. I'm worried about him.

"Yes," I whisper. I lift my hand and press it to his stubbled face. His cheekbone is arched and high, seemingly made of granite as it pulses beneath my palm. "But I'm so tired of it," I admit, and his eyes flare. Fire-breathing eyes. I wonder why I didn't notice it before. It's so obvious now. They never fail to start a fire in my soul.

He crowds me against the wall, as if sinking his hard body into mine, but there isn't any touch involved. His frame sort of hovers over me, heating me up, jumpstarting my nerves. I'm a mesh of live wires, firing lust and adrenaline. I'm sticky as sugar and drunk as whiskey.

Thomas arranges his body and places both his palms on the wall, caging me in. The vein on his bicep becomes taut, a purple string tugging on my senses.

I watch him watch my parted lips, and suddenly, it's the only piece of my body I can feel. My mouth, throbbing, puffy, swollen with the need.

"Me too," he whispers, almost to himself.

I wasn't meant to hear it, but I did. Again, I'm hit by a storm of desire to kiss him better. It's a tornado, an avalanche in my body, and in one breathless moment, I decide to go for it. It's okay. I can take the blame for it later.

I break the rules and reach up and kiss him. A feathery peck on his plump lips, it's a kiss of solidarity, a kiss that intends to tell him I understand—but one isn't enough. It only manages to ratchet up my lust. So I give him another, this time on the corner of his mouth, and then another one on his jaw.

It's not *enough*, these small, barely-there touches. I want more, but I won't take it. I'll be good; I'll only give.

Abruptly, he fists my curls and stops me. I look at him fearfully, ready to apologize—not for the kiss, but for being the kisser. His gaze reflects passion, stark, raving need, and I shiver, despite wearing layers and sweating with his heat.

"Are you trying to kiss me, Layla?" he rasps, flexing his fingers on my makeshift ponytail.

He couldn't tell? Blush rises to the surface and I know I'm glowing like a neon sign. Swallowing, I nod. "Yes."

He inches closer to me, still not touching—as impossible as that is—but infinitely closer. "You want to kiss me, Miss Robinson, you do it right."

Oh God, does he have to call me that? Now, here? My spine arches on its own and my heavy tits graze the contours of his shuddering chest.

"H-How?" I ask innocently, belying the daring action of my body. His stern, professor-y voice is doing things to me, making me wild, uncontrolled.

For a second, he's silent, just watching. I'm afraid he'll back out from whatever this is, whatever insanity we're about to commit—but then I sense the shift in the liquor-laced air as he opens his mouth and growls, "Like this."

Twisting my hair in his grasp, he swallows my lips in his mouth. He sucks on the shape of my sensitive flesh and all I can do is let him. I put my palms on his shoulders, feeling the heated muscles under the soft material of his t-shirt. His chest shifts and slides over my breasts, like a wave of water. I want to be drenched with it. I want every drop of his sweat, his lust on every inch of my skin. I pull him toward me so he can crush me with his massive weight.

He doesn't budge though. He stands there, unfazed, still devouring my lips, immobile. His tongue thrusts in and licks me from the inside—the roof of my mouth, my tongue, my teeth. He is after my essence, the special taste that lives deep. He growls when he gets it, my flavor, and the pressure of his grip on my hair increases tenfold.

It's painful, but not enough to tamp down my arousal. I give up my attempts to bring him to me. Rather, I go to him. I lift my leg and wrap it around his waist. My hands creep up and lock around his neck. I climb him like an ivy, toxic and poisonous and shameless.

I press my body to his and kiss him back with everything I am. I pour my soul into it. For these few moments, I become a balm to his pain.

But it doesn't last long. My selfishness and my need for him take over. My core starts leaking and it becomes hard to remember I'm only meant to give, not to take.

I rotate my hips, searching for that magical friction against the ridged planes of his body. Then I feel it—his erection against my upper tummy. It's huge. Hard. A heated rod. It's alive, and when I move against it, I feel it throb. A tortured moan rips out of his chest.

Thomas tears his mouth away from me and even my soul mourns the loss. We stare at each other, gasping for breath. I'm still clung around him and his cock is still nestled between our aroused bodies. I adjust my thigh around his hip, and it throbs with the small movement.

"Don't fucking move," he tells me, emphasizing it with a tug on my hair.

"Okay." I swallow. "I'm sorry."

A pained chuckle. "For what?"

"I made you kiss me."

The legendary tic makes its appearance at the heel of my words. It drums on his jaw like a secondary heart, or maybe a time bomb. "You did, didn't you?"

Unable to talk, I simply nod.

In answer, he lodges his thigh between my legs and presses on my core. It's an electric shock multiplied by a strike of lightning, and I almost burst into flames.

"Wh-What..." I try to speak but he increases the pressure, eliciting a moan from me.

"Why?" he whispers, noting my lusty reactions. "Why did you make me do it, Layla?"

"Because I—"

Again, he repeats his movements, reducing me to wordless, needy moans. *What is he doing?*

"Because you what?"

"Because I do this kind of thing. I-I'm selfish and bad..." I moan, doused in shame and arousal. "I take what I want because I can't control myself. I don't want to."

"And you want me, don't you?" When I don't answer, he tugs on my hair sharply. "You want me, Layla."

It's not a question, but still I nod my head. Yes, I want him. I've wanted him since the first time I saw him. I want him more and more with each passing day. I want him because he's like me. He's in unrequited love and I want to save him, somehow.

His eyes shine with satisfaction, a sense of victory at my answer. He loves my desperation and it makes me hornier.

We're so fucked, my omniscient heart says. I agree.

"I can do whatever I want with you and you'll let me. Isn't that right, Layla?" He licks his lips as if savoring his own words. "I can tell you to jump and you'll ask how high. I can tell you to strip and you'll strip as if your clothes are on fire."

"Yes," I moan.

He rewards me by grinding his muscular thigh and my cunt pulses. My lust-addled brain commands me to move, to chase the friction, and I do it. I slide up and down his maddening leg, digging my nails into his scalp as the pleasure mounts.

I feel the angry and rhythmic jerk of his cock on my stomach and I love it. I love the fact that I've shed all my inhibitions and am reduced to this, a lust-drunk puppet. I love that it gives Thomas pleasure. He isn't sad anymore, or vulnerable.

Yes, I love all that.

His pain has become my pain, and it's going to make me come on his leg. I watch Thomas with hazy eyes. I watch the arrogant slope of his flushed cheeks. I watch his dilated pupils, his wet, parted lips. All the while, I'm moving, humping his leg. Up and down. Up and down.

"Of course you will," he rasps. "Will you come for me, Layla?"

I jerk out a nod. In the back of my mind, I know how wrong this is, how shameful, but I can't stop myself. As Thomas said, I'll do anything for him in this moment.

My movements are haphazard now, jerky, epileptic. I want it so bad. I want my cum to gush so hard it seeps through my panties and leaves a wet patch on his jeans.

The graphic, vulgar thought pushes me over the edge. Hard and moaning, I come, just the way I wanted—no, just the way *he* wanted. I was simply following his orders. My mind is filled with cotton and shooting stars and static. I want to bask in it forever.

Oh God, it's so good. *So good.*

The pressure on my body eases. I don't feel his muscles between my legs, and the harsh grip on my hair has vanished. In the wake of my orgasm, Thomas has let me go, and in turn, forced me to unwind my body from his.

I'm still recovering from my climax, leaning against the wall for balance, but I try to focus. Thomas is watching me, intensely, his flaming eyes working double-time to take me in, his hands on either side of my head.

"Do you understand what I'm telling you, Layla? Can you hear your heart beating? Is it trying to pound through your chest? Do you think you can control it? Tell it to calm down? Your hips are still shaking. I bet you're still leaking cum, aren't you? Do you think you can control any of that?"

I shake my head.

"Yeah, that's right. You'd be surprised to know how many things aren't your fault at all." His eyes bore into mine, as if telling me the importance of his declaration.

For a second, I can't make the connection between what he's telling me and what happened here, but then I get it. He's absolving me. He's rendering me blameless for kissing him, for making him kiss me. I wonder if this absolution includes what happened with Caleb. Am I free of those sins too?

My heart scoffs. *Are you kidding? We tricked him into having sex.*

"I saw you," I blurt out without thinking.

As soon as the words are out of my mouth, I know in my bones that this will destroy whatever kindness he's harboring toward me.

"Through the window," I add, because I can't handle not being blamed.

Everything is always my fault. The broken vases at home. Muddy footprints on the tile floors. The missing bottles of liquor from the cabinet. Caleb's missing underwear. The fact that he ran off to college a month early and won't even visit home. The fact that I shoplifted, drank and drove numerous times, crashed parties, broke my mom's ice sculpture.

It's all my fault. It's just like me to do those things. I want Thomas' accusation too.

"I saw how lonely you were. I saw the anger on your face, the way you...the way you paced around the room, like you were trapped." The scene plays in my head: his frantic steps, his hands tugging at his hair.

Then the scene changes and I'm outside his bedroom window. "And-And then you were with her—Hadley. I... You were talking and you looked so sad and angry, and then she left. I kept watching your back and your shoulders. They were so tight and I could see the effort it took you to keep yourself together. Then you picked up a vase and I thought you'd throw it against the wall, break it, because I know your heart was breaking, but you held on to it. You set it down gently. You were better than me. I-I could never have done that."

Nothing moves on his body. I don't know if he's breathing, if he's even seeing me.

"Thomas, I-I'm sorry. I didn't mean to see it. I..."

Then he shifts on his feet and the overhead light slashes his face into two halves of shadow and light. He appears beastly, like an animal with bright eyes and hard face. For the first time since I began my confession, I feel a tinge of true fear.

I can see he wants to do something, maybe harm me physically. His body is taut with violence. He looks bigger, enlarged with the barely leashed control. For a second, I think he *does* lose control. His hands jerk and ball into fists, but then he takes a shallow, choppy breath.

"Stay the fuck away from me," he says softly, deadly.

With that, he marches out of the storage room.

CHAPTER THIRTEEN

The Bard

My father was a man in love. He's been dead for ten years now, and the only thing I can say for sure about him is that he was in love with my mother.

I never knew my mother. I never heard her voice, never touched her. She died the day I was born. I have seen pictures of her, of course. I have seen her smile, her warm, blue eyes that resemble mine. She was a beautiful woman with dark brown hair and a wide smile.

Other than that, my knowledge about her is fairly limited. I don't know what kind of woman would inspire such devotion from a man who never understood how to love his own son. Whatever I know about her came from my father's poems, which I didn't know existed until I was old enough to understand that my dad was unlike other dads.

He was busy. He was silent. A hunched, unkempt man who stumbled more than he walked.

My father was a poet.

His desk was always covered by a mountain of papers. Many of them had trails of blue ink webbed across them, as if words had dissolved and run down.

He wrote and wrote but never published anything.

That's because he wasn't writing for anyone else but himself. He was resurrecting his dead wife through his words. He wrote about her and only her, and most of his poems were unfinished and rough. They were ramblings about silk-spun hair, a blue-green scarf, a mole on her shoulder, peanut butter cookies.

And I realized this was love—brutal, dark, and never-ending. It's madness.

When I left this town, I knew I'd never come back. All I've ever known here is loneliness and a role model who wouldn't even look at me. This town isn't my home. My father wasn't my father, even though he gave me the gift of poetry—or maybe the burden of it. I am where I am because of it. If I hadn't found the magic of words, maybe my life would be different right now.

But tonight, the kind of madness that has gripped me is different. It has nothing to do with love, and everything to do with a violet-eyed girl who refuses to leave my thoughts.

My fingers splay wide on the tiled wall as the cold water sluices down my body. The air around me is chilly and abrasive but my body remembers Layla's heat.

I shift on my feet and a current zaps through me as my cock touches the cold tile. It's hard and swollen and angry. It's wild like me, like the things inside me, things that feel both novel and primitive, as if they've been in hiding, programmed in my genes, and I'm only discovering them now. The absolute need to possess someone, to be the air they breathe and the universe they live in—I feel both powerful and powerless at once.

My eyes scrunch closed and all I see is her, wrapped around my body, moving, bucking. Like she'd die if she didn't touch me. Like she'd lose her mind. My arousal spikes up and like a reel I can't stop from rolling, I see Layla behind my closed eyelids. But it isn't her face or blush-stained cheeks that I see. It's her spirit. It's the fact that she stood up in a class full of people and read her shitty poem out loud. It's the fact that she had the courage to expose her ugliness to me, to cry in front of me, to be vulnerable. It's the fact that she threw herself at me, knowing I might reject her.

Could I be that vital to someone?

It makes me want to hold her close even as I want to push her away. How dare she spy on me? How dare she make judgments about my life? What does she know about it anyway?

I shouldn't have followed her. I shouldn't have lost control and kissed her back. I've been good at ignoring her all week.

But she *licked* me. In a classroom. In broad daylight. Who does something so crazy? So fucking...erotic?

A sound brings me out of my thoughts. It's a soft thud of footsteps. I know it's her; I'd recognize those light, airy footsteps anywhere.

But how do I face Hadley now?

How do I tell her about yet another mistake I made when I promised to put her first? Like a coward, I want to hide out in here, but we have a pull that's magnetic. If she's around, I can't be far away from her. It's a fucked-up kind of physics.

I shut off the water, dry off, and with the towel wrapped around my waist, come out of the guest bathroom.

As I walk down the hallway, I rush through a hundred different scenarios for how to tell her, whether to tell her or not. I cringe at the idea of hiding this, though I'm left wondering why that is. Is it because I want to be honest with my wife, or is it because that kiss meant more than a slip of judgment and deserves acknowledgment?

Before I can dissect this absurd thought, I see her. Hadley is at the front door with a small bag in her hand.

At the sight of her, I'm back in this world, in my reality. It makes Layla feel like a creature from a distant, alternate universe.

"Hadley?" I say her name in a questioning tone, though I know the answer to my unspoken question.

I've never felt a complete shutdown. I've never had my breath suspended or my heart skip a beat. People talk about it, the symptoms of falling in love, but this isn't love. This awful feeling—it's pure, unadulterated fear. It occupies every corner of my body.

Hadley is leaving me. For good.

She turns and her face is wary but blank, somehow. Her posture is both delicate and firm.

"I'm going to Beth's."

It takes me a second to hear her with the absolute silence pervading my body. "What?"

"I'll be back Wednesday."

"You'll be back."

The frown that drew me to her for the very first time makes an appearance. Strangely, I don't have the urge to ease it off her forehead.

"I need some time to myself," she says. Her soft voice screeches at my skin, like claws dragging across my body.

"What about Nicky?"

I've asked this before. We've had this conversation before. The night Layla saw me through the window was the night Hadley and I argued about this very thing. I wanted her to stay, and she wanted to take off for a few days.

Hadley shakes her head. "He doesn't need me."

What about me? I need you.

"Are you saying your son doesn't need you?"

She swallows as an odd look enters her eyes. "He has you, and Susan can stay here for a few days. I just...need to get away."

"From what, exactly? What do you want to get away from?"

"I don't want to argue, Thomas. I just... I want to go."

"Is that why you're sneaking out at night? Because you didn't want to argue?" I don't give her a chance to talk. "Guess what, you can't escape the argument. You can't fucking escape me."

I know I should control myself. I should. It's not her fault she wants to get away. It's me. I'm the one who ruined everything.

But dammit! Can't she see how much I love her? How her leaving would fucking destroy me? And if she loves me, how can she do this to me?

She doesn't love you.

"Thomas, I don't—"

I take a step forward. "What is it that I'm doing wrong? Tell me. What do you want from me? What do I need to do to get you to stay? Because I'll do anything." I reach her and before I can talk myself out of it, I grab her bicep. She flinches at my touch and my gut burns with anger and resentment and fear.

She can't leave me. She can't. I can't be alone.

"I've been a fucking asshole to you in the past, but I've changed. Tell me what you want from me and I'll give it to you in a heartbeat. Just...don't leave."

My words are right, I know it, but my voice is all wrong. The emotions inside me are wrong. Everything about this feels wrong. The darkness, the silence, the fact that I'm wearing a towel, begging my wife to stay. The fact that she's still unmoved. The look in her eyes is that of being trapped.

Hadley feels trapped with me.

"I want you to let go," she whispers.

My frightened fingers grip her even tighter. "No. No, I won't. I'm going to fight for us. I'm going to keep my promise because I love you."

I say it like an accusation. It lashes out of my mouth as an attempt to make her understand, make her stay.

"I don't want you to. Just let me go," she says again, and this time, her plea holds all the power in the world. My fingers loosen and then drop to my side, limp and useless.

She's leaving me.

She's. Leaving. Me.

A burn makes a home in my eyes and I swallow thickly. Hadley notices it, raises her hand, and caresses my cheek. I shudder and latch onto it, as though I could physically keep her here.

"I don't want to hurt you," she says with flickers of emotions in her voice.

"Then don't go," I whisper raggedly. "I need you."

She shakes her with sadness. "I just need a little bit of time. Please."

I gave up everything for her. Everything that mattered to me is gone. I kept my end of the bargain. I put her first.

So why can't she do the same? Why can't she love me back?

My bigger hand clenches around her smaller one. For a brief moment, I want to keep going, keep squeezing until I crush her tiny fingers. Maybe that physical pain will tell her how I'm burning inside. Maybe then she'll stay.

But I let go and step back.

"How were you planning on getting there?" I ask with a ticking jaw.

She studies my face silently. I show her all of my anger, my pain. I hope she sees the devastation she's going to leave in her wake. I hope she sees this in her nightmares like I'll see her indifference in mine.

"I called a cab. It's outside," she tells me.

"Give me a second to put on some clothes. I'll walk with you."

"You don't have to."

I shoot her a look and she quiets down. If she wants to leave, I'll escort her out myself. A few minutes later, we're standing at the door of the cab. Hadley puts her bag inside and then slides in herself. Without looking at her, I shut the door and tap on the roof, alerting the cabbie to pull out. I feel Hadley watching me through the window but I don't return her look. I simply turn around and walk to the house—the pile of bricks I want to take apart with my own bare hands.

Last time Hadley left, it took me two days to notice she was gone. I'm not proud of it. In fact, I'm downright ashamed that I never noticed her absence. My sole focus was the collection of poems I was working on. I had a deadline and I didn't see anything beyond that. I can't remember if I ate or even moved from my desk, although of course I must have.

I can't remember anything of those frenzied forty-eight hours until the knock that came at my office, jarring me awake from my dreamy, fugue-like state. After that, I remember everything clearly. I remember Hadley entering the room. I remember wondering about how clean everything looked, despite the fact that I practically lived in there for hours on end. The trash was in the trashcan. The papers were organized on the desk. I felt a momentary happiness, a momentary pride at how different I was from what I've known, from my father.

I was a real poet. I had published poems, won awards, and I was organized and neat. As I looked at Hadley, I remember thinking I had a family. It was a moment of sheer arrogance for myself and pity for the man who'd failed in every aspect of his life. It was a moment of sheer anger at him.

But with Hadley's next words, my world cracked and then crumbled. She told me she wanted a divorce, and like a fucking moron, I stilled, became speechless. She told me she had been gone for the past two days. She'd needed the time to think. She said our love had died and it was better to part ways, that it was no one's fault. It was just something that happened.

We're in awe of each other, Thomas. We admire each other, but we don't love.

What the fuck did that mean? Of course I was in fucking awe of her. She was my wife.

The jingle of keys followed by the click of the door brings me out of memories, and tells me Susan has arrived. It's morning now. Hadley has been gone for a few hours, but it feels like years.

Susan sets her bag down on the coffee table and pads over to where I'm sitting on the floor in front of Nicky. My son sits on the carpet, his toys strewn about. His favorites change every week. At the moment, it's the elephant I bought a few days ago.

"He's up early." She sits beside me and coos at Nicky. He gurgles at her. With his red cheeks and messy hair, he appears impish. I wonder if he feels the change in the air. Does he feel the absence of his mom? I want to pick him up and hug him, tell him I'll always love him, no matter what. *Just don't leave me.*

"Thomas?" Susan puts her hand on my shoulder.

"Yeah, he was sort of fussy. I should've tried to put him back to sleep but I just…didn't. I guess I wanted to play with him."

"It's okay. He'll be a little cranky, but nothing I can't handle." She smiles.

There was a time when Susan knew me the best—she was my nanny too, when I was growing up—and I think her motherly understanding is still intact. She studies me, my face, my posture, and I want to hide myself...or maybe break down and tell her everything, like a child does to his mother, hoping she'll solve all the problems. At least, that's what I imagine a mother feels like.

"Are you okay, Thomas? What's going on?"

Her concern touches a deep part of me. It soothes me to see that she cares, but even so, her sympathy is grating. It further proves that I fucked everything up.

"Everything's fine," I reply curtly as I stand up. "Would it be possible for you to stay here full time for a couple of days? I'll pay you, of course."

She frowns. "Of course I'll stay, but why?"

I can see that she probably knows why, and I hate that. I hate that she knows there's something wrong in this house, in my family. I've never known one. I've never wanted one, but now I can't seem to let go of it.

"I'll need you to start today. Let me know when you're ready and I'll drive you to get your stuff."

I walk away then, but Susan catches up with me at the bottom of the stairs. "Thomas, get back here."

It's her stern tone, one she has used on me countless times when I was a kid. *Thomas, walk slowly. Thomas, don't disturb your father. Thomas, your father is busy.*

I stop but don't turn around. I hear her footsteps approaching. "What's going on, Thomas?" At my silence, she puts her hand on my back and I tense at her soft touch. "Is it...Hadley?"

At the mention of her name, a weird sense of possessiveness rises in me. I can't explain it, but I don't want Susan to be talking about her, knowing she left me, knowing she left her seven-month-old son. As if Nicky knows I'm thinking about him, a sharp giggle echoes in the air.

"Let me know when you're ready to go," I insist, taking a step away from her, about to climb up the stairs and do...something. Anything. Words are coming to me, begging me to make something of them, but I won't. I *hate* them.

"She left, didn't she?" she says, effectively stopping me in my tracks. Her long sigh makes me turn around. It's an unsurprised sound. It's a sound that says it was expected. My anger is about to burst now. I feel hot, hotter than I've ever felt.

"Do you have something to say?" My voice is calm and soft, unlike the jagged, furious edges inside me.

"Thomas, I..." She sighs, her hands wringing in front of her. "I know it's hard to hear, but I think there's something wrong with Hadley. I think she's going through something big and she needs help, Thomas. She might be suffering from baby blues or something similar. I read up on it the other day. It's very common in women. They don't show interest in their children. They are... depressed." She reaches out and clutches my bicep. "It fits the bill. I think Hadley should see a psychiatrist."

"My wife is not crazy," I say with gritted teeth.

"No, of course not. I'm not saying she is, but she needs medical help. I have seen her, Thomas. Nothing about her indifference feels right. I—"

"We're not talking about this."

"We *need* to talk about this. We need to do something. Do you know where she went? We need to find her. I should've said something sooner. I—"

"*We* don't need to do anything, and Hadley hasn't left. She's just gone for a few days. She just needed a break. She'll be back Wednesday." As I say it, I realize how hollow it all sounds. Do I really believe she'll be back?

"A break from what? You don't leave your baby to fend for himself like that—"

"You do when you never wanted that baby."

The declaration thuds like a landslide. It crashes against the air and boomerangs, hitting me in the chest. I know the reason why Hadley can't bring herself to care about Nicky. I *know* I'm responsible for it.

"What are you talking about?" Susan asks, frowning.

"She wanted to get an abortion but I convinced her not to." I plow my hands through my hair and finally break down and tell her. "She'd found out she was pregnant so she went away for a couple of days, but I didn't even notice she was gone. I was too busy writing my next fucking masterpiece. When she got back, she told me she wanted a divorce. She wasn't even going to tell me about the baby. She didn't want him, said it wasn't the right time for a baby because we hardly loved each other. Things would get messy, she said. She didn't think she could raise a child alone because I was too wrapped up in my own shit." A bark of a laugh escapes me and with an aching throat, I confess, "I'm like my father, Susan."

I feel dizzy and I grab the railing to keep myself upright. If it wasn't for that discarded pregnancy test, I never would've known I was going to be a father. She would've killed my baby because I fucked up. I can't describe the anger I felt then. I wanted to kill her, kill myself for not loving her right.

But all I did was beg and beg until she gave in and decided to try again.

My gaze swings over to Nicky, who's still playing on the carpet. His coos and gurgles cut me as sharp as a knife. Somehow I've failed again. She's gone, and Nicky is left motherless.

Susan puts her hands on my tight cheeks. "Thomas, you're not like your father. He loved you and your mother, but he didn't know how to show it. You do know. You know how to put your child first. You know how to be there for Hadley." She squeezes my arm. "Do you hear me? You're *not* like your father."

"Then why is she gone?" I whisper.

Susan understands and steps forward to hug me. I deflate within her motherly warmth, like a fucking child. I hate it. I hate being this weak, being such a failure, but I don't have the strength to step out of her embrace yet.

After a while, Susan leaves to get Nicky something to eat.

He is playing with Layla's purple Russian hat, chewing on the fur, drooling. It triggers the memories of last night and before I know it, I'm thrown into another dimension. I'm flooded with Layla. I haven't thought of her or the kiss since Hadley left, but now it's all I can think about.

A hunger rises in me, a wrong, dirty, angry kind of hunger. It just wants to take and take and take, because I'm tired of feeling like this, like I have no control over my life.

I'm ravenous for Layla. I'm ravenous for the power she gives me. I want to abuse that power, unleash it, use it against her. I want to destroy her like I'm destroyed in this moment. She is too brave for her own good. I want to destroy that bravery, that pure courage.

Maybe Susan is right; maybe I'm not like my father.

My father never thought about anything else besides his wife, and the sudden burning in my bones, the volcanic eruption in my gut has nothing to do with Hadley.

It has everything to do with Layla Robinson.

PART 3
THE HARLOT

CHAPTER FOURTEEN

Emma is with Dylan at the dorms and the school is closed due to the snowstorm. I am home alone and restless. Normally, I wouldn't care about being stranded alone, but over the past month, I've forgotten how to live that way. Emma has spoiled me and now she's gone.

I hate her.

And I hate Dylan.

And I hate the fucking snow.

I hate everyone and everything.

I'm sitting on the couch. My body feels tight and awkward, like it doesn't know what to do with itself. I try to remember what I normally do when alone. There's a half-eaten packet of Twizzlers on the coffee table, and I begin stuffing my face with it.

Okay, what else?

"Aha!" I shout to the empty room then scroll through the music on my phone and put on something by Lana Del Rey. Blue Jeans.

The song reminds me of Thomas—no surprise there. I curl up on the couch and make myself miserable listening to it. Flashes of storage closet bombard me as the song progresses.

The kiss. The orgasm. My confession. The devastation when he left.

I brought it on myself. I never should've kissed him in the first place. I never should've come apart on his leg. It was wrong on so many levels...even though he seemed to enjoy my moans and desperation.

The song stops and a shrill ring echoes in my apartment. I have half a mind to ignore it, but my fingers clumsily hit accept before I can see who it is.

It's Caleb, and I'm staring down as the seconds pass on the screen. Slowly, I bring it to my ear and stammer, "H-Hello."

I should've prepared myself for the sharp intake of breath on the other side at the sound of my voice. There's a rattle in my chest. I feel my ribs shaking as my heart tries to squeeze out of my chest and latch on to the phone.

"Hello?" I say when I don't hear anything else.

"Hey," he says with a world of hesitation. "I-I wasn't expecting you to pick up."

I let his voice—a little scratchy, a lot boyish—wash over me. It's been two years, two *years* since I've heard it, since he's spoken to me. I pinch myself and curse at the sting.

"Lay? You there? What's, uh, what was that?"

It's hard to speak against the tidal wave of emotions rolling through my throat to my mouth. "Um, I just kinda pinched myself. I'm okay though."

A shy chuckle. "Okay. Good to know." He clears his throat. "I hope I'm not interrupting anything, but in my defense, I was hoping you wouldn't pick up."

"No. You're not interrupting anything." I look around the empty apartment. "It's a snow day so I'm pretty much free."

"Ah, yes. I bet it's coming down hard over there. I hope it stays that way. I know how much you love unexpected holidays."

Not anymore, I want to say. Now I hate them. I hate being trapped inside the apartment. I hate not being in Thomas' class.

Caleb doesn't know me. He has no idea what's going on in my life. I derive a certain satisfaction from that. "Yeah," I say instead, and leave it at that.

We fall silent. I listen to his breaths—they're more like sighs—and I feel like a bitch. I ruined everything between us. Me. What I did was a felony. No apology would make up for it. Even though I called and called, he never picked up.

I shake my head and break the silence. "So, how's Boston?"

"Good...I hope. I'm back in New York."

"Yes. For the party." I lick my lips. "Did you bring me anything?"

"I-I actually—"

"Relax. I'm kidding." I throw out an awkward laugh. "Wow, Boston sucked all the humor out of you, didn't it?"

He laughs and I picture his dirty blond hair and green eyes. I picture his smooth fingers gripping his cell phone—is it an iPhone?—while he talks to me.

"Where are you staying?" I want to complete the picture, see what he sees. My hungry heart wants information.

"At your mom's. In fact, I'm staying in your room."

"No way." I sit up. "Ugh. Why? They've got enough rooms. My room is messy."

"Lay, you don't still live here. They cleaned up after you."

"Oh, right." I fall back and prop my legs on the coffee table. "Sorry I panicked."

"What for? I've seen your room before. I know you're a slob."

"Hey! I'm not a slob. I'm just a little disorganized."

"No, you're a slob. You lost your phone in your room for two whole days because of your supposed 'disorganization.'"

"Well, excuse me for acting my age. Not everyone is as perfect as you, wiping off water rings." I shudder.

This time our silence is much lighter. I take the time to complete the picture. Caleb is in my room right now. It's hard to imagine my room clean, but still I see him sitting on my bed, propped against the white headboard, maybe even staring out the left window overlooking Central Park. This time of year the trees must be bare, and today, they must be covered in freshly falling snow.

"So I've been calling because I wanted to see if you were still coming to Henry's party," Caleb says, after a while.

That's why he's been calling. He wants to see me.

I press my palm to my stomach, trying to squash the onslaught of butterflies, the fluttering of their soft wings. It's been a long time since I've felt that. Did I imagine it wrong or have the sensations always been so...light with dulled edges?

It's nothing like the sharp tug of my belly button or the firecrackers over my skin, or the urge to smash my thighs together and grind my hips.

"I can't." It comes out agonized, pained. "I've got some stuff to do at school. I already told Mom."

"Oh." He is disappointed. I can hear it in his voice. "Well, maybe I'll see you some other time then."

"Are you planning on sticking around?"

"I think so, yes. The company needs me. I mean, I've been groomed for it forever, you know. I think it's time."

"Sure. Yeah. The company. Well, I'm glad you're gonna be around."

"Me too," he says with a quiet voice.

It's the end of our conversation. It's time to put down the phone, but nothing feels resolved. What was the point of the call? Somehow I know it's not the usual check-in about the party.

"Why did you leave me?"

Did I just say that? I did, didn't I? I'm such a fucking moron.

"Lay, I..."

"You never even said goodbye. Were you...that mad at me?" I hear the rush of air as he prepares to say something, but I don't let him. "I mean, I know you were. Why wouldn't you be after what I did? But I thought... I don't know, I thought we could maybe fix it, or if not that, then maybe you'd give me a chance to apologize, but you never even answered my calls. You never came around. You know, Mom was devastated that first Christmas when you wouldn't come home."

I know I'm rambling, but I can't stop the word vomit. It falls out of my lips, rolling down my tongue.

"She was completely depressed. She didn't even throw a party, and she always throws parties at holidays. Henry was so worried about her. He was, like, you know your mom well—what's happening to her? I told him I didn't know, but I *did* know. She was missing you." I sigh. "You know, I never feel bad for the things I put her through. She's not the mother of the year, as you know better than anyone, but I felt bad then. I felt like I broke up our family. You never even shouted at me or told me you hated me. I mean, I don't wanna hear that, but silence is way worse. I don't..."

I press the heel of my palm to the center of my forehead. "I'm sorry, for lying, for taking advantage of you...for everything."

"Lay, stop, okay? Please just stop," he whispers in a guttural voice, and I know, I *know* he has tears in his eyes. They jab behind my closed eyelids as if in answer to his pain.

"You don't have to say sorry. It...It wasn't your fault."

I'm hit with a tiny déjà vu. *You'd be surprised to know how many things aren't your fault at all.* Thomas' voice, even in my imagination, makes me shiver.

"Lay?"

"Yeah, I'm here." I gather my thoughts. "Caleb, it...it was my fault. I knew you were drunk and that cigarette I gave you...that was pot. I knew you weren't interested in me, but still I...forced you to—"

"God, is that what you think? Is that what you think happened? You forced me?" A sharp gust of air and I can almost hear him cracking his knuckles like he does when he's agitated. "Layla, I knew it was pot. I knew what I was doing. I wanted it to happen, okay?"

"You-You wanted to have sex with me?"

"Yes."

"Wh-Why?"

"Because...Because I wanted to know what it would feel like."

"You mean having sex? You hadn't had sex before? You were a virgin too?"

See, this is the kind of thing you should know about your sexual partner. I'd always assumed Caleb was more experienced, though it's true that I never saw him with a girl. He was one of those guys who spent time reading, doing homework, sometimes hanging with friends.

But I thought he'd done it. I'd heard rumors about it. I never had the courage to ask, only the courage to throw baseless tantrums. Yeah, I fought with him over a stupid thing because I'd heard he'd slept with someone. I even broke his lamp and spilled water on his biology homework. Boy, that was a big fight.

"No, I wasn't."

"You weren't a virgin?"

"No, Layla. I wasn't."

"But you just said you wanted to see what sex would feel like."

"You know what, this isn't the way I pictured having this conversation. I was hoping you'd come to the party and we'd talk. I've missed you, Lay. I've missed you so much and I've got so many things I wanna tell you, and I'm tired of not talking to you. Are you sure you can't make it? I mean, it's a Saturday."

"Tell me what you meant." I'm sitting on the edge of my seat, my legs bouncing on the floor, impatient.

"Don't do this, Lay. I don't want to do this over the phone."

"We're gonna have to, unless you wanna drive up in the snow."

"Please, Lay, just—"

"What did you mean, Caleb? You know I'm not gonna let this go. I'll keep calling you and drive you crazy until you tell me."

This time his sigh is resigned. "I wanted to see how sex would feel like...with a girl." I remain silent at his declaration. Things seem even more tangled now. "I'm gay, Layla."

"No you're not," I blurt out.

"I am."

"No, you're not. You slept with me."

I'm repeating myself and my voice is high, but I can't seem to wrap my head around what he's saying.

"I thought...no, I *knew* that if I was going to fall in love with a girl, it would be you, Lay. You were everything to me. My best friend. My go-to person. I knew you were in love with me and I thought if I could just push all those weird feelings away, I'd fall for you. I thought if I just...touched you, I could, maybe, fall in love."

"But you didn't."

"No," he whispers.

"So it failed, your experiment," I mutter, talking to myself. "It was an experiment for you, sleeping with me."

"No. God, no. Layla, it wasn't an experiment. I could never do that to you. I—"

"And you left." My voice seems dead to me. Flat. Without any inflection. "You left me in that strange bed. With people I didn't know. By the time I got back home, you'd already gone. You know, when I was lying there in that bed, for a second I thought you'd gone out to get me coffee or something, like in the movies. I thought you were falling in love with me. I thought things were going to be perfect."

"Layla, I'm—"

"Don't. Don't say it."

"But—"

"I think I'm gonna hang up now."

My entire body sags as I end the call. The phone slides out of my limp fingers and falls on the ground with a clatter. I sit on the couch in a daze. It's hard to focus when the buzzing is loud in my chest, my ears, my stomach, even my arms.

Caleb can't be gay. I love him—*loved* him. Whatever. I pictured our wedding, our honeymoon in Paris, our babies: one violet-eyed boy and a green-eyed girl. I pictured him making love to me countless times. Even though our first time was a fucking disaster, I knew we'd improve with age, like wine or...or some kind of alcohol I can't think of right now.

How can he be gay?

I hear a crash then, in the distance...or maybe it's inside me. I spring to my feet, but I can't stand still. I keep changing legs, as if prepping myself to run. Somewhere. Anywhere. In the snap of a moment, I dash to my room. I'm dragging clothes over me. Tights over my sleep shorts. Leg warmers. A fuzzy white sweater over my camisole. My purple fur coat. A hat. My boots. Gloves. Three pairs of socks under my snow boots. And I'm out the door.

A snowstorm is easier to battle with, than my empty apartment.

CHAPTER FIFTEEN

He stole my notebook. The notebook I write my poems in. The notebook I had with me on prompt night.

That asshole.

How do I know it's him? Because I'm not an idiot. I've looked fucking everywhere at home. I had to clean my apartment—twice—to get into all the corners. I've got blisters on my palms to prove it. My knees are chafed from kneeling and fishing out clothes hiding under my bed.

I still didn't find my tiny blue spiral-bound notebook.

After my sojourn in the snow yesterday, I started thinking rationally. The pain and the sting of the cold cleared my head.

Caleb is gay. The guy I've been in love with all my life is gay, and I never noticed it.

Never. Not once. I've been so absorbed in my fantasies that I never bothered to come out of them. How selfish and stupid and unobservant do you have to be to not notice that your best friend is gay? I grew up with the guy, for God's sake. How did I not know this?

I sat at my bench—the bench where I saw Thomas for the first time—and pondered. And cried. And pondered some more. It was an awful cycle, until I thought I'd die of the cold weather. So I trekked back, and by the time I reached home, I was itching to read or write or both.

And since then I haven't been able to sit still, because my notebook is missing. *Missing!*

I know it was Thomas. He stole it when we were in the storage closet. It has to be him. I know I didn't simply misplace it, and he's the only human being I've come in contact with in the last three days.

Since it's Tuesday, our poetry class isn't meeting. Even so, classes are back on, so I walk to the Labyrinth. He must be there. He has other classes, after all.

I *need* my notebook back. I need that stupid poem back. I remember every single word of it, and I just hope he isn't able to figure out it's about him. I don't want him to insult it like he did my last poem.

As I reach his door and stare at the *Poet in Residence* sign, I realize how stupid it is to think he doesn't know. Of course he knows I wrote it for him. He knows *everything* about me. I try the knob, feel it turn, and suddenly, I'm standing in front of him.

Thomas is at his desk but he looks up as I enter. He doesn't appear surprised to see me here, as if he knew I'd come. This makes me even more sure he's the thief.

Without looking away, he puts his pen down and sits back in the high-backed leather chair. It creaks slightly. The sound, oddly, feels illicit, like breathy pants behind closed doors or a loud rustle caused by hasty shedding of clothes in the dark.

Should I feel shy around him now? Should I want to look away from his beautiful eyes now that he knows I'm a crazy stalker who comes on people's legs? Because, honest to God, I don't feel any of those things. I feel famished. My skin thrums. It's more than awareness. It's like he's...in me. A part of him is breathing inside my body.

I step in and close the door behind me with a *click*. The hood covering my head falls, swishing down my loose curls. These inconsequential sounds feel even more illicit than the creak of the chair, something out of a thousand imaginations I've had.

"So, apparently you don't even knock," he murmurs.

Shit.

"I was just checking to see if the knob would turn." I lick my lips. "And it did."

"And it did," he repeats.

My hands are at my back, gripping the very knob. *I'm sorry* is on the tip of my tongue, but I know it won't do any good. Somehow I know that if Thomas is angry, no matter what I do, he won't budge. Should have thought of that before I confessed all my crimes to him.

"You have my notebook." My words waver.

Thomas shifts in his chair, causing it to creak again, causing my thighs to quiver against each other.

"Your notebook."

"Yes?" I wanted to make it a statement, but my voice betrays me and comes out squeaky at the end, turning it into an unsure question.

"I'm in possession of it, yes."

My hands fall away from the knob. *Huh. That was...easy.* "Are you saying you have it?" A stupid question.

He rubs his lips with his index finger. "Is there any other way of saying it?"

There's a tiny spark in his eyes. If I hadn't spent copious amount of time studying those twin flames and cataloging them, I would've missed it.

"Wow, so you did steal it from me," I murmur to myself.

"If by stealing you mean the way you *stole* the book from my office, then yes, I did steal it."

The mention of the book conjures up the image of it sitting on my nightstand. I've read it numerous times. I've read it so much that it's mine now. I can't give it back to him. I mean, I can go buy a copy for myself, but that won't have his words in it. I won't know what sentences he holds dear, how he defines himself and his unrequited love.

I grip the knob again, ready to turn it and leave, but I manage to stand my ground. "Look, I'm not here to make trouble. I just want my notebook back and you won't..." I pause for a split second before completing the sentence. "You won't have to see me again."

Yes, this is the right thing to do.

He is married. He is a father. He is a teacher. He is *not* a distraction. He is not fleeting. I don't understand what he is to me yet, but I know I can't afford to find out. Already, I am in too deep. We have crossed too many lines.

"I'm going to drop the class." I nod, having made up my mind. "Which is a relief because I obviously know nothing about poetry, or writing in general. So, if you'll just give me my notebook, I'll be on my way."

Something flashes across his face that I don't understand, and he shifts in his chair again. The creak, the whisper of his clothes against the leather gets my heart whirring. I ignore it though. He fishes out my notebook from the drawer and places it in the middle of his neatly organized desk. He uses his ring finger to slide it across the surface, until it sits at the edge.

"Take it."

With shaking legs, I walk farther into the room. I extend my hand and curl my fingers around my notebook. It's unusually hot to touch, as if he left his heat-print on it. I pick it up, ready to tuck it away in my coat pocket, but his fingers snap around my wrist and halt my progress.

"Not so fast," he says softly. "Read it to me."

"What?"

His fingers are so long that he can encircle my tiny wrist completely, and I'm shivering at his power. On top of that, he stands, towering over me. I have to crane my neck up to look at him. "The poem. Read it to me."

My eyes bug out of my skull. I must look like a cartoon because *Holy shit!* I can't.

"No."

Thomas lets go of my hand but I'm not relieved—not when I can see how bunched up his body is, how coiled with restrained strength.

I lick my dried lips and his eyes follow the action. They are charged with erotic electricity, and a silly hiccup jerks out of my throat as I draw in a breath. I slap my hand over my mouth in mortification and walk backward.

For every inch I move away, he gains two. He is advancing on me, blocking out the meager light and the view of the snow through the windows.

Clutching the notebook to my chest, I keep walking until I'm right back where I started—at the door, my spine pressing into the wood and the knob digging into the small of my back—only this time Thomas is right there with me. He is so close that I can feel his fire and the flames dancing on his skin, but not close enough to touch and burn.

Fire-breather.

"Don't make me repeat myself."

His stare is making me fall apart. What is happening? Unable to return it, I eye the patch of skin on his throat, which is directly in front of me. "I can't."

He goes still at my threadbare voice but then his Adam's apple bobs, hitches, like his throat is inundated with swollen emotions. "You wrote it for me."

His thick whisper compels me to lift my gaze. My first reaction is to deny it, but I reject the idea as soon as it comes. Some weird intuition tells me he needs it, like he needed my orgasm, my desperation at the bar.

Hypnotized, I nod. "I did."

"Then do it," he bites out.

My eyes go back and forth between his face and his throat, watching the odd intensity of his expression and the savage pounding of his pulse. It's difficult for him, this display, but I'm guessing his emotions are too big to contain. He can't stop them from bleeding out, and I can't stop myself from absorbing it in my pores.

My hands tremble as I open my notebook and flip to the page I wrote the poem on. I could recite it without looking, but I need this barrier because *God, this is crazy*. It's fucking crazy and it's turning me on.

Words blur as a full-body tremble clutches me in its grip. I grab the knob behind my back with one hand and tighten the hold on my notebook with the other. Somehow I focus and get the words to stop swimming.

"It-It burns when you look at m-me," I whisper, my tongue feeling heavy.

"Flames dance in your eyes, in them the fire resides.

Turning me into ashes. Black and p-powdery.

It...It's a slow process. My disintegration."

I stop to take a breath. My breasts are heavy and so are my thighs, heavy and needy. I rub my ass against the smooth door, which does nothing to abate the thick lust in me.

"Keep going."

"It-It begins with a spark of heat, a sizzle so tiny." I jump when I feel something brush against my throat.

I almost drop the notebook when I see his finger grazing the top button of my coat. Every time, I'm hit by the fact that his fingers are so long and thick. Tiny curls of hair sprout from his knuckles, making them look masculine. They feel *right*, which means it's probably wrong.

"What are you doing?"

Thomas is focused on the task. "Unbuttoning your coat."

"Wh-Why?"

"Because I want to." He shrugs. His reply is both arrogant and boyish.

The top button opens, revealing a sliver of my skin. "Thomas. Don't... please."

"Keep reading." He unbuttons the second one and then the third, followed by the fourth. Out of habit, I expect cold to rush in any minute, but I know it won't. Thomas is close; the sun follows him wherever he goes.

I let go of the knob and curl my hand over his, stopping him from going further. "Please. Stop."

His eyes lift and I can't draw in a breath. If I thought he needed me to read the poem for some bizarre reason only he's privy to, then I was wrong. That wasn't need. That wasn't...anything. This is need. *This*. The flush of his cheeks. The clench of his jaw. The flare of his nostrils dragging in a bucketful of air as though his lungs are starved. He is starved for me.

I've never been looked at this way before, never been someone's blazing focus of attention. My body, my very soul pressures me to move my hand from on top of his.

Oh God, I'm going to let him do this, aren't I? I'm going to let him unbutton my coat.

My hand falls away and he continues his task. The silence is too much, and the only way to fill it is by reading the poem, so I do it.

"A warmth..." My coat is completely unbuttoned now. My chunky green sweater shows through the gap. Guess what, it has buttons too. He parts my coat, careful to not touch my skin, and pushes it over my shoulders. I roll them and it hangs lifelessly, awkwardly from my body.

Thomas runs his finger along the V of my sweater, feeling the soft but fuzzy cloth before stopping at the top pearl white button.

A drop of sweat skates down my spine and I arch my back—only a fraction, but he notices. The vein on the side of his neck pounds in answer.

"*A warmth invisible. It leaps and grows,*

Turns my skin red and roars.

Then I burn. Slow and steady.

It hurts when you look at me."

Thomas has reached the middle of my sweater and there is no way I can focus on reading. I let the notebook fall, along with my coat and grab the knob with my other hand. I'm sliding down. My thighs are slippery, my hands sweaty. There's an inferno in my stomach courtesy of the fire-breather.

"Finish the poem, Layla," he says, his fingers about to reach the last button.

I attempt to shake my head but in reality, it lolls from side to side against the door. "I-I can't. I can't do it. It's too much."

I look to the ceiling and scrunch my eyes closed when I feel him pop the last button. Tamping down a needy moan, I clamp my quivering thighs together.

"Next time." I hear the smile in his voice and latch on to his words.

There's going to be a next time? I snap my attention back to his slightly bent head. He is clutching the edges of my green sweater in a tight fist. The color on his knuckles is leached out, leaving them white and almost trembling with need. I can see he is as desperate to unveil my skin as I am to expose it to him.

His gaze sweeps up to my rather exposed chest. The swell of my breasts is showing over the boat-necked black shirt I'm wearing, which *also* has buttons. The longer he stares at them, the heavier my tits become, much heavier than their usual B-sized weight.

Thomas shoots me an irritated look through his lashes. "Another?"

At first I'm confused as to what he means, but then I realize he's talking about my shirt. "Layers. Sorry."

He doesn't smile but his irritation is gone, replaced by amusement and a tinge of warmth. His fists loosen and he begins again. One by one he pops the buttons of my shirt. I gasp when his knuckles skim over my breasts. They swell and tingle on the side, as if expanding, and my nipples itch, growing hard. A strange soreness grips them.

Just touch me already.

He reaches my stomach and it hollows out as I lose my breath. Then finally, *finally* it's done. My shirt hangs open, exposing my white bra and the wide expanse of my stomach. He takes me in with greedy eyes and at the sound of his harsh breath, I whisper, "What? What is it?"

He is focused on my belly button ring and then it happens. He touches me, but only with his pinkie. It hooks through the ring and pulls. "Fuck," he mutters.

"Do you...not like it?"

"No. I fucking love it."

At his unguarded and guttural words, I give in to the pull of his finger and bow my back off the door. Our hips crash and I feel his cock against my belly.

"Oh God, it's so big," I moan, unable to stop myself. As soon as I say it, I'm ashamed, probably blushing; my skin feels hot.

Thomas tenses. "I never knew. I wondered, though."

"What?"

His eyes roam around, from the tops of my breasts to my belly button ring. "That you blush with your whole body." I blush harder, making him chuckle.

My heart sighs at the rich sound. I want to live here, in this moment. It's honest and almost fantastical. It's a different world altogether, a land of no rules, no past or future, just the present.

With his other hand, he snaps the clasp of my bra and lets the cups dangle on the sides, exposing my swollen tits and rosy nipples.

My skin combusts. I'm breathing with my entire body now, shaking and undulating. I want to cover myself even as my nipples itch to be touched, pulled at, sucked on. No one, not a single person has seen me this way, not even the night I gave Caleb my virginity in darkness.

Thomas licks his lips and gulps in a shuddering breath.

He needs me. And that makes me need him more.

"I'm so achy," I whisper, and he stares at me with dark and dilated pupils. "Please, you have to touch me. You just have to."

My begging arouses him and that, in turn, arouses me, so much so that my innermost muscles clench and gape repeatedly.

Thomas presses his thumb at the base of my neck. My pulse skitters and then pounds. With hooded eyes, he trails his thumb down, bumping over my collarbone, traveling through the valley of my breasts. Just his thumb.

"Oh God..." My voice doesn't sound like mine; it's throaty and abraded with lust.

He circles around my breast, caressing the top, winding around the side, and scratching the bottom.

"Like this?" he asks in my ear, his shirt whispering over my skin. My right leg lifts up and hooks around his hips, cradling his cock close to my covered but needy pussy.

"Yes, but more." I press my half-naked body to his clothed one, getting off on the friction.

He repeats the motion on my left breast, over and over. My nipples jut out in anticipation of his touch, but it never comes. He tortures me with light caresses, never giving me something to hold on to, reducing my skin to a canvas of goose bumps.

"You're so mean," I tell him, frustrated but leaning into him nonetheless.

"But you like it." He blows a hot breath in my ear.

"I shouldn't."

"Yes."

"I should just leave."

"Yeah."

"This is wrong," I moan, circling my hips, bumping against his cock. "The wrongest thing I've ever done."

Of all the times, he picks this moment to pinch my nipple and give it a harsh pull, much like he did with my belly button ring. Like before, I give in to the call and rub my pulsating breasts against his chest, searching for that magical friction.

"God...what are we doing?" I pant into his shirt.

"The wrongest thing we've ever done," he says, repeating my words. "So yeah, you should leave. You should just go, and don't ever come back." I look up at him and witness something splitting open in his expression, leaving him completely exposed.

Flicking his thumb over my nipple, he massages my entire breast in his palm. "Because I'm selfish, Layla. I'll ruin you, set you on fire, and won't even look back. I'll take and take until you're empty and hollow." He keeps at his slow torture. "You should push me away, shout at me for undressing you, and then you should slam the door in my face on your way out. And when you're out there in the hallway, knock three doors down and report me."

"Never. I'll never tell on you."

One side of his lips quirks up. "Never is a long time, Miss Robinson."

"Maybe."

Both of his hands move up and cradle my cheek. "Sometimes I forget how young you are."

"I'm not that young," I say insistently, pressing myself closer to him, trying to climb up his sexy body like I did at the bar.

"Go, Layla." He doesn't let me go, though. "I'll probably steal your naiveté too."

Yes, I should go. I should go, drop the class, and never come back.

I should.

I should.

It could be that I'm stupid and young as he says I am, but I feel the loneliness in his teasing voice. I see the clenching of his back muscles when Hadley left him in the room. I hear his never-ending battle with his impulse.

Boldness strikes me and I circle my arms around his neck, flattening my breasts on his hard chest. "Then *maybe* I should just give it to you so you don't have to steal—my naiveté, I mean, so you could help me grow up."

He is silent for a few seconds and I'm scared I crossed a line. It's such a funny thought after the way I'm wrapped around him that I bite my lip to stop an inappropriate, hysterical laugh from bubbling out.

"You want me to make you a grown-up, Miss Robinson?" His eyes smolder, and I'm glad I've got my arms around him or I would've dropped to the floor in a puddle. Something is so...weirdly erotic in that sentence.

I don't have time to analyze it because he begins moving his hips, giving me that sweet friction, and *Jesus fucking Christ*, it's the best thing I've ever experienced. The pressure is making my wounded pussy bleed cum.

He leans into me, curls his large body around my small one. "How do you suggest I do that?"

"I don't know." I gasp, rocking along with him.

"Well, if you don't know then I can't help you." He pauses his movements.

"P-Please, don't stop. I-I..."

"You what?"

I look at him with drugged eyes. He appears darker, bigger, like he can absorb the world into his body until there's nothing left but him and me. "I need it. I need you..."

"To do what?"

"To move."

"And that's it?"

"No. I want more." I push my hips against his and flex my thighs around his waist. "I want you to fuck me."

I can't believe I said that. I can't believe it was my voice, desperate and small, like that of a little girl.

He breathes in sharply. There's excitement in his eyes, dark and mean and so fucking irresistible. I feel things change between us. Whatever dynamic our non-relationship relationship had has now shifted.

"Fuck you, how? With my big, hard cock?"

I'm shocked and so fucking aroused. There are alarms ringing in my head, blaring, honking, bellowing. This is so wrong, but his guttural voice still penetrates through and shakes a thick drop of cum out of me. I feel it roll out of my pussy and soak into my already wet, white innocent panties.

"Yes. God, please." I rotate my hips once more against his stationary body.

"Are you sure you can take it?" He grinds his forehead into mine. "Maybe it won't fit in your tiny pussy."

I jerk at his words. "No. No, it will. I know it will. It'll fit," I whine, hungry and eager and playing my part in this weird game.

"What if it's painful? What if it stretches your hole so much that it hurts?" His fingers twitch and flex around my face. He's loving the rush of power. He's getting off on the control he has over me.

"I don't care. I don't care about anything. I'll take the pain. I'll do anything."

"For my cock?"

He is the sexiest thing I've ever seen, big and brooding, his face a mosaic of lust and need.

Yeah, I'll do anything. For you.

I nod my head and say in a small voice, "Yes. I'll do anything for you to make me a grown-up."

Thomas growls and his hands settle on my hips. I'm expecting him to haul me to his chest, but he keeps me pinned to the door and moves away.

"Not today." His chest shudders with difficult breaths. "Go home, Layla."

"But—"

Thomas tucks my unruly hair behind my ear. "You should probably hold on to your naiveté a little while longer. So just go home."

CHAPTER SIXTEEN

I had a bad dream, and now I can't go back to sleep. I've been tossing and turning for hours.

I pull myself up, sighing in frustration. In the past, before Caleb went away, I'd call him, no matter the time, and ask him to hold me. I can't imagine us ever getting back to that place.

I feel so lonely. I haven't felt this lonely since Emma moved in.

Turning on the light, I reach out, pick up my notebook from the nightstand, and open to the last page I wrote on. I thumb the tiny curls of paper around the white spiral where a page has been torn off.

My poem.

Before sending me on my way, Thomas tore the page and kept the poem for himself. He didn't say anything, just folded it and slid it into his pocket while staring at me.

I shiver under the blanket as if his eyes are still on me, hot and hooded with desire. It makes me aware of the lingering wetness between my legs, how I threw myself at him and he denied me, never even touched me with more than a finger on my chest and belly, a palm on my cheeks.

I'm dying for him. *Dying*. It's all I can think about—that, and how immoral this is. With each passing day, I'm crossing more and more lines.

Where does it stop, I wonder. *How* does it stop? Why can't I control myself?

I thump my head on the headboard, try to put pen to paper, but nothing comes out. Nothing feels right. I want to write but I can't bring myself to, so I try to read. Maybe Barthes or Plath will have some insight.

Barthes tells me it's okay if things are hopeless and Plath tells me to kill myself, so I shut them down.

Then I drag my laptop from the desk and look up Thomas on the university's website. I've seen this page a million times since classes started, but still my breath halts for a moment when I take in his face. Handsome, unsmiling, unattainable.

My eyes home in on his office phone number, the tiny ten-digit number located under his office address. I have seen that number before but have never really *seen* it, never really thought about it.

I sit up and look for my phone. It's wedged between the mattress and the headboard. I swipe across the screen, ignoring messages from Caleb, and dial the number. It's crazy. I don't even know why I am calling. What am I going to say to him? Besides, I don't even think he's going to be in his office this late at night, but I need a connection with him, even if it's flimsy, even if it's with his answering machine. In fact, I'm counting on it. I'll say whatever I want to say and then hang up and go to sleep.

On the third ring, there's a click, and then his sandpapery voice fills my ears. "Hello?"

I almost drop the phone. "Th-Thomas?"

"Layla?" The creak of his chair sounds. "What... Why are you calling me this late at night?"

"I was... I didn't expect you to pick up."

He is silent for a few seconds, maybe just as stunned as I am, or maybe thinking about what happened between us only a few hours ago.

"See, if you don't want me to pick up my phone, then don't *call me* on my phone."

I puff out a breath and fall against my pillow, grinning like a fool at his teasing tone. "I just thought you'd be at home."

This time the silence is loaded, as if I stepped on a landmine, but his voice doesn't reflect any turmoil. "Now that we've established that I'm not, do you mind telling me why the hell you are calling?"

"I..." I want to ask him about what's going on with him, but I don't. I know he won't tell me. He's only honest in those stolen moments, in my desperation.

"I can't sleep," I blurt out instead, and funnily, it sounds pouty. He hears my strange voice, which apparently only comes out when he's around, and sucks in a breath.

Where is this coming from? This ache, this restlessness, this boldness. I can't stay still. I'm rustling my legs together, playing with the neck of my white cami.

"And you thought talking to me would put you to sleep. Your flattery knows no end, does it?" His voice is hoarse as he makes the joke, and just like that, the loneliness is gone.

"As I said, I didn't expect you to pick up. I just...I didn't know who to call." I let him adjust to the truth. Meanwhile, I brace myself for his signature rudeness, but deep down, I know it won't come. Thomas isn't deliberately mean; he just pretends to be for some reason.

"Why can't you sleep?" he asks in a low tone, proving me right.

"I had a bad dream," I say, snuggling into the pillow. "About Caleb. Well, not a bad dream, per se. I mean, he was happy in it, or at least he looked like it from where I was standing. He was kinda having sex." A deep breath, mine, before I confess, "With a guy."

Nothing. No sound on the other end. I decide I don't need him to say anything, not yet. I want to get this out first.

"He's gay." I throw out a short laugh. "The guy I grew up with, the guy I've loved all my life is gay—and you know the worst part? I never knew. I never even saw a hint that he might be gay. He never told me and I never took the time to notice. He said sleeping with me was his way of checking if he could switch teams." Another short laugh bubbles out of me, this one harsher. "I'm an idiot, aren't I? A complete moron. A selfish moron."

That felt...good. My chest isn't caving anymore. The weight of this secret isn't mangling my bones.

Thomas is silent again so I coax him. "Say something. No, wait—say something *helpful*, not one of your sarcastic comments that help no one but you."

"And why should I withhold for you?" I like that he's teasing me, not treating me with kid gloves—not that he is even capable of doing so.

"Because I've decided we're friends. That's why the word vomit."

"You hump all your friends?" he growls.

Oh God. My eyes flutter and I squeeze my thighs together. "No. We're not *just* friends."

"Is that right?"

"Mm-hmm." I nod and open my mouth to say...something, but it doesn't matter what because I'm struck by a revelation, an epiphany.

"We're soul mates." I can't breathe, and at the same time, I feel light as a balloon.

"Excuse me?"

"Yes." My eyes widen as everything slides into place. "That's it. We're soul mates."

"I... You... What?"

"Oh, would you relax?" I can imagine the vein on the side of his neck pulsing. "Not the kind who end up together or live happily ever after. We're not that kind of soul mates. Even *I'm* not *that* naïve. What I mean is, we understand each other. We're similar—well, similar in all the ways that count."

Thomas sighs, long and hard, and shifts in his chair. I know he doesn't believe me, but it's so obvious.

"We both understand one-sided love better than anyone we know," I explain. "And I know you don't like to hear about it but the other night, when I saw you through the window—for which I apologize once again, by the way—the expression on your face, it was like...I was looking in the mirror. It was like I could read your every thought. I could *feel* your every thought. I felt it in my stomach." I clear my throat. "So you see? We're soul mates."

"You're right."

Excitement bubbles inside me. "I am, aren't I?"

"Yeah. I don't like to hear about it."

"Oh." I swallow and deflate against my pillow, staring at the white ceiling.

He shifts in his chair again and I imagine him mimicking me, head pushed back, staring at the blank ceiling. I don't know how long we stay silent this time, hearing each other breathe. I can't let him go though. I can't be the one to break this connection.

And neither can he, apparently.

It's such a soothing delusion that he wants me to breathe in his ears so he knows he isn't alone. Maybe it isn't a delusion at all.

"Do you know what a vestigial organ is, Layla?" he asks, after I've made countless patterns around my belly button with my middle finger.

"What?"

"It's an organ that's useless. It serves no purpose. It's defunct, extra baggage. It's just there because we haven't evolved enough."

"O-kay."

"But they are quite capable of giving you pain. Oh yeah, they might even kill you...slowly, until you're begging for it."

"Why are we talking about useless organs?"

"Because unrequited love is like a dead, useless organ. It's functionless. It's sicker than a disease. You can cure a disease, but you can't fix a defective soul. That's the most frustrating thing in the world, to be that powerless."

I'm all dried up. Parched. Every cell in my body hurts for him. For me. For us. His pained words haunt my insides.

"Why aren't you home, Thomas?"

"Because it's not home when she's not in it," he admits quietly.

I dig my nails into the soft flesh of my belly, trying to translate his emotional agony into my physical discomfort.

And I'm struck by another epiphany.

I don't know what he is to me, but I know what I am to him.

He needs me. He needs to exert his power over me because his love has made him powerless. He needs me begging because his love has made him a beggar himself. The lust he feels for me comes from the love he feels for her.

A thick tear skates down from the corner of my eye to my hair. I bite my lip to keep from making any sounds.

"Go to sleep, Layla."

I wipe my nose with the back of my hand and swallow the jagged lump in my throat. "Will you stay on the phone while...while I sleep?" His breath slips before getting heavier. "Please?"

"Yeah. Okay."

I sigh in relief. "Thank you."

He hums his assent.

"Good night."

He hums again. I close my grainy eyelids, feeling comforted. I hope he does too.

Time passes. Questions flit through my mind. *Where is Hadley? Is that what I heard through the window that night? Where's Nicky? He's my soul mate too.*

"You know, we should get matching bracelets or something. Soul mates should definitely have a matching something," I mumble, warm and drowsy.

"Okay, but I don't like purple."

A weak chuckle escapes me and I burrow my nose in my purple blanket. "Don't worry, it'll grow on you. I'll get one for Nicky too."

He grunts, as if he's falling asleep right along with me.

As I slide deeper into sleep, I feel it in my resting and cozy heart. Thomas and I are meant to be. This thing between us was supposed to happen.

Because I'm a girl who's not supposed to be the love of someone's life, not with my selfishness. I was meant to live in the shadows and secrets. I can be Thomas' secret, for a little while, at least—until I absorb all of his pain and set him free.

It's well after midnight, the exact time I spoke to Thomas on the phone a couple of days ago. I should be staying in bed, trying to sleep. I shouldn't be running toward him, but I am. I have to show him something, something I got for him in a very impulsive decision.

Oh well, when am I not impulsive?

The Labyrinth is quiet and sleepy when I enter with a swipe of my ID card. This is the first time I've seen it so empty, without its noisy activities. The walls feel intimate, carrying a million secrets, or maybe it's just me.

I climb the stairs and walk down the hallway until I'm standing in front of his office door, panting in the cold. My nose is running in a very unflattering manner. I get a handle on my reaction to the freaking winter before I turn the knob; it gives with a soft click.

He is here.

My gut told me he would be and there he is by the window, illuminated by the lamp sitting on his empty desk. He turns, a cigarette in his sexy mouth, as he hears me enter. He looks exhausted, his energy extinguished in a certain way I can't explain.

He sucks in a drag and blows out a long strand of smoke. In the dismal lighting of the room, with shadows flickering on the wall, he doesn't even look like he belongs in this world. He is too beautiful, too haunted to be human.

I swallow, a lengthy shiver rolling through my body as I enter and close the door behind me. My hair must look windblown after running through the streets to get here. My cheeks must be red and flushed, and so must be the skin of my thighs where my fur coat and knee-high boots don't meet, leaving them bare and unprotected.

"I want to show you something."

I lick my lips and lock the door with a click.

I've always thought of my body as a curse. It has incessant needs, the wrong kind of cravings, but after meeting Thomas, I realized my body could be a tool. It could be *his* tool.

So there is no shyness in me when I open the buttons of my coat, staring into his unblinking, unmoving eyes. I watch for his reactions. Does he like my boldness? Hate it? The color of his face is heightened and the lean muscles of his chest twitch as he looks on. It bolsters my courage, gives me reassurance that this is the right thing to do. I part the lapels and roll my shoulders to take the coat off me. It falls to the floor and I jerk at the sensation of my thick curls teasing my naked back.

Um, yeah...I'm naked—except for the black knee-high boots and, of course, the ankle-length purple polka dot socks under them.

Goosebumps coarsen my skin as I stand in front of him for his perusal. My curves are slight. My breasts are small and my waist is tiny. In preparation for tonight, I shaved everything so my skin is smooth and pale, and my cunt bare.

His gaze sweeps over my face and then skates down, down and down, and then he stops. I know what he's staring at. I did it for him.

The tic in his jaw throws me for a loop. Is he angry or horny? I can't tell. I hope for the latter. I hope tonight is the night he ruins me, steals away my naiveté and finds some peace in it.

In a snap, he throws the cigarette out the window and shuts it, muffling the sound of snow-laden wind. He faces me again, and with his eyes trained on my stomach, he prowls forward. My core clenches at his lazy but charged steps.

He stops a few feet away and reaches out his hand. I gasp as his cold fingers touch my quivering stomach, the reddened skin around my newly-gotten tattoo. It's the circle of a flame around my navel, and I switched out my belly button ring for a sapphire-colored stud.

His thumb moves over the shape of the flames and I whisper, "It's the color of your eyes."

The flames are blue, just like his gaze. I wait for the shame to pour out of me. I'm showing the guy I haven't even slept with that I've permanently marked him on my body. You don't get any clingier than that.

But I feel no shame. I feel no need to hide from Thomas, not like the way I've always felt with Caleb, hiding my feelings, watching him from the shadows.

"I... You remind me of some kind of fire-breather," I explain further.

Thomas snags my gaze with his intense ones. They mimic an inferno with savage emotions as he comes down to his knees.

"Thomas?" I clutch his shoulders to stay steady.

He breathes heavily, noisily, as if in reply, and then his mouth is on me. His tongue lashes over the jeweled stud as he wraps his arms around my waist to bring me closer.

My head falls back on a low and heavy moan, and my hands travel up from the swell of his shoulders to his thick, silky hair. I thread my fingers through the strands and pull on them when his open-mouth kisses and the suction of his hot mouth become too much.

Is it possible to get wet from someone sucking on your tummy? Maybe it's crazy, but who cares? I'm wet, and getting wetter by the second as he laps at my skin with hungry, ravenous licks. The area around my tattoo is still tender, and his tiny nips make me feel like he'll break my fragile body open. The thought oozes out a thick drop of cum from my clenching pussy.

Thomas growls as if he knows what my core is up to. I'm riding the high caused by his needy grunt when my back crashes into the door, and my leg is lifted before settling on his shoulder.

He kisses and bites my lower tummy, sucking in the soft skin, leaving what I'm sure are red marks all over. I look down just as he scrapes his stubble on the inside of my lifted thigh, and cradles it between his arm and his neck. The action is simultaneously arousing and tender, and my eyes are very close to watering. He splays the fingers of his free hand on my other thigh and parts it open. My pussy clenches shyly at being on display before him, making his shoulders bob with a long breath.

Thomas looks up at me, his eyes dark and smoky, burnt all the way through with lust. "I'm going to suck on your pussy, Layla."

They're the very first words he's spoken since I came to him. They sound raspy and guttural, ripped from the depths of his soul. They are enough to make me come and my eyes strain to flutter closed, but I keep them open. I want to see him. I want to see the beginnings of my ruination.

"Okay," I whisper unnecessarily.

Still staring at me with a fevered look, he nuzzles his nose just over my pubic bone, sending electric shocks to my core. Slowly, he moves down, his lips breathing over my skin. The first contact of his mouth to my freshly-shaven pussy is a shock. It sears me. I feel it everywhere, inside and out.

Thomas sweeps his tongue from the clit right down to the entrance that is aching, has been aching for him. At my moan, he burrows his face closer, rubbing his nose, his mouth into my wetness. He takes a long sniff, smelling me, breathing me in. It's enough to make me go crashing to the floor, and I would if he wasn't holding me in his arms.

With a gusty breath, he latches on to my clit and sucks. I moan out his name, my head thumping on the door and my lower body bowing off. It's too much, the suction of his mouth on that tiny bud. I've never had it in someone's mouth and God, *oh God*, I'm shaking.

"You taste like cherry. Plum, sweet cherry," he murmurs into my pussy before smothering it with his lips.

A tiny smile blooms on my lips at his rumbled declaration, but soon it turns into a turned-on grimace. I massage his scalp with my fingers, making him grunt low and gather me close—even closer—in his arms. I arch into his mouth, digging the heel of my boot into his back. My needy actions spur him on and his hardened tongue rains down on me with all its might.

"Oh God, Th-Thomas..." I break off at a moan that originates in my belly. "I can't... It's-It's too much. It hurts."

He pulls on my clit before letting go of it with a pop. "Good. You make me hurt too."

With that he dives back in and vacuums my wet, sticky lips. My entire pussy fits into his greedy mouth as he eats it, nibbles on it, chews it out. All I can do is take it, let him make a meal out of me.

Oh God, it stings so good.

"Fuck." His agonized whisper brings my attention to his bowed head. I loosen my fingers from where I've been strangling the beautiful strands of his hair. "Your pussy is so tight, tighter than I ever imagined it to be, and I've imagined a lot."

My breath evaporates as he looks up. He is aroused, flushed and sweating, yet he appears godlike. How's that possible when he's the one on his knees? He's a beautiful, sexy god who has my sticky juices painted on his mouth and chin. It glistens in the yellow light like liquid fire.

"I'm not proud of it. I don't want to think about it, but you tempt me, Layla, so fucking much. You make me feel crazy."

With that, he falls on me. That's the only way to describe it. His lips lock around my clit before going back down to my sopping entrance. He crams his tongue in my channel and *Jesus*, it hurts so bad, but in a very, very good way. The sting is what makes this entire thing real, and I wouldn't trade it for a comfortable, all-pleasure fuck for anything.

Now that Thomas is inside, he swirls his tongue, feeling me up. He alternates between thrusting his tongue in and out and bumping it across the crevices of my cunt. The lashing, the suction, the way he growls—it's all rolling into a big ball of fire inside my stomach. The blue flames around my belly button burn bright and alive.

"I'm...I'm going to come," I wheeze out, rolling my hips, pulling on his hair. He doubles his efforts—if that's possible—and pushes me off the edge.

I fall off the tightrope I've been walking and come. I fly, shaking and quivering and chanting Thomas' name.

My heart races and bursts into a million pieces, traveling to every corner of my body with the furious rush of my blood. I become my heart, a pounding mess, and my heart becomes me, sleepy and peaceful in the midst of my climax.

I think I black out for a few seconds because the next thing I know, Thomas is standing up, dragging my previously fallen coat over my arms. My orgasm-addled brain is confused as he buttons up my coat. My mind goes to the last time I was here and he kept opening them. His actions are so not what I was expecting when I came here, not after what he said to me about imagining my pussy.

I put my hand on his as he is about to close the last button beneath my chin. "What...What are you doing?"

He looks up. His eyes are still burning, his cheeks slashed with red. He wipes his mouth against his arm, making me catch my breath. That move was so masculine, so fucking primal that I can't help but be affected by it.

"Taking you home." His voice is scratchy, as if he hasn't spoken in a while.

"What? Why?"

"Because you need to leave." He knocks my hand off his and finishes buttoning my coat. The gesture is aggressive, angry, and I can't breathe for a second.

"But...I—"

He straightens the collar of my coat as if I'm a child and stares into my eyes. "If you want someone to fuck you, you need to look somewhere else. Don't come back here. We're not friends. We're not anything, you understand?"

I remain quiet. My ability to form words is gone. Thomas isn't happy, and neither is the tic flickering on his hard jaw. "Do. You. Understand, Layla?" he asks again, with gritted teeth and flaring nostrils.

"Y-Yes."

He moves away from me, cool and unapproachable, and breathes deep. "Let's go."

CHAPTER SEVENTEEN

How the fuck did it go so wrong? *I thought...*

What did I think? Yes, *what* was I thinking? That he'd sleep with me? That his pain is so big, so agonizing that he'd commit the sin of adultery?

Not everyone is like me. Not everyone is selfish and impulsive and a goddamn moron.

I sob and groan and cover my face with my palms, even though I'm alone in my stone-cold bathtub. Thomas dropped me off an hour ago, without saying a word. The entire ride took less than five minutes, and from the inside of his car, campus looked even more forbidding and dark and desolate. I didn't even wait for the car to come to a full stop before I jumped out and dashed into my tower, and now I am here, drowning in embarrassment and guilt and anger.

We're not anything.

If he didn't want me then why did he make me come? Why did he put his mouth on me and let me shatter in his arms only to kick me out the door?

My tattoo is buzzing with heat. How crazy does someone have to be to do something like this for a man who isn't even her boyfriend? Thomas has to be the most confusing man I've ever met—not that I've met many men in my life. My love for Caleb took care of that.

I slide down and lie on my side, bringing my legs to my chest and curling into a fetal position. I spend the night in my bathtub, oscillating between sobbing and being angry. In the morning, I hear a crash and I'm jerked upright. There are angry noises and I run out of my room to see what's going on.

"I'm not taking their side. What's wrong with you?" Dylan booms, shaking his head.

"I don't want to talk about this. Can you just leave?" Emma is holding the front door open, her face tight and inflexible.

Dylan runs his hand over his face and sighs. "Fine. Whatever. You're being unreasonable." With that, he strides out of the apartment.

I decide it's safe to speak. "Hey, what's...what's going on?"

Emma is still holding the door, staring down the hallway. She turns to me slowly and closes the door behind her.

"Sorry, did we wake you?" She drags her feet to the couch and plops down on it, dejected.

I sit beside her. "No, it's fine. Tell me what happened."

"It's nothing. It's stupid."

"It's not stupid if you kicked Dylan out of the apartment first thing in the morning because of it."

She turns to me and seethes. "He was being a moron, that's why."

"Okay. About what?" I realize this is what normal life feels like—fighting with your boyfriend, kicking him out, and then bitching about it with your friend. These are normal problems to have. I wish I had normal problems. Normal problems are so much better than what I have.

"About spring break," Emma replies. "My mom wants me to come home. I don't want to, but Dylan is insisting that we go. He wants me to bond with my mom or something."

"And that's a bad thing, why?"

She sighs and peers up at me. I've never seen her this serious and this calm. It's kind of scary. "My mom... She is not a nice person. I don't like her, and that's *never* going to change."

My heart is beating anxiously. Is that why she never talks about her parents? I remember the heated phone call she had when she first moved in. Dylan was the one to calm her down. Since then I've never seen her talk to her family.

"Did...Did she do something to you?" I ask, apprehensive.

"No, not to me. To my dad." She sighs, looking away from me and staring at the wall. "She cheated on my dad, and he had no clue. None." Air rushes out of me and I feel like I'm collapsing on myself as she continues, "It hit him out of nowhere. He was devastated. I mean, how could you do that to a person you promised to spend your entire life with?"

My throat is dry and scratchy. It's rejecting words, but somehow I manage to mumble, "I-I'm sorry."

She shakes her head and goes on, as if she didn't hear me. "She destroyed our family. My dad lost his job because he couldn't keep up with it. They spent months fighting over custody of me. I was a minor so I didn't have a say, and my mom won because my dad wasn't 'stable' enough to take care of me. On top of that, she married the man she cheated on my dad with. As soon as I turned eighteen, I decided I'd never step foot in that house again." She turns to look at me, her eyes glassy. "I'm never going back. Never. I hate her and what she did to us."

"How's your dad?"

Emma shrugs. "He's fine. He's dating someone. As much as I'm happy for him, it's too weird for me, but I don't begrudge him that. He deserves all the happiness, you know?"

"Yes." I nod, too ashamed to do anything else, too guilty. How would she react if she knew what I did last night? Is there any way to justify cheating? Is there any way I can ever tell her, my new friend, my *only* friend who seems to like me, what wrong I almost committed last night?

Last night will be another one of my many, many secrets. I can never tell her. I can never tell anyone. I can't...I can't go back to being lonely again. It's too scary now.

"Hey, you okay?" Emma puts her hand on my shoulder. "I'm sorry. I didn't mean to unload on you like this. It's way too early for that."

"I'm fine. I'm just...I'm sorry."

"Not your fault." She stares at me with a critical eye now. "Why do you look like a raccoon? When did you get home last night? Where did you even go?"

I'm terrified, panicked, a statue of shame and guilt. *I went and offered myself up to our married professor because I thought he was lonely like me and I thought extramarital sex would be just the thing to cheer him up.*

Oh God, I can't even say it in my head without wanting to kick myself.

"I-I just...went out. For a walk."

"With all that makeup on?"

Oh yeah, the makeup. Along with grooming myself, I also attempted to put makeup on. It's all ruined now.

"Um, yeah. I do that, sometimes." I stand, unable to bear her shrewd eyes. "Do you wanna get coffee? Let's get coffee."

Emma knows I'm hiding something but doesn't push, just leaves to get changed for our coffee run. Thank God. If I have my way, last night will be the only secret of mine for a long, long time to come.

It's night again. Emma is sleeping in the next room. She's still mad at Dylan, even though I've tried to reason with her. Dylan was just being a caring boyfriend who wanted Emma to give her mom another chance. I called Dylan and he told me that it was simply a casually thrown idea that got out of hand. One of those arguments that escalate, unexpectedly. And now, even he doesn't want to talk to her.

I'm trying to go to sleep but I can't do it. I can't fall asleep.

I'm staring at the ceiling, trying to stay put, and then my phone rings. A gasp catches in my throat and I have to shoot up to a sitting position to be able to breathe. It's Thomas. It's his office number.

I'm too shocked to pick up the call and the ringing stops. It's visceral, the loss I feel at a mere missed call, but...he's never called me before. I jump up from the bed, shed my pajamas, don a skirt and t-shirt, pile on my winter gear, and I'm out the door.

Like last night, I run and run and don't stop until I'm at the Labyrinth. I climb up the steps and reach Thomas' office door with an urgency I didn't have last night. I turn the knob and it gives, exactly like yesterday, and I enter.

This time, Thomas is sitting on the chair, staring at the phone on his desk. He jerks his eyes up when I close the door. I'm panting, drawing in difficult breaths as his gaze tangles up with mine. It's angry, furious, blazing, as if he's on fire.

He takes in a sharp breath and stands, nostrils flaring. My heart is pounding. It doesn't understand the role it needs to play. Should it be afraid or thrilled to be the subject of Thomas' intensity? Can it be both?

"I told you not to come back here." Though his voice isn't angry like last night, the cutting edge is still there. It still manages to stutter my breath and douse me in shame.

"You called me," I tell him, angry and aroused.

Thomas rounds the desk and advances on me. "So?"

"So why did you do that if you didn't want me here?" Another step toward me and I press my spine to the door. "Well? Why did you call?" Before I can stop myself, I add, "A-And if we aren't *anything* to each other, why did you..."

He stops in front of me. He is close, too close, and I'm caged between him and the door. All of this is déjà vu, repeated history. I can still hear his words. I can still hear him telling me we are nothing to each other. That's what hurt me the most.

"Why did I what?"

I lift up my chin, even though I want to shrink into myself. "Why did you make me come? If you hate me so much, why did you do that?"

Thomas puts his palms on either side of my head and strains down on them, bringing his face extremely close to me. "You think I hate you?" A short laugh escapes him, resembling the bark of an animal. "I don't hate you, Layla," he grits out. It sounds exactly like he hates me.

"So you like me?" I squeak.

My naïve question seems to have angered him more. His face is red, the vein on his neck bulging out. It's scary.

"God, you make me so fucking mad." He shakes his head. "Do you think this is a joke? Huh? Do you think we're in high school? Do you think I'm going to kiss you and make out with you and take you to the movies or something? Is that what you think, Layla?"

"N-No."

"Then what do you think is going on here?"

"I don't...I don't know."

"You don't know? You got a fucking tattoo for me. You came to me naked. You can't seem to stop throwing yourself at me." He mocks me, and my eyes water. "Are you telling me you have no clue what's going on here?"

Tears spill and track down my cheeks. I hate him. I *hate* him so much. This is what he does to me—pulls me forward one second and then pushes me to the ground the next—but this time, I do the pushing. I put my hands on his chest and push him away with everything I am. He doesn't budge.

The nerve on his jaw jumps and he cradles my wet cheeks. "Do you have any idea what you're doing to me?" He wipes my tears off with his thumbs. "Do you have any idea what *I'm* going to do to you? You don't want this, Layla. You don't want me to touch you."

I curl my palms on his chest, fisting his shirt. Regret clouds his features, dulling the aggression in his eyes. "Why not?" I ask him through the tears.

"Because you're going to regret it. You're going to regret what happens if you don't leave. You have to stop coming back."

"But you called me."

"You don't get it, do you? I'm not a nice man, Layla," he warns.

"I don't believe that." I fist his shirt tightly. "You're just lonely, like me. Lonely and brokenhearted." I let go of his shirt and caress his heated, chiseled jaw and cheeks. "You can touch me, Thomas. I won't regret it, I promise."

He shudders under my touch, as if coming apart. This is the most vulnerable I've seen him. But then he steels himself, goes rigid. I'm afraid he'll push me back and send me away, but he hauls my body flush with his.

"Don't make promises you can't keep." He breathes over my lips. "*When* you regret this—and I know you will—just remember that you asked for it."

In the next second, he puts his mouth on me and I forget my every thought.

CHAPTER EIGHTEEN

I stand naked in the middle of Thomas' office, bare except for the pair of polka dot ankle-length socks on my feet.

The only source of light is the lamp sitting on the desk, illuminating my meager curves. There's a shadow of me on the wall. I wonder what these walls have seen. Is it something new to them? A girl—a student—naked and horny in this room. Has this ever happened before? For a second, I can't imagine any other girl feeling like this for her professor, as if I'm the only girl in the history of this college, in the history of this world, to ever feel this way.

I'm panting, opening and closing my fists at my sides, wracked with insecurities. Any second now, I expect Thomas to reject me, to send me home, but he stands there like a statue, staring at my body. His chest is heaving and his frame is tight, too tight, too brittle.

While kissing me, he tore my clothes away in a mad desperation. It was frenzied and urgent, and now they lie in a pile by the door. Here I am, displayed in front of his eyes, and I'm going crazy with the wait, with the embarrassment and arousal.

He walks closer to me; putting his hand on my cheek, he tips my face up and makes me stare at his gaze. I see desire lurking there and my heart skips a beat.

He wants me. So fucking much.

As if to prove it, he leans down and resumes kissing me. This time it's even hungrier and more urgent, if that's possible. I lean into his clothed body, my skin brushing over the warm fabric. It makes me wet and horny and so powerless that I'm exposed and he's not.

It makes me feel like a slut. His slut. Horny and shameless.

For the next however many minutes, Thomas becomes my lifeline. He breathes air into me through his mouth, feeds me his lust with his lips. I'm slowly getting drunk on him. My blood is replaced by his essence, until all I feel is him.

He lifts me up, grinding our pelvises together, and my legs instantly go around his waist. His palms splay over my bare ass and I jerk in his arms. I'm so lost in his kisses that I don't mind when the world tips on its axis, and I find myself lying on my back on the coarse grey carpet.

Thomas breaks the kiss and raises himself up, kneeling between my spread thighs. He's so fucking sexy that I can't help but inhale a sharp breath at his beauty.

Swallowing, he takes me in, starting from the dark hair spread out around my face and neck. He travels down, his eyes caught at the base of my throat. My pulse pounds so I feel it beating against my skin. Then he goes lower, to the valley of my small breasts. I feel a tiny piece of my heart beating at the tips of my nipples.

By the time he reaches my vibrating stomach, he is drenched in sweat and shaking. The vein on the side of his neck stands taut, as if in arousal, just like his cock, which juts out in his pants. I bite my lip at the pain it must be causing him.

"I-I want to see you," I whisper, watching a thick drop of sweat roll off the side of his forehead. "Please."

I can't imagine not seeing him when he fucks me for the first time. He understands the gravity of my need and unbuttons the top three buttons of his shirt. He fists the back of the white, slightly wrinkled fabric and yanks it right off, throwing it away.

"That's so fucking sexy," I moan and roll my hips on the floor. A slut—yeah, that's what I am for him, writhing and naked.

The side of his lips tips up in an arrogant smirk, but it does nothing to banish the intensity of his expression. Unlike him, I'm impatient, and I take him in, in a hurried fashion. The tight planes of his pectorals covered by just the right amount of hair. The grooves of his ribs giving way to his smooth, hard abdomen. That trail of thick hair leading to the huge bump barely contained by his blue jeans.

I gasp as I realize the significance of his attire: blue jeans and white shirt, just like the song I love so much.

"What?" he asks, his arms on either side of my hips, his palms splayed open on the carpet. I watch the dance of the muscles on his shoulders and arms. They are strung so tight right now.

"Nothing. You just...remind me of a song I love."

"Yeah? What song is that?"

"'Blue Jeans,'" I say. "Uh, it's by Lana Del Rey. It's...It's about how she can't look away when he walks into a room, about how much he makes her burn."

Thomas crawls on top of me, his strong arms walking from my hips to either side of my head. He lowers himself as if preparing to do a pushup, and the tendons on his neck stand out in stark relief.

"I know what's it about," he whispers over my mouth, his entire body whispering over mine, not touching but looming like a shadow.

I rub my naked thighs over his bare sides, making him shudder. His head dips as his eyes close at my touch, telling me he likes it. I like it too. His skin is smooth and so fucking hot to the touch. I knew it would be. I knew it. He is my fire-breather.

"Are you going to fuck me now?" Need has made my voice both husky and small.

His face remains bowed; only his gaze moves up to me. "Yeah."

With that, he pushes up and stands over me, divesting himself of his jeans and underwear.

And then he is naked, like me, his cock thrusting out of his body, so big and long and *oh God*, I'm going to hyperventilate from how much I want it inside me and how much it's going to stretch my little hole out when it *does* get inside me.

What if it stretches your hole so much that it hurts?

I hear his words from the other day and decide I don't care. I want him.

I want to study his cock more, study him more, his taut thighs, the runner's calves, analyze all the ways the light is hitting his sleek, cut body—but he isn't in the mood to model for me. He crashes down on his knees, much like last night when I showed him my tattoo.

His desperation leaches into his movements as he fumbles for his discarded jeans, and fishes out a condom from his back pocket.

My mouth dries out as he sits on his haunches and rolls the condom over his hard, jutting shaft, and then he covers me with his body.

I halt all movements, breathing evenly to absorb the sensation of his bare muscles rubbing against mine. It feels so good. His skin on my skin. His cock tucked between us, pressing against my belly button.

But I want more. I need it.

I arch under him, making his cock throb between us, and he clenches his teeth. He grabs a chunk of my hair in his fists and stares down at me. There's anger and satisfaction in his eyes. "You can't stay still, can you? You can't stop tempting me for one fucking second."

"No, I can't," I admit. "I don't know how."

"You're always hungry, Layla. Always starving." He rocks into me, drags his weighty arousal against my stomach, and blows a breath into the nape of my neck. "Why's that? Huh? Why are you such a cock-hungry girl?"

I moan at his dirty words. God, he's such a poet, speaking filthy poetry to me.

"I don't know. I just want it so much. I want your cock." I mimic his action and fist his hair in a hard grip, my voice begging. "Put it in me, please. My pussy is so hungry for it."

I don't really know where it came from, but Thomas makes me so wild. He feels so right above me that wrong words taste like sugar in my mouth.

Thomas' control snaps and he rears back, forcing me to let go of him. His body arches, the muscles slanting taut, and I see every tight, hard curve of his chest and abdomen. He fists his cock and positions it in front of my entrance. "Then I'll fucking feed it to her."

He forces his way in with a long grunt. My back bows off the floor and I hunker down on his cock with a pained scream, my nails digging into the rough carpet.

"*Fuuuuckk...*" He draws the curse out and drops his forehead over mine, almost falling over me.

I'm whimpering with his invasion. It's painful, *so* fucking painful. I feel the brilliance of it in every corner of my body. My legs are shaking as a cold sweat grips me in its clutches. I don't even remember it hurting this bad when Caleb took my virginity. Why is it hurting so much now?

"Have you been lying to me, Layla?" Thomas is angry, clenching and unclenching his jaw, grinding his teeth. "Have you been lying about your virginity all this time?"

I shake my head furiously, rolling our sweaty foreheads against each other. "N-No. No, I wouldn't do that." I scrunch my eyes in pain and somehow manage to speak. "This isn't my first time. It's the...second."

My hips jerk from side to side and my toes flex inside my socks, trying to find a comfortable position, but the pressure isn't easing. Thomas digs his palm into my hip and halts my movements. "Stop moving. You're going to make it worse."

"But it hurts," I whine, biting my lip.

"I know." He grinds his forehead into mine and closes his eyes on a grunt. His chest undulates with a long breath, meant to gather himself. "I can't do this. We—"

My limbs move before he can finish and twine around his body. It's not the first time I think of myself as a toxic, wild plant that never knows when to quit growing. His cock slides in deeper due to my movements, but I don't care about the pain. I don't fucking care about anything as long as he is inside me.

"No. We can. I can take it."

"Let me go, Layla." I shake my head and a pulse starts on his jaw. "Don't make me pull your arms off. I don't want to hurt you. Just...let go."

"No." I cling to him tighter, until I'm almost hanging on to him. "You don't understand. I don't remember anything. I don't remember my first time except that it was dark and I was drunk and I couldn't even see him. I don't remember the pain. I don't remember if there was any blood. It's like..." I search for the right words, praying they won't fail me. "It's like I made love to a ghost. It might as well have been a dream or a nightmare, but this is real. This is so fucking real, Thomas. You are real. I want the pain. I want the discomfort. I want all of it."

I tighten my hold around him, feeling the muscled planes of his body shifting. It feels like I'm holding on to an impending earthquake, seismic waves bobbing beneath my grip.

"I want this to hurt because I want *this* to be my first time," I say, looking him in the eye.

His cock throbs inside my tightness and I feel the brush of his shuddered breath over my heavy tits. I *feel* him coming to a decision.

"Put your hands on my back." His voice is hoarse. "Dig your nails in when it hurts. I'm going to go slow, but I can't..." His nostrils flare. "I can't promise that there won't be any pain."

"Okay." I nod, doing as he says, sliding my arms down and uncrossing my ankles so he has room to move.

Closing my eyes, I prepare myself for his thrust. I'm ready for the fire but it never comes. Instead, I feel a flick, a pleasurable flick, over my clit. Gasping, I whip my eyes open and look at him. He is braced on one elbow, his other arm hidden between where our bodies are joined. Another flick of his thumb and I'm biting my lip to keep my lusty moans in check.

Thomas doesn't smile but something loosens in his harsh face. I stare at him in awe. His fingers are, indeed, magic.

"Do you like that?" he asks.

I swallow and moan, "Yes."

"I've thought about you like this," he says in the thinnest of whispers. "Under me, naked and desperate. You moan when I touch you like this but I tell you to be quiet. I tell you to keep it in because I want to hear something else." He presses his thumb and I bob under the pressure. His erection jostles, reminding me that I'm stuffed full of him.

"Do you know what I want to hear, Layla?" The pressure on my clit increases and I can't keep the moan inside.

"Thomas... Oh *God*."

"Shh. Tell me, do you know?" When I shake my head, he clarifies, "The poem you wrote for me."

His thumb is circling, flicking, feeding me pleasure, and I forget to be embarrassed about my poem. He is making me hungry and though it's still painful to move, I do it. I bow my back, lodging his cock farther in.

I hear his strangled curse and watch the tendons of his neck tighten at the cost of staying still. "Ah, God, you're a tease. You're such a fucking tease."

I moan and manage to ask, "How do I tease you?"

"The way you stare at me, like you want me to kiss you. The way you follow me around. The way you take everything I give you, never complaining, never backing down. You're asking for it, aren't you? You're daring me, *begging* me to do all the bad things to you."

I'm shaking my head on the floor, moving it side to side, mindless, insane, drunk on him.

"Isn't that why you came here? Isn't that why you keep coming? You want me to ruin your pussy, make it bleed like it's your first time. Isn't it?"

"Yes," I hiss. "That's what I want."

I'm wet, *so* wet down there, and suddenly we're moving against each other. He is rocking into me, in and out, long, lazy strokes that I feel in my stomach.

My desire ups with every slide and I forget about the pain. I wrap my legs around his waist and bring him closer. Thomas speeds up his thrusts until he's slamming into me, grunting like a man possessed.

"Oh God. Oh God. Oh God," I chant as his hips smash into mine, as his balls slap against my ass. I am sobbing with every jab.

Thomas has gone speechless as he stares down at me, at my rebounding breasts. He is feeding off my moans, my pleasure, my restlessness like a demon. My desperation spurs him on as I meet him stroke for stroke.

I watch him over me, his stomach contracting, his hips pumping, his skin flushed and glowing with sweat. It seems the fire inside him has come to the surface. It burns beneath his skin, creating a reddish sheen over his body that is accentuated by the yellow light.

The sight brings forth a gush of cum from my pussy. I pretend it's blood, my virgin blood, instead of the creamy arousal.

I moan and shift under him, and the angle of his thrusts changes. He's hitting an elusive spot inside me, and shivers start down in my toes. They spread to my thighs and I know I'm going to come. I want to warn him, but words are trapped inside my throat with my breath. It doesn't matter because he doesn't need any warning anyway. His strangled groan acknowledges my climax.

My sock-covered toes curl and my muscles lock tight. Only my core is spasming with life while the rest of my body might as well be dead.

Thomas drops his head on my shoulder, his thrusts erratic. It's a mad race to his own climax, the jerky movements, the rotation of his hips—and then it all stops. Orgasming, he throws his head back, exposing his neck.

I don't think I've ever seen anything more beautiful than this, than him. I've never heard anything more melodic than his animalistic grunts. He grinds his cock inside me, wringing out every drop of his cum. I wish I could feel it without the barrier of the latex.

My hips twitch in unison with the heartbeat in his cock, and I wind my arms around his neck, never wanting to let him out of my pussy.

For a long time, we breathe in sync, in and out, in and out, as if our wild, aroused breaths are fucking now that our bodies are at rest. It's a poetic thought, a little fanciful and a whole lot of impossible, but it's nice.

Then Thomas heaves himself up and away from my body. He removes the condom, wraps it in a tissue – to hide it? -- and throws it in the trash, before snatching his pants from the floor and putting them on.

Again, I can only catch a glimpse of his corded thighs before they are covered by the frayed denim. He leaves them unbuttoned, as if it's too much of a hassle to do such a mundane task, and walks to the window, lighting a cigarette.

Like a moron, I keep lying on the floor; I watch him take a drag. The slopes of his carved back twitch with his actions, and so do his bulging biceps when he rakes his hands through his thick hair.

The longer he is silent, the more my anxiety grows. Something's wrong. Something's going on in his head, and I want to know what it is. I drag myself up, barely suppressing a hiss as the rug burns make their presence known. I stand on jellied legs and go to pick up my discarded clothes by the door, but the sight of the couch stops me.

It's sagging and wrinkled, so unlike the pristine condition it's usually in. Frowning, I take the room in for the first time since I entered. Papers are scattered on the desk, so unlike him. Cigarette and ash litter the floor as if he's been bingeing on nicotine all day. It makes me think that the cleaning crew is going to hate him in the morning.

"Are you...Are you sleeping in here?" I blurt out the question at Thomas, my clothes forgotten. His back tenses, grooves and digs appearing out of the knotted muscles, and that's my answer. *Yes.*

"Thomas?" I press on. "What's going on?"

Nothing. Just a swirl of smoke that scatters into thin wisps as it touches the window. If anything, he's become even more statue-like, unapproachable and cold. I clench my fists at my sides and dig my toes into the carpet, stopping myself from going to him. I know he won't respond kindly to it and I'm feeling oddly vulnerable right now, naked and anxious.

"Where's Nicky?" My voice is hoarse with fear, and that's the first thing that pops up. "Did she...take him?"

This elicits a harsh laugh. "No. She wouldn't."

"Why not?" He doesn't answer, so I ask another question. "So where is he?"

"He's fine. He's with someone who can be there for him right now."

"And you're not that person?"

"No. Not right now."

His callousness presses down on my chest and a strangled question emerges. "Thomas, wh-what's happening? Have you even been home in the past two days?"

Sighing, he turns around. His face is lined with impatience. Looking me up and down, he sucks in a long drag, pinching the cigarette between his index and middle finger. His eyes are both harsh and lazy and despite my anxiety, my pussy clenches. I wince at the dull pain.

My flinch doesn't go unnoticed and his gaze drops to the juncture of my thighs. It makes me hypersensitive to the wetness still lingering there, so much so that I rub my soft, fleshy thighs together.

"Put your clothes on. I'm dropping you off."

"No, not until you tell me what the hell you're doing."

He lifts the half-smoked cigarette and points to it, his voice laced with dry sarcasm. "Trying to kill myself." Then he flicks it away, adding to the litter and walks to the side of the desk, picking up his keys. "Now, shall we?"

I don't think. I don't even tell my body to move. It just does, and in the next second, I'm lunging at him, climbing his sturdy, powerful body. He *oomphs* at the impact and shifts his stance to brace my weight.

My arms are around his neck and my thighs clamp around his waist. My wet cunt is sliding over his ridged stomach, the curly hair around his belly button tickling my clit, making us both shudder. I put my forehead to his and stare into his eyes.

"She'll come back, Thomas. You'll see." My reassurance scrapes my throat and tongue, but I keep talking. "She'll realize how much she loves you and she'll come back, I promise. I just know it."

Thomas settles his arms under my ass, his hot palms stinging the tenderness caused by rug burns.

"Yeah? Is that what you know?" His gravelly voice is making me restless, and the fact that he is massaging my ass, soothing the soreness, as if he cares that I'm hurting, doesn't help. He's looking at me like I'm something...precious but irritating. Like I confuse the fuck out of him. Like he can't believe I'm talking about his wife while clinging to him naked, rubbing my core against his stomach like a slut.

"She will. She loved you once, and she'll love you again. You can't fall out of love. You just can't." *Love has to be enough.*

I don't know whom I'm trying to convince, him or me.. Thomas can't ever stop loving Hadley, and I can't wrap my head around the fact that anyone would willingly *not* love this man. It's incomprehensible to me. It makes me hurt.

Thomas flexes his fingers and smashes our bodies together. I feel his hardness in the crease of my ass, and my core clenches in response. We're stuck to each other's bodies, slick and hot with lingering sweat and ever-expanding lust.

"She told me she'd be back Wednesday, but she isn't here, and I...don't know what to do."

It's such a vulnerable, almost childish statement that I can't stop myself from kissing him and drinking his pain away.

When we break apart, he says with intense and glassy eyes, "I don't deserve her, not after neglecting her for a long time. I don't know when it happened, but I lost sight of her. I forgot about her. I forgot everything but my words. No one deserves that. No one deserves to be forgotten."

I didn't even realize I was crying until I hiccup and his features slash with regret. This is why I come back to him time and time again. This is why I don't care if I'm breaking every single rule and deeming myself a slut, a harlot. Because he's lonely. Because he's in unrequited love. And for some unfathomable reason, it *kills* me to see him like this.

I rotate my hips against him, wondering if I've lost my mind. How is it possible to be so, so sad and filled with lust at the same time?

Thomas brings his hand over to my cheek and tries to wipe the salty water away, but I'm filled to the brim with emotions. God, I hurt so much right now. For Thomas. For myself.

"So you see," he whispers over my lips, ghosting the wet, soft flesh over my plump, salty ones. "You can fall out of love if you're in love with someone like me."

As he hauls me even closer and fuses his lips with mine, I can only think of one thing.

If I ever fell in love with Thomas Abrams, I'd never fall out of it.

CHAPTER NINETEEN

I promised Thomas I wouldn't regret what happened, and I don't. I truly, honestly don't. I don't regret it, but it's hard to keep things in perspective when the world around you is booing Hester Prynne for having an affair. They even slapped a scarlet letter A on her chest because of it.

I want to jump and shout, *Her husband was playing dead. She was alone. Didn't she deserve love?*

But I can't, because I want to throw up.

Turns out the theatre people upstairs were practicing a play based on the novel *The Scarlet Letter*, and tonight they are performing it in the university's Lincoln Auditorium. Emma and Matt are sitting next to me in red vinyl seats and are engrossed in a whispered conversation. I really don't know what they'd be talking about that requires such a level of privacy. Dylan isn't here, because apparently they still haven't made up, and that makes me feel wretched, as if their fight was my fault.

But isn't it my fault, or at least the fault of someone like me? Like Emma's mom who cheated on her dad and destroyed their family?

I look away from them and my gaze falls on a couple sitting two rows down. They are kissing in the darkened theatre. Like a perv, I watch their tender embrace. The guy has his hands buried in the girl's hair and she is holding on to his shoulders. It looks soft and loving and so unlike what happened between Thomas and me.

But still, it manages to burn up my lust for him.

Now the urge to throw up is even stronger. Suddenly, I stand and make a beeline for the exit. Matt and Emma are busy with themselves so no one notices me slinking away. I search for a bathroom frantically, and throw up whatever I ate in the toilet when I find one.

God, I am Hester Prynne. I am a harlot.

I have a strong urge to hide myself and never show my face again. My bathtub has become my best friend because I've spent two nights hidden away inside it. I feel so ashamed. I feel like people will take one look at me and know, as if my skin is glowing scarlet.

I want to go back to yesterday and live there. When Thomas is close, nothing feels wrong. What we did was not shameful. It was survival. I need Thomas right now. I need him to make me feel better.

How ironic is it that the only person who can make this go away is the very one who turned me into this shivery, anxious mess?

Panicking, I sprint through midnight streets, barely paying attention to my surroundings. I reach the Labyrinth, standing tall and shadowy. Once inside, I take the stairs two at a time and keep dashing until I reach Thomas' office. I turn the knob but it doesn't give. I try it again, and again and again until I'm rattling the door, pounding on it with my fist.

Oh God. Oh God. Oh God.

I'm hyperventilating. My breaths sound too loud for the tomb of silence.

Where is he? Why isn't he here?

An illogical thought rises in my head: *What if Thomas is gone? What if I never see him again? What if he left like Caleb, without saying goodbye?*

My tattoo burns.

I know it's stupid. Thomas won't leave. He can't. He lives here. He's got a job here. He can't leave mid-semester, can he? But I'm not listening to my own rationale. All I can feel is the sense of abandonment, the betrayal I felt when I found myself alone in a strange house, packed with drunk-dead bodies.

I can't...I can't take it. Not again. I want to fall on my knees and sob but my panic won't let me. It's filling me with a bizarre sort of energy that vibrates through my legs. Before I know it, I'm sprinting again.

I hit the same streets, until I'm traveling deep into the residential area where the snow covers the grounds in a white sheen, making it look uninhabited. I don't slow down until I reach his house. It's dark, deserted. The naked branches of the tree hovering over the roof sway with the wind, all lonesome-like.

Hiccupping with cold and loss of breath, I walk toward the driveway. My feet drag. The pavement beneath my boots turns into sand, clutching at my heels with sticky fingers. I don't want to finish this walk, don't want to see what's at the end of the road, but I put one foot in front of the other.

I keep my eyes on the house, willing the bricks to show signs of the life contained inside it, but there's no movement. The windows are as dark as ever. Only the white door shines under the yellow porch light.

Swallowing and breaking a million rules, I become a trespasser once again. I jog across the yard, around the house. I remember the window in the back, through which I saw Thomas with Hadley only a few days ago. So much has changed since then. I have too many secrets now. About Thomas. About myself. About who we are and what we're capable of.

In my haste to get to the window, I slip on the wet and snowy earth, falling with a yelp. *Shit.* Tears well in my eyes as I try to stand up, but in the process, I scrape my knees against the pebbles and the icy patches of snow.

I'm brushing the muck off when a force pulls me back and I slam against something hard and warm. Something moving, growling. Something that smells like sweat and chocolate.

Thomas.

He is here. I sag against his heaving chest, relief making me weak and pliable.

Thank God. Thank God. Thank God.

The tips of his fingers dig into my arm and he spins me around to face him. He is sweating. A puff of wintry breath escapes his parted lips as sweat rivers down his forehead. His gorgeous dark hair is hidden under a black hood, but a few strands fall over his forehead, framing his fire-breathing eyes.

I'm so relieved to see him that I smile—a lazy, you just-saved-my-life kind of smile. The anger in his features intensifies.

"What the fuck are you doing here?" he growls, yanking his earbuds out with his other hand. A muted melody wafts around us, the muffled sound of a beat I want to listen to, too. I want to see what kind of music does it for him.

"Layla," he warns, his face dipping toward me, no doubt to intimidate. I'm so mellow with relief that nothing he can say or do will make me fear him.

"Thomas," I breathe, feeling giddy and ridiculous. "You weren't in your office so I thought—"

He shakes me, effectively cutting my speech off. "So you thought what? That you won't get fucked tonight? Are you that hard up for it?" he bites out as if disgusted.

His disgust hurts me more than anything I could've ever imagined. All day I've been wracked with guilt and hatred for myself, and honestly, that play didn't help either. All day I thought Thomas was the only person who'd put me at ease, who'd make me feel better.

Before I can say anything, he speaks, his harsh voice changed to a serrated whisper. "Why can't you let me save you, Layla? Why do you make it so fucking hard?" The flash of agony and regret is so thick and bright on his face that I see his true intentions.

He wasn't in his office because he knew I'd come. He knew I wouldn't be able to stay away from him. He wasn't there because he was trying to...yeah, save me. Me. No one has ever done that for me before. I've never been that important to anyone.

His patience seems to be stretching thin and I put my palm on his stubbled cheek. "I thought you'd left and I'd never see you again...like Caleb did."

Something changes in Thomas. I don't understand it, but I know it's different than his anger just a few seconds ago. His fingers burn hot on my arm and I can feel it through my coat. I wonder what I said. His scowl matches the black sky, and I can actually hear him grinding his teeth.

He whips his hood off, messing the sweaty hair even more, and wrenches my arm, pushing my back against the tree. The bark is rough and soaked with liquid snow, and I feel the chill seeping in.

I crane my neck up to stare at his beautiful, glittery eyes. The impact of their beauty doesn't lessen no matter how many times I look at them.

"Caleb." He rumbles over my mouth and I grab his sweatshirt at his waist.

He kicks my feet apart with his own before invading the space between my thighs and pressing my hip against the tree. My fingers flex where I'm holding on to him, itching to get under the heavy material and touch the ridges of his abdomen.

I want his mouth on me.

Maybe he knows what I want. Maybe he can see it in my face, because he hovers close and ghosts his lips over mine. Wildness grips me and I go to snatch them up with my mouth but he moves away, leaving me panting.

He rocks against me, letting me feel his hardness. "Do you think your Caleb can do this?"

"Wh-What?" I'm dazed with arousal. I don't want to talk about Caleb, not right now. He yanks me to his body and rubs me against his cock, groaning, controlling me like I'm his doll. His little fuck doll. I moan. Why does this arouse me so much?

"Do you think he can get hard for you, Layla?" His hot breath grazes my forehead, making my spine tingle.

"No. Not for me," I whisper against his neck, feeling the jerky bob of his Adam's apple as he swallows.

"Yeah? What about if you stroked it? Long and nice." He unclutches my hand from his sweatshirt and puts it on his cock. I massage his achy hardness through his sweatpants. "Do you know how to do that? Do you know how to stroke a cock so it's hard and painful, ready to fuck you?"

His shuddering chest crashes against my tits, until my body is mimicking his actions, shuddering in return, taking in quivering breaths. "N-No. I've...I've never done that." I shake my head and rub my nose into his neck.

Thomas moves away then and I squeeze his shaft, trying to stop him. He clamps his jaw shut and looks at me with dangerous, passionate eyes. Now I'm scared, shivering with a good kind of fear, waiting for his next move, blinking up at him.

Without a word, he almost tears the buttons of my coat open and the cold air punches me in the chest. I gasp, losing my breath.

"Th-Thomas, it's...it's cold." My teeth chatter when his hand goes under my skirt and fists my tights. "Please, I'm so cold."

He pulls on the material and brings me closer to his body heat. "I'm reminding you."

"About what?"

"What I said about trespassing."

A fleeting thought touches my mind. A long ago memory of us bantering at The Alchemy on poetry night. *Bad things happen to those who trespass.*

"I'm sorry. I panicked. I thought you'd leave me too. I—"

"I know, like Caleb." He pins our foreheads together. "And that's another thing I'm going to remind you of—that I'm not Caleb."

"Oh God, you have to stop. Please."

A smile sits on his lips, one as cold as the winter around us. He lets go of my tights and I'm left disappointed even though I asked him to do so. Then he hooks his fingers around them and pulls them down, leaving my thighs vulnerable and bare, and I lose my breath to the chill all over again.

"Caleb wouldn't do that, would he?" He adjusts the waistband of the useless material so that it cuts into the soft flesh just above my knees. "He'd stop if you asked him to, but who am I, Layla? What's my name?"

"Thomas," I answer, quivering as he circles his hot hands along the back of my thighs. My frozen insides begin to melt under his touch. The cold has no meaning, no power over me.

"Yeah." He rumbles, as if pleased. My breaths shake with the pleasure in his voice. "I won't stop even if you beg me to. I'll make you strip in the cold, put you on your knees on the ground and fuck you till I fill you up. You know why, Layla?" I shake my head, hypnotized by his voice. "Because you want me to. Because that's why you came here, scared out of your mind. You want me to fuck you in my backyard, isn't that right? You want me to bend you over and pound into you so you scream and wake everyone up. And you know what'll happen then?"

"Wh-What?" I shudder when his hands go to my ass and squeeze it.

"They'll open their windows, all sleepy and irritated, ready to call the cops on whoever is making all that noise, but then they'll see you, on your hands and knees, getting fucked, taking my cock and screaming. Your face all scrunched up. Tears streaming down your cheeks..." He pauses, groaning into my neck, getting aroused by his own story. "And they won't be able to stop themselves. They'll stroke their cocks to the rhythm of your moans and when you come, they'll come in their pants. Won't they, Layla? They'll see you on the ground, naked and writhing, and they'll lose it."

I could die at the shocking words falling from his mouth. I'm so tangled up in the erotic web he's woven that all I can do is moan. All I can feel is the imaginary eyes looking at me, looking at us, and I want to put on a show for them.

"You love that, don't you? You love being wanted." He's as much gone as I am.

"Yessss," I hiss, imagining the lewd picture he just painted with his words. He's a wordsmith, a filthy, commanding wordsmith, and I don't ever want him to stop.

"And what's my name?"

"Thomas."

I open my eyes to look at him. A half-smile blooms on his lips, making me even hornier. The elastic of the tights bites into my skin as he pushes my feet even farther apart.

"Hold up your skirt for me," he whispers over the fluttering pulse of my neck, then licks it, sending electric waves to my core.

He is massaging my ass cheeks, infusing warmth into all parts of my body, and I don't even think twice before doing as he instructed. I give up all control and hold my skirt, white-knuckling the checkered woolen fabric, exposing my panty-covered pussy. Thomas runs his fingers over the seam of my plain cotton underwear and I let out a moan, rubbing the back of my head against the tree.

"You're so fucking wet." He bites the juncture of my neck and shoulders, then soothes the sting with his tongue. "Ask to suck my cock." Another whisper followed by another bite on the neck and a lick of his tongue. He is running his finger up and down my pussy before sliding under the fabric to play with my wet hole, but he never makes contact with my tight bud. He doesn't give me relief.

"Come on, Layla. Beg me."

The need in his voice supersedes the need in me, and I'll do anything for him. I'll forget about my own pleasure and suck his cock, just so I can feel him pulsing on my tongue.

"Please, Thomas, can I suck your cock?" His eyes squint in desire but he holds his silence. I know he wants me to beg more, and I do. "Please, I want it so bad. *Please.* Won't you...Won't you put it in my mouth?"

Thomas grits his teeth, hard—harder than I've ever seen him—and squeezes my ass with such force that I can't stop the whimper from escaping.

I lick my lips. "Please, Thomas? Put your cock in my mouth."

He lets go of my ass and shoves me down. The sting I feel as my bony knees fall to the ground isn't a normal one. I think I cut my skin when I fell before, and now I'm going to grind that wound while sucking him off...but that's okay. I'll do anything for him.

"Since you asked so nicely." His growly voice makes me wetter.

Then I forget all about my own arousal because his hard cock is before me. Thomas has shoved his pants down enough to reveal the giant...thing in my face. Fuck. *Fuck.* No wonder it hurt me so much last night. It's huge, and thick and wide and...so many other things for which words haven't been made yet.

There's a groove in the middle of his purple head and I can rest my tongue against it if I want to. A vein snakes down the length, the skin becoming darker as it reaches the wide base. And those two balls he's got? *Wow.* Are they supposed to be this huge?

I try to remember all the porn I've watched, all the naked cocks I've seen, but I can't.

"Scared, Miss Robinson?"

I whip my eyes to his smirking mouth. *Asshole.* I want to give him a piece of his mind for laughing at me, but I don't, because he's drowning in lust. I can see it. His tensed shoulders. His panting chest. The tight grip of his fist in my hair. He needs me.

"It's so big," I tell him truthfully, like he doesn't know, and I touch the knobby head with my finger. It jerks up in reaction. "I don't think it'll fit in my mouth."

His hand flexes in my hair at my small voice and he drags in a deep breath. "Then we'll keep trying until it does..." He forces my head back, straining my neck muscles, and nudges my lips with his cock.

I open my lips to suck on the tip and moan at the first taste of him—salty edged with sweet and something masculine and hard. His skin is so soft, so delicate. I'm scared of nipping it. Oh, and it's hot, so very hot that all thoughts of winter, of the chill winds battering my chest, are gone in an instant.

I lave his head, flicking my tongue on the groove, trying the texture of it. Thomas groans over me, both his hands holding my hair prisoner now. A sudden burst of salt overtakes my tongue and I whip back.

Right. Pre-cum. Of course.

A drop sits at the crown and I let my tongue catch it.

"Fuck," Thomas rasps.

I go back to sucking on the head, but this time I don't stop there. I take him deeper, until he's wedged between the roof of my mouth and my tongue.

"Shit," Thomas curses again and I lift my eyes to him. The twin flames are roaring right now. He's staring at me like he's going to fuck the life out of me. I lick the underside of his cock to reward him for that look, to tell him he can do whatever he wants with me.

His stomach clenches and I reach out to touch the muscles under his hoodie, but Thomas shakes his head. "Uh-uh. Keep your skirt up. I want to see those thighs shake with the force of my thrusts."

I lift up my forgotten skirt as Thomas pushes inside my mouth, almost leaning over me until my bare ass hits the snow-covered tree. I jump at the wintery sting. He keeps pushing in until my jaw is wide and aching, and then he begins to move. Short, grinding jabs.

Even though he's only inside my mouth, I feel him all over, like I'm bursting at the seams, full of him, his essence.

"God, that feels..." He trails off on a grunt, moving in an erotic, horny rhythm.

"Fuck, you're good at this. If I didn't know any better, I'd say you've done this before."

Despite my strong gag reflex, I'm flushed with pleasure, but it doesn't last long. Thomas whips his cock out while keeping my jaw prisoner in his strong grasp. He is bent at the waist, looming over me. "Have you done this before, Layla? Did someone teach you?"

Teach. The word means so many things between us. If he wasn't so serious, shooting fire from his very touch, I would've laughed at his question.

But I shake my head—or try to, since he's holding it still. "No. Never."

You're my only teacher.

I'm not bold enough yet to say it, but it's implied. I lick my wet lips, surprised to find a glob of saliva sticking to my lower lip, and blink up at him. The pressure of his hold on my jaw and my hair increases, making me whine, "Thomas, it hurts."

It doesn't, not really, and even if it did, I wouldn't mind. I only say it to make him go crazy. Mission accomplished.

His demeanor becomes even harder as he straightens and stabs his cock back inside. He goes in even farther than the last time until I start coughing with the invasion. He retreats immediately, letting me gulp in air. Once my breathing is stabilized, he repeats his actions, punctuating my breaths with coughs.

"This is what happens, Layla." His speech is both slurred and cutting at the same time. "This is what happens when you do something I specifically told you not to. This is what happens when you strut in here in your short skirt and purple fucking coat and give me those big, violet eyes."

He is panting, keeping up the punishing pace that feels anything but punishing. It feels...intimate, out of control, desperate, and I love it. Every inch of my body loves it. My thighs shake as he predicted they would. My breasts dangle heavy and full, and my tattoo burns bright on my stomach.

"You make me do this." He rolls his hips, making my eyes water with the pressure. "You make me abuse your mouth."

The way his voice breaks at the end makes me moan, and I caress his cock with my tongue. With a curse that echoes right down to my bones, he wrenches my mouth away and comes on my chin and throat. His cum splatters on my face in thick drops, sliding down, some soiling the neck of my white sweater and some reaching my chest.

Over me, Thomas props one hand on the tree, the other stroking his still-jerking arousal. His head is bowed and his eyes scrunched shut. If I didn't know any better and if I hadn't sucked him to completion, I'd think he was in pain. But no—this is the aftermath of his lust for me, agonizing and glorious.

Thomas focuses on me. "Goodbyes aren't my forte, but I won't leave you like a coward either."

CHAPTER TWENTY

Thomas' words rattle inside my brain, and it takes me a moment to get it. When his meaning settles over me, I sag with relief and swell with tenderness. He is giving me a non-promise promise that he won't leave me like Caleb did, not without telling me first.

I let go of my skirt and rub his cum over my neck and chin in circles, hoping to get him under my skin. I lick a few drops clinging to my mouth. It tastes like the best kind of chocolate, salted and thick.

His lips part on a harsh breath and he yanks me up by the arm, at the same time pulling his pants up. I squeak at the sudden pain in my knee as the pressure of kneeling lifts off.

"What's wrong?" Thomas asks with a frown. "Did I...Did I hurt you?"

His concern for me eases the pain. "No. It's just... I think I busted my knee when I fell earlier. It's nothing."

Before I can finish, Thomas is the one on his knees, examining my injury. He lowers my tights even farther and inspects my knees—they're bleeding. He curses and unzips my right boot.

"What are you doing?" I brace myself on his shoulders as he lifts my leg and takes the boot off. The ground is freezing—like, literally freezing—and it makes me shiver. I feel like a bleeding Cinderella who just sucked off her dirty Prince Charming, and now, instead of fitting my boots on my feet, he's taking them off.

"You can't go home like this," he replies while working on my other boot. "You need to be cleaned and bandaged." After my boots are off, he strips off my leg warmers followed by my tights, until my lower half is exposed to the chilled air. He stands. "Come on, I've got a first aid kit."

Like the weather, I freeze at his words. They punch me awake, dispersing the insanity. My actions become crystal clear, as if I hadn't committed them myself. I sucked him off in his backyard, right in front of the window I watched him and his wife through.

God, I'm such a slut, and even Thomas' presence can't ease the guilt right now.

"Layla."

I focus on him, the languidness of his frame, the flecks of arousal still coloring his cheeks. "I can't...I can't go in there."

He is silent, like he understands why, like he sees the craziness of what we've just done. We can't break all the rules. *I* can't break all the rules of being The Other Woman and step foot in his house.

He runs his eyes over my legs and pauses a beat on my stomach, as if seeing my tattoo through the sweater.

"I made you bleed, so I'm the one who has to clean you up." He says it like a punishment, but it still manages to sprout butterflies in my cartwheeling stomach. With that, he turns around and begins walking to the back of his house, carrying my tights, boots, and leg warmers.

I stand immobile for a fraction of a second before righting my coat and taking off after him. Thomas is at the door, waiting for me to catch up. He unlocks it and stands aside to let me in first. Entering his house through the back door makes the whole situation even more illicit. It feels like we're breaking in. His shoulders are tensed as if he realizes the same thing as me. We're like thieves in the night, trespassing together.

The stove light is on and the fridge makes a dull whirring noise. It's a typical sound of a typical kitchen, but I'm in awe—because it's Thomas' house, and I'm in it.

Thomas stands still at the island, not for a long time, but long enough that I notice and wonder. Why does he look lost in his own house?

He comes out of his trance then, and tosses his phone, wallet, and keys on the marble island. "Take a seat. I'm going to get the first aid kit."

I hear him walk down what must be the hallway and I use my time to absorb everything about the place. There's a coffee machine right by the door with a stand for mugs. He's got an NYU mug hanging at the top and I touch the cold ceramic, missing the city with an ache. Thomas went to NYU when I must've been eight or nine. He lived in the same city as me. It floors me to think we might have crossed paths, the poet in the making and me. Soul mates. Maybe I saw him through the crowd but never took notice.

His house has an open floor plan and the living and dining rooms are both visible from the kitchen, lit by tiny nightlights. I trace the leather couch with my hands, the couch he sits on at night while grading papers.

To the left are the stairs and the hallway down which Thomas disappeared. I can hear him rattling things in the bathroom. I pad down the hardwood floor, my bare feet hardly making a sound. I stop at a room with a half-open door. It issues an unspoken invitation for a trespasser like me.

Swallowing, I open it wider to reveal a room full of boxes and a sprawling desk, illuminated only by the moonlight streaming through the window. I trace my palm over the surface of the wood and feel the scratches, the rough texture of it. This is a desk with history, with a certain character to it. It's unlike the glossy, polished surface of the desk in his office. I like this one better.

The top is empty except for a dusty small lamp. Not even a pen resides. I wonder if it's his organizational skills at work or something more. It feels like more.

I glance at the boxes, the whole mountain of them by the wall. They are labeled *Old*, *NYU*, *Poetry*, *Literary*, and so on. I stop at the one labeled *Anesthesia*. It's taped up. I want to tear it open and see what's inside. What are the chances of him noticing if I steal something from here?

"Don't even think about it."

Jumping, I whirl around. "Think about what?"

Thomas switches on the light on the desk, throwing the room into stark relief. The yellow light is the same as his office, reminding me of our fucking in the shadows. I press my hand on my stomach where I feel something moving.

"Taking my things without permission."

"I wouldn't," I scoff. "I was just looking around."

"Strangely, I'm not surprised." His tone is dry. "Sit." He points to the desk, and that's when I notice he's carrying a first aid box.

I walk over and shimmy my ass onto the surface. He watches my every move, making me very aware of my own body, especially my bare thighs and calves.

He sits at the chair, which creaks under his weight, and a shot of arousal runs through my core. If I get any wetter, I'll leave prints on his desk, and this isn't the time. I'm trying to be good, respectful.

Lusting after Thomas in his own home is wrong, more wrong than anything we've done till now. Isn't a house supposed to be a safe place? And I'm invading that safe place with my sullied, ruined presence.

Thomas puts his hand on my right knee and it jerks. It isn't even a sensual touch. There's a no-nonsense, clinical quality to it as he puts my foot on his thigh. He does the same with my other leg, barely touching me, barely lingering on the skin, but I feel it all the same.

The silence is thick, thicker than the delicious muscles of his thighs that I want to rub against—but I won't. I might be a slut, but even I have limits. *Not here. Not here. Not here.*

He reaches over and fishes bandages and other stuff out of the box with tight, jerky movements. I have a feeling that, like me, he's holding on to his control by a thread.

"Uh, did you always want to be a poet?" My voice is squeaky, but I need to fill this stupid quiet.

He doesn't answer for a while, dabbing alcohol onto a ball of cotton and then putting it on my wound without warning, making me wince and curse. He watches me through his lashes before focusing on my trembling thighs.

"I'm not good with words," he says, startling me. "Or rather, talking. When I was a kid, I'd go days without talking to anyone at school, buried in textbooks, comics, and stuff. Sometimes I felt like I had a lot to say but didn't know how." He pauses to clean the wound on my other knee. This time I'm prepared so I don't jump too much. "Then I found my dad's journals, his poems, and I knew."

"Knew what?" My hands are holding on to the edge of the desk. It's my way of stopping them from sinking into his gorgeous hair.

"That this was the way for me to talk."

"Your dad was a poet too?"

"Not a real one." I'm confused at his meaning and he explains, "He never published anything."

"Oh," I offer lamely. His definition of a "real" poet doesn't sit well with me, but what do I know? I'm not even a fake poet. "He must be super proud of you, then."

"He's dead." He finishes bandaging my other knee. "Besides, I'm not a poet anymore."

Before I can ask what he means by that, he asks a question of his own. "So did you always want to be a stalker?"

His fire-breathing eyes...they are smiling, slightly. I should be offended that he's laughing at me, but I'm not. In fact, I genuinely think about it. "Well, I guess, yeah. It was kind of inevitable. I've always been invisible to everyone, to my mom, my dad. I don't even know if he remembers me." I shrug. "And to... Caleb. I always watched them through the shadows. So, yeah, it made perfect sense for me to become a crazy stalker."

By the time I finish my explanation, Thomas has a permanent tic in his jaw like a livewire crackling with dangerous electricity. I think about the cause for it. Is it because I mentioned Caleb again? I tamp down a delicious shiver at how he convinced me that he is different than him.

"Thomas?"

His name called out in an unfamiliar, a *feminine* voice chills me more than the winter ever can.

Is it...Is it Hadley? Is she here? How could Thomas do this to me? Bring me in his house when his wife was here all along?

Thomas stands up. The creak of the chair sounds more like a death knell this time.

How could he do this to us, my heart cries.

"Susan, this is Layla."

For a second, I sit there. It's Susan. Not Hadley. *Susan.*

Oh God, who's Susan?

I jump down from my perch like someone injected me with a shot of adrenaline. Susan is an old but beautiful woman with the face of what I imagine a warm grandmother would have. My grandparents—too many of them—have faces carved out of Botox.

"H-Hi." I move away from Thomas and stand to the side, hands primly folded in front of me.

"Hello." She is confused. She looks from him to me and then back again. "Is everything okay?"

We weren't doing anything. I wasn't even touching him.

"Yes." Thomas' face is blank. "I'm going to take her home now. Is Nicky still sleeping?"

"He is. I just woke up to get a glass of water."

"Okay. I'll see you in a bit then." Without looking at me, Thomas issues his command, "Come on."

I give Susan a tremulous smile, which she returns, and follow Thomas. I feel her stare on my back and I don't know if it's my newfound paranoia or if she really knows something is going on. I collect my clothes from the island and Thomas drives me home.

The ride is silent and tense. I don't know what happened. I'm freaking out, breaking into a sweat and slathering his leather seats.

When he stops the car in front of my tower, I turn to him. "I'm sorry. For…For showing up the way I did."

He stares ahead, his fingers flexing on the steering wheel. "You should be."

"It won't happen again. Ever," I tell him. "Will… Is Susan—"

"You don't have to worry about Susan." He looks at me, and something in his eyes puts me at an uneasy sort of ease. She won't tell, but she'll know, and that's even worse. Silent reprimand. How *does* she know, though? Could she tell just by looking at us? Are we that transparent in our lust for each other?

Thomas is waiting for me to get out, but I can't go. Not yet. "What did you mean when you said you aren't a poet anymore?"

His sigh is sharp and long. "Nothing. I didn't mean anything. Now, go home."

"Last night you told me you forgot about her, because…because you were too busy with your words." A dreadful feeling makes a home in my chest as I put all the pieces together. "Are you… Did you quit? Is that why you came here?"

How is that even possible? How can he quit writing? How can anyone?

"Get out."

But I don't budge. "Thomas, that's ridiculous. I mean, you're too good to quit. You love this stuff. And how can you even do that? How can you un-become a poet?"

Thomas turns to me, his face stark and white within the tinted windows of his car. "Get the fuck out."

I should be offended. I should be. Really. There are many things about him that should offend me. He is rude and mean and made of thorny, jagged edges, but I'm crazy enough to see what he doesn't show me—his raw and unpolished pain.

"Thomas—"

"Just…go, Layla. Just go. Leave. I… It fucking hurts me to hurt you, but I'll do it. I'll keep doing it because that's just who I am, so you need to cut your losses and move on."

Like Hadley, I add silently. The love of his life, for whom he's given up the very thing that defines him—his words.

Right here, in the confines of his car, I hear my innocence shatter. Whatever I've believed in is gone. Apparently, love *isn't* enough.

And right here, I decide I'll never leave Thomas. I'll never abandon him like his wife did.

CHAPTER TWENTY-ONE

I'm being sneaky this morning. I told Emma I had an early appointment with a made-up professor. She didn't question it because, well, she is out of it these days. I'm waiting for Dylan outside our poetry class. I called him a while ago and asked him to meet me here. He's already late, and we only have just about thirty minutes before class starts.

The sound of hurried footsteps alerts me to Dylan's arrival. He is cold and panting and clutching a mug of hot coffee as he comes closer. "Hey, sorry. I got a little held up."

I stare at the mug and strangely, I don't have any urge to steal a sip from him. Thomas is the only person I want to steal things from now.

"So what's up? You said it was something important?" Dylan asks.

"Yes. Why are you being so stupid?"

His brows draw together. "What? What are you talking about?"

"I'm talking about how you're being stupid with Emma." I fold my hands and lean on the wall. "Why are you guys still fighting?"

"I'm not fighting with her."

"Really? Then why's Emma always moping? And how come you don't come around?"

It's been a week of fighting between them and Dylan hasn't shown up at the apartment. It's always Matt, and he always steals all my Twizzlers—which is so not good—but mostly, I'm worried about Emma. I'm worried that something that isn't either of their fault is causing a rift between them. It's really silly to fight over something her mom did such a long time ago.

"I think you guys are being really stupid and dramatic," I add, without giving Dylan a chance to talk. "I mean, you guys love each other. Do you know how rare that is? Why can't you get over it?"

Dear God, I could slap him silly for squandering away something so precious.

"Hey, I'm fine with it, okay? I'm fine with patching things up, but she's being unreasonable. I even apologized about the whole mom thing, and what does she do? She agrees to go to Florida with Matt for spring break."

"What?"

"You didn't know about that?" I shake my head, stunned. "Well, apparently Matt and Emma are going to Florida for a few days to chill out, all because we had a stupid fight. If she wants to make me jealous, she can go ahead and do that."

"But that doesn't sound like her. That does not sound like her at all."

He shakes his head. "I don't even care. It's just too much hassle to begin with. We never should've started going out."

I stand up straight and widen my eyes at him. "What? No! You guys are great together. And you love her. And she loves you. There's obviously more to the story."

Dylan goes quiet and stares at me. It's weird, the way he's looking. He's gone all shy and awkward as he runs a hand over the back of his neck. "Your eyes are...huge."

"Huh?"

"I mean, they are...they are beautiful."

"O-kay. Dylan—"

"I had a crush on you last semester. I mean, I liked you. Crush sounds so juvenile." He throws out a nervous laugh and somehow comes even closer to me.

"Dylan, that's just—"

"I always thought you were beautiful, and well, when I saw you in Professor Abrams' class, I-I wanted to ask you out..."

He trails off and bends his head toward me. I know what's coming. I know he's going to kiss me before he even puts his mouth on my lips. He smells of coffee and cold, and his lips are soft, and maybe a little bit dry.

I am frozen under him. It's not fear—I know he won't hurt me—it's something else. Maybe shock? I'm stunned at his actions, but as he slips his tongue out to trace the seams of my lips, I jerk back.

He is hurt—it's there in his eyes—and slightly ashamed, not because I didn't reciprocate, but because of his fight with Emma. He is jealous and he wants some control back. *God, men are so simple.*

Before I can tell him my conclusions, I feel someone staring at us. Dylan feels it too, and he moves out of the way and turns around. It's Thomas. His gaze is pinned on me and his jaw is locked shut.

It's obvious he saw the kiss. *Shit.* I move away from Dylan because nothing happened between us. I want to go to Thomas and tell him it didn't mean anything. I even take a step forward, but then I remember where we are—and more importantly, who we are to each other.

I can't run across the space and jump into his arms. I'm afraid to even smile at him. My lips might spill our secret. It hits me how we can't do the little things that normal couples do. We are not even a couple.

"Hey, Professor," Dylan greets, nervously.

Thomas barely spares him a glance as he begins walking toward us. What is he doing? I swallow a thick knot at his hardened expression, his determined strides. My legs move of their own accord and take a couple of steps back.

He pauses in front of me. His eyes are so blue, so flaming. I can't stand it. I open my mouth to say something—anything is better than this aggressive silence—but Thomas cuts me off. "Excuse me."

I blink up at him. "What?"

He studies me for the length of four beats. "You're in my way."

I lick my lips and his eyes flare, become even bluer, if possible. An answering tug in my belly makes me want to arch up to him—and that's exactly the kind of thing I can*not* do. It serves as a wake-up call and I look around. I am, indeed, in his way. I'm blocking the door.

"Sorry," I say, looking up at him.

As soon as I move aside, he passes me and enters the room.

The class goes by quickly. We discuss *Satyr* by a seventeenth-century poet, John Wilmot. According to him, men are beasts and society civilizes those beasts. So fuck society. Fuck rationality. Do whatever you want to do. Don't judge your impulses, just act on them. I'd believe him if it weren't for the fact that he had a steady stream of mistresses and that he died of an STD.

Thomas never looks at me once. He appears normal, no signs of anger or anything, as if the scene from earlier didn't happen. Am I the one making a big deal out of it? Maybe he didn't mind. Maybe it didn't even register on his radar. I should be happy about this because it was, in fact, nothing, but I am not. I am the opposite of happy right now. I am... I can't tell what I am, but it's not good.

When the class is done, I decide to talk to Thomas about it, but I don't get the chance. A couple of girls—whose names I don't even know—surround him, asking questions. Usually, Thomas is reserved. He never encourages discussion, dashing out of class before anyone gets the chance to ask him anything, but today he is lingering, answering all their questions with patience. He is smiling at them, nodding and talking. He never does that. *Never.*

It's making me feel worse by the second. I have too much useless, restless energy inside me. It's making me horny. It's making me crazy. I just want him to look at me once. Just once.

When I can't take it anymore, I jerk out of my seat and dash out of there. I run across campus to my next class. I sit beside the window, looking out at the snowy courtyard. The serenity of it all is making everything worse. Why isn't the world exploding with me? I know I should channel all this frustration into something productive, like writing. But fuck writing. Fuck everything.

Why wouldn't he look at me? Why would he talk to those girls? Why didn't that meaningless kiss affect him?

I stand up and my chair screeches loudly. The professor halts midsentence. People are staring at me, but for once, I don't care. I collect my things and address the professor, hastily saying, "I, uh, I'm not feeling well so I'm gonna leave."

I don't wait for his reply as I bound down the stairs of the lecture hall and run out of there. Ten minutes later, I'm inside the Labyrinth, dodging the crowd that always lingers in the corridors as if the classes are too small to fit this many people. A flash later, I'm standing in front of his office, my hand on the knob. I open the door and find Thomas in his chair, his head bent over some papers.

I close the door behind me, shutting out the noises, or at least dulling them. His attention usually makes me calmer. It soothes something inside of me, the animal that growls when he isn't around.

But I'm not calming down today.

"It didn't mean anything," I say without any preamble. "The kiss. Dylan was just angry and...well, he kissed me, but I moved away."

Apart from putting his pen down, he remains silent, but something lurks on his face, a softening of his features. I can't explain what it means. My mind is clouded. Thomas stands up and rounds the desk, but he doesn't approach me.

"You're mad, right? You're mad because he touched me, aren't you? You have to be. You have to be angry and...and jealous, because *I'm* angry. I'm so fucking angry that I can't think straight." I come to stand before him. His smell invades my lungs and I shiver. "You never talk to students. You are never nice to them. So why were you being nice to those...girls? I don't even know their names but I hate them."

"Melanie," he says in a gravelly voice.

"What?"

"That's one of the girls' name."

"It's a stupid name."

"You don't like it?" His lips bloom into a mocking, lopsided smirk.

"No. I hate it. And I hate you right now."

His eyebrows arch and I move even closer. The tips of our boots are touching. He's wearing the same boots from that night long ago, a lifetime ago when I thought I had a crush on him and when I thought he was a man who had everything.

It was a foolish thought. I never had a crush, and Thomas might be the poorest man alive. What I feel for him is indefinable, and I have no desire to think about it right now.

"Then what name would you like me to say?"

"Mine. Say my name."

I shudder thinking about yesterday when he forced me to remember his name as I sucked him off. Oh God, his cock. His taste. The length of it, the weight. I could write poems about it, and I'm not even a legit poet yet. And his words. My cunt is still wet from his filthy poetry, as if my lust never went to sleep.

In fact, it has evolved into something stronger, angrier.

My fingers fist his shirt and I jerk him closer to me. "I'm hungry."

He watches me with hooded eyes. "Is that right?"

I hook my leg over his waist, going up on my tiptoes, and pout, "Yes. Starving. And I want to eat your cock. I promise to not use my teeth."

I wonder when I became so bold as to say such things. I wasn't so courageous last night. I wasn't this courageous even a minute ago. Maybe it's him. Maybe it's this achy feeling inside me.

His swollen flesh jerks between our bodies. "Why should I let you do that? What's in it for me?"

I want to slap him. Stomp on his foot. Shake him.

Can't he see how mad I am right now? How fucking jealous? I'm out of control, but now I know what game to play, what game will make him lose his mind.

I tuck my face between his shoulder and neck, and toy with the top button of his shirt. "Because I'm gonna make it good for you."

"Yeah? How are you gonna do that?" His lazy, indulgent voice is making me see double right now. The lust is so thick and potent in my veins.

I become a poet in this moment and describe my filthy thoughts in detail, in my tiny voice—the voice he likes so much.

"I'll give it a lick first. There's this...this groove in the middle. I'm going to pay special attention to that, and then I'll nibble on it so that white stuff? You know the stuff that's salty and slippery? Your pre-cum? It'll ooze out, and then I'm gonna lick that up too. Then I'm gonna suck and suck until I get my prize at the end, and then I'm gonna swallow all of it."

Our breaths have escalated. His fingers on my ass flex and knead and run in circles. Every time they lift up more of my skirt. I wish I weren't wearing my tights. I wish I were naked underneath.

Christ, what's wrong with me?

It's the middle of the day. This building is alive. There's a tap, tap, tap of computers. The ringing of a phone somewhere. Footsteps. All of this should make me want to stop and turn back, but it just makes me even hornier. The fact that people around us are unaware of the depravity inside these four walls makes it even more appealing.

His face is harsh, nostrils flaring. Maybe the same things are running through his head as he growls, "If this is your way of driving me crazy, then you better make it good, Layla. Because my cock is hungry too, and it won't be full until it feeds on your pussy and eats out all your cum."

I want to smile with victory but I'm busy being super turned on. I move away from him and watch his body go lax, as if he's surrendering himself to me. It's such a surreal moment that I feel dizzy, with power, with lust.

He knows what I want.

He can see how hard up I am for his cock and in a very, very surprising move, he is giving it to me, letting me be in control.

I push him back and he goes easily. I keep going until he drops into his chair, making it squeak like crazy. I almost moan out loud. I crouch on my feet, careful about my banged up knee, and tuck myself under the desk. It's enclosed on three sides, turning it into a dark, erotically claustrophobic space.

I rest my palms on Thomas' thighs, bringing him closer to me. His muscles strain under my fingers and I can't stop myself from tracing the hard patterns with my hands. Up and down. Up and down. His muscles grow tighter by the second. The bulge of his cock is thicker.

In this moment, my hands mold him. I'm the sculptor who creates him.

I manage to open his belt, followed by the zipper. He maneuvers himself and helps me take out his cock. He hisses as I run my hands all over it. I answer him with a long sigh.

Last night, he took my virgin mouth and abused it, but today, I use it against him. Today my mouth is greedier, hornier, a seductive beast of teeth and tongue that sucks him and sucks him like my life depends on it.

The veins in his forearms are ready to jump through his skin with the need to touch me, yet he doesn't move his hands from the armrest. My body feels heavy with the power. I yank off my coat and top and expose my tits.

Thomas almost jumps off the chair at my actions. The creak of it hits my cunt, making it pant with need. He's mesmerized by my body, hypnotized by it, and I put on a show for him. I play with my nipples and he curses, says my name in a helpless moan.

A rush of power douses me and the world loses its meaning. I don't care about anything but sucking his cock forever. I never want to stop, not for anything.

Not even for the jarring knock at his door.

CHAPTER TWENTY-TWO

Thomas rips my mouth away from his shaft and sits upright. There's a click and I realize I forgot to lock the door. Shit.

"Thomas," a man says.

"Jake." His voice is tight, tighter than usual, but nothing that would suggest there's a student hiding under his desk. I put a fist over my mouth to muffle the sounds of my breathing. As if Thomas knows I'm hyperventilating, he puts a reassuring hand on my head.

Electric current runs through my spine as he keeps talking, while maintaining contact with me at the same time. "What do you want?"

"Whoa, is that how you talk to your boss?"

Thomas caresses my hair, petting me as he takes a deep breath and replies, "What do you want, Jake? I'm a little busy right now."

"Really? Too busy for a coffee run?" There's suspicion in his voice.

God, I'm terrified and so fucking turned on at the same time. His wet, hard cock is right in front of my eyes, and I want to touch it so bad.

"Aren't you gonna die without your chocolate fix?" Professor Masters continues.

Biting my lip, I eye the angry head of his dick, glistening with my saliva. What would Thomas do if I licked it right now? Sucked it? Would he be mad for making him lose control in front of a colleague, his boss? Or would he be as turned on as me?

As I advance toward him, I realize I don't care. I just want to suck his cock. I'm hungry. I need it in my mouth, and if he loses control, then so be it. He makes me feel out of control pretty much all the time.

"I think I'll survive," Thomas says. "Now, if you'll excuse me, I've got papers to grade."

"Why the fuck are you sweating?"

I latch on to his shaft just as Professor Master's suspicion-laced question reaches Thomas. A creak sounds as he jumps under the double assault caused by me and the inquiry, his hand fisting my hair.

"Are you okay?"

"Y-Yeah." Thomas clears his throat and tightens his fist in my hair to the point that it hurts, and I take it out on his throbbing cock. "I'm a little tense, that's all."

"Why?"

"Upcoming audit," he clips. I suck and suck and play with his balls. I feel them tightening in my hands to alert of the impending orgasm. Even though it's my mouth that's going to receive his cum, my pussy is getting excited, pushing out juices.

Professor Masters says something to soothe Thomas' fake worries and Thomas tells him he'll be fine in a while. They talk some more but I tune them out except for Thomas' voice. Lust is leaching into it, making it brittle, breakable.

I've never been this horny in my life. Graphic images of Thomas spraying his cum on my face flash through my mind, images of him losing total control and yanking me out from under the desk, and fucking me in front of Professor Masters and the whole goddamn world like he talked about last night. I trap a furious moan in my throat. I picture his ass flexing as he drives into me and I look every single person in the eye, especially that Melanie, and tell her how good his dick feels inside me. *He hurts me so good. Sooo good. I'm such a slut for his cock.*

It's strange that my jealousy doesn't extend to his wife. Maybe because I've always known that Thomas is hers, but seeing him with someone else messes with my crazy heart.

I'm the only other woman in his life.

And then my heart jumps in my throat and all thoughts are forgotten. Thomas pulls me by the hair and I'm yanked out of the dark hole I've been in. Panic and excitement grip me in equal measures as he turns me around and pushes me on the desk, crushing my bare tits on the surface. Professor Masters is gone. The door is closed. *When did that happen?*

"Stay there," he orders. I see him striding across the room and locking the door. Then he is behind me in a flash, his hand in my hair as he pulls me away from the desk.

"You like playing games, Layla?" he hisses in my ear, his chest moving against my arched back. "You like making me mad, huh?"

His voice makes my nipples throb and I have no choice but to squeeze my breasts as I answer, "I just...I just wanted to show you how I feel around you."

"And what's that?"

"L-Like a loaded gun. Like I could go off at any second. I just wanted you to know what it feels like to be so wild."

His bitter laugh stirs my hair. "Wild like this?" He thrusts his cock into my skirt-covered ass, letting me feel his swollen desire. His hands cover mine where I'm squeezing my breasts and smash them together. "Or like this? Like you can't stop playing with your tits for one fucking second? You think this is what wild feels like?" He is crushing them and I arch up to my tiptoes to get closer to him. *Always* closer. I want to fucking crawl under his skin.

"You have no fucking idea, do you?" he says harshly. "I'm gonna show you though. I'm going to show you what it feels like to be wild, what it feels like when *you* are around me."

A sob breaks free when he plasters me back on the desk. He flips my skirt up and pushes my tights and my panties down, exposing my ass. My cheeks are trembling with anticipation when he puts both his hands on them, and squeezes them like he did my breasts. I turn my face to the side so I can see him.

He is bathed in sweat. It trickles down his forehead, the side of his face, and disappears down the collar of his shirt. Even his eyelashes shine with the salty fluids. They look so thick and black framing his downcast eyes.

I release a puff of breath as he grabs a handful of my ass cheeks and pull them apart. My eyes scrunch closed, imagining what he must be looking at: my pussy and my...asshole. I go on tiptoes again, this time inching away from him as he circles a thumb on that forbidden place. It clenches and unclenches with his every stroke.

His chuckle is dark, shiver-inducing. "Is that what you want? You want me to fuck you in the ass right now? Is that why you're winking your tight little hole at me?"

I whimper when he presses his thumb, poised to get in. "Answer me, Layla. Is that what you want right now?"

"No," I whisper. "I don't...I don't know. It's...It's going to hurt."

"Yeah. It will." He leans over me. "But tell you what, I won't spoil the fun for you. I won't take your ass right now. One day when you're so mindless with my cock pounding into your pussy that you don't know up from down, I'll shove it in your tight little hole, making you scream." I'm quaking beneath him, hypnotized by his voice, by *him*.

"Remember when I told you I'll set you on fire and won't even look back?" He strokes my sweaty hair and whispers in my ear, "That's how I'll do it, while fucking your ass. I'll pour the gasoline, light the match, and watch you burn, Layla—and trust me, you're going to love it. I'm going to ruin you for every other man out there and you're going to love every second of it."

God. *God.* I think I'm dead. I'm in heaven and hell. In another stratosphere. I'm everywhere. He has shattered me with his dark promises, broken me, and I don't think I'll ever be pieced back together.

"Not today though." He moves away, one hand on the nape of my neck, keeping me down. "No. Today I'm going to show you something else. Today I'm going to show you how *I* burn."

With that, he shoves his cock in me and I bite my lip to keep from screaming. He isn't gentle. He doesn't give me time to adjust to his size. He is hurting me—my pussy is going to be sore for a long time—but nothing matters when his hips are slapping my ass with every stab of his cock, when he is grunting over me, probably sweating and panting. I wish I could open my eyes and look at him, but the hurt is so good.

Winding his hand in my hair, he jerks me upright, changing the angle of his thrusts. He is pressing against the upper wall of my cunt, making me feel him in my stomach. The force of his hold is so tight, so mighty that my neck is arched up and I'm looking at his fierce face upside down, my chin tucked under his.

"I feel like I'm sick, Layla. Burning up. Sweating. Like every cell in my body is vibrating." His teeth are gritted, his words infused with his lust and exertion. "It starts in my gut. Then it travels up to my chest and shoulders, and I feel a raging pain in the back of my skull. That's when I know I'm going to catch fire any second if I don't get it under control, if I don't stop thinking about you."

The pressure in my stomach is unrelenting. It feels like I'm going to burst or pee or something. "Th-Thomas. Too much. It's..." I trail off with watering eyes.

"Not enough. It's not enough." He jams his cock inside, probably touching my insane heart, and rotates his hips. It's a good thing his other hand goes to cover my mouth because I can't keep the scream inside this time. Neither can I keep my tears held up. They stream down, wetting his palm.

His nostrils flare at the sight but he doesn't stop. God, he does *not* stop. He keeps going, keeps jackhammering, and I...

"You love it. Yeah?" he rasps, completing my thought. "Maybe that's why you forgot to lock the door the first time around. Maybe you wanted to get caught, wanted people to see how much you love my cock. Isn't that right? You want everyone to see you like this."

I blink in agreement. That's all I've got the strength for. He lets go of my hair with a grunt and drops his forehead in the crook of my neck. His strokes are erratic now, like he's inching closer to his climax.

Now that my neck isn't stretched tight, I can take full breaths. My fingers sink into his hair. It's peaceful like this. His violence, his aggression put me at ease. I never want to leave his arms, this room. I want to be with him forever.

My eyes jerk open at the thought. *No. Not forever. This is* not *forever.*

"Rub your clit. I want you to get yourself off."

All thoughts evaporate at his commanding voice and I do as he says. I flick my clit and play with my puffy nipples.

"This is what I think about," he bites. "It doesn't even matter if you're around. *This.* Bursting every door down so I can get to your pussy. All I can think about is fucking you, Layla. All the time. Every time. You're in my fucking blood, and I'll tear apart anyone who dares to fucking touch you."

That's when I come. My body strains, goes rigid as I come at his confession—a confession that seems to be torn out of his very soul. It sharpens my orgasm, makes it that much more painful and fulfilling.

I feel him come inside me. It's only then I realize he's wearing a condom. I was so gone in my lust that I didn't even know when he put it on. His climax is a silent one, probably because he said too much before.

He lets me go and strokes my sweaty spine in soothing circles. His touch finally calms me, and I smile a sleepy smile.

Thomas was jealous. It did affect him.

I don't remember having been this happy for a long, long time.

CHAPTER TWENTY-THREE

Words are powerful. Words are fucking magnificent. I love all things words.

I'm flying today with Lana's voice in my ears, all because Thomas gave me the words. *You're in my fucking blood, and I'll tear apart anyone who dares to fucking touch you.*

I never knew something as potent and ugly as jealousy could invoke such happy emotions in me. I could kiss Dylan again just to feel Thomas' aggression. It makes me wonder if everyone is like that, if it's normal to feel this way, to be so needy for something.

I open the door to my apartment and all thoughts about kissing Dylan vanish when I see Emma crying on the couch. I rush to her side. "What's wrong?"

She sniffs. "Dylan and I broke up."

"What?" I give her a side hug. "B-But why?" *Is it because he kissed me?* I want to add, but I can't, because it's going to hurt her—and what if she blames me?

"Because he's being a jerk."

"What happened? What...What did he do?" I pat her back in circles. Any second now, she'll knock my hand off and break up this friendship.

"He accused me of cheating." She scrunches up her face. "As if I'd ever do such a thing. I'm not a slut."

"With Matt?"

"How do you know that?" Emma is suspicious.

Shit. My big mouth. I don't know if I should tell her what happened this morning, how I lied to her so I could meet Dylan and then he fucking kissed me. *That idiot.* I'm lying to her so much as it is, or rather not telling. *I'm like your mom—well, I'm the female version of the man who wrecked your family. Now, can we be BFFs?*

I look at Emma's tear-stained face and think of all the troubles she's been having these past few days. Whose fault is that? Theirs for fighting over something that happened in the past? Or her mom's for doing something terrible years ago? Or is it mine? Did I do a wrong thing by getting them together? But they loved each other. It was so obvious. If you love someone, you should be with them, end of story.

God, things don't make sense anymore. I can't tell what's right or wrong. Is love even worth all this trouble?

I decide I can't lie to Emma more than necessary. She's my friend. "Uh, I...well, I know that because—"

"I know he kissed you," she informs me.

I tense up. My heart is pounding like a jackhammer. *Please, don't let her blame me. Everyone always blames me.*

"I'm sorry, okay? It was stupid. It didn't mean anything. He barely touched me. Just..." My voice is shrill with panic. "You have to believe me. It was nothing."

"Hey, Layla, of course I believe you." Emma is the one calming me down, patting my back. "Why wouldn't I? I know you would never do such a thing, move in on my man or whatever, so relax."

Her words are reassuring, but my heart is still racing as if it doesn't understand what the fuck is happening. "You do?"

She throws out a sad laugh. "Yeah. It's his fault that he kissed you, his, not yours—and to throw that in my face because he thinks I am cheating on him with Matt?" She shakes her head. "It feels like I don't even know him anymore."

"It was stupid, Emma. I think he was just jealous. Please don't break up because of it." I'm ashamed that not ten minutes ago I was floating around on a high that jealousy caused. I can't see her like this. I can't take any more heartbreak.

Why can't people just get along? my heart whines.

Tears start flowing anew as Emma whispers, "I mean, I always knew he had a crush on you, so maybe I was stupid to get together with him in the first place."

"No. You weren't stupid. There is nothing stupid about loving someone." I grip her hands. "There has to be a way for you guys to work this out. This can't be the end."

"I don't want to." She shrugs. "I've been thinking these past few days and I think maybe, it's okay to not get what you want. Yeah, I loved him, or I thought I did, but getting together with him was not better. I thought it would be, but I think we were closer to each other as friends. We shouldn't look for love stories where there are none to be found."

I have a new shadow. Her name is Sarah Turner. She follows me everywhere.

One day she caught me in the ladies' room up on the second floor of the Labyrinth. I've always felt it's too risky to go there, but I'm known for not heeding my own advice. I had just come out of Thomas' office and I needed to put myself back together after he made me fall apart. She was at the sink when I entered and shot me a curious look.

"Are you here to see Professor Abrams?"

"Y-Yes. We, uh, I had a few questions."

The running water filled the silence as I averted her eyes. Then she asked, "You're new, right? Creative writing isn't your major?"

"No, it's not." I don't have a major yet, but she didn't need to know that.

Closing the tap, she rolled out a tissue and wiped her hands. "So our star poet pulled you into this?"

Yes. "No. I have a friend who insisted I take the class."

"Well, good luck. I'm here if you need me for anything. As I said, I'm great at gender roles in literature."

She left then, and it took me a minute to understand what she meant. Suddenly, I remembered that long ago fib Thomas told outside of The Alchemy, back in a time when I barely knew him.

Anyway, after that encounter, I see Sarah everywhere around campus. She waves at me from the corridor or smiles at me from across the street. I don't like that. I don't like that she sees me. In those moments, it's hard to keep my promise to Thomas of no regrets. In those moments, I wish I could wear him on my skin so he could curb my anxiety and this heavy, dark feeling inside my chest.

Because it doesn't matter. No amount of accusations or looks or guilt will ever make me give this up, whatever Thomas and I have. I won't give this up, because Thomas is happy. Well, not *happy* happy. He is too abandoned for that, too much in unrequited love, but he laughs without bitterness. A laugh that actually sounds like one. I thought I'd never see him laugh that way.

But he does with me. His laughter is rich and dark, like everything else about him, and I bring that out of him.

"Your office is so boring, Thomas. I mean, beige, really?" I told him one night when I was there, sitting on his lap.

"What would you prefer? Purple?"

"Duh, what else? Though I could be persuaded by blue too. You know, the color of my tattoo, the tattoo I play with when I'm alone at night." I undulated my hips, feeling the bump of his erection between my thighs.

"Is that right?"

"Mm-hmm."

"Except it's my tattoo and you're here every night and I play with it with my tongue." He licked the side of my neck and whispered in my ear, "Until you're begging me to stop but secretly hoping I don't. Is that the tattoo you're talking about?"

"You're such an ass."

He laughed then, threw his head back and stared at the ceiling. I was stunned. I'd never seen him do that before. The sound rolled over my flesh, drenching me in fresh lust and arousal, but it was more than that. It was the fact that I'd said the same line to him countless times in the past, but he'd never laughed at it. I wasn't saying anything new or particularly funny, but he heard it that way.

Thomas was happy. When you're happy, you laugh at the lamest jokes.

How can happiness be wrong?

How can any of this be wrong if the end result is laughter and momentary peace?

When I'm in doubt or when I can't fall asleep in my soft bed and have to curl up in my cold bathtub or inside my closet, I think about his laugh.

I think about how he laughs when I climb up his body like a monkey in desperation. He laughs when I get mad at him for stealing my Twizzlers, like I steal his cigarettes. He laughs when he sees my polka dot socks. He laughs when I insist on wearing those ridiculous Russian fur hats—his words, not mine. He laughs when I tell him he's the worst teacher anyone has ever had, that his home assignments are stupid. He laughs when he fucks me and I get too needy for my orgasm. He laughs when my words stutter while reading my poems and riding his cock.

He laughs and laughs and laughs, and it makes me wonder, if I hadn't pursued him with a single-minded insanity, would he have deteriorated in Hadley's absence? Would the lines around his eyes and mouth have deepened into permanent scratches?

So maybe all of this is a good thing—all the sneaking around, breaking rules, fucking with the universe. Everything is worth it.

For Thomas.

Even though it's inadvisable, I still build castles in the air. I still think of myself as a Cinderella and him as my tarnished, broken, kinky Prince Charming.

I just wonder what's going to happen when the real Cinderella comes back and makes him all shiny and whole. He won't need me then. He won't need his slutty fake princess.

Bathed in the yellow light of the lamp, Thomas is sprawled in his office chair, having a smoke with his shirt unbuttoned and hair mussed up by my fingers. I'm on the floor, propped against his couch, my notebook in my lap, my eyes on the tight curves of his sweaty muscles.

I've gotten used to this arrangement—being with Thomas, inside a sleepy building, in the dead of night, cozied up in his fire, writing while he smokes. Sometimes I listen to the music on his phone. It's all instrumental, songs without words. They help me write whatever nonsense comes to my head.

My gaze falls on his tie, lying by my side. It's maroon in color. He never wears a tie but today was some sort of a special staff meeting and Professor Masters insisted. Not half an hour ago, I wore it around my neck with nothing else but my polka dot socks as I rode both of us to our climax. I squirm in place, probably leaving a wet patch on his coarse carpet.

On his desk, against the wall, on the couch, on the floor—he has had me everywhere. As I look around the room, I can see our merged silhouettes on every surface. I can hear the things he whispered in my ears. I can smell the musk of our raging, borderline lunatic fucking. I can see the wrappers of Twizzlers alongside his discarded bags of chocolate croissants. I always litter and he always picks it up and puts it in the trashcan, with an exasperated but indulgent look. Maybe I do it just so I can see that look.

I realize that this is my home, made of my moans, my cum, and my sweat. This is more my home than my tower, than my mom's house in New York. I don't have to hide in here. I can be myself. Whatever fucked-up self it is, I can be that.

Thomas is all quiet and introspective. I want to ask him what he's thinking about, but I'm afraid to hear his answer. He's probably thinking about her, about Hadley. He's always thinking about her.

It has been ten days since she went away. I know she will be back. I know she'll come to realize how much Thomas loves her. There's a power in him, a power in his love. It reflects in the way he fucks me. How he slakes his frustration with my body. How his body laps up my moans, my orgasms to subdue the fury in him. How he uses me to be happy.

"I thought you were trying to quit smoking," I say. I need his eyes on me, and that's the first thing that comes into my head. His muscles wake up and strain as he turns the chair in my direction, and blows out a giant cloud of smoke.

"I thought you were trying to write." His rumbly voice tells me he was on the verge of falling asleep. I can't help but notice that there's something endearing about that, and so like a man. They fuck. They sleep. They fuck again.

"I'm stuck."

The air changes from lazy to tightly strung. Thomas is still sprawled in the chair, giving the impression of being relaxed, but the twin flames in his gaze flicker. "Are you?"

Nodding, I get up on my knees, my notebook falling to the ground with a thud. My back arches—a default reaction now—when he looks me up and down. My winter gear along with my undergarments are lying somewhere in a heap, leaving me in a thin, see-through sweater and a wool skirt. My nipples pout, much like my lips.

"So are you gonna help me?" I ask in my tiny voice, the voice that never fails to get a reaction from him.

Last time I asked him to help me with my poem, he told me to sit on his cock and read it out loud while riding him. All the while, he sat there like a king, never moving, simply watching me with a hunger that drove me to jump on him, up and down.

I come to my hands and knees and crawl toward him, watching him through my lashes. Cigarette clenched between his lips, he follows my every move with hooded eyes. Every flutter of my loose hair around my face. Every little sway of my dangling breasts that are barely hidden by my top. I reach him and he shifts his chair to face me. My hands grip his calves through his jeans, massaging the muscles as I sit up on my haunches.

"So?" I crane my neck up and hug his leg between my breasts, moaning out loud at the delicious friction of his pants.

He whips the finished cigarette out of his mouth and it lands in the trashcan. Leaning down, he breathes the smoke over my mouth. I suck it in like I'll never breathe again. Oh God. *God.* I can't take it. This hormonal, chemical explosion inside my body—it's too much.

Then his hands band over my biceps and he hauls me up and makes me straddle his lap. The chair creaks with both our weights. My hands caress his stubble as I murmur, "That sound is going to kill me."

"What sound?"

"Your stupid chair." And there it is, his laughter. It makes every corner of my body smile. "Whenever I hear it, all I think about is you fucking me in it so it's screaming with our weight."

A side of his mouth tips up in the wake of his short laugh. "I'm kind of getting the feeling you want me for my body rather than my poetic genius."

Genius—yup, he is that. I don't know how, but words come to him out of thin air. He looks at the ceiling and describes it in ways I never even thought of. Despite our frenzied fucking, he does teach me things. He calls me out on my poor word choice, tears me apart over overly flowery language, and I think he likes it. Other than sex, that is the one time he's animated, his eyes dripping with another kind of passion. He glows when he talks about poetry.

Coming back to the moment, I say, "Actually, I also want you to bump my grades up." I move against him, my bare pussy sliding along the hard bump, barely hidden by his unzipped jeans. "Because, you see, I'm not very good at writing. My work is choppy, and my word choice sucks." His eyes smolder and his hands come to grab my undulating hips.

"Is this your way of getting a compliment out of me?"

"Yes," I admit shamelessly. "Give me a compliment. I challenge you."

He digs the pads of his fingers into my hips to stop me from moving. "Fine. You don't irritate me as much as you did before."

"Wow, stop, I'm blushing." I swat at his naked chest. "You're *so* good with words."

He swats at my ass in retaliation, making me moan. "I told you I'm not very good at talking. You want compliments, you should hang out with your friends instead of being with me."

It's a joke, I know, a dry, sarcastic comment. I should forget about it. I shouldn't ruin the moment—I'm on borrowed time as it is.

But my stubborn heart isn't in the mood. It's remembering his words from the other night when I was in his unpacked study. *I found my dad's journals, his poems, and I knew...that this was the way for me to talk.*

Perhaps he notices how rigid I've become in his hold, because he tenses too. After my last attempt at talking about it in his car, I haven't broached the subject of his lack of writing.

"What's wrong?" he asks, frowning.

"Nothing." I smile and massage his shoulders, trying to do what I do best—distract him.

"Layla," he warns with that voice of his. It's not fair. I can never resist that voice. Never.

I simultaneously sag and tense in his hold. "I...I want to see you write. Something. Anything. I just want you to write."

A beat passes. Then two. The urgency in my chest is increasing. I don't want the silence. Silence is ruining. "I can't see you like this. Thomas, I know. It's obvious. You—"

He doesn't let me finish as he lifts me up and puts me on the desk, my legs dangling. I try to sit up but he presses his palm on my breastbone, keeping me still. He stands over me, some kind of god of wrath with his thunderous frown and sparkling skin. My chest rises and falls under his palm, like he's the one making me breathe. If he removes his hand, I'll die.

"Take off your top."

What? No.

"Thomas—"

"Take it off." He licks his upper lip.

Shivering, I obey his order. My tits come into view and he breathes deeply. "Lift your skirt up to your waist."

I do that too, squirming, revealing my naked pussy and my tattoo. This time his breath splinters as he takes it in. He circles my tattoo with his knuckles, jerking the flesh of my stomach. With both his hands, he spreads my thighs, his thumb rubbing my soft skin, grazing my pussy lips and the fragile flesh around it. I move restlessly, bucking my hips at his touch, making my heavy tits jiggle.

Thomas is aroused by the sight. He loves seeing my breasts shake, so I do it over and over, bucking, writhing, stoking his lust. It's turning me on too, even though a part of me weeps at this. I want him to talk to me. I don't want to be a distraction or a fake Cinderella. I want to be the real deal. It scares me so much that I forget to breathe.

It's not the first time I'm thinking this, and I don't know how to stop.

The air comes rushing back when Thomas retrieves a pack of cigarettes from his pocket. He takes one out, pops it in his mouth, and lights it up.

His nostrils flare and my mouth dries out when his entire hand grabs my pussy and squeezes. It's such a vulgar gesture, vulgar and owning and possessive and...erotic.

With his other hand, he takes the cigarette out of his mouth and sends the smoke spiraling up. His hand on my pussy moves, and I almost shriek when he inserts two fingers inside and curls them up.

I reach my arms out to hold on to a part of him but he shakes his head. "Grab the edge of the desk."

Swallowing, I do, and I watch him take another drag while playing with my core. He bends at the waist and hovers over my breasts, his cheeks hollowed out, the cigarette stuck between his lips.

"Th-Thomas?" I'm scared. The burning end of the stick is too close to my body. It looms over my left breast, my heart. *Is he...Is he going to mark me with it?*

He lifts his eyes at me, holds the stare. Something shifts in them, something dangerous, and I struggle beneath him, afraid. Then he takes the cigarette out and blows hot smoke over my tits before he latches on to my nipple and sucks. My hips buck, lodging his fingers deeper.

Moaning, I open my legs wider. My dangling feet come up on the desk, my heels digging into the edge.

"You were saying..." he rumbles over my quivering flesh, sending a frenzy of arousal everywhere in my body.

"What?" Tilting my head, I ask the dark-haired head currently bent over my breasts.

Thomas pinches my clit as he looks up, an arrogant brow arched. "You were saying something that you know, about something that's obvious."

My head falls back down, defeated, maybe even in anger. I don't want to be his fuck doll anymore.

Thomas notices the tightness in my body and blows another mouthful of smoke on my other breast, before plumping it up and sucking on the nipple. Despite myself, my pussy shoots out thick strands of arousal.

"You're so fucking wet, Layla." Thomas groans into my skin. "You're always so smooth and wet and hot. I like to think you keep it that way for me. You keep your pussy warm for me, don't you? You sleep with your hand tucked between your legs, cupping your cunt so it stays warm and toasty for when I fuck it."

My legs come around his back as I writhe beneath him, loving this, hating myself, hating him for doing this to me. "I've seen you in class, Thomas. I've seen you...looking at them wh-when they talk about writing. I have seen how you talk about writing and art and how talented you are. I've seen the longing on your face. You want what they have and it-it breaks my heart," I whisper, tears rolling down my cheeks. "I want you to write so you can *talk*. You have to talk, Thomas. No one can live like this."

A shudder goes through him at my words and his forehead drops to my breastbone. I sink my fingers in his gorgeous, lush hair and clutch him to me, in longing, in tenderness. Maybe I did make a difference just now.

But then he stands up, flicks his finished cigarette away. Crazily, I think that it's going to leave a mark on the carpet. He takes his cock out of his jeans. It's hard and angry and red—just like him. I know he's going to use it to punish me.

Yes, punish me for being selfish enough to want more, to want to talk.

I deserve it. I'm beginning to think I'm the worst harlot ever.

I tip up my chin and open my legs, ready for him. Thomas clenches his jaw and in one stroke, jams his cock inside me. I nearly come off the desk, my nails skating along the hard wood. Gasping, I go back down and grab the edge to brace myself, because in the next second, I'm in danger of flying off and crashing to the ground.

His slams are punishing. Brutal. Borderline violent. My teeth chatter with every stroke. My breasts heave and rebound. His grip on my thighs is going to leave marks, I know it, but most of all, it's the obvious pain of his hip bone hitting the desk that jars me. He is punishing himself as much as he's punishing me.

But, no matter what, no matter how brutal or violent he becomes, he never fails to make every fucking cell in my body sing. He never fails to send my pulse hurtling. I want to melt into his violence. I want to dissolve myself in the moment so he can absorb me in his body and find some peace.

His eyes are narrowed to slits, his jaw clamped as he presses his palm on my lower abdomen, increasing the pressure on my organs. My head lolls, insanity washing over me. I want to tell him to stop but I won't. I'll take it.

The *slapslapslap* of our flesh is interlaced with the slurping, wet sounds of my pussy. The sloppiness of my core makes me blush all over. As if that's not enough, he looms over me, bringing my thighs to his shoulders, deepening his thrusts.

He frames my face with his hands so I have nowhere to look but him. "Do you hear those sounds, Layla?" he whispers thickly. "That's me talking to your pussy." Then he changes angles, holds himself inside me, rotating his hips, bucking up and down, hitting me in just the right spot. In turn, I hear the sloppy gurgling of my core, a slightly different tone than the previous sounds, wetter and angrier.

"And that's your pussy telling me she likes it, saying she loves to feel me inside her." He stops grinding at that and starts ramming with a savage force that doesn't let either of us breathe. Sweat drips from his forehead, plopping onto mine. "That's all the talking we need to do. That's all the fucking talking we *ever* need to do."

He fits his face in the crook of my neck and bites my skin, launching my climax through my body. My hips arch up and become rigid in the air, the muscles of my thighs locking around his shoulders. My loss of control brings out his own and before I can blink, he whips out his cock and comes on my stomach, groaning.

In a fog, I realize he forgot the condom. He never forgets it. He's always so careful. He never discards his cigarette on the carpet. He never litters. Never. Never. Never.

The anomaly scares me, terrifies me more than anything ever has.

His sweat-soaked chest and torso contract with every heaving breath. He lets go of my thighs and grabs hold of my chin, looking deep into my eyes. For once, I don't want them on me. I don't feel any pleasure in their blazing, fire-breathing look.

"I'm not your boyfriend, Layla. I'm not going to hold your hand or take you to a movie. I'm not going to *talk* about my feelings with you." His fingers flex on my jaw. "Tell me you understand this."

I blink my heavy lids and tears fall from the corners of my eyes. They make him even angrier. There's a harshness in him I haven't seen before. Maybe he's been fooling me all along. Maybe I never made anything better. Maybe it was all an insane dream I made up to keep doing this.

"Tell me," he says harshly.

Afraid, I jerk out a nod, but he shakes his head. "No, say it. Give me the words, Layla."

I hear the shatter of my heart. I hear that sound from long ago when I broke the bottle of that expensive champagne when Caleb left. But this time around, the sound is like a gunshot, more jarring and deafening. It's the sound of my castle falling through the air and crashing to the ground.

"You're not my boyfriend and you won't take me to the movies or hold my hand, and you won't talk to me about your feelings," I say in a monotone. I say it without halting or stuttering. I say it clearly.

His grip loosens and a look flashes on his face, but it's gone before I can decipher it—and I don't want to decipher it. I just want to leave. Thomas moves away, goes to the window, and lights another cigarette, like he did that first night he fucked me. Everything is coming full circle now, but I'm a lot different than what I used to be.

Swallowing, I try to sit up. Wounded and battered, my body is a warzone, a torn-up village after a sandstorm. I dress myself while Thomas is busy watching the darkness. Usually, he takes me home in his car and I'm under my purple blanket within ten minutes, sleepy, dreaming of him. Tonight, though, it looks like I'll be walking home. It's no big deal. Midnight streets and I are old friends.

Before I turn the knob, I face Thomas. "You know I want you. I'm the crazy girl who lets you fuck her however you want. You can see it in my eyes. That's what you said, isn't it? *It's in your eyes.* You can play with me. You can play with my body because you know how much I get off on it. I'm an open book to you." I take a deep breath and unlock the door. "But I can read you too. It took me a little while. It took a lot of staying awake at night, thinking about you and yeah, stalking you, but I finally figured it out. You're suffocating yourself, hoping to breathe life into your relationship, into your love. You're holding on too tight, and maybe you need to let go, because if you don't, you might just... kill everything."

I close the door behind me, and then I walk away. From him. From the only home I've ever known.

CHAPTER TWENTY-FOUR

The Bard

It takes me a few minutes to come out of my stupor.

She's gone.

She left, all alone, in the dead of the night. I see her running through the darkened streets, crying, her wild curls flying, in disarray. What if she stumbles and falls? She has a knack for doing that. What if she bumps into a boy? A drunk boy who can't see straight, let alone understand the meaning of the word no?

Layla is just…a child. So young and fragile, but brave too—brave enough to be with me, to take my abuse. Her courage floors me. Her courage highlights my own cowardice.

I can't let her go like this. I can't. I *can't* let her go. Period.

As I throw the cigarette out the window and button up my shirt, I become still. I become afraid. Am I not always that way?

All this time, all these nights that she came to me, she has always been alone. She has walked those streets all alone, unprotected, probably without a care because she was eager to get to me.

And I have been just as eager. I have been just as bent out of my head for her to get to me that I never once questioned it. I never once questioned how she got here. I never asked her if she was being careful or if she met someone on the way over, or if it's safe for her to walk at night.

I never once asked her anything. I just took and took, like I always do. I become so wrapped up in my head that I never care about anything else—but didn't I tell her this already? Didn't I warn her? Why did she keep coming back? Why did she keep offering herself to me like a fucking sacrifice?

I told her she'd regret this.

My head is aching, burning up. I need to make this right, but I stubbornly don't move from my spot. I won't move. I *told* her. It's not my fault that she left crying, that she thought this was more than what it was.

I'm rooted in the middle of the room when there is a click and the door swings open. For a fraction of a second, I think it's Layla, and my body comes out of its deathly stillness—but it's not. It's Sarah.

She has a bundle of papers tucked in the crook of her arms. Even so late at night, she appears put-together, her hair polished and well-kempt.

"I came to get some last-minute printouts from my office for tomorrow," she explains, motioning to the papers.

Tomorrow, Sarah and I are heading to New York for a poetry convention. We'll be back Monday, hopefully with a bunch of signups for the coming semester, given I'm the bait—the youngest poet to win the McLeod genius grant.

"Layla Robinson," she says, her demeanor cold. "You're having an affair with her."

The flame flickers to life in my abdomen, and I tighten my body for the first electric rush of heat. No matter what the situation is, her name is powerful enough to affect me deeply.

I neither confirm nor deny. Affair isn't how I'd describe what Layla and I have. No, it's more...complicated than that, more layered. Sordid. Pure. It's more than I could ever put into words.

And right now, she's out there alone because of me.

It's not my fault.

"What, no response? What happened to all your sarcastic wit?" Sarah smirks, shaking her head.

"Get to the point," I manage to croak out, gritting my teeth.

"So you're not denying it, then. You are, in fact, sleeping with one of your students. Jesus Christ. You know, I didn't believe it. I knew something was fishy with all those meetings you had in here that strangely required her to go to the ladies' room after, and then, imagine my surprise when I find you here in the dead of the night after I saw Layla running out of the building." Her eyes are shooting icy daggers at me. "Congratulations, Professor Abrams. You're both an incompetent teacher and a pathetic human being."

She was running. That's all I can think about. She was running when she left, and I know she'll slip or stumble and she'll fall. I need to get to her before that happens.

My feet move but then come to a halt at Sarah's next words. "You're such a piece of shit, Thomas. You're married. You just had a kid and this is what you do to your wife? Sleep with a student behind her back?"

Yeah, a piece of shit. That's what I am. I'm a motherfucking piece of shit who only thinks about himself. I am selfish, incompetent, pathetic. Her insults sound like my own conscience—the conscience that was buried under my anger at Hadley and my need for Layla. It's surging now, along with the nausea.

"What do you want?"

"What do I want? Is that all you have to say for yourself? You've broken a thousand school rules, not to mention successfully wrecked your marriage. Hadley will never forgive you for this—you know that, right?"

"What Hadley will do is none of your business." *She left me.* I fist my hands to curb my impatience. "What I want to know is what you plan to do with the information."

"Sure, let me give you a step-by-step description." She smiles tightly. "First, I'm going to go to Jake and tell him everything. I'm sure, being your friend and all, he'll try to save you somehow, but I won't stop there. After Jake, I'll go to the chairman. I'm sure he'll have something to say when I tell him his star poet is sleeping with a student."

The headache explodes. "I'm asking you again, what do you *want* from me?"

Her face is streaked red with her anger. "What I want is for you to quit your job. I deserve that position more than you ever will."

"And if I don't?"

"Then be prepared to get fired anyway, because I'm not going to sit on this. So, it's really your choice, Thomas: do you want to get fired and be disgraced, or do you want to go quietly?" Before leaving, she adds, "Go back to where you came from, Thomas. You don't belong here."

I squeeze my eyes shut. White stars pulsate behind my lids, temporarily blinding me with the pain and anger.

I can't go back. I need this job. I need to stay in this town.

The thoughts float inside my head by default, like some sort of a memory that won't stop playing. They go on and on and on, until the words change and become something else. *I don't want to go back, because where I came from, there is no Layla.*

The shock of it is enough to get my legs working, and I take off at a run.

I run and run, doing exactly what Layla has been doing every night, exactly what she did tonight. I come to a stop right in front of her apartment building. I don't know what floor is hers because I never bothered to stop long enough to find out. I'd drop her off and rush out of there.

Panting, I crane my neck up and stare at the top of her building. I can't imagine her living anywhere else but at the top. She belongs in the sky. She belongs with the stars. She is bright and loud.

But more than that, she is scary.

Layla Robinson is fucking scary, and I don't know what to do with that.

Now that I am here, I don't know why I came. What was the purpose of it all? What was I hoping to do? Go up to her apartment and knock until she opens the door? And then what? Apologize? For what? For telling her the truth? For setting her straight? No, this is better. We have no future. Maybe I told her those things because I never want her to come back to me.

I'm not brave. I don't know *how* to be brave, and I don't fucking know how to talk.

Gritting my teeth, I turn around and walk away.

I'm woken up by the light footsteps. They are moving toward me. I know them, that light tread.

Hadley.

Am I dreaming? I don't even remember falling asleep. My body is curved in an unnatural angle on the floor. I open my groggy eyes and realize I'm in Nicky's room, sitting under the window. Last night, for the first time in a long time, I came back home before dawn. I checked up on Nicky and then crashed on the floor.

I blink and find Hadley on the threshold.

She is back.

I spring up to my feet, any sleep forgotten, the entire world forgotten at the sight of her.

I whisper her name.

Now that she is here, her absence glares even more. I remember all those calls I made, frantic and panicked, the voicemails I left during those first couple of days. She never got back to me. After that, I was too blinded by my rage to call her.

Or maybe it wasn't rage. It was the weight of all the wrong things I've been doing. It was my lust, my need for someone else. When she left, it was a small kiss, but now my lust has a life of its own. It has a body, a heart, and a soul. It is strong and vibrant, and she needs to know. She needs to know the person I've become in the last ten days.

"Thomas," Hadley whispers, walking forward.

We meet in the middle of the room.

"Hadley, I need to—"

"Will you hold me?" she asks, delicate and vulnerable. Her words shock me. It's a zap to my already chaotic system. It's everything I've been dying to do. Just hold her. My arms, my chest, they tingle with memories of holding her... but there's something else too. There's relief. I don't have to tell her about Layla right now. I can hold her. I *want* to hold her.

Selfishly, I take the out she gives me. "Yes."

"I missed you..." she whispers.

I nod but the reciprocating words won't come out.

She wraps her fragile arms around me and I do the same. She slides into place, tucking her face in my neck, and I breathe her in, her sweet, feminine scent. I let her sagging posture sink into me. I nuzzle the soft skin at the nape of her neck and my gaze falls on my son. He sighs in his sleep as if he knows this is it. This is where Mommy and Daddy have made up, and now everything will be fine.

At last, I have everything.

This hug has all the makings of a new beginning. This right here is what I've been waiting for.

Still, my stomach churns. Still, I gasp for breath. Still, my lungs are suffocating as if I'm holding on too tight. Still, I feel like this is the end of something and I'm dying.

PART 4

THE FIRE-BREATHER

CHAPTER TWENTY-FIVE

A few days ago, when everything was perfect, Nicky said his first words. *Lay-la.* Yeah, that's what he said.

He looked right at me with Thomas' eyes, gave me a drooling chortle, lifted his pudgy hand in the air, calling me to him, and said, "Lay...la."

I remember tearing up, and then laughing, and then tearing up again. It was a weird thing to do in the middle of Crème and Beans on a Saturday morning.

"Did you just say my name?" I asked, and then I looked up at Thomas, whose lips were twitching. "Did he just say my name?"

"Lay...la. Layyy...la!" Nicky jumped up and down on his dad's lap and laughed again, bumping his head on Thomas' chin.

"He did!" I remember being astonished. "Oh my God! He did. Am I his most favorite person or what?"

"Don't get too excited. He's probably just making up words like he always does." He ruffled Nicky's hair. "And in his defense, your name does sound made up. Two randomly put together syllables." Thomas shrugged. I remember the dark strands of his hair catching the winter sun and hitting me right in the chest.

I pretended to be outraged. I don't remember what I said in retaliation, something like, *Oh yeah? And what is Thomas? Tho-mas. Isn't it, like, a lame modification of Christ-mas?*

He laughed. I remember that because I was bursting with pride in being the one who brought it out in him.

It's Saturday again, and it's all I can think about as I enter Crème and Beans. Nicky's voice is all I hear, and Thomas' glinting hair and amused eyes are all I can see—and it's a good thing, too, because if I think about whom I am here to see, I might turn back and never come out of my room.

As if he senses me standing here, he looks up from his mug of coffee. My chest is caving in on itself as I take in his face, a face I haven't seen in more than two years. God, he looks…older. So much older, as though he's let himself go, given his body permission to grow out on him. Longer hair, broader shoulders, shadow of a beard.

But then he smiles, and it's the smile I've seen in my dreams forever, a smile that never fails to make *me* smile.

And then we're running toward each other like a couple of kids. I jump into his arms, laughing and crying. It's like the last two years never happened. It's like all the awkwardness in the world can't overshadow the fact that he's the closest friend I've ever had.

Caleb Whitmore, my very first friend.

We break apart, still laughing, and he lets me down on my feet.

"Hey," he says in a voice that's so familiar to me, so fucking familiar that all I want to do is break down and cry.

"Hey," I whisper over the ruckus my heart is making. I'm so damn happy to see him.

"You look…fantastic." He tucks my unruly hair behind my ear.

"You do too." I poke his wispy beard. "Where did that come from?"

Caleb gives me a sheepish grin, rubbing the spot. "I'm going for a mature look."

"What? Why?"

"People take the beard seriously."

"You're kidding." I frown. "They're giving you a hard time over at your dad's office?"

"Eh, it's not too bad, but you know, extra muscle helps." He rubs his barely-there beard again, making me laugh.

"Do you want me to kick their asses for you?"

He laughs, an indulgent look in his eyes. "God, I missed you." He swallows, growing serious. "So much."

"Yeah," I admit on a broken whisper.

We walk to his table and sit across from each other. Caleb watches me expectantly, and I shoot him a questioning look. He glances at his coffee and then at me. "You don't want to steal it?"

No, I don't steal anymore. The only person I want to steal from is not here.

A lump forms in my throat and I chuckle around it, trying to keep things light. "Are you calling me a thief?"

"Well, yeah. You are one."

"I don't think you're remembering things correctly."

"I remember everything about you, Lay."

I glance away. It's too hard to look into his eyes and find my old self reflected back. There are ghosts moving in the depths of them—my ghosts, but I don't look like them anymore. I've changed. I've changed so much since the time he knew me. I've done things, despicable things since then. Then again, maybe I haven't changed at all.

I was crazy then. I'm crazy now.

"Thanks for the gift basket," I say to break the silence.

Yesterday evening, Caleb sent me a gift basket with Twizzlers that I only noticed when I came home from Thomas' office. It was sitting on the coffee table; Emma had brought it in. She grilled me about it, too, asking me who the secret admirer was. I had to laugh at that, though it came out distorted, too much like a sob. I told her it was from Caleb and that he is gay. It didn't hurt to say that. It didn't hurt to say I used to be insanely in love with him but he never loved me back.

In fact, if I'm being honest, I haven't thought about Caleb at all in the past few days. Makes me wonder if Thomas was as much a distraction for me as I was for him.

"You didn't have to bribe me, you know."

"I didn't think you'd want to see me after...what I told you."

"Why *didn't* you tell me?" I whisper, unable to go higher than that. I'm exhausted. Breathing seems like a chore. I just want to stop. Stop running. Obsessing. Blaming.

He clasps his hands on the table. "I didn't know how."

"But it was me, Caleb. *Me.* We grew up together. You were my best friend. Wasn't I yours?"

It's such a petty, childish thing to ask. *Wasn't I your best friend when you were mine?* Still, I feel it's the most important thing I can ask him, more important and vital than *Don't you love me?* I realize now that I might crumble if he answers in the negative; his friendship means far more to me than his reciprocation of love.

He lets out a watery laugh. "How can you ask me that, Lay? When I've spent every second of the last two years missing you like hell. I..." He thrusts his hand through his hair. "I've felt so...guilty. So lonely. So unlike myself. But I didn't know how to face you after...what I did. The way I took advantage of your love. The way I left you."

It's hard to look at him, to look at the naked regret on his face. My heart curls up in my chest and rocks back and forth, hurting. He's blamed himself the same way I have blamed myself. I don't want him to do that. I don't want to think about what happened; it's too fucking depressing. It's time to share the blame and then move on.

"I forgive you," I tell him. "I do. For whatever happened. Do you forgive me?"

He takes my hand in his own and squeezes. "Yes. Although there's nothing to forgive, Lay."

I smile through my tears. It's over. It's done with. I feel light, both floaty and grounded.

We spend the next hour catching up. He tells me how hard it was for him throughout high school, how he thought he was weird. He was afraid his dad wouldn't ever accept that part of him. I tell him he was being stupid because hello, this is the twenty-first century. Who cares if you're gay? Then, I tell him about how bad things got after he left, how my mom wanted me to go to the youth center but I got out of it by coming here. I tell him about Kara. I tell him about my tower, about Emma.

The only thing I don't tell him about is Thomas Abrams. What is there to say about him anyway? He is my professor. He taught me that reading can be cool, that words are the most important thing in the world, and I used to sleep with him and now it's over. I let him vandalize my body, my heart, my dreams. I became a slut for him, but that's okay. He never asked. In fact, he warned me about him, his cruelty. I gave up my morals voluntarily.

I gave him everything, but he wanted nothing from me.

"I miss the city," I say to Caleb, out of the blue.

"Then come back." His expression is hopeful, the green of his eyes shining. "Yeah, come back. They'll easily take you in at Columbia. Your credits will transfer and you can live with me. You don't even have to go back to your mom's."

I smile, thinking of it, picturing living with Caleb. All the movie nights we can stock up on. All the video games we can play. It could be like the old times. I could have a new home. I could *build* a home for myself.

And then, in the middle of Crème and Beans on a lazy Saturday morning, I have an epiphany. It's bone-chilling. It tells me I'd rather be homeless than away from here, this place.

"I can't," I whisper, shaking my head.

"Why not?" Caleb senses the seriousness in my tone.

"B-Because I need to be here."

"Why?"

"Because..." I suck in huge gulps of breath, but am still afraid I'll pass out. "I'm in love."

CHAPTER TWENTY-SIX

The snow has melted—or is in the process of melting—and from underneath it, the earth is emerging, stark and damp and ugly but somehow still beautiful. I like to think we had something to do with it, Thomas and I. The friction we created with our naked bodies made the fire that dissolved the frosty world.

Because the way we came together was magical. It made me fall in love again.

It could almost be a story I'll tell myself when I'm dying. The Harlot fell in love with the Fire-breather. It was beautiful and right. It was wrong and ugly, just like the earth beneath my feet. It was tragic and ecstatic. It was everything I'd hoped love could be.

This time, though, I am going to do everything right. I'm going to change, be a better version of myself. I can't stand the thought of my love ruining anything. It's too pure, purer than any love that came before it or any love that will come after.

It takes me fifteen minutes to reach my destination: the sprawling house with a tree dangling over the roof. I know Thomas isn't in there—he's in New York for the poetry convention—but still his presence lingers. His displeasure drags my steps down. He wouldn't be happy if he knew I was here, uninvited, but this is something I have to do. I *need* to do. This love is my strength, not my weakness.

I knock—once, twice—and stand there, huddled into myself.

The door swings open and it's Susan, the lady I met a few days ago in the most unconventional way. I give her a small, trembling smile, and she returns it with a confused frown.

"H-Hi. I'm Layla." I remind her, even though I know she knows. How could she forget? The girl Thomas brought in at night when his wife wasn't home.

"Thomas isn't here." She purses her lips.

"I-I know. That's why I came." I widen my eyes in horror at how it sounds. "No. No, I don't mean it that way. It just came out wrong." I sigh. "Look, I know you don't like me. I'm not liking me very much either right now. I just... I need to see Nicky." Susan opens her mouth to say something but I rush on. "You can be there the whole time. I know it's an unusual request and you've got no reason to trust me, but I promise you I have no intention of harming him. I love that little guy and he loves me back, you know. I mean, I'm not good with kids. In fact, I don't know anything about them. But he's so... He's kind of my friend, and I just want to talk to him, apologize, and you won't have to ever see me again."

"What did you do to him? That you need to apologize for?" She is looking at me with an evaluating gaze.

"I, uh, I'd rather tell him. Please."

Maybe my desperation to talk to a seven-month-old baby breaks through to her, or maybe she takes pity on a girl with tears stuck to her eyelashes. Either way, she nods and steps back. "Five minutes. I stand there the whole time."

Relief sags my shoulders. "Yes. Yeah. Anything."

I step inside Thomas' house for the second time, and it feels more wrong than my previous visit. Sunlight pours into the living room and there he is—Nicky, playing in his bassinet. The sunrays make him glow, all pink-cheeked and stubby-nosed.

The little guy with his drooling chin and tufts of black hair commands my entire attention, like the room begins and ends with him. Just like his dad. I feel a surge of love for him, something very similar to maternal love, which is the weirdest thing I've ever felt in my entire life. I'm not a mother. I'm barely an adult myself, but as I walk over to Nicky, my arms ache with the need to pick him up and smush his face into my neck.

I come down to my knees in front of him and smile, looking into his blue eyes. He is chewing on a baby elephant and abandons it to grin at me.

"Lay...laaaa," he shrieks.

"Hey, little guy. You remember me, don't you?" I finger-wave at him like I always do and he grabs me with his sticky palm.

I bend down and place a soft kiss on the tiny fist holding my finger. He chortles and keeps chewing at his elephant. I remember Thomas telling me how Nicky thinks everything is food.

"Hey, I've got a present for you. Here." I take my Russian-style hat off, this one white in color. "You can have it, though you already have my most favorite one." I blow fishy kisses at him, making him laugh. "God, you're so adorable. I could just eat you up." I feel Susan's presence so I hastily add, "I won't though, so don't worry."

Nicky plays with his new hat, waving it around in his dimpled hands while I gather the courage to say what I came here to say.

"I broke the deal," I blurt out, much like I do with Thomas when I need to get something difficult off my chest. I cringe. "Ugh. That just kinda came out. I think I should start at the beginning...not that it's gonna make any difference to you." Nicky is busy with the hat and waving his fists while squirming in his yellow onesie. "But I'm going to do this the right way. So, I made a deal with your dad. It wasn't anything formal. It was just...a silent understanding, and trust me, I only made it because I thought...he needed it. I needed it too, but his need was...so much bigger than mine, you know, so much more potent. But, I broke the deal."

Susan shifts behind me but I keep my focus on the little bundle who doesn't even care what I'm saying. "I know you're not gonna understand what I'm saying right now, and you're probably gonna forget all about me because I don't think we'll see each other anymore, but I want you to know I didn't break it on purpose—the deal, I mean. It just happened, okay. I never planned on-on, you know, falling for your dad." I scrunch my eyes closed and breathe out a puff of air.

"But I'm going to do the right thing now. I'm-I'm backing off, Nicky. You don't have to worry, okay. It won't touch you. My mistakes won't come back to haunt you."

I think of the tears Emma has shed for something that was never in her control. Nothing is worth that; I know it now. No amount of excuses can absolve what I did, and if there's even a sliver of a chance that it can touch this little guy, I'm not willing to take it.

Tears gather in my throat and eyes and I swallow to bury them—not that Nicky notices. "Your dad loves you very much. He isn't like my dad. He'll never leave you, and I bet your mom loves you equally, if not more. And you know what, your dad loves your mom just as much as he loves you. So...don't worry about anything." I sniff. "I'm sorry for whatever damage I did." I lean over and kiss his forehead. He gurgles out a laugh. "This is the last time we'll see each other, so take care, okay? I'll never forget you."

With one last look at him, I stand up and find myself face to face with the most beautiful and fragile-looking woman I've ever seen. Hadley.

She's...She's back.

She. Is. Back. Just as I thought she would be. I always knew it, but still, it seems incredible. I want to laugh, and then I want to cry.

Before I really do any of that, the situation becomes glaring.

I'm practically a stranger and I was rambling to her baby like a deranged person. She is studying me with gorgeous golden eyes and I feel so ashamed. So naked.

I'm the girl sleeping with your husband. Me. I'm the one who fell in love with him, who dreams about him, who will probably keep dreaming about him for the rest of her life. So, you can kill me if you want to. In fact, I'd advise that myself.

"You're good with him," she says in her classic, melodic voice.

"What?" I squeak. In comparison, I'm a hyena with broken vocal cords.

"With Nicholas. You're good with him."

The musical notes of her voice stumble over the name of her son, going off-key. Now that the initial shock of seeing Thomas' love in the flesh is gone, I study her with as much objectivity as I can.

Her eyes are swollen and red-rimmed, and her blonde hair, though beautiful and smooth, looks too threadbare. She has on a large white sleep robe that swallows her petite body. She appears even more fragile than the last time I saw her, but she seems to be at peace. She glows with an odd light.

This is the woman who left her seven-month-old baby alone and went away. This is the woman who left Thomas. I want to shake her, shout at her. In this moment, I'm so fucking jealous, so angry. She has everything that I want and she doesn't even care.

Before my anger turns harsher, I remind myself that I'm in the wrong here. I took what belonged to her. I have no right to feel this way.

"I, uh, I've got no experience with kids, but Nicky makes it easy, I guess." I add, "You have a beautiful family."

She stiffens at my answer, and I regret saying the last part. My anger was apparent just then. Maybe even my jealousy...*I don't know.* I need to leave before I blow our cover and make trouble for Thomas.

Just then, I hear Susan coming back. "Here." She thrusts a book at me and I stare at it in confusion. "The book. It was right on the desk and I was looking for it everywhere." When I still don't take it, she goes on, "Thomas doesn't like when someone touches his books, but you must be failing pretty badly in class if he wanted you to have it for the exams, no?"

There's a mischievous twinkle in her brown eyes, and I wonder how she is even capable of it at a moment like this. I take the book. "O-kay."

I practically run out of there and speed walk until the house is out of sight. Then I come to a stop in the middle of the road and look up. The sun is out, and I can't remember the last time it was sunny like this. It feels like it's been ages since I saw the sun.

The world is brighter, and I feel that I did something right. I restored all the balance I'd tipped. The broken rules are patched up. The universe is right again.

I send a wish up in the clear sky. *Please, let Hadley be back for good this time. Please give Thomas what he wants. Please God.*

And then I cry all the way back to my tower. I hate the fucking sun.

CHAPTER TWENTY-SEVEN

It's Sunday night and I'm alone in the apartment. Two months ago I would have used this time to binge on Twizzlers and porn. I'm still bingeing on Twizzlers, but instead of porn, I'm typing like the wind.

My fingers are flying on the keyboard, words pouring out of me, and I'm thinking, *No one has ever written a story like this.* For weeks, I've had this girl in my head. She is loud. She has a neon green backpack. She is adventurous and she wants to see the world. Her name is Eva. For weeks, I ignored her, because hello, I want to be a poet, not a fiction writer. Fiction writers are lame. Poets are geniuses. They change the world. They make you think. They are magical. Like Thomas.

But I can't ignore her anymore. I can't ignore her need to take shape. Besides, I know if I don't write, I'll never stop crying. I might even slip back to my destructive ways. I might drink all the liquor and smoke all the pot, and then I'd die, and I don't want to die. I want to live. I want to write.

Tap. Tap. Tap.

Then, I hear a shrill noise—my phone. I jump and turn around at my desk. My room has exploded. Clothes and books and empty candy boxes are on every surface. I have half a mind to let it go to voicemail, but for some unknown reason, I don't.

The noise is coming from my bed, and I dive for the phone before the ringing stops. It's an unknown number but I pick it up anyway. "Hello?"

A growly voice crackles through, making my heart flounder. "Layla."

"Th-Thomas?" My legs give out, and I plop on the bed.

"Are you alone right now?"

"Yes." I look around as if checking, as if I didn't already know I was alone.

"Open your door."

"You mean, my front door?" I stand and walk to the threshold of my room, eyeing my closed front door in confusion.

"Yes, your front door."

"O-Okay."

There comes a long sigh. "You should probably also tell me which door is yours." His voice somehow sounds both indulgent and self-deprecating, like he's ashamed that he doesn't already know which door is mine.

"The last apartment on the right."

"What floor?" he asks patiently.

"Uh, t-top floor."

His laugh is broken and sad, full of resignation, and I don't even know how a laugh can be all of that. He clicks off the call before I can ask him anything else.

I'm glued to my spot, watching the door. Shouldn't he be in New York? *Oh no.* I'm worried that maybe he found out about me going to his place this morning, but before I can completely freak out and lose my shit, a knock comes, commanding and loud. My phone falls to the floor, my legs break into motion, and I throw the door open.

Thomas stands at the threshold, his arms propped on the frame on either side. Our eyes clash like a bolt of lightning. At first, my heart stutters at the wealth of emotions brimming in his gaze, and then it pounds. It pounds as I take in the rest of his appearance—wrinkled shirt, messy hair, stubbled jaw.

He looks undone. The strings holding his body together have come apart, unraveled. A shiver wracks his frame. Startled, I whip my gaze back up and find his eyes solely focused on my face—drinking in my features, devouring them. He is eating me up with his magnificent gaze, but I don't understand why.

"Thomas? What, um, what's going on?" My voice brings on another bout of shivers, and I notice for the first time how tightly he's holding on to the door frame. His veins are vibrating from the effort.

"Thomas, you're scaring me. What's happening?"

Whatever anger I had at him, whatever self-preservation I had is gone, and I walk closer to him. All I know is that he needs me. That's all I understand as I uncurl the fingers of his right hand from the frame using both of mine. It's a struggle, but I manage to unclasp his grip and hold his hand tightly.

Only then does he move his eyes from my face and look at our joined hands. My small pale ones are enclosing his thick, darker one. I feel the undercurrent of energy through his skin. I feel the chaos, the mayhem running through his veins.

"You live in a fucking construction zone," he mutters.

"I call it my tower." The tightness in his hand loosens and I take an easy breath. "Why aren't you in New York?"

"Because I have to tell you something."

"Wh-What?"

"You're beautiful, you know that?" he says, instead of answering my question. Somehow his voice shivers too, a rumbly sort of vibration that I feel in my tattoo. He lets go of the door frame and crowds me, forcing me to take a step back.

He brings his other hand to cup my cheek. His fingers tremble over my skin and I put my hand over them to give them stability. "Thomas, please, tell me what's going on."

His Adam's apple jumps up and down. "No, that's...that's not right. You're not beautiful. I think you're the most exquisite thing I've ever seen." He licks his lips, his eyes flitting back and forth. "No, not a...not a thing. You're more than that, Layla. You're...the poem I can never write. Yeah, you're the piece of poetry I can never hope to finish, no matter how hard I try."

"Thomas," I whisper, a fat tear rolling down my cheek. My wounded heart squeezes in my chest. It's like he's caressing the walls of it, leaving his fingerprints forever for me to carry. The way he's stumbling over his words... I can't bear to see it.

He leans into me, grabbing both my cheeks now, wiping off the tears. "The first time I saw you at the bookstore, you had these crazy headphones on and you were dancing to the music. I saw something pop over your head, a word. I couldn't place it—not until I saw you in my class. That's when I realized that you were so bright and loud and shiny like..."

"Like what?"

"Scarlet," he whispers, his breath misty over my tear-drenched lips.

This time, *my* laugh is broken and sad and full of resignation. "Yeah, I'm that, right? Like Hester Prynne. I bet it's clear to everyone."

The force of his grip increases, flattening my cheeks. "No it's not, because it's not true. Do you understand me? It's not. You're nothing like her or anyone else. You're not..."

"A slut?"

He grits his teeth. "Fuck no. You're not. You'll *never* be that. Tell me you know that. Say it, Layla."

His face is a blurry painting through the lens of my tears, a labyrinth of emotions and expressions I can't place. The only thing grounding me in this moment is the vivid color of his eyes. They are jarring in their sincerity. They beg me to give him that, to believe him, and when have I ever been able to refuse him?

"I'm not a slut."

He nods his head, sighing, sending a burst of his chocolatey breath into my lungs. "That's right. You're not."

"I can't do it anymore," I blurt out. "I know I promised I wouldn't regret it but I-I do. I regret all the things we did and the way we did them. It wasn't right, Thomas. We broke all the rules. I..." A sob wracks my frame.

"Shh... Hey, we're not. We're not doing it anymore, okay? It's over."

"Okay." My hands find his shirt and fist the fabric. I sob on his chest, bringing him closer to me when I should let him go. It's over. All the illicit things we've been doing. All the things I've been hiding from Emma. All of it is over, but I don't feel relief. I just feel enormous amounts of pain and hurt and burn.

He rocks me in his arms like a child, and I clutch at him harder. He's the only thing keeping me together and making me fall apart, and no matter what I said, I don't want to let go. I don't regret falling in love; I only regret how it happened.

At some point, I stop crying and simply hold on to him because I don't want this to end. I breathe him in and he does the same. His arms are shaking around me and I look up at him. I've never seen his face so expressive before, like a battered page of an ancient book. There are stains of agony and regret.

He stares down at me with half a smile, a pathetic attempt to appear nonchalant. He looks like he wants to say something but he stops himself. Then, he bends down and places a soft kiss on my forehead, lingering for about two seconds before he takes a step back. It was tender and soft and all the things I've always wanted.

He takes me in, one last time, and then turns around and begins walking to the elevator. Astonished, I stand there, immobile. That's it? Is this how it ends? He never told me why he came here.

A beep sounds, signaling the arrival of the elevator. The steel door whooshes open but before he can get on, I dash to him and cling to his strong body, twining my arms and legs around him. He jerks to a stop, one arm grabbing my wrist on his chest and the other resting on the small of my back.

We both shudder with panting breaths. Then, as if he whispered the words in my ears, I hear them clearly. This is goodbye. He came to say goodbye, like he promised he would. *Goodbyes aren't my forte, but I won't leave you like a coward either.*

It's enough to send me sobbing again but I remain silent and wrapped around him, simply breathing him in. I won't make this harder than it has to be.

I won't. I *won't*.

Thomas tries to unwind my arms but despite everything, I hold on to him tighter. "Let me go, Layla. I need to go."

"I know." I burrow my nose in his neck, run my teeth over his skin. His flavor explodes over my tongue, making me all drugged up and crazy. "But before you go, could you stay a little while?"

As soon as I say it, I'm filled with shame. I shouldn't have said that. I made a promise to his child that I wouldn't break up his family, but my brain is sluggish right now. My body is dying for his.

Even so, I untwine my arms and legs and slide down, feeling the ridges of his back, the patterns of his muscles on the gentle hills and valleys of my front.

I'm waiting for him to leave. He's waiting for it too, if his accelerated breathing is any indication.

And yet, Thomas spins around and faces me. The hunger in his expression is unmistakable. I'm rendered speechless by it. He bends down to plant a hard kiss onto my lips. A ticking pulse starts down below, in my pussy, a bomb that could blow up at any minute.

"Last time," he growls over my mouth. "Ask me to promise you that this is the last time."

I don't want to, but it needs to be done. We're going to be over by the time we both come. The amount of time we have left is the length of one fuck. This is how we began, right? And this is how we'll end. I want to laugh at the rightness of it all. I want to cry.

"P-Promise me that this is the last time?"

Tectonic plates shift under the harsh surface of his body, juddering and rearranging themselves. "Yeah. I promise."

After that, there isn't any need for words. He hauls me up in his arms and strides over to my apartment, our lips fused together, my fingers holding on to his hair. He kneads the globes of my ass as he kicks the door shut, and his long legs eat up the distance to the opposite wall. My back thuds against it, a sharp pain shooting in my skull, but I just kiss him harder. I latch on to his lips like I'll never let him go.

He props me against the wall with his hips, fitting his hardness over my core. His greedy hands wander up and down my bare thighs. He tucks his thumb inside the hem of my polka dot sleep shorts and edges closer and closer to my wet, hot center.

His tongue slides down my neck and he takes a bite out of the swell of my right breast. This is what happens when we're in close proximity—we combust, we burn. He yanks down the straps of my cami and exposes my puffy tits, lashing my nipples with his tongue, one at a time.

"Oh God..." I arch against the wall, bending myself into a taut half-moon.

He lets go of my thighs and frames my face with his hands, forcing me to look at him. Our chests move in sync. One breath in and one breath out. Our lips are parted. Our eyes swirl with animal lust. In this moment, we're more than soul mates. We inhabit each other's bodies. We are one. One skin. One heart. One need.

He smacks a hard and fast kiss on my lips and whips my shorts off, leaving me half dressed in my cami, which is bundled up beneath my breasts. On his knees now, he bands an arm around my waist to keep me steady, and with the other, he parts my trembling thighs.

Then he falls on me. Tongue, teeth, and mouth—I get them all. He slashes my core with his decadent, dirty touches. A long suck on my clit. A couple of jarring rotations of his fingers inside me. All the while, he murmurs dirty nothings to my quivering cunt. He tells her how much he loves her taste. How much of a good girl she is to respond to him this way. How he's never going to forget how tight and hot she is. How she hugs his cock like a glove a size too small but somehow, still right.

I come in the wake of his filthy words, his dirty poetry to my hungry cunt, and it's glorious. Magical. Potentially life-altering. All I can do is tangle my fingers in his hair and chant his name over and over. He presses a soft, fluttering kiss on my tattoo and stands up. His arms lift me from the floor and carry me bridal style in the general direction of my bedroom, which I waved at in my half-drowsy state.

I nuzzle in the hollow of his throat as he enters, and lays me down on the bed. He then proceeds to make enough space around me so we can get comfortable. I watch him with hooded eyes as he unbuttons his shirt halfway, then snags it in the back and pulls it over his head. His jeans come off next, leaving him magnificently, heartbreakingly naked.

My hands twitch with the need to traverse the solid pack of muscles of his chest and abdomen. The raven curls sprinkling his chest exude sheer masculinity. He runs his gaze over my body, from the cloud of my hair to the tips of my flexing toes. He's committing me to his memory, like I'm doing to him.

I arch my back for him and his cock gives a jerk. Licking his lips, he grabs it at the base then pumps it once, twice. His touch on his own cock translates to the erotic sensations in my core, and a trickle of cum seeps out.

The muscles of his thighs bunch as he bends down to retrieve a condom from his jeans.

"No. No condoms." His displeased frown makes me rub my thighs together. "And no pussy either."

Now his frown is more than displeased. It's thunderous. He locks his palms on my knees and applies pressure until my thighs are parted, and my needy flesh is open to his eyes. "You want to repeat that?" His voice has dropped an octave lower, scraping my senses, arousing them even more.

"I want it in my ass."

Bold, *bold* words for someone who's pinned down on the bed simply by the intense look of her lover. I bet if he told me to stay still so he could cut out a piece of my heart, I'd obey him. I'm so far gone for him that he could fool me easily.

He arches his eyebrows and prowls over my body, his sculpted arms putting on a show for me. "What?"

My toes dip into the springy hair of his calves as I reply, "If this is the last time then I want you wh-where you've never been."

His hair falls over his forehead as he lowers himself over me, propped up on his arms. "It's going to hurt."

"I know."

A fierce expression flickers over his face, not yet taking hold but lurking. "I don't want to hurt you."

I would laugh if I weren't on the verge of crying—again. He's already hurt me a million times before. What's one more? I want the hurt. I want to burn. He told me once that he'd ruin me for any other man, and that this is how he'd do it. I want him to do it. I want this. I want to be ruined for every other man out there because no one is like him. If I can't have him, then no one will ever have me. I'll be alone. The very thing I was running from...I want it now.

I whisper, "It's okay."

A drop of sweat from his forehead plops down between my breasts and he watches its descent. His breathing is erratic. He wants this as much as me. In fact, he might be afraid of how much he wants it.

"I might not be able to stop..." He is measuring each word, striving to make them just right. "Once...Once I get in."

I cup his harsh jaw and rub his calves with my feet. "But you'll make it good. You always make it so good for me. Please, Thomas?"

My pouting lips are his demise. That fierce expression overtakes his features, darkening his eyes and flushing his cheeks crimson. He moves away and hauls me up by my arm. I yelp as I go up on my knees, facing him.

We take each other in, panting, mad with lust. My eyes home in on the mole on his collarbone, the mole I somehow missed during our previous encounters. I reach out and touch it and then splay my hand over his chest, feeling the tattoo of his heartbeats on my palm. I watch the interplay of his abdominal muscles as he sucks in deep breaths, throwing the lines of his ribs in sharp relief.

If I focus really hard, I can pretend we're two people in love. This is what happens when your love is requited. You control each other; you live for each other.

He grabs my arms and yanks them over my head, then takes off my barely-there cami. Now I'm as naked as him, shivering under the deluge of goosebumps.

His hands close over my breasts and knead the flesh. My breath picks up, and so does my heart. I feel it ballooning in my chest, pressing against my ribcage. My arousal seems bigger than me right now. The more he massages my achy tits, the more restless I become. I rock my lower body, grazing the head of his cock with my stomach, making him grunt.

Letting go of my breasts and moving away, Thomas grabs the back of my neck and pushes me toward the bed. I go down willingly, until my elbows hit the messy sheets and I'm on my knees, my butt in the air.

He moves behind me, palming my ass, massaging and kneading. A slew of tingles pools down my lower back, spreads over my flesh. That dark, uncharted hole clenches.

Moisture dribbles down my core and along my inner thighs. Thomas swoops it up with a finger, bringing it to my pussy and painting it over my dripping lips.

Mini jerks float down my body, making me hump the air. I look behind to find Thomas focusing on the movements of his finger. His brow is furrowed as he adds his other hand to the mix, inserting a thick digit inside my core. He stretches my tight hole and my swollen lips using his fingers and thumbs. My cheeks are parted and I'm exposed to his eyes.

But I can see he isn't happy. He wants more. It's in the way his body shifts with impatience.

His nails dig into my ass as he stretches me farther. The tight ring of my asshole pops open; I can feel it. I can feel my pussy gushing and dousing me in a weird combination of arousal and shame. Then he does something that throws me into a different stratosphere of lust.

His lips pucker and he spits on my asshole. As soon as the warm liquid hits me, my hips twitch. Thick, knotted ropes inside my lower tummy unravel, and I almost come, falling on the bed, face first.

"Can you feel how tight you are here?" His fingers work to lubricate me, spreading his spit over my tight ring, all the while playing with my other hole. "I knew you would be. I know you won't rest until I completely lose my mind over how tight and untouched you are."

He stops playing with my pussy and focuses only on my ass now. He inserts his wet thumb and a tiny crumb of pain darts through my spine. It screams that I want this. I want him to take my ass and be my first.

Arching my hips, I rest my cheek on the soft bed. I bring my arms back and put them on my ass cheeks, helping him stretch my hole.

"Fuck," he curses on a shuddering breath. "You're trying to kill me."

"No," I mumble into the sheet, suddenly extremely horny and shy. "I'm trying to get you to fuck me already."

A pained laugh escapes him. "Yeah, I'll be dead before this is over."

Now that I hold myself open for him, he lets go and palms his cock. It hits my ass, the heat of it seeping into my skin. He spits again, this time on his head, and rubs the saliva all over his shaft. The view of it is hidden behind my raised ass but I can imagine his rod shining, the foreskin sliding up and down, creating the magnificent friction I feel when he flicks my clit.

The flex of his biceps relaxes as he halts the movement and looks up at me. I bite my lip, my chest fluttering up and down with anticipatory breaths.

With his eyes, he tells me he is ready to take me. No words pass between us. This moment is too big for words. It can only be described in actions. He is going to claim the last part of me now.

Thomas grips my waist with one hand, keeping me in one place, and with the other, nudges the head of his cock against my dark, tiny entrance. He pushes in, trying to breach the compact ring of muscles. It's hard, a struggle, during which I squirm and scrunch my eyes shut, and he breathes in loud pants. Then a pop sounds and he is in.

The sting of it. The pressure of it. I feel it fanning over my entire ass and spine. Hissing, I buck my hips, almost dislodging him, but he tightens his grip around my waist and keeps me steady.

He keeps sliding his cock in, and I swear I hear the muscles stretching, peeling away from each other. *Oh God.* Tears form as I breathe through my nose, trembling with pain.

This was a bad idea. Bad. Bad. Bad.

"Shh..." Thomas caresses my spine with his other arm, trying to soothe my skittish body. "It's gonna be okay. It's gonna be okay. I'll take care of you."

"Is it...all in?" I whimper.

"No, baby, not yet." He whooshes out a long breath. His strong thighs vibrate against the back of mine, telling the tale of his control and exertion.

That slip of his tongue, that casually thrown in endearment makes me open my eyes and look at him. Every hollow and crevice of his body stands taut and highlighted. He appears to be made of stone. My fire-breather. My stone god.

And I'm his baby. *Baby.*

His head is dipped as if in prayer, his brow furrowed as if he can't afford to lose control and hurt me in the process, but I don't care anymore. I want him however I can get him.

"It hurts," I tell him in a small voice.

His body jerks and his hazy eyes lift up. I pop my thumb into my mouth and suck on it, imagining it's his cock that I'm using as a sucker, like a good girl.

I play his favorite game one last time and his nostrils flare. He suddenly grows larger, bigger, tenser. I smile on the inside when his sweat-slicked palms grab both sides of my hips and he pushes through. I bite my thumb, moan around it, and close my eyes. The pain is excruciating but as I surrender to it, I realize it ebbs in slow measures.

Thomas grunts as he bottoms out, the coarse hair around his cock prickling the smooth skin of my ass. I imagine him watching me suck on my thumb, being still, being good for him. My heart pounds as I picture him gathering himself once again to pull out so he can push back in, smoothing his way through my tight chamber.

He unclenches one hand and brings it to my clit, strumming the bundled-up button. My hips buck again, but as always, Thomas keeps me balanced. While playing with my clit and making my pussy bleed cream for him, he withdraws almost fully then pushes back in. He huffs and I grunt.

Sweat pools on my back, skates down to my neck, tickling me. Moaning, I rub my heavy breasts on the soft bed, seeking friction for my engorged nipples as Thomas finds his slow but confident rhythm. The pain is there, but it's bearable, pleasurable even.

One last time, he tells me a story, dirty and pornographic. He tells me how tight I am, how amazing I feel. He tells me men would kill to get inside my pussy, my ass—it doesn't matter which.

As I listen to him and lose my mind, I know I don't care about any other men. I only care about him.

Our flesh is sliding together, oiled with sweat and my own juices. Then Thomas shifts onto his knees to bring his leg out and around my hips, changing his angle. Weirdly, I feel his cock in my spine. I feel it bumping against the ridges of my bones, and I explode.

Spurts of cum burst out of me, drenching my thighs and his, too, I'm sure. My body is tight and loose at the same time, bucking and shivering, a beast I can't control. For a second, I'm scared it won't ever be over, that I'll never regain control of my own body. A shriek echoes in my throat but his hand over my mouth tamps it down. I put my own hand over his and grab on to it.

Behind me, Thomas jerks. He rotates his hips in a telltale sign of his climax, and I squeeze his palm over my mouth to tell him I'm here, that it's okay to let go.

He falls over me as his cock pushes out hot cum. I sigh under his delicious weight and we lie in the puddle of our orgasms. His shuddering chest bumps with my back, his arm thrown over my shoulder. I smell his skin, nuzzle my face in the coarse hair of his forearm. His sighs scatter the hair on my neck.

For the first time in a long time, I feel sleepy on my bed. I don't need the hard surface of the bathtub. My eyes are on the verge of falling shut when I hear him whisper, almost distractedly, "You bring them back...my words."

It's so soft and thin that it could almost be a dream. In that dream, I could almost imagine that he came here not to say goodbye, but to tell me he loves me.

I fall asleep in the wake of those three imagined words.

CHAPTER TWENTY-EIGHT

When I woke up this morning, Thomas had left. I'd expected him to, but I wasn't expecting to find myself tucked under my purple blanket, sleeping soundly on the bed. At some point during the night he moved me, put me under the covers, and crept out silently. For some reason, that hurts me more than anything we've ever done.

My coffee sits on the kitchen counter, untouched and cold. I had all the plans of holding my head up and moving on, but everything hurts.

Hurts. Like I've been run over by a car.

Emma's door opens and I quickly wipe away all the tears. Turning, I greet her with a fake smile. "Ready to go?"

"No, class is canceled. I just got an email."

Relief is my body's first reaction. I don't want to go. I don't even have a plan in place as to how to face Thomas, how to be normal around him after everything. Then my brain catches on. "What? Why?"

Her expression is both horrified and confused. "I...got a text from Samantha, who got a text from Brian. He says he actually saw it or maybe heard it from somewhere. It-It doesn't matter. But Professor Abrams... His wife's in the hospital. She-She tried to kill herself."

A buzz enters my mind.

A constant sound of static that invades my ears, and it doesn't stop there. It floods over my body. I see Emma. I see her lips moving. I see the frown on her face, the agitated lines around her mouth. But it doesn't register.

Nothing does.

Thomas.

He needs me. I know he does. I need to go to him. I need to find Thomas. This...This can't be happening. I saw her yesterday and she was fine. I saw her with my own eyes and *oh my God*, he loves her. He loves her so much and... Did I do this? Was it me? Did-Did my going there bring this on? Maybe she realized how much I love him too. Maybe she found out about us. It's my fault, isn't it?

My world screeches to a halt and then shakes, shakes violently.

"Layla? What the hell are you talking about?" Emma is closer to me than before. How did she get here? I look down and see coffee spilled all over the floor, some of it splashed over my bare feet with shards of my broken mug scattered around.

"I need to go see him," I tell Emma.

"I don't understand. When did you see his wife? Why is it your fault?"

I realize I was saying it all out loud. I don't have time to explain things right now. I need to go find Thomas.

"Do you know where..." I take a puff of breath, trying to make sense of words, which are failing me right now.

"She's at the hospital. She's fine. At least, that's what I heard. It's all over campus."

"Okay. Okay." I walk around her. "I need to go to the hospital. Right now."

Emma stops me then. "Layla, there's more."

Her tone sends a chill down my spine. Cold curls around my bones and hunkers down. "What? What is it?"

She is wringing her hands, agitated. "I-I heard that their baby, the one we met at Crème and Beans all those weeks ago?" She is shaking her head.

Why is she shaking her head?

"Layla, he's in the hospital too."

"What does that mean?"

"I don't know... I heard he's in the ICU or something."

"Nicky?" I shake my head at Emma's sympathetic, pitying face. "Why? I mean, what happened. How can he be in the ICU? Isn't...Isn't that serious?"

She puts her hand on my shoulders and rubs my skin in circles. "Shit, Layla, you're shivering. You need to sit down for a sec, okay?"

"No." I stop her from pushing me down on the barstool. "No. Tell me where Nicky is."

"Layla, I really don't know, honey. I told you what I heard. I've got no idea how any of this happened."

I break out of her hold, numb and charged at the same time, ready to stride over to the front door. "I need to go. I need to find Thomas, okay? I n-need to tell him Nicky is fine. He must be freaking out right now."

"Layla, you need to listen to me. Just please, listen to me." She goes to grab my arm and I spin around.

"No," I shout. "No. I don't *need* to do anything but find Thomas, okay? He needs..." My voice breaks and I take in another breath. "I just need to get to the hospital. Right now."

Emma nods. "Okay. I'll take you. I'll find out what hospital they were taken to and then we'll go."

I nod, and then my legs give out and I crumple to the ground.

L*ay-la. La-laaa.*

Yes. I'm Layla...or Lala. Whatever. I sip my coffee and he chews on his tiny fists, staring at me in fascination. His eyes are big, wide pools of blue water. He's adorable.

You wanna drink my coffee, little guy? He gurgles. *Okay, tell you what, I'll give this to you if you say coffee. Say, co-ffee.*

Thomas sends me an exasperated look. *What? I'm teaching him a new word.* I look at Nicky. *Come on, Nicky, don't let me down. Say, coffee. Co-ffee.*

He chortles. Thomas is pursing his lips, holding back a laugh. *Oh, you're enjoying this, aren't you? You wait and see, the day will come when Nicky's going to say coffee and love me more than he loves you.*

"We're here, Layla." Emma's voice brings me to the moment. We're at the parking lot of the university hospital, and I'm surprised to find tears tracking down my cheeks.

I don't know why I'm crying. They told Emma that Hadley is going to be okay, and... I *know* Nicky is going to be fine. I know it. Even though they said that he's in the PICU and chances are he won't survive the night. I mean, what do they know. They said *chances are*. Right? Chances could mean anything.

So my tears are stupid.

I jump out of the car and make my way toward the front entrance. When I see Thomas, everything is going to be okay. I chant it to myself, over and over. Emma talks to the lady at reception but she is refusing to give us anything. We're not family.

A movement in the periphery catches my eye, and I turn to find Susan walking down the hallway to the left of the reception desk.

"Susan."

She is startled to see me walking toward her. "Layla."

"Why are you crying?" Her cheeks are tear-stained, similar to mine. It makes me feel…panicky. "No. Don't cry. There's nothing to cry about. Everything is gonna be okay. They told Emma…" I turn to point her out at the desk. "Hadley's gonna be fine."

She covers her mouth to muffle a broken sob. "Nicky—"

"He's fine." My shrill voice surprises her and she looks at me like I'm crazy. "Nicky's fine. Nothing's going to happen to him. He's fine."

"You know he likes to put all his toys in his playpen. Every night he makes me gather them up and put them in one corner." She hiccups. "He looked like an angel this morning, playing with his little elephant." She looks like she's going to fall so I put my arm around her shoulders.

"Then Hadley woke up early and I-I asked her to watch Nicky while I ran to the store to get the formula. I didn't want to. I didn't want to leave him alone but I don't know h-how I forgot to stock up on it and he needed it. I thought I'd be back soon, but the store didn't have it so I had to drive a little farther."

Susan is full-on crying now. I want to snap at her but just then Emma walks over to us, puts her hand on my shoulders, and shakes her head once, telling me to rein it in.

"B-By the time I got back, he was…he was almost…gone. I called 911 and then I looked for Hadley. She was in the bathroom unconscious." Susan's sobs are dislodging something inside me—my stern, stark belief that Nicky is okay—and I don't like that. I don't like it one bit.

I move away from her. "Where's Thomas?"

Susan takes a while to answer, a while that stretches thin and brittle. She tells me he's on the third floor where the PICU wards are located, in the waiting room. I dash upstairs, unseeing, barely conscious myself.

My feet stop when I catch sight of him. His back is to me. The wide berth of his shoulders is the only thing I see. He's standing in the middle of the empty waiting room, facing the glass doors that lead to the hallway containing the wards.

It reminds me of the night I saw him through his window. Even through his grey shirt, I see the bunched-up muscles, the tensed patterns on his back. That night I couldn't console him. I couldn't touch him or tell him everything was going to be okay.

But I'm going to do it now.

I walk toward him, slowly, my steps quiet like a flickering, dying breath.

"Thomas?"

He doesn't move. I don't think he even heard me. I walk around and come face to face with him.

Or something that looks like him. Something that's as tall and as wide but somehow shrunken. A husk of a man, pale and haggard with barren eyes.

"Thomas," I call again, this time louder than before. His gaze snaps away from whatever tortured vision he's been having and settles on me. "Everything is going to be okay," I repeat for the millionth time. The more I say it, the more dusty and scraping it feels in my mouth, as though I've swallowed a sandstorm and my body is filled with crunchy grains of the desert. But, I push on. He needs me. "I'm here now. Everything is gonna be fine. Hadley's fine."

I swallow and get close to him. My neck strains as I look at his face, immobile and dead. "Thomas, d-don't worry. They're all lying about Nicky, I know it. Trust me, okay. I—"

I'm shocked at the release of a shattered sob. It sounds so much like Susan's, the woman who thinks Nicky is almost gone. I'm not that woman. My sob shouldn't sound like hers. I know Nicky is gonna be okay. He has to be. There's no other option.

The sound of my pain wakes Thomas up, but he still doesn't see me. He's too occupied in his own head, too overcome with his grief. I never thought sadness could be violent and savage, but on Thomas it is. His devastation is brutal. I'm readying myself for it to rain down on me. It never comes, however.

He walks away.

His legs eat up the distance and he's opening the door to the stairwell. I run after him. I snatch his arm and stop his progress just as he reaches the edge of the greenish stairs. "Thomas, wait. Just look at me, please. It's going to be fine. I'm telling you. Just please, look at me," I beg, and then he does.

He looks at me, and fury blazes through his eyes. He grabs my bicep and shakes me, jarring every single one of my bones in the process. "My son's dying, Layla." He spits out my name like a toxic curse. "They won't even let me in. They won't even let me see him. He almost *choked* to death on a fucking button, and they won't even let me see my own son."

He's at a stage where everything looks like food and drool-worthy. I sob again and it is broken and strangled, with enough power to destroy me.

"Do you know why no one was there to stop him?" His grip tightens on my arm and he pushes me, walks me backward, thumping my back and my head to the cold wall. I bite my lip to stop from crying out in pain. "Because my wife was busy killing herself," he snarls. "She was busy swallowing down a bottle of sleeping pills." By the time he finishes, his snarl has become a roar as he belts out his pain. He slaps his palm on the wall beside me.

But then the fight is leached out of his body as if that one slap to the wall was all he had in him. His voice loses its violent quality and is now fraught with torture. "I thought everything was fine. I thought if she let me touch her, then she must've forgiven me. She asked me to hold her a-and I thought she must love me back. Maybe not a lot – God knows, I don't deserve that, now more than ever – but at least a little. And now...everything is broken. My entire family is torn apart when I just got it back."

There's a crack in his voice, right in the middle of it. It breaks my heart, crushes it into a pulp. I'm bleeding on the inside.

I remember the odd glow I saw on her yesterday. She was tired but...peaceful. She was happy, and I fucked it all up.

"It was me." I swallow. "I-I did that. It's my fault. I went to your house to see Nicky. I wanted to tell him I'd back off, that I broke all the rules and fell in love with you, and I saw Hadley and I—"

"You fell in love with me," he says. It's a flat statement. I would've been fooled by the calmness of it if not for his pulsating cheek.

"Thomas, I –"

"My family is dying because you love me," he says matter-of-factly, and I go speechless at the inferno bursting through his red-rimmed eyes.

Thomas is burning up. His thick fingers are going to leave a burn mark around my bicep. It wouldn't be anything I don't deserve. I'm bracing myself for it. I'm bracing myself for whatever punishment he wants to dole out. His gaze tells me that I disgust him.

But again, nothing comes.

The pressure of his grip eases as he whirls around, momentarily dazzling me. His dismissal is confusing. His restraint increases my urge for the punishment. I don't want his control; I want his fury. All I can think about is that he's hurting because of me and he needs this. He needs to hurt me back so he can get some closure. I'm both calm and frantic in my thinking.

I go to grab his shirt—to stop him? Tell him to hit me? Punch me in the face? Kick me to the ground for murdering his family? I don't know—but he jars to a halt, and the impact of it makes my boots slip on the shiny floor of the stairwell. Suddenly, I'm airborne.

I'm flying.

Falling—literally.

My body is bounding down the stairs and as I hit the ground, all I think about is how fucking sorry I am, how fucking right it is that I'm going to die now because my love is so toxic.

And then the dark, sticky fingers pull me under, and I go to sleep.

I come to, surrounded by the *beep beep beep* of machines and that clean but diseased smell of the hospital. Before I even open my bleary eyes, the bone-deep despair rises to the surface. The panic. The helplessness. It all stampedes on my chest and I gasp, trying to sit up.

"Hey. You're awake."

I focus on a sleep-ruffled Caleb. "Wh-What..." *Oh God, the pain.* I press my fingers to my throbbing head.

"Here." Caleb produces a cup of water with a straw, urging me to take a sip. I obey, the water soothing the dryness in my throat.

He puts the cup away and faces me, shushing me when I try to speak. "Don't. Your head's gonna hurt for a while. Just give it a rest for now."

"I...c-can't." I groan. Even that small whisper rattles inside my skull, tears prickling my eyes. I've got so many questions, so many, many things to ask him.

He strokes my hair. "Hey, it's gonna be fine. Everything is going to be okay."

Helpless, I lie there, crying with bitter irony. I can't believe I said those very things not long ago. *It's gonna be okay. It's all fine.*

Nothing is fine. Not a single thing. I don't even know how long I have been out.

"Th-Thomas?"

His face hardens. I have never seen him with that expression. "He's gone."

I shift on the bed, struggling to get up, but Caleb pushes me back down. Somehow, I manage to ask, "Why?"

"Are you fucking serious right now, Lay?" I sink into the hard pillow, horrified by his cursing. Caleb never uses bad words. Ever. It ratchets up my anxiety even more.

There's some advantage to knowing a person for a lifetime, because Caleb can read the emotions on my face without me having to spell it out. "You fell down the stairs. It's because of him, isn't it? Do you remember that?"

Words scrape my throat as they struggle to come out. "N-No. He didn't do anything. It was me. I was g-going after him." *And this is right on so many levels.*

Caleb's face hardens even more before going slack. "It's not your fault."

Tears are streaming down and my head is buzzing with the pain. "You don't know. Hadley, she tried to kill herself because I went to their house." Caleb shakes his head but I forge on, "She knew, Caleb. She could see I was in love with her h-husband. And Nicky... Is he..."

It's getting harder and harder for me to talk. My head is going to explode and I can't breathe with all the snot running down my nose. Caleb hands me a tissue. But I don't care about the tissue. *Please, please, please let him be okay. Please God.*

"He's fine. He made it."

Caleb's voice breaks through the mayhem in my head. He's nodding, repeating what he just said. *He made it. Nicky is fine.*

"He is?" I whisper.

"Yeah. He, uh, he's okay. He's out of the critical care, and so is Hadley. Everything is okay now."

I nod and nod again. I keep nodding, and my tears keep rolling down my cheeks.

Thank God. Thank God. Thank God.

I can't form the words, the feeling of relief is huge inside me. So fucking huge. The pressure evaporates from my chest. Suddenly, I've become loose, flexible.

But it's all wrong, isn't it? I need to feel the pressure. None of this would've happened if not for me. I went to their house, their safe place and fucking destroyed everything.

"I almost killed him." My words are thick and wet with my salty tears.

"Layla, listen to me." He waits till I look at him. "What happened to Nicky is not your fault. If anything, it was Hadley's. They're talking about a psych eval for her."

"What?"

"She tried to kill herself, Layla. That's a serious thing. Not to mention, the kid almost died on her watch. She'll probably get slapped with charges of neglect, or maybe more. None of that has to do with you. You couldn't have brought it on by just being there."

Caleb doesn't know. He doesn't know the extent of it.

My family is dying because you love me.

He didn't see Thomas' face. He didn't see how I took everything from him when he'd just gotten it back.

"Do you know where Thomas is right now? Can you take me there? Please Caleb, I really need to see him." I grab his hand, pleading.

"No. I wouldn't tell you even if I knew. They flew Nicky out to a different hospital in the city, and they both left with him, Thomas and his wife. That's all I know."

Panicked, I try to scramble up. I need to see Thomas. I need to apologize. I need to do something. He might hate me, but I *know* he needs me.

Caleb overpowers me easily. He pushes me down on the bed and holds me there. "Jesus, Layla. Look at yourself. You need to take care of yourself. Shit." His face crumples then, almost crying, but not yet. "When your mom called me, I-I was… God, I've never been so scared in my life. And to come here and find out the man responsible for your…accident is your professor? Is that the guy you love? Is that why you wanted to stay here instead of moving to the city?"

I never told Caleb who I'm in love with after dropping the bomb on him when he came to visit. I just ran out of there when I had the epiphany.

I struggle to get up once again. This time, however, Caleb doesn't have to come stop me, because I collapse all on my own.

"He's hurting, Caleb," I cry, fisting the sheets covering my frail body. "I-I need to go to him."

"What you need to do is rest. You're gonna need your strength. Your mom's here, and so is your dean, and they know, about…everything." Again, I don't have to ask. Caleb understands on his own. "Someone told them."

"Who?"

He sighs, rakes his fingers through his hair. "Sarah Turner? Does that name make sense to you?"

I nod. "She wants his job."

"They want to talk to you. There will be an investigation." He gives me a meaningful look.

"There's no need for one." I avert my eyes. "I pursued him. I literally stalked him. Went to his house. I fell in love with him. It was all me."

"He was right," Caleb mutters.

"Who was right?" I ask, but I don't really care about the answer. It's all automatic. I feel the animation and emotions leaving my body. I actually feel lighter, thinner because of it, like a little tap would turn me to dust.

"He told me not to say anything, but I know you. You're insanely stubborn so... Thomas was here last night."

I whip my gaze back to him as my heart drums from beyond its grave. "Thomas?"

"You were out cold. He told me to tell you it isn't your fault. I wasn't supposed to tell you that the message came from him though."

"He...He said that? That's what he said?"

"Yes. Among other things."

"What things?"

Sighing, he turns his face, and for the first time, I notice the left side of his jaw is swollen. "He punched me. Told me it was because of what I did."

My eyes widen and a pounding starts in my head again. Caleb puts a calming hand on my shoulder. "Relax. You're gonna make yourself worse."

"And he just left after that?"

"Yes." He stares at me with pity. "He wasn't going to stick around anyway."

Caleb doesn't say it but I can read his expression. *What were you thinking? Sleeping with a married professor?*

"Of course, yeah. I know that." I shake my head as tears fall down in a thick stream. "Why would he?" *I almost killed his family,* I want to add, but my voice shuts down, along with every other function of my body. I become useless and limp as Thomas' words swirl around in my head.

My family is dying because you love me.

How could I have done this to him? How could my love be so toxic? Selfish and greedy. A fucking demon.

It isn't your fault. I don't believe Thomas. How can it not be my fault? I went there when he specifically asked me not to. Maybe he was just being kind to me while I was unconscious, and that kills me even more.

I thought I did everything right this time. I thought my love wouldn't eat me from the inside out. I thought it wouldn't hurt anyone.

Turns out, my love is cannibalistic. Turns out, I don't deserve to love anyone, much less have that love reciprocated.

CHAPTER TWENTY-NINE

The Bard

Four Months Later...

He looks at me with bright blue eyes. His dark hair falls to his forehead and drool hangs from his lips. Yeah, I might need to get that later. But for now, he's happy to be a free agent. He's on all fours, grinning at me, or rather the purple blanket I'm holding in my hands.

"Come on, buddy. You want this?" I wave the small blanket at him and his grin gets wider. "Then come get it. Come on."

I egg him on and he shrieks, and crawls over as fast as his knees and dimpled palms will allow. I laugh at his enthusiasm and haul him in my arms when he reaches me. His shrieks and mirth get louder as I lift him up.

He's lighter than air but I know he's put on weight. His red cheeks have become fuller and healthier. He is happy and oblivious. He doesn't know that mere months ago he almost died, that the button from his favorite purple elephant, almost killed him. And I wouldn't want it any other way. I don't want anything tarnishing his pure innocence.

Nicky gurgles when I put him down on the floor and give him his blanket. Muttering to himself, he snatches it from my hands and begins to rub his face on the soft fur. Then he proceeds to blow raspberry kisses on it, and I chuckle. A strained, almost choking sound. Something about his playful actions, about the fact that he can do this... that he gets a *chance* to do this, lodges something sharp in my throat.

I look up when I hear Hadley come into the room. She's freshly showered, her hair up in a neat bun, and her smile in place. Like Nicky, she has grown healthier too.

"Do you want to eat now?" I ask. "We can think about unpacking a few things later."

The boxes are stacked up by the wall of the living room. A lifetime of possessions, a *life* contained inside the four cardboard walls somehow fails to do justice to what we've all been through.

This is our new home now. We've been living in Jake's empty apartment in the city for the past few months. But it was time for a change, to move forward. So we got a new place in Brooklyn.

Hadley gives me a shy smile. "Okay."

I leave Nicky to play on the floor, and pad over to the kitchen and start taking out containers from the bag. I sense Hadley coming closer. She stops at the island, still standing. I look up at her and find her watching me. I swallow and almost drop the container, my hands going weak. It's still surreal that she is here, that my son is alive, that we are a family, again.

I focus on the food, dishing the perfect portions of the kung pao chicken out.

"Thomas?"

I halt my movements, the fork dangling in the air. There's something about her voice that gives me goosebumps. My entire body goes into defense mode and the attack hasn't even come yet. It's the subtle steel, the soft authority in her words. It's a tone she has rarely used with me. We never had any use for it. Even during the early days when we'd only just met, we never clashed. Now I realize that was because she gave in to all my demands.

"Yes."

She rubs her arms—a gesture so like her that my chest hurts—but her eyes are determined. "I want a divorce."

A beat passes. Two. Someone laughs on the street. A car whooshes by. A woman shrieks followed by more laughter. My eyes go to Nicky. He's still playing with the blanket, crawling with it tucked close to his chest. A chest that's moving up and down, as he breathes. My own chest begins to heave, one shuddering breath after another at the sight of my son alive and breathing. Focusing back on Hadley, I admit that I've been wondering when she'd say those words, when she'd be strong enough, mentally and physically, not to need me anymore.

Not need me to get her meds, feed her, hold her while the nightmares make her cry—the only time I have the courage to touch her—and silently pray my own tears away because she needs me to be strong.

"I see." I rub my fingers over my mouth, oddly stunned that the moment is here.

She smiles then. Slowly, she leans over, puts her hand on my shoulders and tells me to sit. I do, like I'm a child, incapable of thinking for myself or doing even the simplest things.

Hadley takes a seat and we sit at the island across from each other. "This feels nice," she says. "It feels like old times."

I clear my throat. "Yeah."

"Look at the size of this thing. It reminds me of the tiny island you had in college."

"It does."

"You don't remember it, do you?"

"I—"

"You don't have to agree with me on everything, Thomas. I won't...I won't blow up or anything."

"I know."

For the next few minutes, we keep mum. The silence is familiar, comforting even. This is how we've spent the last four months, with silences, occasional conversations. Yet, I know this moment is more. Something is coming; I can feel it in my bones, in my soul, even.

"I need to leave, Thomas," Hadley says, after a little while. We both haven't touched the food, but we're both gripping the white plastic fork. For what? I don't know.

But at her words, my grip tightens. My fists are shaking. It's not as if this was unexpected. It's not as if...we've been happy. With a sigh, I unfurl my palm and let the fork go.

"Right," I say, robotically.

"I need to leave. At least, for a little while."

"What about Nicky?" I repeat the question from long ago. But there is no heat in it. Maybe I'm going through the motions.

Her face crumples slightly and she squeezes my hand on the table. Hadley has always been good at hiding her emotions. She is soft and subtle, everything opposite of who I used to be. But now I can read her easily. I can see emotions playing on her beautiful face, like her porcelain skin has turned transparent and suddenly I can look inside.

She sighs, as if bracing herself for something big, and I'm on alert.

"He has you." She smiles. "And Layla."

The dulled embers inside my gut heat up at the mention of her name. The fire in my blood fans. My mind goes to the piece of paper tucked in my pocket—her poem from long ago. The poem she wrote for me, in another lifetime maybe. I carry it everywhere with me. I carry *her* everywhere with me, like a forgotten penny in my wallet. Most days I don't even clap my eyes on it, but it's there, safely buried.

It's been four months, four long months since I saw her at the hospital, since I left her with one, pathetic line: *It's not your fault.* I wasn't even man enough to stay back and say it to her face. I ran. I couldn't see her broken. I couldn't see that I'd finally managed to push her too far.

"Hadley…"

My entire body is trembling. *Fuck.* I'm not prepared for it. I'm not prepared for talking about this. I'm not prepared to talk about Layla with Hadley.

"I-I… If I could go back, I'd—"

"I'd want you to have that all over again." Shocked, my gaze flies up to her. "You fell in love. I'd never begrudge you that."

Love. I fell in love with Layla Robinson.

In the frenzy of the last few months, I never got the chance to tell Hadley myself. She heard the rumors though. She heard why I quit my job, why we moved back to New York, other than for her and Nicky's treatment.

I had an affair with my student.

It's true that I ended up falling in love with her, but I never confessed this to Hadley. It feels foreign to hear it from my wife's mouth. It feels…like relief. I haven't felt it in a long, long time.

"I should've told you," I rasp. I want to look away but I won't. I'll at least give her the courtesy of looking directly into her eyes when I confess.

"Yes." She nods. "But I wasn't there."

"I should've waited for you to come back. We should've…should've talked about things."

"Yes, but honestly, I didn't want to. I didn't want to face what I was going through. I didn't want to face anything. I-I thought that if I left for a few days, things would be better, but they weren't. And I missed you so much when I was gone, but when I came back, I felt even worse."

It's not easy listening to it. It's not easy listening to how by forcing her to be with me, I almost destroyed her, how she lied to me. She never went to Beth's. She simply ran away, lived at a motel someplace upstate.

"Susan... She told me. She kept saying something was wrong but I never...I never thought... My mind never even went there. Or maybe I didn't want to see it. I felt..."

"What did you feel?"

For this, I don't have the guts to look at her. "I felt relieved."

I felt lighter when she left, like I didn't have to tiptoe around her anymore. I didn't have to pretend things were okay. I was angry at Hadley for so many things, for hiding the pregnancy, for not loving me, and when she left, I felt better. I felt like I could breathe, and that's the worst thing I could've done. Worse than cheating. Worse than breaking our vows.

I look back at her to find her eyes wet. She sniffs as she continues, "Me too. The moment I stepped out the door, I felt like everything would be okay. Like I didn't have to see how much I was killing you. I didn't have to get up every morning and *be* there. I didn't want to be there. I didn't want to...to even look at Nicholas."

Both our hands jerk at his name, like the hold is the only thing keeping our bodies together. If we let go, bones and skin will fall apart.

"And I thought that if I could just stay like that for even a day, I could be happy. I wouldn't feel so...so down all the time. Every time I looked at him and he looked at me, I thought he was judging me, like he was saying I couldn't be a good mom to him. I couldn't take care of him."

I want to reach out and wipe the tears off her face, but I can't. I can't let go of her hand.

"His cries." She bites her lip, to keep herself from sobbing, I suppose. "The way he'd break down, screaming. Red-faced. His fists clenched. Oh God, I couldn't take it. I'd ask myself *Why doesn't he stop? Just make him stop.* And at the same time, I'd be terrified of picking him up and...and soothing him."

"What if...we never had him?" It seems sacrilegious to say it, to say that the only way to prevent Hadley's depression was to never have our son. What if I never forced her to keep him? What if I hadn't been so afraid of being alone like my father? What if I had let her go the night she told me she wanted a divorce?

I swivel my gaze to Nicky. He has abandoned the blanket and now, he's playing with his firetruck. These days, he never stops talking or rather muttering. He's always saying something, crawling all over the place, laughing. He is *living*. I hate it when he goes to sleep because I can't hear him then. I can't hear the signs of his life. And I have to touch his chest or listen to him breathe just so I can breathe myself.

I bring my gaze back to Hadley. She's watching me watch our son.

"I wouldn't trade it for anything," she says softly, putting me at ease. I wouldn't trade my son for anything either.

"You know, mothers are supposed to take care of their children. They are supposed to stay up all night for them, feed them, nourish them, keep them alive. I never did those things. Those things scared me and he didn't even know it. He didn't know he had a terrible mother who couldn't even look at him, but he saved *my* life, Thomas. If he wasn't... Susan would never have come to get me. She would've thought I went back to sleep like I used to do and then I'd be dead. He almost died to save me. What kind of a mother am I?"

This time, I risk falling apart and release our hold. I take her face in both my hands and kiss her forehead. "A great one. I know it. Just give yourself a little bit of time."

My eyes burn with unshed tears and I look to the ceiling to keep them inside. I can't play the blame game with her, I'm tired. I'm tired of feeling like this, of trying to keep everything together, only to have it fall apart.

Hadley has become a better Mom. She holds Nicky now. Sometimes she even puts him to sleep. She still gets afraid, looks to me when he cries or when he needs something. But I know, I *know* she'll get the hang of it. Her depression almost took her away but she's getting better.

"Do you know what kept me alive all those months?" She moves away. "This. You. Your complete dedication. Your stubbornness to work on something that was almost gone. You loved me, Thomas, no matter what, and every day that gave me the strength to open my eyes when I didn't want to. I didn't want to face that I was one of them, you know. My entire family has depression of one sort or another. They can't hold jobs. Most of my sisters are divorced. I didn't want to be one of them."

It was a couple of days after the incident that we found out she was suffering from post-partum depression. Textbook case, they said.

"There's nothing wrong with it. There's nothing wrong with going through what you went through, Hadley. It's not something to be ashamed of."

"Yeah, I know now." She nods, tears shining in her eyes. "But I need to forgive myself first. I couldn't touch Nicholas before because I just didn't know how. I was afraid or...sometimes I'd feel nothing at all. It's different now. I feel too much. I love him with all my heart. I never even thought this kind of love was possible, you know. So when I want to touch him now, I can't. Because of what I did, of what I almost let happen."

"Hadley --"

"No. Don't say anything." She swallows. "I can't do this. To you, to him. Even to myself. I need to figure things out for myself. I need to see where I can go from here. How do I come back from this? How do I come back from almost killing my own baby?"

"It wasn't you. It was your depression. You were sick. What happened was an accident."

"Yes. But I'm not sick anymore. My head's clear. It's my turn to do the right thing." She squeezes my hand again. "You need to do the right thing too. All these months, you've been there for me. But now, you need to be there for yourself, and for her. Layla."

The fire roars at her name, roars and flows just under the surface. I feel a tidal wave of pain coming on, and it's harder to control my emotions.

"She's fine," I tell her with gritted teeth. I let go of Hadley and sit back. Touching her while thinking of Layla seems wrong, although it's tame in comparison to the sins I've already committed.

"Actually, she's not. She's not at all fine."

I sit up. I feel like I'll explode out of my skin. "What's wrong with her?"

Hadley stays silent for a beat, before saying, "I don't want you to punish yourself anymore."

I open my mouth to say that I'm not, but something else comes out. "I don't know what else to do. I've done so many things I'm not proud of. I've betrayed you. I broke all my promises but...but it's worse." I swallow. Then I swallow once again. I try to push down words, a lump, a jagged rock of emotions and a million things that just won't stay buried.

"She said...She said she regrets everything. Everything we did. She regrets it and I don't blame her." I scrub my face with my hand. "I've been bad *to* her, *for* her. I've hurt her in so many ways."

When Layla fell down the stairs, I realized that I loved her too. I've always loved her, and she was on the ground, broken, because of me.

"Then go fix it."

"I can't. She's better off without me."

"I told you she's not."

"What does that mean?"

"I went to see her."

"What? How?" The piece of paper in my wallet suddenly seems heavy and bloated.

"Today." At my confusion, she explains, "I didn't have a doctor's appointment today. I lied. After you and Nicky dropped me off, I took the train to her school. She goes to a community college in the city."

"She's..." I lose my voice for a moment. "She's in the city?"

"Yes. I asked Jake and he asked someone else and he came back with pretty thorough information. She's here. She's taking summer courses to make up for the lost credits from last semester."

She's here. In the city. Somewhere among the millions of people who live here is the violet-eyed girl I'm scared to dream about. But I do. I do dream about her. I smell her sometimes in my sleep, hear her muted laughter. I keep her there, contained behind my closed eyelids. I don't dare think about her any other place. I can't. Not after the things I said to her. Not after I carried her broken body only to leave her in the hands of strangers, like a coward. I told her I wouldn't leave without saying goodbye but that's exactly what I did.

"What did you... How's..."

"She was shocked to see me. She didn't even move for a few minutes. Looked like she was bracing for something, like she was expecting me to go off on her. I made it look like we met accidentally, and I told her."

"Told her what?"

"That what happened wasn't her fault."

I wince as if there was a gunshot. My ears start ringing. *My family is dying because you love me.* Every now and then, I hear my own words. I'd be doing something in the middle of the day, and suddenly, they would burst forth, jarring me completely. Those words are one of my demons. My son's almost-vacant eyes, Layla's laugh, my cruelty, Hadley's frail body in the hospital bed— I have so many of them that I don't even feel human anymore.

"She blames herself, doesn't she?" Hadley says.

"That's why I can't go to her. I need to let her move on. She needs to move on. She'll forget about me after a while."

"Are you going to forget about her?"

"I can't."

"Then what makes you think she's going to forget you?"

"She's young, Hadley. And there's Nicky to think about. I can't...I can't ask her to..."

I can't even say it. How can I ask Layla to...be there for Nicky? And as what? As a stepmom, a mother figure, what? I can't burden her.

"You and me both know that she loves Nicky. She's probably more qualified than me to take care of him."

I run my hands through my hair and make a punishing fist. I know that. I know, and yet...

"I've hurt her so bad," I say, at last. "I don't...I don't think she can ever forgive me."

"Then that's a chance you're going to have to take." She reaches forward and caresses my jaw. "You can't hold back because you're afraid."

I've heard this countless times, have probably said it to people myself. Somehow, it never registered in my psyche. Somehow, until now, I hadn't really listened to it. They say sometimes you need to hear something at the right time for it to make an impact, like a book you read at a certain age in order to really appreciate it.

Maybe this is that moment.

Hadley must see the change in me before I even figure it out myself. "She's like you, Thomas. She's strong and bright, and she loves you."

For the first time in months, I don't hold myself back. I don't choke the tears that come to my eyes. I let them fill to the brim. "You think so?"

"Yes. She has what you have."

"And what's that?"

"Fire." Hadley nods. "She has your fire."

I think of her smile, her raven hair, her violet eyes. Her smooth, creamy skin. Her slender limbs wrapped around my body. Her tattoo. Her laughter. Her courage. Her words.

We're soul mates, Thomas. You're like my favorite song. You have to talk. You can't live like this. You're holding on too tight. You remind me of some kind of fire-breather.

Layla Robinson, the fire-breather.

My fire-breather.

PART 5

THE RULE-BREAKER

CHAPTER THIRTY

We don't make a circle in this class. Even though it is a critique class. The professor here doesn't insult anyone or doesn't comment on horrendous word choices. He is not rude or mean or arrogant.

He is also not a genius.

I like him, though. He's a good teacher, encouraging, full of kind words. 'Like' is the best thing, the *right* thing to feel for someone who teaches you. Anything other than that...anything even close to love or even hate? No. That's a big no. It only complicates things.

So I'm happy with my new professor. He is not Thomas Abrams. But, that's fine. That's more than fine. I don't want a professor like him. Ever. I don't want to go through what I went through ever again. I never want to do all the bad things that I did.

My family is dying because you love me.

It's not your fault.

Thomas' last words haunt me and frustrate me and I hear them all the time. They are always loud and clear, and always send my numb heart spiraling, so much so that I want to hunt him down and shake him and demand all the answers. *Was it my fault or not?*

But it's better this way. I don't want to look to him for answers. I don't want to be dependent on anybody for that.

Dr. Apostolos says we have all the answers, always. We just need to look for them, and in order to do that, we need to love ourselves. *Love yourself and the rest will follow.*

She is my therapist, and she is a legit one, not like Kara. I met her at the youth center in New Jersey, after I confessed everything to my mom and the dean.

I told everyone it was me. I was the one who pursued Thomas. I was the one who stalked him, went to his house. I showed them my tattoo. Yeah, I stood up in the hospital room full of people and lifted my shirt. They all cringed and grimaced at my shamelessness. Sometimes being crazy pays off, because they dismissed the case and kicked me out of school. Thomas had already quit his job by then.

It's fine. I wasn't going to stay anyway.

My mom had reached her limit though. She sent me away, and I didn't protest. I didn't know where else to go. I didn't have a home, and I didn't have the energy to make one. So, for the next thirty days, the rehab center was it for me.

Dr. Apostolos was nice to me. She never judged, only listened, and then handed me tissues when I was all cried out for the day. I told her everything. About Thomas, about the affair, about Nicky. About Hadley, and the fact that she was suffering from post-partum depression. This I found out from Emma when she called me early in my stay. There were rumors going around and she wanted me to know. We're still friends, though she was hurt I didn't tell her about Thomas.

I told everything to my therapist. She told me post-partum depression isn't something I could've brought on. In fact, to reach a point where Hadley wanted to kill herself, that takes a lot of time and a lot of depression. It wasn't my doing. I didn't trigger it by going to their house.

I know that. I've heard it a million times. I've researched everything about depression, but I don't know why I don't believe it.

Even so, I'm focusing on loving myself. *Love yourself and the rest will follow.*

I'm climbing down the stone steps of the building, having just now finished my creative writing class. The steps merge with a busy sidewalk, but that's New York. Big and loud and crowded, always in a hurry. Everyone is going somewhere. I like that. I like everything about this city.

A small smile blooms on my lips before it drips off. The heat fluctuates in the air. The temperature goes up. There can only be one reason for it. Thomas.

He is here. Despite the mass of bodies, I see him. He's standing at the end of the block, by the red light, watching me. As if, he knew I'd be out here, at this very moment.

Maybe he did know because Hadley was here yesterday. To be honest, I was expecting him. I don't know why he's here, though. I don't even know why Hadley showed up out of the blue like a ghost and scared the shit out of me. I could only stand there and stare at her while she talked about that awful, awful day. She told me how she'd given up and how when she got back, she pretty much knew what she was going to do. It had nothing to do with me. She said that probably five times, confirming what Dr. Apostolos already told me.

The entire conversation, I couldn't look away from her. She appeared so... healthy and beautiful. It was blinding. I'm not proud that I was comparing her otherworldly beauty with my very worldly one, but I couldn't help it. In the end, she apologized for traumatizing me, which made me snort. She was saying sorry to me when I'm the criminal.

Taking a deep breath, I swat my breeze-ruffled hair off my face. I straighten my checkered skirt and my top.

I can't take any more of this suspense, so I walk up to him. He's staring at me with his blue, blue eyes. They never fail to make me heated or cause tingles all over my body. It's like the sun is watching me from the sky. The tingles spread out of my scalp and radiate toward my neck, my spine, the back of my thighs. Everywhere.

His eyes are beautiful but tired. He's lost some weight and his face has become sharper, more bony. His hair, though dark and rich, is overly long, dangling over his shoulders, his forehead. He looks like he hasn't shaved in a while. He looks like he hasn't slept in a long while either.

He looks like he hasn't *lived* in a long while.

I stop a few feet away and in the frenzy of the city, the silence is thick between us. Until he breaks it. "How are you?"

"Good," I say, awkwardly.

Thomas is big, so big that I can't ignore him. I can't ignore his face or his strong chest or the fact that he's wearing a white shirt and blue jeans. I can't ignore any of that.

I remember the first time I saw him on the bench, and then after in the bookstore and in class. Even though he was restrained and stoic, his posture always tight, inside I knew he was brimming with anger, frustration. There was a certain arrogance in him, too. He knew he was the best, even though he hated it. He hated that his passion for his words ruined the passion for his wife.

But all of it is gone now. No passion. It's all despair.

He opens his mouth, and then closes it. His eyes take in the purple bag on my shoulders, and the notebook I'm clutching to my chest. "I... Are you taking any poetry classes?"

"I hate poetry."

"Right." He nods and rubs the back of his neck.

It's weird to see him unsure. I almost want to put him out of his misery. I almost want to break this awkwardness between us and be an easy person to talk to. But I won't. I won't be an easy person ever again.

I won't.

I *won't*.

"How's Nicky?" I blurt out, like the old times.

Damnit! I'm weak. I'm so mushy.

But in my defense, I really want to know how the little guy is doing. I miss him. I miss his laughter, his passion for the color purple. How stupid is that? Nicky isn't even mine. Just like Thomas.

"He's fine. He's doing great, actually." Thomas has a tiny smile on his face. "He's starting to talk. I'm convinced he said *daddy* the other day."

"Yeah?" Despite myself, I smile at him. But when he returns it, I can't resist goading him like he did me, ages ago, "Are you sure it's not some randomly put together syllables?"

Thomas' smile thins out and he swallows. There's probably remorse on his face or something similar but I force myself to peel my eyes away.

And then, I feel someone crashing into me, and I, in turn, crash into Thomas. His arms come around me, and my breasts crush against his hard, *hard* body. God, this has to be the most clichéd move ever. I can't believe it happened to me.

I try not to sniff him, but it's hard not to when we're this close. I do have to breathe, so I take in a breath mixed with his chocolate scent. I keep it tucked away somewhere in my body for later when I'm alone in Caleb's apartment. I jump out of his hold, then. I don't want his stupid scent.

This time though, I can't look away from the remorse on his face. It's sharp and cutting, and it digs into my crazy heart.

My notebook and the papers are scattered on the hot pavement, and I bend down to grab them. But somehow, Thomas is there before me. I watch his fingers -- his large, graceful fingers that I've always been curious about – picking up the papers, one by one. I study the veins on the back of his hands. *Do you still not write?* I want to ask, but I won't.

I keep my eyes on his fingers, observing them do an ordinary thing but looking no less extraordinary, no less naked. I stop breathing. His fingers are *naked*. He doesn't have a wedding ring on.

I know he never takes it off. Never. Not once have I ever seen him without it. It's like he always carries Hadley with him. Even when we...had sex, I'd feel that metal digging into my waist, my thighs, my arms...everywhere, telling me how wrong it was, how he was not mine and would never be mine. I feel the pressure again, as if the ring is still pressing into my body.

Abruptly, I stand. Thomas senses something is wrong and comes to his feet beside me. I can't look away from his...naked hands. "You don't..."

He looks down at his hands as if seeing them for the first time. A beat passes with no words. Holding my notebook in one hand, he rubs the pale spot where the ring used to be. I don't know if it's in regret or relief.

"Hadley and I, we're getting a divorce."

"Because of me?" It comes out before I can stop it, and the cringe that follows is involuntary too. I remind myself that I have nothing to do with them now. I shouldn't even mean anything to them. When Hadley came to me yesterday, pretending it was accidental, I didn't tell her anything. I never even asked about Thomas or Nicky. But she had to know, right? That's why she was trying to put me out of my misery, letting me off the hook.

Oh God, did I ruin things again?

Thomas must see the distress on my face because he moves forward, reaching out his free hand, but I move away from him. My feet step back and he flinches.

"No, not because of you. It's something that should've happened a long time ago. It has nothing to do with you." He pushes a hand through his longish hair. "It was me. I was holding on too tight."

Is it possible to gasp and sigh at the same time? Because I probably just did that. My own words thrown back at me with such gentleness and gravity is... shocking. I never expected him to remember that, let alone say it.

I need to stop jumping to conclusions. Not everything is my fault. *Love yourself and the rest will follow.*

I push my unruly, stupid hair back and his eyes follow my tiny gesture. In fact, he hasn't stopped looking at all. What is he looking for? I don't think I have anything left that can be of use to him.

"Okay. Well, I-I'm sorry." I stare at my chipped toenails and my flip-flops, unsure. "I know you...love her."

"I still do." He shoots me a sad smile. "And I think I'll always love her. But I don't think it's the kind of love that makes people stay together. It was more of an awe of each other than love, and awe can get intimidating and become a burden after a while."

What's going to happen to Nicky? I wish I could ask him that. Divorce is such an awful thing. Look, how I turned out because of my mom's multiple divorces. But then again, how is living together with no love any better?

So maybe it's all for the best.

"Right. I can see that." I nod, unable to stop myself. "You're pretty...awful."

He laughs then, short and succinct and loud, and something flutters in my stomach. I tamp it down. Shivers and flutters have no business coming on right now.

"I gotta go now. I have to get home. So I'm gonna go."

Before I can whirl around and get out of here, Thomas speaks up. "I'm sorry I left without saying goodbye."

"You did." I shrug, jerking my tight shoulders up. "You hated me, right? You didn't owe me anything."

Just then the sunrays turn harsh and expose every inch of Thomas' agonized expression. It makes him look a shadow of his previous, confident self.

"I didn't hate you. I *never* hated you. I don't...hate you." His jaw clenches, but I know it's not anger. It's his attempt to control his unruly emotions.

He doesn't hate me.

It's the kind of statement that should bring a smile or make me feel lighter. I should feel like I have everything now, but tears spill out of my eyes and down my cheeks, tears I didn't know were brimming.

Thomas jerks forward again but stops himself. He shakes his head once, silently telling me not to cry. His bunched fists open and close at his sides. He is dying to touch me – I know. But I won't let him.

"See, that's worse, Thomas," I tell him, getting choked up. "Because if you don't hate me then that means you..." I can't say *love*. I don't think I can ever say love. "Feel something opposite of hate, and if you in fact feel something opposite of hate, how could you not find me before this? How could you not pick up a phone to tell me you don't hate me? I went days and weeks thinking you hated me, that I ruined every fucking thing in your life. I thought because of me, you'd never be happy. People kept telling me it wasn't true, that it couldn't have been me, but I never believed them. I *still* don't believe them. How could you do that to me? How could you let me carry that burden? How could you do that to a person you *don't* hate?"

I don't know how long I've kept these words inside, and how long I can go on now before breaking down and sobbing on this godforsaken sidewalk. My tears show no sign of stopping, and I feel a sob beginning to emerge.

So maybe I'm being selfish. Obviously, he never had the time before this. He was busy taking care of Hadley and his son. I should let him off the hook, but I don't want to. I don't. I can't. Loving myself means fighting for myself, fighting for my sanity, and I will fucking fight. I won't be a martyr even though guilt keeps pouring out of me like tears and sweat.

"You don't. You don't do that to a person you don't hate," he whispers, his eyes red-rimmed. The tears shining in them stagger me. I mean, I know he must cry—he's human—but seeing it in the flesh is…defeating. I feel defeated at his tears. I feel like I'll crumble right here.

"Then why d-did you?"

"Because with you, everything is new. I feel like I've never not hated anyone before."

A broken chuckle escapes me at his deliberate use of my terminology. He doesn't laugh though; no. "With you, I feel that I've never had any feelings before, like it's the first time I'm feeling anything at all. Do you know how terrifying that is?" He shakes his head and answers his own question. "It's very terrifying. I have so many things I want to say to you that I end up saying the wrong thing. I'm so scared of taking the wrong step that I never move at all. I don't know why I do that. I don't know why I keep fucking things up when it comes to you, but all I can say is you make me feel like…I've never taken a breath before, like I've never lived before."

It's spooky how he said the same thing I was thinking about earlier, that he looks…unlived somehow.

We're soul mates, my heart whispers.

Shut up, moron. We don't think about those things anymore.

There's an eerie seriousness in the air, and I don't know how to deal with that. "Well, that was…um, very poetic."

He tucks his hands into his pockets and rolls on his feet, as if embarrassed. "You wake up the words in me."

That stirs a memory from long ago, but I can't quite grasp it. Why does it feel like I've heard that before? And why does everything feel sad and hopeless again? Like even if all of this is true, too much has happened?

"I don't know what to do with that," I tell him honestly.

"I'll wait."

"Wait for what?"

"For you to figure out what to do with it."

"That's…" I shake my head. "You can't do that."

"Sure I can."

"What if I never figure it out?"

"Then I'll keep waiting."

"That's crazy," I scoff. "That's...like the book." My heart bottoms out then. It's exactly like Barthes' book, the one I stole from him ages ago. I still have it tucked away at the bottom of my drawer.

"A lover is the one who waits," he paraphrases. "Then, I'll wait. Forever."

CHAPTER THIRTY-ONE

The Bard

In the months following my divorce, and getting custody of Nicky, I've thought a lot about what bravery means. Is it the absence of fear? Is it the feeling of being invincible?

I realized I already know what it means, that I've already seen it. My father was a brave man. It's an odd and jarring thought, but it's true. All my life I assumed my father was weak, that he wasn't even a real poet, and I did everything I could to not be like him. But, as it turns out, my father was braver than me.

Bravery is picking up a pen and writing. Bravery is gouging out words from inside you and then imprinting them on a page to make them permanent. Bravery is knowing they might not ever be read by anyone, that the art you leave behind, the contributions you make to the world, might never be known by anyone. Bravery is knowing all of that but doing it anyway.

Like my father did. He wrote for himself. He didn't care about the awards or validations. He wasn't a good father, no, but in his own way, he was brave—braver than I ever was. I put so much stock into what I don't want to be that I forgot what I could be.

I've started writing again. It's poetry. It will always be poetry. That's how I express myself. It's the voice of my soul, like *Anesthesia*. The testament to my loneliness even when Hadley and I were together.

I've been working on a collection about Nicky. It helps me deal with things that happened. I don't know where Hadley is. She left, just like she said she would. All I can wish is that she finds the peace she's looking for. Maybe one day she'll be back and Nicky can meet her. But until then, I'll tell him stories about his mom.

Nicky has grown up so much. He is walking. He laughs. He plays. His favorite toys still change every week. It's as if there is no past for him. He doesn't remember being in the hospital or almost choking to death.

I do. I remember those things. They keep me awake at night. I check up on him constantly. I sleep more on the floor by his crib, than on the bed. But that's okay. For now, they make me feel in control.

When I watch Nicky take stumbling steps, I look down at my own feet. I flex my toes to understand the mechanics of walking. There are times when I feel that every step is my very first step. There are times when I look at the world with Nicky's eyes and wonderment.

And I keep coming to the same conclusion: that bravery is not the absence of fear, but the courage to do something despite it—taking that first step despite the danger of falling, creating a piece of art knowing that people might not appreciate it.

Bravery is like falling in love. You don't know if the person will reciprocate, but still you fall.

Bravery is waiting for my Layla. I couldn't ask her to love me back then. It wouldn't have been fair. She'd already given me too much, and in return, I'd hurt her too much.

So I told her I'd wait, and since then, I've been waiting. Fall has become winter now.

Endless days when we meet at her school and I watch her shy away from me. At first, she wouldn't even let me touch her. We'd go to a café nearby and sit at a distance from each other, me staring at her because I didn't know where else to look, and her looking anywhere but at me. She'd play with Nicky, give him hats, laugh with him, teach him words. And I'd be torn between laughing at her antics and shaking her, *begging* her to love me back.

Every day I watch her walk away, saying she has classes or has to be somewhere. Endless nights when I think about her, and then break down and call her. In the beginning, she ignored my calls, until one day she picked up, but the conversation was halting. It took days of my coaxing before she finally started to open up, and I realized how fucking hard it must have been for her when I refused to give in and talk to her.

Endless conversations where we talk about Nicky, about books, about things I never even knew I wanted to talk about. I never even knew I had this many words in me.

I never knew I could wait for someone like this. Until Layla.

It's almost midnight, and she just called me to tell me she's coming over. I told her not to. It's not safe taking the subway to Brooklyn this time of the night. I told her I'd come to her, but she laughed and said, *Midnight streets are my friends.*

The knock comes at my door and I rush to open it. Layla stands there with a huge grin on her face, and I have to clutch the door to keep myself upright. Her beauty is like an explosion, sudden and jarring, but in a way that steals all my breath and thoughts. Sometimes I have to push a palm down on my chest to keep my heart from bursting out.

"I finished it." She hops on her feet as she comes inside my dismal, one-bedroom apartment. I have more books than furniture, but she doesn't mind. The walls are purple, and that's only because Layla thinks white is boring and went with me to pick out the colors.

"Finished what?" I close the door and turn around to find her taking off her coat and her sweater, followed by her hat, her scarf, and then finally, her gloves. She dumps it all on the coffee table and I have to bite the inside of my cheek to keep from laughing.

She shoots me a glare. "What, it's cold outside."

"Right, and we live in Antarctica."

"Ha ha." She rolls her eyes and I feel like I could kiss her from five feet away.

She takes out a fur hat from her childish purple backpack and without a word, walks toward the bedroom where Nicky is sleeping. I follow her. I'll *always* follow her. She tiptoes to his crib, smiles down at him and sighs, clutching her chest. I want to laugh at her dramatic actions but I press my lips together. I don't know why I even thought for a second that she wouldn't love Nicky or think he'd be a burden. She loves him. It's the little things she does for him, how she brings him hats, how she always makes a point to say goodnight to him on the phone, if she's not here.

Layla places the hat by his sleeping form, this one tangerine in color, and walks back out to the living room. She comes to a stop and faces me, beaming. Her skirt reaches mid-thigh and even though she's wearing tights, I'm able to trace out the slope of her thighs and her calves. I remember peeling those scraps of fabric off. It feels like both yesterday and a lifetime ago, with the way I remember it so vividly and the way my fingers ache for it.

"Thomas," she says, her breaths coming out hard and fast. I've never admitted it to her, but I love the way she says my name, like no one has ever said it before, like she invents me anew every time she says it. It's fucking magical, and she calls *me* magic.

The shudders of her chest echo in my cock and I clear my throat. "So what did you finish?"

She swallows, appearing dazed. "Uh, my story."

Layla has been writing a story that she hasn't shown me. She doesn't talk about it, not like she used to do back when she was my student. It stings, the distance, but I'll take it. Unlike me, she likes to work on many things simultaneously, while I like to labor over one thing at a time. She likes to flit from one project to another.

Again, she bends down to root around in her bag, giving me a peek of her tits through her flimsy white top, and I whip my gaze up to the ceiling. I feel like a fucking pervert. Only Layla can make me feel both young and old at the same time.

"Here."

I look at her outstretched hand and then up at her face, all inappropriate thoughts forgotten. "What's that?"

"I want you to read it," she whispers.

She looks at me through her lashes, shy and uncertain. She rubs her foot against the other leg, anxious. She is so fucking young in this moment that if I touched her right now, I'd sully her with my ancient, cynical fingers.

She isn't giving me her story. She is giving me her heart.

I've thought about her heart a lot too. It's big and fierce and soft and bright. It's like a star or the moon or the entire fucking sky, and she's giving it to me. She's giving me the sky.

Everything has led to this. The fear I'm so damn familiar with rises up. I feel the physical effect of it in the way my stomach churns, in how tight my chest becomes.

I push past all of that. I push past the fear, the anxiety, and stalk toward her, stalk toward the only thing I want. "What's it about?"

"It's about how we fell in love." She lowers her arm and retreats, step by step. I would've stopped if I thought she didn't want me to come closer, but her purple eyes are shining. As soon as she reaches the wall, she sort of sinks into it, and I sink into her when I reach my destination. Her.

Our bodies touch and I almost groan out loud. I keep my arms on the wall, caging her in. "What's it called?"

"The Rule-Breaker." Her voice sounds rumbly like it does in the morning when she wakes up, and calls me about the dream she had about Nicky or about me.

"Yeah?" My voice mimics hers, as if she's just jumpstarted my heart after months of being comatose.

"Yeah." She nods her head. "It's not pretty, our love story."

"It's not."

"We break all the rules, and sometimes I hate that."

"Me too."

"But it's ours."

"It is."

A trembling smile appears on her lips and I want to kiss it, but I refrain. "Where does it start?" She looks away from me and I have to chase her gaze. Blush coats her cheeks and I feel the rush of my own blood under the surface. "Where does it start, Layla?"

"Well, see, it starts at midnight when I saw you on the bench, the one by the tree with white flowers."

I lick my lips, stunned. I never expected her to say that. I never even knew that. It's the same spot where I proposed to Hadley.

We're soul mates, Thomas.

I've never believed that until now...or maybe I did, but I've never seen the sheer, magnificent evidence of it. I press my body against her even more, trying to fuse our skins together, and her breath hitches.

My voice shakes when I answer her. "Yeah, I know that spot."

"So the story starts when one night I see you there and you look lonely, kind of like me. I think that you need a friend."

"And then you discover that I'm an asshole."

She bites her lips to keep from smiling but her eyes twinkle. "Yes. But then you kiss me."

This time, I can't stop the roll of my hips against hers, making her whimper. She feels hot, even through the layers of clothing. Our bodies are aroused and ready, waiting for our hearts to catch up.

"What happens when I kiss you?"

"I...I feel like you could eat me alive with your mouth and I've never felt that before. I've never been anyone's sustenance, and I want to keep going forever."

I want to do that to her now. I want to eat her up, fill my mouth with her taste. It's been long, so very long. I'm hungry. Starving. For her. But not yet. Not yet.

"Yeah, but in a classic move, I fuck it all up."

"You do, but you don't stop there. You keep fucking up, until I can't take it anymore."

I laugh as my eyes sting. "I'm a piece of shit. Are you sure I'm the hero of this story?" Fuck, I just want to touch her. Just once. That's all I want. I won't even ask for anything else. I just want to touch her and tuck her into my body and hold her, but I don't dare move my hand. I won't take what she isn't willing to give—even though it kills me, even though *every*thing burns.

"But you make up for it."

"Do I?"

Have I done enough? Have I shown her enough? I don't know. I don't know if she realizes how much I love her. I haven't said those words yet, but I want her to know. I want her to see it in my eyes because I bleed with it, I burn with it, and for the first time in my life, I don't mind it. I wouldn't mind it if she burned me alive or destroyed me. I'd keep on going. I'd keep on loving her.

I hear the thud of her notebook falling, and in the next second, she's the one touching me. She puts her hands on my cheeks and presses back into me with her hips. I shudder, my cock going full mast, and my forehead meets hers.

"Yes, Thomas. You do. You *have*. God, please tell me you know that. Please tell me you think I'm a bitch for making you wait this long."

"Layla," I warn.

"Then you're just stupid." She goes on her tiptoes and hooks one leg around my waist. "You won't even touch me, you idiot. You're still not touching me. If I move back for whatever reason, you back off like it's you I'm running from. You pick me up from fucking college when I can very easily ride the subway like every other person in New York. You stay up all night, helping me study over Skype because you think I don't want you in my apartment. You won't even ask to come over. It's frustrating."

There was a time when her desperation made me feel powerful, but now I admit that I was just as desperate for her. It still holds true. "You said you didn't know what to do with it, so I've been waiting."

"Well, I'm tired of your waiting, you moron."

She jumps and hooks her other leg around my hips. The move is so familiar. So many times she has simply wound her limbs around me, like we have always belonged together, like it's always been that simple.

"I even talked to Nicky about it," she tells me with mischief in her voice.

"About what?"

"That you're taking too long. That I love him so, so much. And I..." She bites her lip and stares at me through her lashes, making my heart skip a beat. "I know I'm not the best person to take care of a baby. I mean, I'm kinda crazy and impulsive, and... But I love him so much and I'll –"

"Hey, you're my everything. Every goddamn thing, Layla," I say, my voice wrapped up in gravel and a million swelling emotions that taste like tears. "Besides, love is enough. It has to be. We can figure out the rest."

Maybe it *is* simple, being together. I want to tell her, but she beats me to it. "I love you."

I sigh, and it feels like the very first time. It's the first time I've breathed. "I fucking love you too."

She beams even though her eyes are wet. "So that's what it feels like."

"What?"

"When someone says those three words back to you. I've always wondered."

"Technically, it was five words."

"I'll take them. It's even better. *Fucking* makes everything so much more... amazing and epic." She rubs her core over my cock and I can't keep the groan inside this time. Smiling, she closes her eyes and breathes me in. "I feel like I can walk on water."

"Yeah? Don't do that, though. That's not real, baby."

"You're such an ass." Opening her eyes, she chuckles and tightens her hold around my body. It's getting harder to support her weight without my arms. They are plastered to the wall, one last barrier between us. I should let go of the brick and wind them around her, but something is holding me back.

"Are you going to kiss me any time soon?"

"Tell me. Give me the words, Layla."

She smiles as a single tear falls down her cheek. "You don't have to wait for me anymore, Thomas. You *never* have to wait."

That's when my arms come off the wall and touch her. One hand goes to her ass, the other to the back of her head, and I kiss her.

This time it's me with an epiphany: I've always been brave. I just needed to look deeply into myself. I was brave enough to bring a child into this world. I was brave enough to love him with all my heart and soul, knowing that life is transient and fleeting.

There are many things uncertain in life. There are many hurdles still to overcome. Our love will grow and change, and we'll change with it. But today, I make a promise to myself.

I'll always be brave rather than fearless.

I'll make my own rules rather than follow them.

And I'll love. I'll always love my violet-eyed girl, Layla Robinson.

THE END

NOTE TO THE READERS

Thank you so much for taking this journey with me. Thomas and Layla are very special to my heart and I hope you enjoyed them. This story was challenging to me on many levels. I am not a poet, and I tried to write poetry with it. Trust me, I feel Layla's pain. I've tried to write *Anesthesia* so many times but couldn't. Thomas is too much of a genius for me to channel his words. I imagine him to be a hybrid of Stephen Dunn and Hemingway.

Anyway, if you enjoyed the story, then please consider leaving a review on Amazon and/or Goodreads. Reviews are the best way to support a story and an author.

EXTRAS

Would you like to be notified when Saffron releases another book or when a sale is happening? Please sign up for her newsletter here.

For signed paperbacks & YBTY merchandise.
Visit Store here.

ACKNOWLEDGMENTS

I have so many, many people to thank with this one. Writing is solitary but publishing a book and being an author take a lot of people. I am thankful for each one of you. Thanks for being as crazy as I am.

My husband: The person who sees me in action. He has survived so many of my writer moods and tantrums. Ever since I started writing four years ago, I've become more sensitive. I laugh too much. I cry too easily. I get mad at the slightest things. My husband has been with me throughout. I love him with all my heart. Thank you! And sorry for making you format this TWICE.

My parents: Thank you for always believing in me. Special thanks to my mom for pimping my books to all her friends. I love you, guys.

My Green Indies turned Fabulous Four: Suzanne, Bella and Kim are my oxygen. I can't imagine this journey without you. Thank you so much for being there for me, sharing advice, your happy moments, your woes. I love you guys so much!

Renate Thompson: My critique partner and the one who listens to every single one of my doubts. I can't believe how far we've come from when we started. You are not only a fabulous critique partner, you are a wonderful writer too. I can't wait for the day when your book comes out and wows the book world. Thank you for being my person.

Serena McDonald: I love you, woman! You're one of those rare gems that shine the brightest. THANK YOU for being my friend, for your passion for the book world, for your sass and sweetness, for holding my hand through this. I hope you know that you're stuck with me. #Saffrena for life.

My beta readers: Mara White, Sunny Borek, Haylee Thorne, Ari Purkayastha and Faith Andrews. Thank you for reading my work in a rough form and offering your advice. Where would I be without you guys? You are totally stuck with me for life.

Ella Fox: For single-handedly saving this book!

Fellow authors: I've met so many great people in the book world who have offered their invaluable advice, support, and inspired me. THANK YOU to all of them.

Sexy Saffronites: This is my happy place in all of the world wide web. You guys rock with all your support and sex talk. I couldn't do this without you so THANK YOU for being sexy and awesome. I love you guys!

ABOUT THE AUTHOR

Writer of bad romances. Aspiring Lana Del Rey of the Book World.

Saffron A. Kent is a USA Today Bestselling Author of Contemporary and New Adult romance.

She has an MFA in Creative Writing and she lives in New York City with her nerdy and supportive husband, along with a million and one books.

She also blogs. Her musings related to life, writing, books and everything in between can be found in her JOURNAL on her website (www.thesaffronkent.com)

www.ingramcontent.com/pod-product-compliance
Lightning Source LLC
LaVergne TN
LVHW041905070526
838199LV00051BA/2507